Scarlet Wilson wrote her first story aged eight and has never stopped. She's worked in the health service for twenty years, having trained as a nurse and a health visitor. Scarlet now works in public health and lives on the West Coast of Scotland with her fiancé and their two sons. Writing medical romances and contemporary romances is a dream come true for her.

Kate Hardy has always loved books, and could read before she went to school. She discovered Mills & Boon books when she was twelve and decided that this was what she wanted to do. When she isn't writing Kate enjoys reading, cinema, ballroom dancing and the gym. You can contact her via her website: katehardy.com.

D0773888

Also by Scarlet Wilson

A Festive Fling in Stockholm
Marriage Miracle in Emergency
Neonatal Doc on Her Doorstep
The Night They Never Forgot

Also by Kate Hardy

Forever Family for the Midwife
Second Chance with Her Guarded GP
Baby Miracle for the ER Doc
Surgeon's Second Chance in Florence

Discover more at millsandboon.co.uk.

SNOWED IN WITH THE SURGEON

SCARLET WILSON

SAVING CHRISTMAS FOR THE ER DOC

KATE HARDY

MILLS & BOON

All rights reserved including the right of reproduction
in whole or in part in any form. This edition is published
by arrangement with Harlequin Enterprises ULC.

This is a work of fiction. Names, characters, places, locations
and incidents are purely fictional and bear no relationship to
any real life individuals, living or dead, or to any actual places,
business establishments, locations, events or incidents.
Any resemblance is entirely coincidental.

This book is sold subject to the condition that it
shall not, by way of trade or otherwise, be lent, resold, hired out
or otherwise circulated without the prior consent of the publisher
in any form of binding or cover other than that in which it is published
and without a similar condition including this condition
being imposed on the subsequent purchaser.

® and TM are trademarks owned and used by the trademark owner
and/or its licensee. Trademarks marked with ® are registered with the
United Kingdom Patent Office and/or the Office for Harmonisation
in the Internal Market and in other countries.

First published in Great Britain 2022
by Mills & Boon, an imprint of HarperCollins*Publishers* Ltd,
1 London Bridge Street, London, SE1 9GF

www.harpercollins.co.uk

HarperCollins*Publishers*
1st Floor, Watermarque Building,
Ringsend Road, Dublin 4, Ireland

Snowed In with the Surgeon © 2022 Scarlet Wilson

Saving Christmas for the ER Doc © 2022 Pamela Brooks

ISBN: 978-0-263-30144-1

11/22

MIX
Paper | Supporting
responsible forestry
FSC™ C007454

This book is produced from independently certified FSC™ paper
to ensure responsible forest management.
For more information visit: www.harpercollins.co.uk/green.

Printed and Bound in Spain using 100% Renewable Electricity
at CPI Black Print, Barcelona

SNOWED IN
WITH THE SURGEON

SCARLET WILSON

MILLS & BOON

To all the people who love Christmas
and Christmas movies just as much as I do.

And to the new member of the family—
Max, the best red Labrador in the world!

PROLOGUE

IT HAPPENED IN a flash. One second Paige McLeod was on her feet, the next she was flying into a wall, smashing against it and landing on the floor.

For a few seconds her brain didn't really compute what had happened. A&E was crazily busy—had been for the last few hours. The waiting room was packed, every cubicle full, and two ambulances were still waiting to offload their patients in the receiving bay.

She tried to breathe, and immediately realised her mistake. The air had been knocked clean out of her. Trying to breathe was a limited possibility. Her hand went to the back of her head, rubbing the spot that had hit the wall.

She was surrounded by feet, familiar voices, shouts and a scramble on the floor next to her.

Leo's face appeared in front of her. He muttered an expletive as he grabbed her around the shoulders and leaned over her, clearly doing a quick assessment.

'Paige? Are you okay?'

She could already feel his assessing eyes on her body. He looked over his shoulder to one of the black-uniformed cops—a familiar presence in a Scottish A&E on a Saturday night. 'Have you got him?'

There was an affirmative nod. Leo sighed and concentrated his gaze on Paige. 'Come on, let's get you checked.' He helped her to her feet.

She started to shake her head. 'It's too busy—' Then stopped as a wave of nausea surged upwards. She put her hand to her mouth as Leo steered her into the nearest sluice room and pulled her hair back from her face as she was sick. His muttered expletives told her just how angry he was.

Then there was another. 'You're bleeding,' he said.

She lifted her hand to her head and pulled it back. Sure enough, her fingers were smeared with blood. Before she had a chance to speak she felt something pressed against her head. Leo had her in a cubicle, a quick clean of her head wound and some paper sutures applied.

She was only glad he hadn't had to shave part of her scalp in order to put some proper stitches in. The wound must be superficial. It would be okay.

A few minutes later she was seated in the comfortable chair behind his desk, a glass of water in one hand, a sick bowl on the desk, as he shone a pen torch in her eyes.

She sighed and leaned back in the chair. 'I'm fine, I'm fine. I'll get back out there in a minute.'

'No, you won't.'

She blinked. She'd been struggling recently but hadn't spoken about it, and didn't really want anyone to know. She thought she'd kept her feelings hidden. But maybe she hadn't fooled Leo.

The comfortable chair didn't feel quite so comfy. She sat up. 'What do you mean?'

He let out a huge sigh and settled in the hard chair opposite. She'd never really thought about it before, but Leo's chair was immensely comfortable, and the chair at the other side of the desk was hard and unyielding— almost as if he didn't want any guest to stay too long. Clever guy. He'd been the head of this Glasgow A&E for as long as anyone could remember. There was a lot to learn here.

His voice was deep. 'Paige, this is the third time you've been assaulted at work in six months. Last time with your head injury I...' His voice cracked.

She leaned towards him and put her hand over his. 'That was *not* your fault.'

Leo lowered his head for a few seconds. Everyone knew the punch that had caused Paige's head injury had been aimed at Leo. For an older guy he was light on his feet and had ducked sideways to avoid it, not realising Paige was directly behind him.

His dark grey eyes looked at her. There was an air of resignation about him. 'Attacks on NHS staff are increasing. We both know that. And they're entirely unacceptable. We all know A&E bears the brunt of this. We have the drunks. The confused. The upset, and the angry. You're a brilliant doctor, Paige. I don't want to lose you. But I also don't want you to accept this as part of your job. None of us should.'

Paige blinked back tears that had formed in her eyes. Things were starting to catch up with her. Her ribs and shoulder were aching a little, and her head was pounding. She lifted one hand. 'But you need me. We're slammed out there.'

Leo nodded. 'We are. But I trust our colleagues. Everyone has been triaged. Those who need immediate care are getting it. Those who can wait, will wait.'

He leaned back and folded his arms. Then she watched him swallow. Oh, no. This was serious.

She was panicking inside. Those words. *I don't want to lose you.* It was as if he'd reached inside her head and seen all the thoughts she'd been having. Her feelings of self-doubt. The early mornings her alarm had gone off and she'd woken with a sensation of dread. The near belief that the last few attacks in A&E had been because she hadn't been completely on her game, and she'd probably deserved what had happened. She'd been thinking about leaving. About handing in her notice. But it made her feel like such a failure. Six years of university, followed by six years of working as a doctor. What an absolute waste. Didn't everyone want to be a doctor?

'Paige, when did you last have some time off?'

The words seemed to come out of nowhere, pulling her back from her thoughts. She blinked and pressed her lips together. She knew the answer to his question but didn't want to say it out loud. She'd willingly cancelled her first lot of annual leave when a fellow colleague had problems in her pregnancy. She'd cancelled her second lot when another colleague had come down with a short-term acute illness. It was what any reasonable human would do.

She lifted one hand. 'We're coming up on Christmas—our busiest time. I'm due to work. There's no way I can have time off right now.'

Leo gave a sad smile. 'Dr McLeod, as the head of this department, I've let you down. You've been assaulted in my department three times in six months, and you've cancelled holidays to cover for colleagues. Your dedication and expertise is not in question, Paige, but your wellbeing is.'

She opened her mouth to speak, but wasn't quite sure what to say. Now she really thought that Leo might know what she'd been thinking.

Leo continued. 'I'm giving you this week as sick leave, then four weeks as annual leave. By the time you come back, the new security staff I've requested for over a year will be in place, and our two new medics from Spain and Ireland will be in post. We'll have a full complement of staff, and we should be safer.'

She swallowed and looked around Leo's office. His walls were decorated with awards he'd been given, and photos of him with his arms around colleagues. All of the colleagues looked at him with admiration in their eyes. He was probably one of the best doctors she'd ever work with. She *was* tired. She was feeling a bit jaded. And all she really wanted to do was curl up in her bed. She was so used to clocking in every day, of doing extra hours to ensure that an elderly patient got a bed in the ward they needed, or waiting for a set of blood results or X-ray to come through so she could finish her care.

She knew exactly what she was doing. It was easy to push the memories of the assaults from her brain and stick them in some kind of box where they could be hidden and ignored. No member of healthcare staff should be assaulted. The whole world believed that. But it *did* happen. And Leo was right. It was time to take stock and ask questions. That was why he was in the job.

She looked down. Her hands were shaking. She hadn't even realised. Her voice shook too. 'What will I do?' she asked.

Work was her life and that was part of the reason she was so scared about the thoughts that had been circulating in her brain. If she didn't have her work, what would she have left? Her family was scattered across the country. Her close friends were all in the health service. All would be working over the next few weeks. She had a very nice flat, but lived alone. She didn't want to be alone right now.

Something flickered across Leo's eyes. 'You ski, don't you?'

She nodded. Paige had always been a sporty kind of girl, and had skied in a number of resorts around the world.

Leo flipped open his laptop and made a few keystrokes. He spun the laptop around. 'What do you think of this place?'

Paige's eyes widened. It was like a scene from a film. A snow-set chalet with large windows, perched on a hillside somewhere.

'It…it's magnificent,' she said simply. 'Where is it?'

Leo nodded. 'Switzerland. It belongs to a friend. He loans it out frequently. Usually to medical staff, or people who need some respite. It's right next to a ski resort.

Perfect for you, really. Let me check the dates with him.'
He tapped furiously.

Paige frowned. 'What?'

Leo waved his hand. 'You can go.' Then he looked up, and frowned. 'Do you have other plans? Am I over-stepping?'

She shook her head as tears welled in her eyes. 'No, I don't have other plans. But...how much is it?'

She hadn't been skiing in two years. She would absolutely love to go, and had never skied in Switzerland before.

Leo smiled at her. 'It's free. You just have to arrange your flights. My friend—he's a baron, an inventor—you might have heard of him. He's usually getting maligned in the press somewhere. His more philanthropic efforts always go unnoticed, but he actually likes that. He doesn't want the world to know he has a whole host of houses around the world that he loans out for people who need them.' Leo shook his head. 'He prefers his more cut-throat image. Helps with business apparently.'

'I don't know,' she said hesitantly. This whole thing was swamping her and her head was starting to pound uncomfortably, just like her shoulder. Part of her wondered if this was some kind of dream. Or a result of the head knock. Maybe she was actually still lying on the floor outside?

Leo's brow wrinkled. 'I mean, would you prefer New York, Bermuda, Hawaii, Gibraltar, or maybe South Africa or Brazil?'

Paige's eyes widened. 'He has houses in all those places?'

Leo rested his hands in his lap. 'He has more. And

it makes him sound frivolous. But this is what he does with those houses. A large number of charitable organisations use them for their clients too. The only condition is that it's kept quiet. He doesn't want journalists swooping in and invading the privacy of those who need it.' Leo looked thoughtful. 'It's been going on for more than twenty years.' He gave a shrug. 'I just thought the skiing place would suit you best.'

She nodded just as there was a ping from Leo's computer.

His face broke into a wide grin. 'Ah, there we are. It's free.'

'He's got back to you already?'

Leo laughed. 'I told you, he's a businessman. He uses every tool available. There's an automatic confirmation booking system for these places. It's yours.'

He pushed his laptop towards Paige again. 'Take a better look and I'll send the details to your phone.'

She really couldn't believe this. One minute she was being knocked against a wall at work, the next, she had five weeks off and was heading to some unnamed resort in the Alps where she could ski all day and sleep in what looked like a luxury chalet at night.

She sagged back in the chair.

'I need to observe you for the next six hours.' Leo's words were said as some kind of aside.

She shook her head and held out her hand. 'No. Give me some of the paracetamol I know you have in your top desk drawer. Check my pupils again if you want. I just had an unexpected knock.'

'You vomited,' he said again sharply, his doctor's eyes narrowed.

'Autonomic reaction,' she replied, equally sharply. 'And Esther is off today. I can speak to her if I feel unwell.'

Leo kept his gaze firmly on her as he pulled his phone from his pocket. Esther Cohen was her next-door neighbour and a fellow medic at the hospital. They had a reciprocal arrangement, with both having keys to each other's flats in case of emergency.

He finally looked down, pressed a few keys and sighed. 'Okay, I've texted her. Asked her to check on you in a few hours.'

She might have known he would have had Esther's number.

He pulled the painkillers from the desk drawer and tossed them towards her and she took two with the water she had. Her phone pinged and she looked down. All the details of the resort, along with details of the nearest airport.

'Text me when you arrive,' Leo said, coming around the desk and shining a pen torch in her eyes again, then nodding in satisfaction. 'Equal and reacting.'

He put a hand on her shoulder. 'How are you feeling? I was being serious. I can put you round in the Combined Assessment Unit for a few hours.'

This was actually real. It wasn't some weird kind of daydream. She was actually being sent home.

Paige stood up, her legs feeling less wobbly now. 'No, I'm good. I'll just grab my things from my locker.'

Leo nodded and held the door open for her. The corridor outside was a complete and utter rabble. Loud noises, shouts for assistance, staff hurrying past.

The temptation to step back into it was strong. Like a heavy commitment hanging over her head. But Leo's voice was right at her side. 'Go home, Paige,' he said quietly.

She pressed her lips together and strode along to the changing room, grabbing her thick winter coat and swapping her light shoes for winter boots.

A few moments later she was outside. It was still dark. A few ambulance personnel nodded at her as she zipped up her coat against the immediate chill in the air. Her breath steamed in front of her.

She took a few steps away from the main entrance, moving towards the orange-tinged streetlights and her home, which was only five minutes' walk away.

As the noise dimmed behind her and flakes of snow settled on her cheeks, the tears she had been holding back for months finally started to fall.

CHAPTER ONE

STEFAN BACHMANN MOVED quickly around the empty building, trying to hide his rage. The contractor could barely keep up with his long strides.

'What about those other rooms—when are they due to be finished? And why is there still equipment missing?'

The private hospital was due to open in less than two weeks. There was no chance of that happening.

'We've had some delays,' murmured the contractor, uttering the same words he had for the last few weeks. 'Seven of the suites are finished. Electricity and water are on in one half of the building. Tiling and bathroom fittings for those seven rooms and the staff area have been completed this week. The three operating rooms and recovery area is completed—but there are a few pieces of equipment still outstanding. Kitchen is almost complete.'

It sounded reasonable. But the luxury private hospital was way behind schedule. Only half of the actual works were complete.

He walked into a large room. It was an old ward—back from when this hospital had been used in the First

World War as rehabilitation for prisoners of war who were sent to recover in the mountain air.

Something curled inside his stomach. His great-grandfather had been one of those young men. Originally from Belgium, he'd been wounded and had met Stefan's great-grandmother here, one of the nurses in this hospital.

When he'd first walked through this place there had been definite echoes of the past. The hospital had been reused in what seemed like a hundred different ways since its original purpose. But this part, the place he stood in, for some reason had always remained untouched. Of course, it was in the plans to be refurbished. This was going to be the gym for the physios to use when required.

Stefan could almost laugh out loud. This whole place was going to be almost a replica of another luxury private surgery clinic he worked in just west of Hollywood. There, stars were photographed with hats on their heads and wearing sunglasses, 'pretending' to hide from the world as they attended, usually for some kind of cosmetic surgery.

This place was part of the same company. But the setting was all about privacy. The stars coming here for their surgery wouldn't want it made public. Most of them would need prolonged stays, some to recover from botched surgeries in other parts of the world, some because they needed treatment alongside their surgery. Not every star wanted the world to know they had some kind of cancer. It could affect contracts and deals for them. Stefan had a leading oncologist working alongside him.

All the latest treatments were available, along with a host of highly trained staff who could administer them and monitor any after-effects.

This prestigious alpine retreat could really do some good. Which was the only reason Stefan was here. He'd been reluctant initially when he was approached about acquiring a premises in his homeland. He'd known about this old hospital all his life, and knew the site would be just what they were looking for.

It was close to an exclusive ski resort and reached by a long, winding road which in some parts, and at some times of year, could be impassable, due to ice and snow. There were a number of private properties that lined this road, and part of the agreement for the re-furbishment of the hospital was that they took on the ongoing maintenance for the road. It was obviously in the company's best interests, but it made Stefan a little uncomfortable. This road had been laughingly called 'Millionaires' Row' by the locals. The people who lived in those luxury houses were more than capable of keeping their own road in a reasonable state. But since the hospital was at the top of the track it seemed to have fallen to them.

There had already been a few issues with the building equipment—much of which was heavy. Some of the trucks had struggled in the bad weather to reach the resort, and a few had to turn back, all adding to the delays.

Stefan paused for a moment and ran his fingers through his dark hair. He wasn't even supposed to be in charge of this part of the process. He was a surgeon, not a tradesman. But their business manager was back in

Hollywood, where his wife was due to have twins. He'd had to fly back, and Stefan had been left to oversee what should have been the finishing touches for the resort.

Time was something that Stefan didn't have. He'd spent his life going from one project to another, throwing himself wholeheartedly into every one of them. He'd never learned to slow down, always saying yes when asked to do extra work or take on extra responsibilities. So the fact that this project wasn't complete—that he suspected the workmen might have been taking longer than they should, felt like a personal failure.

Coming close to home amplified those feelings. When he'd told his parents he wanted to go to medical school they'd both worked day and night to help their son fulfil his dreams. They'd always had a strong work ethic and had passed that on to him.

But when he'd got a phone call from his dad to let him know his mother was sick he'd felt hideously guilty. Even worse, he'd been only halfway home when she'd died from a massive myocardial infarction.

Apparently, she'd been having occasional bouts of chest pain, but hadn't had time to see anyone. That made the guilt even worse. He had nearly completed his training at this point. He should have picked up on it. He should have intervened.

It didn't matter how many people had patted his shoulder and told him how proud his mother would have been. The sadness in his father's eyes still haunted him to this day. It made him want to work even harder, go even faster, to be worthy of the sacrifice his mother had made for him. It left him without a minute in the day, but that was the only way he could cope.

He pulled out his phone and started dictating notes. At his estimate, this place was at least six weeks behind schedule—and that was being optimistic. They couldn't open with only half the place refurbished. The front part of the building looked pristine. The suites were finished to the high standard he'd expect, with ample room for guests to have relatives or staff stay with them. But the rest of the facility was nowhere near complete.

'Do we have delivery dates for the rest of the materials?'

The contractor flicked through the paper attached to his clipboard. Stefan could tell he was stressing the man. But he knew exactly how much this had all cost. They should have been finished on time. He made a mental note to check if there were penalties included in the contract for late completion.

'Some of the materials are arriving in the next few days. There's a big delivery of minor equipment tomorrow. It should have been rescheduled until more of the works were completed but was missed.'

'What about the internet provider? That was supposed to be installed two weeks ago.'

'They had problems with the installation. They're due back tomorrow. I'll check the weather forecast, to make sure there are no problems for the rest of the deliveries.'

Stefan naturally glanced up at the sky. It was dark and gloomy. He knew that some of the tougher ski runs had been closed earlier, due to the high winds. He'd skied since he was a child and always welcomed the chance to return home and get back on the slopes. One look at the sky made him think it was highly unlikely that his favourite runs would open again later today.

He waved a hand at the contractor. 'We'll talk tomorrow. I expect all the tradesmen onsite and ready to move this project along. Enough time has been lost.'

The contractor muttered something under his breath but gave Stefan a nod as he left.

Stefan moved over to the nearest set of doors. They opened out to a balcony that had a magnificent view of the surrounding mountainside. Once the transformation was complete, this hospital would be fantastic.

He could imagine how alien this setting might have seemed to men who had been prisoners of war. A little check through history had shown there had been multiple cases of tuberculosis, amputees and those who were termed as suffering 'shellshock'. Many of the sickest had been sent here—those who were never expected to return to war. The job of the staff here had been to try to ensure the men would regain some kind of quality of life that would help them eventually return home at the end of the war. The alpine air and peaceful surroundings would have played a large part in that, just like he hoped it would assist in the recovery of the new kind of patients they would bring to this clinic.

As a plastic surgeon he could perform many of the popular procedures. He'd reshaped numerous noses, chins, abdomens, breasts and buttocks. But his passion was for the highly specialist skills required to repair babies' cleft lips and palates. He frequently spent time working for Médecins Sans Frontières on a voluntary basis, carrying out these operations all over the world. Not all of these procedures were straightforward. Part of his agreement in his new role was to be able to bring children who required more detailed surgery to either the clinic in the US or to Switzerland for their procedure.

And even though the workload was extensive and exhausting he knew his father was proudest of the pictures he showed him of the children who could eat and speak properly because of his surgical skills. Working constantly didn't give him time or space to think about the guilt he still felt. It meant that he always had something to talk to his father about, rather than acknowledge the huge hole left in both of their lives by the death of his mother.

He gazed out over the white-topped mountains again and leaned backwards, stretching out his tense muscles. He couldn't wait to hit the slopes, but first he had to make sure everything was in order here. He had two online meetings to attend, but the internet had not yet been put into place in the hospital—another thing to add to the list. He'd have to go back down to a hotel at the base of the mountain. He'd come up here today in the hope that things might have moved on in the last two weeks. Stefan glanced at the light backpack he'd brought with him. Although the staff accommodation was ready, without internet, he couldn't function properly. He had another case of belongings in his car. He'd leave the backpack here and hope that by the time he came back up an internet connection might have been installed.

He sighed as he made his way back to his car. It was starting to get dark, and the last thing he needed was to end up driving in difficult conditions. He knew exactly what this mountain road could be like. He made another mental note to check about the activity to maintain and upgrade the road before he climbed into the car, pressed the ignition and started down the darkening road.

'Are you sure this is the way?'

Paige was trying not to appear panicked. The journey from the airport should have taken around an hour, but she'd been in this pre-booked private service car for longer than that. Whilst at first the sleek dark car had looked pristine, she'd heard the wheels spinning a few times on this road—the awfully dark road.

In her head, she'd gone from tired and weary doctor to imminent victim in some crime novel. The kind that as soon as the woman steps into a prearranged car in a foreign country, and heads down some dark country road, has the reader shaking their head in knowing anticipation of what comes next.

The driver mumbled something in reply and gave a wave of his hand. The back of the car was wide and spacious and there was a screen separating her and the driver, which made communication difficult. Her mind started to go into overdrive. She could be dumped somewhere on this mountain road. She could be left in a snowdrift. Or maybe the driver was some secret super-villain and would leave her locked in the back of the car and take off in his helicopter, leaving her to starve to death in the luxury vehicle.

She eyed the small cabinet with soda and nuts. How long would they last? She closed her eyes for a second, hearing Leo's voice in her head, telling her to calm down and give her overtired brain a rest. She'd been up for over twenty-four hours now. For some reason she couldn't sleep last night, wondering if she'd packed the right equipment, and changing her book selection several times, then making sure she had them all downloaded onto her tablet in case she lost her luggage.

Thankfully, her case and her ski equipment were in the boot of the car after being safely retrieved from the airport carousel.

There was a screech and she found herself flung to the left, cheek slamming into the side window. Her body jerked forward as the seatbelt automatically tightened and held her safely in place. The car seemed to move in slow motion, spinning sideways, then moving backwards. Lights streamed directly in front of her. But there was no sound of impact. No metal crunching.

No sensation of falling off a mountainside.

Paige took a few breaths, glad her seatbelt had limited any damage. Her shoulder might be a bit bruised, but that would be nothing new. She was about to ask the driver if he was okay when she heard a stream of angry words. The next second, the driver's door opened and he was out onto the road.

The stream of words amplified. She strained for a few moments as she struggled with the seatbelt release, trying to identify the language. She knew that four languages were spoken in Switzerland—Swiss German, French, Italian and Rhaeto-Romanic. This sounded like her first introduction to Swiss German expletives.

She gave her body a shake and stepped outside the

car into the dark winding road. There was another car's headlights illuminating theirs. The brisk cold air stole her breath and she shivered.

Her driver, a short, grey-haired man, was gesturing and shouting wildly at the other guy. Whoever the other guy was, he was much taller and leaner. It was hard to see properly when the lights were directly towards her, but Paige was too tired to be polite.

She walked between the two men. 'What happened?'

For a second there was silence, probably as they both adjusted to her strong Scottish accent. When she was tired, and annoyed, her voice did tend to come across as very fierce. She took a deep breath and waved towards the two vehicles, trying to speak clearly. 'What happened? Is anyone hurt?'

The taller man turned towards her. 'Your driver doesn't seem to know how to navigate mountain roads late at night.'

He was giving her a strange look, his brow furrowed. If he wasn't quite so angry, he might be quite handsome, but being handsome wouldn't excuse his rudeness.

'Are you injured?' she asked again.

He jerked a little, as if he was just now considering other things, and replied in perfect English. 'No. Are you?'

She shook her head. 'Nothing that won't look after itself.' She folded her arms across her chest. 'Is there a reason you're causing such a scene on a dark road, in the middle of the night?'

'Me?' He looked incredulous. 'Your driver clearly

doesn't know these roads. He came around that bend far too fast. He was halfway over my side of the road.'

She arched her eyebrows and glanced towards his car. It was a large four-by-four, with extremely large tyres with deep treads. It might not have snow chains, but she could bet Mr Arrogant would be able to put them on his car in an instant.

'All the more reason that a local like yourself should drive with more due care and attention—presuming, of course, that you *do* know these roads. You should be used to tourists or strangers on these roads.'

She could see the fury build behind his eyes. She knew she was being cheeky, but she didn't care. His first action hadn't been to make sure everyone was okay. His first action had been to get out of his car and shout. She tried to forget that her driver had done exactly the same.

'Idiots shouldn't be on these roads. He—' he gestured to her driver, who she was sure could follow some of the conversation, glaring at him '—shouldn't be driving at night.'

'*He* didn't have much choice, since my flight was delayed by five hours,' she countered quickly. 'And—' she looked him up and down, trying to ignore his broad shoulders, slim waist, and she definitely wasn't looking at those blue eyes she'd glimpsed as he'd turned his head in the lights '—it appears there is more than one kind of idiot on the roads tonight.'

There was silence. He stared at her for a few moments, and she wondered if the edge of his lip turned up in faint amusement. Then he shook his head. 'Are you always this friendly?'

'I was just about to ask the same.'

Silence again. 'Where are you headed—are you lost?'

Paige looked over at her driver, who had understood every word and gestured to further up the mountain road. 'I'm staying in Chalet Versailles, up the road somewhere.'

The stranger put his hands on his hips and gave her a strange, calculating glance. Did he know who normally stayed at that lodge?

He gave a soft shake of his head again, then gestured behind him. 'It's only a few hundred metres further up on the right. The turning is clearly marked. Don't go any further. The road comes to a dead end at the hospital at the top.'

Her eyes widened and her brain sparked. 'There's a hospital up here?' She couldn't hide the surprise in her voice.

'There used to be—in the First World War, and there will be again in the future. It's not running yet.' He frowned again. 'Anyhow, if you reach that you've gone too far.'

Her stiff shoulders relaxed a little. 'See, you can be nice when you want to be.'

It was his turn to arch his eyebrows. 'Just make sure your driver takes it slowly. And warn him about driving back down the mountain. He really needs thicker tyres.'

Paige heard a distinct tut behind her, and knew instantly it was her driver. She turned back, but the stranger was already climbing back in his car. A few seconds later, he gunned the engine of his four-by-four and swept past them, leaving them in the inky-black road again.

Her driver muttered angrily and showed her back to the car, slamming the door behind her. Paige settled back into the comfortable seat. She should go back into panic mode, worrying about what might happen next. But her brain wasn't ready.

Instead, it was fixated on the tall, dark, handsome stranger. She hadn't even asked him his name. And, for some strange reason, she wished she had.

CHAPTER TWO

SHE'D NEVER BEEN this comfortable in her entire life. Last night she'd barely taken the time to look around after her still-muttering driver had dropped her off. She'd tipped him heavily in the hope it would make up for the road mishap, but had just been too tired to spend time exploring her surroundings.

She'd carried her small bag up to the bedroom at the top of the wide stairs, taken a little breath at the size of it, and promptly pulled on her pyjamas and climbed into the four-poster bed. She couldn't remember a single thing after that, but right now she could swear this was the comfiest she'd ever been.

Part of her wanted to take a note of the brand of duvet, pillows and sheets. But part of her knew it would likely all be widely outside her price range, so she just snuggled a little lower in the bed and let her eyes flicker open.

Just as she'd remembered, the room was bigger than the whole of her kitchen and living room in her flat. Most things were white. Paige cringed. She was quite accident-prone and would likely manage to cover things in coffee spills or chocolate smudges.

She pushed herself up in the bigger than king-size bed. The room was wide and inviting, a large wooden dresser, wardrobe and chest of drawers against the walls. A door leading to what she assumed was a bathroom was ajar. A television was mounted on the wall in front of her. She leaned to the side and picked up the list of instructions for all the electronics in the room. A few presses on a remote control changed the lighting from warm, to bright white, to pale pink, then violet, then green. Another button set off a low rumble. Paige watched in wonder as the blackout blind on the large window slowly lifted.

She pulled back. Bright white wasn't just in her room, it was directly outside. It was already morning and the Alps stretched in every direction, as far as the eye could see. It was like something directly from a Christmas card. White, dotted with bits of green, and a few buildings spaced out across the view.

She flung back her covers and walked over, taking a deep breath. This was absolutely gorgeous. Her overtired body was suddenly invigorated. Look at that snow! She hadn't skied in over two years and couldn't wait to get out there.

Paige stuck her feet into her slippers and washed her face, brushed her teeth and wrapped herself in the luxury bathrobe that was behind the door of her en suite bathroom.

Ten minutes later she'd toured the whole chalet. Luxurious beyond words. Seven bedrooms, all with en suite bathrooms. Two other spacious bathrooms. A formal dining room, sitting room, study, nook, library and two other 'lounging spaces'—she didn't even know what to call them. A large pantry filled with stacks and stacks of tinned food, spices and bakery ingredients.

The modern kitchen gleamed, full of state-of-the-art appliances, with a few instructions in a folder at the side. In the middle of the kitchen table was a huge basket, packed with groceries and some fun snacks. The fridge had all the essentials for breakfast, lunch and dinner. She followed the instructions and flicked the switch on the coffee machine as she prepared some eggs on the stove of the range cooker.

This place was really out of this world. She could swear she was in a Bond movie. Any minute now some super-villain would walk through one of the doors and ask what she was doing in their house. She glanced at the clock on the wall. It was after seven. The slopes here were already open.

She picked up the phone and dialled the number connecting her to the resort to arrange a pickup at the chalet. The owner really had thought of everything.

Running upstairs, she pulled on her ski gear, goggles and gloves. Her ski equipment had been left at the front door last night, so she was good to go.

She moved through to the main room and stopped. A Christmas tree. She hadn't even thought about that.

She smiled and moved over, touching the beautiful, colour-coordinated decorations. Of course, these would have been done by a professional decorator. Not the normal hotchpotch that she put out year after year, which had started to look bedraggled. A large glistening star crowned the tree and Paige looked around, wondering if she was actually still sleeping in the bed upstairs. This was too good. Too perfect.

She sank down into the large red sofa for a moment, overwhelmed by it all.

It all seemed too much. Too much for one person. Too much for one little doctor who was here on her own. Too much for someone who should probably just have given themselves a shake and gone back to work, instead of agreeing to take some time off. When Leo had told her this place was used for respite, had he known that she was contemplating whether she still wanted to be a doctor? Or maybe the Baron only wanted health professionals in his resorts—would he be angry if it turned out Paige didn't want to be one any more? Had Leo known how spectacular this place would be when he'd sent her here?

Somehow, she thought that he might.

The thoughts just kept swirling round and round in her head.

She breathed for a few moments, trying to get some perspective. Telling herself that the local police were not about to show up here, demand to see her papers, and accuse her of breaking and entering. The code that she'd been sent had opened the door, and turned off the alarm with no problem at all. This was definitely where she was supposed to be.

There was a large fireplace in front of her. This spot would be a spectacular place to snuggle tonight. She could eat some of the chocolate in the giant basket and find a book in the library she had yet to properly explore. It didn't matter that she'd brought several of her own—exploring someone else's library would be fun. This really was her idea of heaven.

She wandered back to the main door. There was a smiley face on the store cupboard at the entrance and she pulled it open curiously, then stopped dead.

It wasn't really a 'store' cupboard. It was a full ski equipment closet. She could see boots, poles, skis, clothing, goggles and other equipment lining the walls and methodically stored. As she wandered along the walls her hands reached out to touch some of the items. She'd brought her own ski equipment, but instantly recognised that this was prestige equipment. Items she'd never be able to purchase in a million years.

She moved back and looked at the list on the wall, naming everything in the store cupboard. If she had the time, she could cost up the entire contents and likely weep. The list also had instructions, stating that all equipment was free to use, a request to keep the store tidy, to follow guidelines for care of equipment—there was a shelf with a variety of products, including boot-liners and ski wax.

Paige walked back down the rack of skis, her hand automatically lifting to touch some. There was a distinctive gold logo that she recognised. The phrase *Fastest skis on the planet* was the tagline of the exclusive brand. She ran her fingers down the top of the ski, her mouth slightly dry. She'd probably never get a chance to try this brand of ski again. There were six pairs in a row, all of varying length, some on-piste, some all-mountain. Of course, there was a pair just her size.

There was a buzz at the front door. It must be the

driver from the resort. She didn't let herself think too much, just lifted the skis carefully, along with a set of matching poles, and made her way to the door.

The driver gave her a cheerful nod. He lifted his hands. 'Bad weather expected,' he said. 'Best get in as much skiing as possible.'

Paige was surprised but, then again, she hadn't even looked at any weather reports. 'Today?'

He shrugged. 'Definitely tomorrow and a few days after. High winds and storms expected.' He lifted her equipment and carried it to the vehicle. 'They didn't mention today, but look at those dark clouds.' He pointed to a dark smudge in the distance. 'At this time in the morning? I think the weather might be coming in early.'

Paige frowned but then looked back towards her chalet. 'If I have to stay inside for a few days, it won't be a problem.'

'You have food? Wine? You might want to get some supplies before you head back here.'

She climbed into the front seat of the vehicle next to him. 'I might grab a few things. But the chalet came fully prepared. I think I'll be okay.' She leaned forward as he started the engine. 'Tell me about the slopes. What's your recommendation?'

The driver began talking and Paige settled back into the comfortable seat to listen. Even if she only had one day to ski to begin with, it would still be a good start.

She watched as they started down the twisting road, her mind flashing back to last night and the grumpy handsome man. She was a little fascinated about the hospital being renovated up the road from the chalet. Maybe, if she got a chance, she could take a walk up and have a look around. If it had been used in the First World War she could only imagine the history of the place.

She was trying to pretend she wasn't a little curious about the guy too. Why had he been up at the hospital at night? Did he work there? Was he a businessman? The suit had been a bit flash. An accountant maybe, or someone overseeing the work? If a hospital was being renovated, shouldn't it have been tradesmen and contractors that she'd come across, instead of a man in a suit?

Paige leaned back and looked out of the window at the winter landscape. She could think about the mystery of the hospital, and the man, later. Right now, there were slopes to explore.

He loved it. The sensation of moving at speed, making tiny adjustments with his weight and the curve of his body, all to enhance the smoothness of his run. He could do this in his sleep. Skiing had been part of his life since he was a child. For Stefan, skiing was as easy as breathing.

He'd been on the slopes since first light. It was starting to get busier now, and that always slightly annoyed him. He'd skied on some of the most difficult runs on the planet: Harakiri in Austria, Corbet's Couloir in Wyoming, La Grave in France, and Delirium Dive in Alberta. There were, of course, equally challenging black runs at the many resorts in Switzerland but, unfortunately, today's weather meant that all black runs in the local vicinity were closed. Stefan had to content himself with an easier red run, and it was busier than it should be.

He expertly glided around someone stuck midway down the run. Another skier who'd moved up from the beginner slopes before they were really ready to. It was common here, which was why Stefan usually stuck to the black runs. Of course, they too had their fair share of skiers who tried them before they were ready; however, the traffic was always a bit less frantic on the tougher runs.

He'd stayed out longer than he'd intended to. Serious skiers, like himself, were usually first on the slopes and finished while most of those at the resort were still eating breakfast. The late starters had now all caught up with him and the slopes seemed cluttered, and just waiting for accidental collisions. There was a weather warning for the next few days, extremely high winds and general storms. It was unlikely most of the people here would be able to ski then, so, like them, he was trying to get as much time in as possible.

Part of his early morning run today had been about shaking off his frustration at the delays in the project. His frustrations had boiled over last night too, when what seemed like another tourist had been driving on the twisty and precarious mountain road without enough due care and attention. It had turned out to be one of the private drivers from the nearby airport—but that still didn't excuse the fact he'd come around the corner with half his vehicle on the wrong side of the road.

It hadn't helped that his very feisty passenger had called Stefan out on his behaviour almost immediately. He couldn't get that accent out of his head. He'd worked with doctors from all over the world, but the Scottish accent was entirely unique, and sometimes almost impossible to understand. Whoever she was, she'd been headed for the billionaire chalet just down from the hospital. He'd never had time to find out who owned it—maybe it was her?—but, whoever she was, she had a fiery glint in her eye, and a take-no-prisoners attitude.

He'd liked it. Pity he hadn't taken the time to find out her name. But last night his temper had been shot, and his mood irritable. When he'd finally got to bed, his mind had been fixated on the brown-haired, dark-eyed woman who'd put him firmly in his place.

A flash of red crossed his vision and he momentarily slowed, before realising the skier had passed him as if he were barely moving. Something twisted in his guts. Whoever this skier was, they were skilled, and fast—very, very fast.

There was a well-known signature gold flash from the back of the skis they were using and he groaned. Ten-thousand-dollar skis. Of course.

He lowered his body, moving closer to the white packed snow beneath him as he curved into the slope, picking up speed along the way. He didn't want to catch the other skier. That would be juvenile. But he didn't want to be passed as if he were an absolute beginner, or the oldest man on the slope.

Wind whistled past him, hitting his cheeks in a satisfying surge. His tinted ski goggles kept his eyes protected and his vision clear as he continued down the slope, gaining speed all the way.

He pretended he wasn't fixated on the figure in red. It was a woman. He could tell that now from the curves. She was starting to slow down, clearly getting ready for the end of the run. But Stefan had never been the guy to slow down. Adrenaline made him remain low and still hugging the slope as he neared her.

He passed others on the way down, all slowing, but Stefan waited until the end before pulling up sharply, turning sideways and sending a huge spray of snow into the sky above.

Several people behind the barrier at the bottom were showered lightly with snow. A few glared as they wiped their sleeves. He turned his head from side to side, but the skier in red had already disappeared.

He shook his head. It was too busy now, and his concentration was going. There was a thud behind him as someone misjudged their speed and crashed into the safety barrier. Stefan clicked off his skis and stepped over to pick up the crumpled heap of a teenage boy. 'Okay?' he checked.

The boy pulled his helmet off and groaned, rubbing one of his legs as his two friends glided to a more elegant halt next to them. Stefan bent a bit lower to check the boy's face. 'Really, are you okay? Can you stand?'

The boy put his weight on his legs and grimaced. 'Sorry, I thought I could stop in time.'

He looked completely embarrassed, and his friends weren't helping as they started to barrage him with good-humoured abuse. Stefan appreciated it. He'd been this teenager once.

'You live and learn,' he said simply. 'You'll be covered in bruises tomorrow though.'

The boy nodded and Stefan left him with his friends, picking up his skis and heading towards the two coffee shops. One was flash and fashionable, with light colours and floor-to-ceiling windows after being refurbished in the last few years, but Stefan headed into the other. Filled with wood and with smaller windows, this place was a mixture of café and bar. All orders were taken at the broad wooden bar, with customers expected to collect their drinks and food when they were ready. There were two traditional fireplaces, one at either end of the brick building, both surrounded by an array of worn armchairs and sofas, all in a variety of colours. Stefan's favourite was probably the most worn in the entire café. It was dark grey, some kind of velour that had patches on the arms and the imprint of probably twenty years' worth of skiers' behinds.

He moved to the bar and ordered a hot chocolate—a drink that just didn't work well in the Hollywood Hills, but as soon as he reached here it was the first thing he ordered.

For breakfast, he ordered a large bowl of muesli. Through the small windows he could see dark clouds rolling in from the west. If he ate now, he'd be able to concentrate when he got back up the mountain to see if the contractors were all on site. It was essential he ensured the work moved along on time.

As he waited for his order, he could hear chatter and laughter from the other skiers. There was what looked like a school party gathered near the entrance. Some families, lots of couples and groups of friends. The chair lift constantly hummed with figures with their dangling skis on their feet methodically ascending the mountain. The parallel ski lift had the odd mishap, resulting in someone landing on their back and a single rogue ski generally disappearing in inevitably the wrong direction.

Stefan smiled as he lifted his hot chocolate topped with cream and bowl of muesli, making his way in pure habit to the large grey chair with its back to him. As he moved sideways to sit down, he noticed the figure in his chair, a red ski jacket lying on the nearby sofa. Because he hadn't realised anyone was sitting there, he was far too close and his leg bumped an elbow, sending coffee sloshing to the floor.

He spoke instantly in German, apologising profusely. His eyes caught the stack of toast on the table in front of the armchair, butter and jam next to it. He realised his second mistake. This person had to be from the UK. He switched language. 'I'm so sorry. I didn't realise someone was sitting here.'

Dark eyes looked up at him, scanning his ski gear. There was a real flare of annoyance, and then her forehead creased and her gaze narrowed.

'You,' she said accusingly.

It took him a few seconds. Red ski gear. He looked sideways to where all the skis were currently stowed for the patrons of the café. Sure enough, the gold-logoed designer skis caught his eye.

'Do you always ski like some flash idiot?' the female voice continued.

The thick Scottish accent slayed him as pieces started to drop in place. The woman from last night.

'Do you always hire a driver that drives like an idiot?'

Her mouth fell open and her mug tipped to the side again, sloshing more coffee. He caught it and wrapped his hand around it. 'Apologies, let me get you another.' He gave a quick order to the woman behind the bar and slid the red jacket along the sofa, sitting down in its place.

The woman looked at him again. 'Do you just steamroller yourself through life?'

He smiled. Spark. And sass. Relief washed over him. After he'd finished his training as a doctor, he'd completed two six-month placements in the UK, one in London, one in Edinburgh. He'd loved the people, their straight talking and no messing around. He actually missed it. Surgery in the Hollywood Hills with a prestigious client group was a very different ballgame.

He leaned over and held out his hand. 'Stefan Bachmann.'

She eyed his hand as if it were growing microscopic bugs, before wiping her own palm on her red salopettes and shaking it firmly. 'Paige McLeod.'

'Where are you from in Scotland, Paige?'

'Oh, no.' She wagged a finger at him. 'You don't get to sit down all smug after, one…' she counted off on her fingers '…you tried to blame us for a near miss last night. Two, you tried to drown me in snow with your flashy and, may I add…' she leaned forward '…unsafe stop earlier. And three, you just bulldozered past me and spilled my coffee.' She pointed to the table in front of her. 'If you'd knocked my toast, it would have been game over.'

He laughed. 'Don't get between a Scots girl and her breakfast. Is there anything you don't want to blame me for?'

She looked at her half-filled coffee cup. 'Nope, I

think everything is absolutely your fault.' Her dark eyes
flashed and it was the first time he really got a chance to
look at her properly. Last night had been too dark. Even
now, the light from outside wasn't particularly good and
the lighting in the café was deliberately dull. But that
couldn't hide how attractive this Scottish woman was.
Her long, dark brown hair was pulled back in a ponytail.
Her pale skin was clear, but revealed fine bones and dark
brown eyes that had a lot of fire in them. There was no
obvious surgery. Who was this woman? She was skiing
with very expensive equipment. She was staying in one
of the finest properties on the mountainside, one that no
one really knew anything about. Was she the billionaire,
or was her husband? His eyes took a fleeting glance at
her hand. No ring. He was surprised by the fact he liked
that. She moved her head slightly and something twisted
in him. Was that a faint bruise on her cheek?

The waiter behind the bar gave him a wave and Stefan stood up to collect the fresh coffee, setting it down
next to Paige's toast. 'Coffee can be replaced. Here you
go. Anyhow, it's partly your fault. You are, after all, sitting in my seat.'

She'd started buttering her toast and looked up in-
credulously. '*Your* seat?' He could tell she was enjoying this sparring.

He lifted his bowl of muesli and shrugged. 'It's my
favourite. Whenever I come here, it's where I like to sit.'

'So, you think you own everything?'

He shook his head. 'No. But don't you have a favourite chair in a favourite café back home?'

She thought for a moment and nodded. 'Actually, I

do. There's a café with old-fashioned bench seats opposite where I work. They have a special of the day, apple or blackberry tarts, custard doughnuts, caramel cakes, Victoria sponge or homemade Swiss roll. I make it my business to make sure the special is up to standard.'

It was a longer answer than he'd expected. She clearly did have a favourite café.

'So then, we're not so different.' There was a hint of satisfaction in his voice.

But it was clear she was not letting him get away with that. 'Don't bet on it.' She arched her eyebrows and then changed the subject. 'You're local?'

'Yes, and no.'

She opened the jam. 'Are we talking in riddles now?'

Stefan wrinkled his nose. 'My family are from around here. I grew up here, but I've worked away for most of my adult life. I come back at least three times a year, and I hope to be back a bit more.'

Paige looked at him with interest. 'Because of the hospital.'

He nodded. 'Because of the hospital.'

She took a bite of her toast and closed her eyes. 'Bliss,' she sighed, then took another bite.

After a few seconds, she brought her attention back to him. 'So, what do you do? Do you own the place—the hospital?'

'Yes, and no.' Then he laughed, realising what he'd done.

She leaned back in his chair. 'Let me just get comfortable in *your* chair. Because it's clear you're going to talk in riddles all day.' There was something about the grin on her face as she said it. He liked the fact that Scottish Paige had kept him on his toes from the moment she'd met him.

Paige turned her head to the window momentarily. In the last ten minutes snow had started pelting the windows outside and a dark cloud had moved over the area, causing the inside of the café to look quite gloomy. There were a number of people leaving the slopes now and heading back down to the town beneath.

'Looks like we came in at the right time. My driver this morning warned me to go and pick up some provisions down in the main resort as the weather forecast wasn't good. I don't think I'll bother now. The chalet has more than enough food for the next few days.'

'You're staying alone?'

She blinked and looked straight at him. It was a straightforward question, but she immediately wondered why he'd asked.

She gave a nod. 'Yes, there's plenty of room for more people. But it's just me. As far as I know, there won't be anyone joining me.'

She could almost hear her friend from work screaming in her ear. Red flag. Why would you tell a stranger that? You've told him you're alone, in a remote chalet, in a strange country. But, although she'd just met Stefan, she didn't feel wary of him. She wasn't at all worried about him knowing she was alone in the chalet. In fact, it was probably good that someone who was working further up the mountainside knew she was alone, just in case she needed help with anything.

What would she do in a power cut? If the pipes froze? She didn't know the answer to any of these questions, although she had a sneaking suspicion the answers might actually be in one of the very organised folders in the chalet. But it would be nice to have a backup plan.

A few other skiers were standing at one of the small windows, glancing up the slopes and having a worried-looking conversation. It made her a little uncomfortable, so she turned her attention back to Stefan, who was finishing his muesli. 'Hey, you didn't finish your riddle.'

He set his bowl down and then held up both hands. 'Yeah, the hospital was bought by the company I work for, but I'm also a shareholder. They were looking for a property in the Alps and obviously I knew of the place because I'd been brought up here. The company bought the old hospital with the purpose of refurbishing it into a new respite facility.'

'So, who needs a very expensive respite facility in the Alps these days?'

He gave her a careful look and she realised the words might have sounded judgemental—the last thing she was.

'The main people using this facility will be those requiring, or requesting, some kind of surgery, and those who need to undergo treatment of some kind and don't want to do it in the public domain. But not everyone coming to the clinic will be a private patient.'

She frowned. 'Who else will be coming?' Her head was already full of international models, actors and pop stars. Maybe even a few politicians.

There was a strange noise. A kind of shift.

'I work for another organisation...' Stefan's eyes widened and he stopped mid-sentence.

Then she could swear the ground moved beneath her feet.

'Everyone get down!' yelled Stefan. 'Avalanche!'

Paige did the opposite. She stood up. There were people outside. Lots of them. Next minute there was an arm around her middle, pulling her down and behind one of the sofas.

The noise was simultaneously increasing in volume to a loud roar. Everything around her was shaking. Plates and glasses were crashing to the ground. She was conscious of the full length of Stefan's body tucked behind hers. He had one hand still around her waist, and the other over the top of her head.

The noise was so loud now, people were screaming and then there was an almighty crash and everything went dark.

Paige was frozen. A punch. A ricochet off her head. Pain in her shoulder and side. She was having flashbacks to her attacks in the hospital.

She pulled her hands over her head and curled inwards, trying to stave off the panic that was threatening to take over her body. Her heart thudded in her chest as a quiet voice said in her ear, 'Paige, just breathe.' It was calm. It was steady. And warm breath hit the skin at the side of her neck. She was lying in an almost intimate position with a perfect stranger, who could clearly feel her starting to panic.

Someone was crying and the sound seemed to flick some kind of switch inside her. Paige took a deep breath and sat up, pushing her hair out of her eyes and taking in the chaotic scene around her. Most people were on the ground, a few were clutching arms or faces. Broken dishes were strewn across the floor. The lights flickered.

She felt a movement behind her. A hand on her forearm. 'Okay?'

She nodded, realising that Stefan had moved. In a dazed silence she watched as he moved across the room, going from person to person. It took her only a few seconds to realise what he was doing.

She stood up, steadying herself on the grey armchair, which was still upright. She moved over next to Stefan, where he was wrapping something around a woman's arm. 'You're a doctor?'

He looked up, obviously surprised to see her on her feet. 'A surgeon,' he said quietly as he tied off the makeshift bandage.

Of course. He wasn't some kind of businessman involved in a hospital. He was a doctor—probably what a lot of people needed right now.

'What can I do?' she asked.

His gaze narrowed. 'Do you have any training?'

'I'm a doctor,' she replied. 'I work in A&E.'

Surprise flashed across his eyes and he nodded in the other direction. 'Take a look at the people on the other side of the room. Check for anything major. We can leave the minor stuff for now. We need to get outside.'

Paige swallowed. Outside. Oh, no. She grabbed her red jacket and stuffed it under her arm, following his instructions to do a quick check on the people across the room. There were lots of dazed and scraped people there. But there were no major head injuries, no obvious broken limbs. Most people just needed to be picked up, assisted into a chair and told to take a breath.

Within a few minutes she was back, red jacket on, and standing next to the doorway, waiting for Stefan. His black ski gear now seemed ominous, but she tried to push those thoughts out of her head.

'Stay next to me,' he instructed, 'until we assess the situation.'

The door opened with a few hard pushes. Everything was white.

But not quite. There were trees, branches and bushes. Pieces of twisted metal—probably the chair lift—poked in awkward angles out of the snow.

'Oh, no,' Stefan said quietly, and Paige turned quickly to look in the same direction as him.

'What?' she said automatically.

And then she saw it.

The avalanche had swept down the mountainside, mainly to their right. But the road that led down the mountain, and back to the civilisation, was completely blocked. They, and all the potentially injured people around them, were trapped.

CHAPTER THREE

STEFAN BLINKED. A COMPLETE DISASTER. He couldn't remember the last time there had been an avalanche in this part of the Alps. But nowhere was ever completely safe. Where there was snow, there was a risk of avalanche.

He didn't even want to think about how long the road would take to clear. All he could see was mounds of rubble underneath the snow. He started praying there weren't people in there.

A shout caught his attention, and he realised one of the staff from the resort was shouting instructions. He turned to Paige. A doctor. When she'd told him, for a moment he'd been surprised. He'd been fairly certain that in the few seconds of the avalanche she'd seemed as if she was having a panic attack. He really wanted to know more, but now just wasn't the time.

'Can you assist?' he asked.

She nodded without hesitation. He reached over and grabbed her arm. 'Then come with me.'

When it came to an avalanche, the usual rules went out of the window. You didn't take time to assess. You didn't think about all the risks. You didn't wait for help. You immediately tried to rescue those around you.

He strode towards the man who was shouting—a large man, dressed in dark snow gear with yellow flashes and a bright hat on his head. Stefan didn't waste any time. 'Stefan and Paige, both doctors. Where do you need us?'

The man replied rapidly in German. Stefan could see the confusion on Paige's face, so listened carefully, gave the man some more information, then nodded in agreement. He turned to Paige.

'Franco, works here, he's a ski guide, but is also part of the mountain rescue scheme. He's going to organise teams to identify anyone injured or stuck. We've to set up a base back in the café, and they'll bring them all to us.'

'Shouldn't we dig too? Isn't it more important to get those who are trapped out?'

Stefan hesitated. He didn't really want to stand around right now. There were a few injuries already in the café. But none seemed imminently dangerous. People could suffocate in the snow. If they needed to dig first and provide medical aid later, that was fine with him.

Hysterical voices and shouts were everywhere. This was a chaotic scene, and they needed to be systematic here.

He spoke again to Franco, who at first shook his head and then sighed. He finally nodded, then directed them to where another man had appeared with some shovels and probes. Franco directed small teams of willing volunteers to different parts of the piled snow, with another man bringing out some equipment from the dismantled hut at the bottom of the chair lift.

'What's that?' asked Paige.

'I assume it's a radio receiver for any emergency locator beacons.' He looked at her, wondering how experienced she was at skiing. She'd certainly come down that slope like a pro, so he was assuming she had some knowledge. 'You do carry an avalanche transceiver?'

He could see recognition on her face. 'Of course.' She tapped her shoulder. 'It came with the jacket, sewed into the lining.'

He nodded. 'I'm hoping everyone who was skiing today had one in place. It might be the only way we can find them. Time isn't on our side.' Something dark crossed his face.

Stefan grabbed two shovels and turned to Paige. 'We go to the patch we're allocated and dig where we find any sign there might be someone underneath. In the meantime, the experts will search for signals. They'll redirect the teams if they pick up a signal.'

Franco turned to face the mountain, lifted his hand and drew invisible lines in the air, mapping out eight large squares. There was no time for anything else and they all knew it.

Stefan turned to a few other adults who were standing, shocked, near the café. 'Can you help? Can you dig?'

His voice seemed to jerk them out of their shock. One woman appeared, with tears streaming down her face. 'Yes,' she said, nodding. Another few people seemed to realise that Franco was trying to organise a rescue and came to help.

Paige looked pale. She was already fair-skinned, but now appeared a little sickly. Stefan touched her shoulder. 'Can you do this?' She might be a doctor but Paige, like everyone else here, could be injured. Maybe he hadn't been able to protect her in the café the way he'd wanted to. Or was he pushing when he shouldn't?

She tugged her bright hat a little further over her ears. 'Absolutely. Let's go.'

It was clear that many people were still dazed, some searching for friends or family with no idea where they might be. Stefan's instinct was to run over and try to help everyone. He saw Paige glancing in one direction, with the same thought practically written on her face.

He put his hand on hers. 'I know,' he said in a low voice. 'I know. I want to run over to them all. But we have to be methodical about this. And we're time-limited here.' He hated saying that out loud. But people buried under snow could suffocate. They were absolutely time-limited here. Digging people out as quickly as possible was essential. 'We have to stick to the patch we're allocated. Franco seems the most experienced here. Let's see if we can help.' He looked further up the mountain. 'We have to remember this could happen again.'

Paige gave a visible shudder but lifted her shovel and followed him. Two other people joined them. The snow in their area was littered with debris. It was hard to determine what everything was. He extended his probe. The collapsible fibreglass pole was like a tent rod and could be used to determine the location and depth of snow where a person could be buried. Stefan dropped to his knees, tugging at anything sticking up in the snow.

There were a variety of shouts. The man next to him tugged at part of a ski. It was still attached to a leg. The four of them dug frantically to reveal a shocked woman, who coughed madly as soon as they pulled the snow from around her face.

Stefan gave a few instructions to one of the men, then looked at the other three. 'Time matters. We can dig her out completely in a few minutes. Let's check if we can find anyone else.'

Another dark blotch was the elbow of a man's jacket. It only took a few moments to free his face from snow and let him take a few breaths. The second man stayed with him as Stefan and Paige moved on.

Franco gave a shout. He came running over. 'Signal in your area.' He turned his receiver and pointed at one specific point. 'There!'

He used the probe a few times, until finally he got a hit. It could be anything—part of a tree or rock, but, with the assistance of a beacon, he hoped it was a person. Stefan started shovelling straight away. Digging frantically was difficult, and he had to still all his senses. The last thing he wanted to do was cause someone more harm by shovelling too near their face.

Within seconds he saw a flash of pink. 'We've got something.'

His stomach lurched as he and Paige dropped to their knees again and started to pull snow away with their hands. The flash of pink enlarged, and Stefan quickly realised by the size of the limb that this was a child.

Franco met his gaze. 'You got this?'

Stefan knew that he must have picked up another signal. 'Absolutely,' he replied. 'Go.'

Paige was shaking. Her hands moved rapidly, throwing snow away from the pink ski suit as they tried to determine which way was up for the little person underneath them. 'Foot!' she yelled and moved instantly, elbowing Stefan to push him further along so they could scoop out the snow nearer where this child's head would be. The little leg hadn't moved yet.

Stefan was trying not to think about the time. Was it more than five minutes? If an experienced skier had been caught in the avalanche they might have had an instinct to create some space around their head. Some might even have an avalanche airbag haversack—a device that would inflate and bring them to the surface of the snow during the actual avalanche. Some parent, somewhere, had clearly had the sense to put an avalanche transmitter on their child. He only hoped they would find the parent too as he continued to dig.

Curly blonde hair appeared under his hands. Paige let out a gasp and immediately helped move the packed snow. The girl looked around seven or eight, her face exposed and skin cold. Stefan moved forward, his face right next to the little girl's. He was hoping and praying she was in shock right now. He breathed on her face, talking quietly, then tried to position himself to give her some rescue breaths.

'Let me,' said Paige. She knew exactly what he was trying to do. But she was slimmer and lighter and slipped her head into the tight space next to the child. He couldn't see properly but, after a few moments, there was a sound from the child. A splutter, followed by a loud howl.

Stefan had his head down next to Paige and the child. His eyes caught sight of something else. He touched Paige. 'I think I have someone else—can I leave you?'

She nodded and he moved quickly, grabbing his shovel and probe again. Was he imagining something or were those fingertips?

Darn it. He would have missed them. Experienced skiers knew to try and create a space around their face, to put one arm upward in the hope of being seen, and even to mimic backward swimming during an avalanche. Stefan had read all the stories, heard all the advice, but he'd never experienced anything like this before.

Sure enough, fingertips were just barely protruding through the snow. He shovelled quickly, shouting over to the rescuer who was next to the woman they'd first found to give him some help. This man was clearly deeper than any of the other people they had found.

Sweat was pouring off Stefan. He still hadn't done a time check. He knew that the best chance of survival for anyone caught in an avalanche was for them to be found in the first fifteen minutes. Chances of survival decreased sharply after that. They must rapidly be approaching that now. He could also remember that somewhere, deep at the back of his mind, he'd read something about the best way to dig people out. Stefan was cursing that he couldn't recall the details. He kept going, even though the muscles in his arms were burning. He didn't even know the name of the guy digging next to him, he just knew that this stranger was working every bit as hard as he was.

There was a high-pitched wail and it cut right through him. He looked up, just in time to see a woman drop on her knees next to Paige. She started helping to dig the little girl out. It must be the mother. He was relieved. He'd half-expected her to be buried in the snow too.

The wind was picking up, making it difficult to anchor himself in place. It also resulted in the light, more powdery snow swirling around him like a smokescreen. He kept digging, finally seeing some dark hair and moving quickly to delicately scoop the snow out from around his face. The man made a huge splutter, coughing and choking, and almost immediately Stefan could hear the wheeze in his breathing. He would bet this man had broken some ribs.

A few other people came to join them. 'What's your name?' asked Stefan, first in German, then in French.

'Rafe,' came the spluttered reply.

'I'm Stefan. I'm a surgeon. I'll take a proper look at you when we get you out of here. I think it's going to take a little time.'

The man gave a nod but didn't reply. At least he was conscious. Franco tapped Stefan on the shoulder. 'Let these other folks do the digging for a moment, Doc,' he said. 'I need you and the other doc inside, assessing the patients.'

Stefan straightened up. It was difficult to see around him right now. The wind and swirling snow meant he could only see a few feet away. Paige was closest to him and he could see her assisting lifting the blonde-haired little girl from the snow. The mother was understand-ably hysterical, but also getting in the way.

He couldn't see properly, and he certainly couldn't hear but, from the actions, he could tell Paige was talk-ing to the mother, trying to placate and calm her down in order to look after her daughter. Within a few seconds, it was clear she'd had some impact. The mother stepped back a little, allowing Paige to bend over the little girl and do something else. She'd told him she worked in A&E. Paige clearly had experience dealing with upset and anxious relatives.

He nodded at Franco and stepped back himself to allow the other men to take over. He gave a few instruc-tions about taking care around the man's chest and torso and followed Franco back to the entrance of the café.

The café on the other side thankfully had its floor-to-ceiling windows intact. Whilst Stefan might have never known of an avalanche in these parts, the planners had clearly taken no chances and he imagined the windows had specially toughened glass. It was a blessing.

'We've taken everyone with injuries in here. Another few people have come forward who can help, two who are nurses and one who is a physio.'

Stefan nodded. 'Are there any supplies?'

'We have a medical station with a bit more than is usual in a first aid kit. Some splints, and inflatables for fractures. A few stitching kits.'

Stefan nodded. Fractures and wounds requiring a few stitches were probably the most serious injuries usually dealt with here.

'I may have to go up to the hospital,' he said. 'I have

more equipment there, and that part of the road looks as if it's not blocked.'

Franco pointed to the road horizontal to the resorts, café and lifts. 'The avalanche seemed to come down almost diagonally. Look at the amount of snow. It will take days for them to clear the road and get us out of here.'

Stefan looked up. His skin prickled as he realised just how serious their situation was. Paige appeared at his shoulder as Franco started to speak again. 'And, with these high winds, it's unlikely we'll be able to get any helicopter assistance.'

His mind was working overtime now. He'd have to come up with some kind of plan. He nodded to Paige. 'Let us see how everyone is doing and then make a decision about what comes next. Do you think there is anyone else buried in the snow?'

Franco's expression was deadly serious. 'It's impossible to know. We're trying to do an account of everyone, to establish if anyone is missing from any party. But if there were any solo skiers, then unless I find a beacon signal we'll just never know.' He laid his gloved hand on Stefan's arm. 'Leave that part to me. We can chat later.'

'What's happening?' asked Paige, 'I got pulled away before I was finished.'

Stefan nodded and led her inside the café. Three other people were standing near the doorway, waiting for them. 'Are you the other medical personnel that can assist?'

They nodded.

'I'm Stefan, I'm local and a surgeon. This is Paige, a doctor from the UK who works in A&E.'

A woman with fair hair spoke next. 'I'm Lynn, a nurse from England. I work in orthopaedics, and this is Joe, my partner, who works in Theatre.' Joe was already stripping off his jacket and hat, getting prepared to work.

The third person spoke up too. 'Cathy, I'm a cardiac physio, but just ask me to do what you need. I'll tell you if I need instruction.'

Paige stepped forward. 'Let's do this as a triage system like we use in A&E. Anyone who is okay, or has minor injuries and can wait, can go into the café next door right now. Any head injury, abdomen injury, possible break or wound that needs cleaning and stitching stays here.'

Stefan watched with interest. Paige had pulled off her red jacket again and tugged her dark hair from her knitted hat. Her ski goggles seemed to have disappeared. She turned to Stefan. 'Will we be able to get to the hospital if required?'

He nodded. 'I think so. I also have a vehicle up there. Once we've treated everyone, I can hike up and bring my car down to transport anyone up. From what Franco and I could see, that part of the road above looks clear.'

Paige nodded thoughtfully. 'My chalet is probably accessible too. If people need somewhere to sleep it might be useful. And there's lots of food too.'

Stefan lifted his hand, hating to say these words. 'A bit of caution. The hospital is only halfway renovated.'

'What does that mean?' asked Joe quickly.

'There's water and electricity. Several rooms and staff areas are ready. There are functional operating theatres and a number of stock and equipment should have been delivered today before the road was blocked.'

'What kind?' Joe was clearly thinking ahead.

'The furnishings were already in place, but some surgical equipment, medical supplies, pharmacy goods and sundries were all arriving early this morning. The hospital was supposed to open soon, and these deliveries had never been cancelled.'

'Lucky,' breathed Paige.

'Only lucky if they arrived,' said Lynn.

'Let's get started,' said Stefan, praying that by the time he got up to the hospital he wouldn't find the place empty.

They moved quickly, assessing all the people. 'We've been lucky,' murmured Paige. 'Someone told me this place is usually much busier, but it looks like a number had already left because of the weather warning for later today.'

'Thank goodness,' agreed Stefan. 'I bet some of these people wish they'd left earlier today too.'

'Don't you?'

He looked at her and shook his head. 'No,' he said honestly. 'I'm glad I'm here. I'll do what I can to help.'

She pressed her lips together and he thought he glimpsed a sheen of tears in her eyes. But Paige was determined. She'd pulled her long hair back in a ponytail and pushed the sleeves up on her thermal underclothes. She'd removed her ski boots and was moving around in thick socks. As they continued to work, they moved away from each other.

Every few minutes the main door would open and

Franco or some of his team would appear, carrying someone who'd been dug out of the snow on a portable stretcher. Thank goodness the resort had equipment around.

When they'd assessed everyone in the room, Stefan met with Paige and the others. 'What do you have?'

Paige looked worried. 'A seven-year-old female with a fractured tib and fib, a forty-year-old male with a suspected head injury that we need to observe, a thirty-eight-year-old woman with suspected rib fractures and a definite ulna and radius fracture.'

Stefan nodded. 'I've Rafe, the man who's just been dug out. His temperature is borderline hypothermic, breathing erratic. He has rib fractures too. I've two other females with suspected ankle fractures.'

Lynn, Joe and Cathy listed their patients, the majority requiring stitches, one woman in the early stage of pregnancy with cramping but no bleeding, an older man with known angina who'd lost his meds, and a diabetic whose insulin pen had shattered.

Franco appeared next to them, the door banging loudly behind him and the high wind whistling in. 'What's the verdict?' He had a satellite phone in his hand.

'I've got nine people I should take up to the hospital if I can. And a whole host of others we need to clean up and stitch.'

Franco nodded and handed him the phone. 'We have three satellite phones, so this one is for you. The cafés have plenty of food and are comfortable enough. Those who are well enough can stay here with myself and the rest of the staff.'

'How long until help arrives?' asked Lynn.

Franco and Stefan exchanged glances, which Paige didn't miss. 'What does that mean?' He could hear the tension in her voice.

He turned to face her. 'The road block is extensive. I have no idea how long it will take for them to move the snow and rubble so there is access again.'

'Surely there's another way to get people out?' People. Not her, he noted. She wasn't worrying about herself, she was worrying about their new patients, and potentially the rest of the people who could be stranded here.

Franco's deep voice interrupted his thoughts. 'In normal circumstances the emergency services and mountain rescue would be able to bring helicopters to get people in, and out. But...' he gestured towards the sky '...no one can fly in those winds. Too dangerous. We probably don't even want anyone outside.'

Realisation dawned on Paige's face. 'So we're stuck here?'

'For now,' replied Stefan. 'I'm sure we can manage.' He was saying the words without really knowing if they were true. He could only hope the supplies that were ordered for the hospital had actually arrived.

'I'll be able to do some X-rays, put the plaster casts on, even set some bones if required.'

Stefan nodded. He was actually glad she was here. Most docs who worked in A&E had some experience of plaster casting—particularly any who'd covered a Saturday night shift and had to patch up those after a drunken night out. There wasn't so much of that in Hollywood. He'd put plaster casts on arms and legs after cosmetic surgery procedures, but they were few and far between.

Paige gave him a wary look. 'So, what you're basically saying is we're trapped here, with all these people, and the hopeful medical supplies left in a half-finished hospital, for an unknown amount of time.'

The thing he'd first noticed about her and admired— the way she was blunt and to the point. All eyes were on him and Franco gave him a half-smile. For the next few days these were his staff, and it was up to him to deal with them.

'When you put it like that, yes, we're stuck here and have patients to deal with. I'm sure we'll all be fine.'

Paige's gaze met his and she straightened her shoulders. 'In that case, let's finish our stitching, check all wounds are sound and not leave anyone behind we think might deteriorate in any way. It will be difficult enough to get everyone up to the hospital safely. We don't want to make unnecessary trips.' She sighed, put her hands on her hips and arched her back. 'Is there a kitchen?'

He nodded.

'Okay, on the last journey back up, we'll stop at the chalet and collect all the food and take it up with us.' She nodded at Cathy and Lynn. 'I also have some clothes there that we can share out.'

It was as if someone had flicked a switch in her. He'd seen it a few times now. Once, just after the avalanche had hit. Then again for a few seconds, when she'd been asked to help. On both occasions it was as if Paige went on automatic pilot and started performing as a doctor.

And it wasn't just that. She was good. From what he'd observed, her decisions seemed clinically sound, and it looked as if she was an empathic practitioner. Was there something else going on with her?

Yet another thing he didn't have time for.

Stefan took a deep breath and pushed aside the horrible thought. Paige seemed to have gone into overdrive. She was giving orders and checking patients. He pulled his ski equipment on again. Even in bad weather, he was confident he could reach the alcove part way up the road where he'd parked his car early this morning. It wasn't far on foot. It should only take five minutes to drive up to the hospital to open it up and ensure he'd be ready to host these patients.

When he turned back, Paige was standing behind him in her bright red gear, and a pink hat that she'd obviously borrowed from someone else.

'I'll head up. I should be back in half an hour. You decide which patient we should move first. Either Lynn or Joe will need to come up with the first patient, so they can stay with them in the hospital while we transfer the rest.'

She raised her eyebrows. 'I've already decided which patient should come first and left instructions.'

'You're not coming with me,' he said steadily, seeing the glint of determination in her eyes.

'Yes, I am,' she said with equal force. 'You're not going up alone.'

Stefan felt his skin prickle. It was the way she was looking at him. It was setting off charges that hadn't been alive in…

'It's not sensible for both doctors to leave together. If something happened to both of us on the way up the mountain, who would look after these patients?'

She pressed her lips tightly together. He knew it made sense. And so did she.

'Okay,' she said finally, then lowered her voice. 'But don't think you'll win on everything. It might be your hospital, but this is an emergency situation. And we're equal partners here.'

There was a grim determination to her voice, an edge to her, that he hadn't seen before.

And it sparked his curiosity even more. Who was this woman, and why on earth did she intrigue him in ways he hadn't felt in…for ever?

CHAPTER FOUR

THE TRANSFERS WERE smoother than expected. It wasn't easy taking one patient at a time, climbing over snow to reach Stefan's four-by-four, then taking them up to a half-renovated hospital. But they got into a rhythm.

Between herself, Stefan, Joe, Lynn and Cathy, they managed to work out a way to keep all the patients safe. Whilst the hospital was surrounded by snow, the top part of the road was clear and the building was completely undamaged.

Her first sight of it took her breath away. The outside was beautiful and imposing. While parts of the building looked original, including some delicate stained-glass panes at the entrance and some old-fashioned stone pillars and steps leading up to impressive doors, the rest of the front of the building had clearly had a complete overall. It meant that the front had a pale stone façade, with brand-new windows. It looked like a prestigious and impressive place to be treated.

Stefan had quickly ensured all power and water supplies were working before showing them the main patient suites, which were already set up. All they had to do was make up the beds with the linens already stored in the closets. She was impressed by the way he swept around the place and his attention to detail. Every now and then he caught her gaze and held it for a moment longer than expected. She wondered what might have happened if it had been a normal day and their sparky conversation had continued in the café. Might it have led to drinks? To dinner?

It was clear he was frustrated that the place wasn't finished, and she wondered what Stefan the surgeon would be like to work with. She imagined he would have exacting standards about everything—the arrogance of surgeons always made her smile. In the frantic environment of A&E she'd seen a few cut down to size, and she wondered how he would have fared in her Glasgow department.

Paige gave herself a shake. She was too interested in this guy by far. She needed to get a message to her family to let them know she was safe, and she had patients to treat.

He showed them where the rest of the deliveries had arrived. There were boxes and boxes, it looked like medical sundries and supplies, all of which would be needed but could be examined and unpacked once all the patients were comfortable. Joe had already found a locked delivery of medicines for immediate use.

By the time the last patient had arrived, Paige was waiting outside for Stefan, still in her ski jacket.

'What's wrong?' he queried.

She could tell he was tired, and ready to get inside and get warm.

'One last trip,' she said. 'Down to the chalet so we can collect some food. It shouldn't take too long.'

Recognition sparked in his eyes. 'Of course.' He sighed. 'I'd forgotten about the food.'

'That's why you have me,' she said with a smile as he turned the car around and headed down the dark, twisting road.

'Think our nurses and physio will be okay?'

'I think they'll be great,' answered Paige sincerely. 'They seem so switched on. You were lucky some of the medical supplies had arrived and you were able to give some pain relief.'

He shook his head as he drove. 'I actually can't believe how lucky that was. We need to do X-rays, other tests, probably some surgery. But I'm hoping the pain relief will let a few of our patients get settled and over the shock of all this.'

Paige swallowed and breathed. 'Well, if you find a magic wand to get over the shock of all this, can you wave it over me too? I keep thinking I'll wake up in that really comfortable bed and realise this has all just been some crazy dream.'

He gave her a curious look. 'If only,' he said in a voice that was heavy and regretful. 'This couldn't have happened at a worse time.'

She turned her head and looked at him, about to query the comment. But of course, his new business was about to open. 'Hopefully it won't delay things for too long,' she said in an attempt at some kind of comfort.

But Stefan shook his head. 'It's more the knock-on effects of everything else. The clinic opening late also delays my other plans for the patients I have through Médecins Sans Frontières. We'd planned for twelve surgeries this year. I hate the thought of a child having to wait for surgery because of things that are out of my control.'

'You work for Médecins Sans Frontières?'

He nodded. 'I do two spells for them a year, and then the surgeries for children—mainly those with cleft lip and palate. The surgeries for cleft lip and palate need to be done in order, and they're complicated. Delays can impact on a child's eating, or in a developmental delay of their speech. I hate for any to fall behind.'

She looked at him carefully. 'Between here, Hollywood and your other work, you lead a pretty busy life. Do you ever have a break?'

'Do you?' The words came out instantly and his head whipped around to glance at her, before turning back to the road.

Paige pressed her lips together. She'd clearly struck a nerve. Maybe others had mentioned something to him too.

After her experiences in the last few months, should she be nervous driving back to the isolated chalet with a guy she barely knew? Maybe she should. But all her instincts around this guy in the last few hours were good. He was dedicated, and caring. He certainly seemed to work hard. But there was more than that. Rather than just considering her safety, she was actually quite curious about him. Who was Stefan Bachmann? She'd barely scratched the surface.

The drive was less than five minutes and Paige quickly put in the code to open the chalet door and showed Stefan into the kitchen. Thoughts could wait, they had priorities right now. She opened the fridge. 'We have everything in here.' She pointed to the welcome hamper. 'We have this.' Then she walked over to the large larder cupboard. 'And everything in here.'

Stefan's eyes widened as he noticed the supplies. He walked over and looked at her. 'Pasta, soup, tins, rice, flour, sugar. You've certainly got this stocked as if you expected to be stranded.'

He was looking at her in a curious way and she realised he'd never actually asked her if this place was hers. She was suddenly very self-conscious. Did she look like the kind of person who could own a place like this?

'Not me,' she said quickly. 'I'm only a temporary resident. But the owner seems to have thought of everything to keep people comfortable—even though I don't think he ever stays here.'

'Who does own this place?'

Paige took a breath, suddenly unsure of what to say. But they were in the middle of a disaster. Surely it wouldn't matter.

'I think they like to keep it quiet.' She named the well-known baron.

Stefan let out a low whistle in surprise. The baron was pretty notorious worldwide.

Paige was quick to jump in. 'Apparently he has places like this all over the world and he lets people like me use them. Health staff who need a holiday. And others, I think, who need some respite.' She tilted her head to the side and looked at Stefan. 'Maybe a bit like what you mentioned about your hospital. Some place out of the way, where people can get some privacy and a chance to relax. He just likes to keep things quiet.'

Stefan rolled his eyes. 'Well, this place is definitely relaxing in luxury.'

'And just for that,' said Paige, 'I won't show you the ski equipment cupboard that residents are free to use.' Something jolted in her brain. She had no idea where the very expensive skis and ski poles were she'd left with this morning. 'Darn it. I might have lost some of it.' She licked her lips and blew out a long breath. 'Okay, I'll send an email when we get back to the hospital, letting the owner know that I've emptied the store cupboard and—' she pulled a face '—likely misplaced some ski equipment.'

She pulled open a drawer she'd found earlier. 'Here. There's some bags you can use to transport the food out to the car. I'm going to nip upstairs and grab some of my clothes so Cathy and Lynn have some spares.'

Stefan nodded and by the time she came back down it was clear he'd made numerous trips to the car already. As he came back through the main door in a blast of icy air she could see the lines around his eyes. She looked at him and was thoughtful for a moment before gesturing to him and pulling open the ski equipment store.

'Listen, there's some extra ski jackets in here. Boots too. Do you want some for yourself and Joe?'

'You're offering me a ski jacket from Baron Boastful?'

Paige frowned and pulled a face. 'It's interesting that's his nickname, isn't it? When my experience is entirely the opposite. He doesn't want anyone to know he consistently does good deeds like this.'

'Maybe it's a tax dodge,' said Stefan over his shoulder as he walked back to the kitchen to grab more supplies.

'You're such a cynic.' She closed the door on the equipment store. 'That'll be a no, then?'

Stefan walked past, his arms loaded. 'I think we're taking enough of his stuff. Both Joe and I already have jackets. We'll dry them well enough, and hopefully be able to stay inside until the road's cleared.'

As he smiled she noticed how his eyes creased. He'd been surprisingly good company. She liked his occasional teasing, and the way he didn't take himself too seriously. He clearly didn't shy away from hard work either. She remembered the athletic build of the man she'd seen on the ski slope before their meeting at the café, and she tried to push it aside. Now wasn't the time to think like that.

They packed up the car and made their way back to the hospital. The lights were bright and it seemed more welcoming now. Stefan backed the car up so it would be easier to unload. The surrounding area was dark, and as they stepped out of the car a sharp gust of wind nearly blew her off her feet. She grabbed onto the car again. 'Whoa!'

He moved around beside her and put his arm around her waist and ducked his head down as they pushed through the door. The others were close by and came over at their arrival.

'Everyone okay?' asked Stefan immediately.

Joe nodded. 'Need some help?'

'Be careful out there, everyone,' said Paige quickly. 'The winds are still dreadful.'

Cathy zipped up her jacket. 'Once we've got the food, we can close up and stay inside. Depending what food we have, Lynn and I will try and pull something together, so we can feed everyone before they get to sleep.' She turned to them both. 'We'll give you a rundown on them all, but all are settled with their painkillers. Why don't we leave any casts or surgeries until the morning, when we're all over the shock of what's happened?'

Stefan gave a slow nod. 'Franco gave me a radio. We can get back in touch to find out if they've made contact with emergency services. It might be we can get everyone out of here in the next few hours. As long as everyone is comfortable, I'd rather not start anything, if that's an option.'

They all nodded and, after a few trips out to the car, deposited the food in the kitchen.

Lynn looked at them both. 'You two are freezing. As you can tell, the heating is working, so is the hot water. Go and grab a shower while I make a meal.'

Paige looked around. 'I'll show you,' said Stefan quietly, clearly realising she hadn't quite got her bearings yet.

He took her down a corridor and they both stuck their heads in the rooms, saying hello to their patients to make sure all were fine.

Although the rooms had really been designed for one patient each, because there was space for private staff, two or three had been put in each room. Cathy, and Lynn and Joe had taken other rooms, leaving one last suite.

Stefan clearly realised this and looked awkwardly at her. 'Do you want to bunk in with Cathy?'

It made sense, of course it did. But she didn't know Cathy any better than she knew Stefan. 'Why don't we worry about that later? Just show me a bathroom with a working shower and let me find some clean clothes.'

She dumped her bag on a nearby chair, trying to hide her surprise at the size of the suite. It had the largest hospital bed she'd ever seen, clearly with all modern accoutrements. The floor was some kind of luxury vinyl, easy to clean, but as she pulled off her boots and socks she realised it was warm and oddly soft underfoot.

Blinds had been pulled over the large windows, and there was an array of other doors leading off the main room.

Stefan had walked through one and she could hear running water and see the visible steam drifting out through the door already. Bliss. She couldn't wait.

There was a pile of bed linen sitting on another chair, along with towels and bathrobes.

Stefan stepped out. 'All yours.' He looked down at the pile she was looking at and waved his hand. 'There are two other rooms for staff and private nurses. I'll make up the beds, you grab a towel and go ahead.'

She considered pausing and offering to help, but was exhausted and felt grimy. 'Thanks,' she said, taking her clothes with her and heading into the bathroom.

Like everything else in this place, it was luxurious, with pristine white sanitary ware and gleaming gold taps. The mirror was already steamed up, and Paige sat her towel and fresh clothes near the basin and stripped off her clothes.

As her bright red and now grimy salopettes dropped to the floor she realised how little she'd been prepared for today as she'd hit the slopes. Her thermals and other clothes soon joined the pile on the floor and she stepped under the streaming warm water. It was bliss, heating her chilled skin instantly. She looked around for some soap or shower gel, but it seemed that those extras hadn't been found yet. It didn't matter, she was happy enough just to rub her face and body with her hands. After a few seconds' contemplation, she pulled her hair from the ponytail and let the water stream over her hair too. If no hairdryers existed, she could just tie it back up.

Ten minutes later she'd dried herself and pulled on her clean clothes—fresh underwear, a pair of jeans and a pink T-shirt. It was such a relief. She gathered her dirty clothes and towel and headed back out—and stopped.

Stefan was sitting on top of the bed. He'd removed his boots and jacket but was still wearing all his layers. His head had sagged forward with his chin resting on his chest. Was that a tiny snore?

She froze, not wanting to disturb him.

After a few moments she bit her lip. She couldn't stay here with a pile of dirty linen in her hands. Her stomach growled loudly and Stefan's head jerked up.

Paige started to laugh. She couldn't help it, particularly as her uncontrollable stomach decided to make yet another loud growl.

Stefan's eyes widened as he took in her position. Realisation flooded his eyes and he started laughing too. He pointed. 'Is that what woke me up, your stomach?'

Paige kept laughing as heat flooded her cheeks.

'How long have you been standing there?' he asked as he swung his legs off the bed.

'Hours,' she replied promptly, moving over to the bag she'd brought.

She saw the tiny flicker of panic. 'Minutes.' She waved her hand. 'Your turn for the shower and I'll go and claim one of the other bedrooms.'

She moved through to a very comfortable room with a hastily made bed. Hospital corners weren't Stefan's forte. She'd remember to tease him later.

Everything else in the room was great, including the small en suite bathroom she hadn't even considered might be there. She shook her head. In future she would take a shower in here, and she hung up one of the bathrobes on the hook behind the door.

She paused in the main room, wondering if she should wait for him. But it would be better to recheck all the patients and do whatever she could to help feed everyone. As she went to leave, the satellite phone lit up and she grabbed it, taking a few seconds to work out how to answer.

Franco's voice was a little patchy, but it was there.

'How is everyone?'

'Well, we're here. The electricity and heating are working, and I picked up some food from the chalet. Stefan wondered if there was any chance of transport, before we start any procedures on the patients.'

'Yeah, about that…' Franco paused and she heard a huge sigh.

'What's wrong?'

'Obviously, it's night-time now and difficult to make a full assessment. But the avalanche and landslide has completely blocked the road. They can't get a helicopter in the sky to get a proper look at the damage, due to the high winds. Bad news is, the winds are due to get worse—they think it might not be safe to get a helicopter up for the next few days.'

Her heart sank. 'So we could be stuck here for days?'

Franco cleared his throat, and there was a pause. 'We could be.'

Panic prickled Paige's skin. She licked her dry lips. It took a moment for her to collect her thoughts and ask the question she should. 'Is everyone who stayed with you still okay?'

'Yes,' Franco replied quickly. 'All good. We'll just need to get comfortable and wait.'

'So, I guess we'd better go ahead with the X-rays and treatments,' she said, more to herself than Franco. Her stomach was twisting and it was nothing to do with being hungry. It was dread. Fatigue. Worry.

'Yes, I'll get back to you once I speak to the authorities in the morning. They'll likely be in touch to see if you require any medical supplies.'

'Okay, thank you.'

She ended the call and leaned against the wall, breathing, trying to stop her heart racing in her chest. She couldn't quite understand why she was reacting this way.

Paige had never been a panicker. Always managed in a crisis at work. Kept a cool head.

'What's wrong?'

She spun around as she heard his voice. Stefan was standing in the doorway of the bathroom, a towel around his hips.

Her mouth fell open. He was lean and muscular, with defined biceps and dark hair scattering his chest. He seemed completely comfortable with the fact he wasn't wearing much.

He looked down. 'Sorry, forgot to grab other clothes. I have a rucksack I left here yesterday. It has some spare clothes, and I think there might be scrubs along at the theatres.'

Paige was having trouble constructing words.

'What's wrong?' he asked again, moving over to the bed and picking up another bathrobe that was lying there.

For a moment she wondered if the towel might drop while he put the bathrobe on, but no, of course not. He slid the bathrobe on, tied it at the waist, then tugged the towel from underneath. Perfectly covered. She wasn't sure she liked it.

'Paige?'

Her brain seemed to have a jolt of recovery. She held up the phone. 'We could be stuck here for a few days. Weather is closing in and it's unlikely any helicopters will be able to fly and get our casualties out.'

'Darn it,' and he muttered something else under his breath.

'We'll need to treat everyone.' The words came out with a slight tremor to them that she couldn't explain.

He nodded. 'Let's check everyone. We can decide if we need to do anything immediately. If it's safe, we'll let them eat, ensure they are pain free and get a good night's rest. I want to double-check what equipment, tools and drugs we have before we start.'

Paige raised her eyebrows. 'And you need some clothes,' she added.

He sighed, looking down at his white robe. 'I can't go in this?'

She gave a laugh. 'I don't want to be responsible for what happens if that bathrobe accidentally opens.'

This time it was Stefan's eyes that rose in surprise. 'I'll keep that in mind. I'll meet you in the kitchen in five.'

Paige turned and walked down the corridor, half cringing at her careless comment. At a moment of natural disaster, was she flirting?

She shook her head as her stomach grumbled again. She put a hand on her stomach. 'I'll blame it on low blood sugar.' She smiled to herself as she tried to get the image of Stefan and his towel out of her head.

There was something slightly off about Paige. She looked good. She looked well. He was well aware that they'd been out in the cold for some time. It was likely that every patient and staff member here could have suffered an element of hypothermia, and letting everyone rest for a few hours would give them a chance to get warmed through. Could it just be that which was wrong with her?

There was so much he didn't know about this doc. He'd been shocked to see how slim she was, now that she'd shed all her skiwear. The bones around her neck and shoulders were prominent in her pink top, and was there a hint of a bruise too?

Of course, that might be developing after today's events. But his gut told him it was a little older and was fading instead of just emerging. He could remember having a similar thought at the café earlier.

He'd grabbed some underwear and pulled on a set of navy scrubs. It wasn't the warmest clothing, but the boiler had definitely kicked in and the temperature was rising gradually. The corridors were still cold, but each of the rooms was at a comfortable level of heat.

Lynn and Cathy had taken the eggs and bread that had come from the chalet and made scrambled eggs and toast for everyone. It was simple and not too heavy for bodies which had been under strain today.

The most worrisome patient was Rafe, the man who'd been buried deeply under the snow. He was on low level oxygen and had been given pain relief for his likely rib fractures. Cathy, the cardiac physio, had found an ultrasound machine. Whilst she was familiar with the technology for looking at hearts, she'd adapted and been able to show their pregnant woman who had cramping that there was a definite flickering heartbeat in her uterus and put her mind at rest. Eva had shed tears of relief and agreed to keep resting.

The newly flung-together staff were currently sitting

in the kitchen, on stools at one of the preparation stations. They could have made it into the formal dining room, but it was distinctly lacking any furniture.

Joe came back along the corridor with a makeshift head injury chart he'd made on paper, a pen torch in his hand, and slid it in front of Paige. 'Bruno seems stable.' He gave a smile. 'But, as a theatre guy, conscious patients aren't really my forte.'

Stefan smiled. 'I'll be glad to have you tomorrow. And Lynn, thank goodness you work in orthopaedics. We'll have two ankles to maybe pin. A tib-fib fracture to sort, and an ulna and radius. All will need casts. All will need X-rays, as will our two people with likely fractured ribs.'

Joe nodded. 'Are you okay if I go for a look around your theatre, and your surgical equipment?'

'Absolutely. Some of the surgical packs arrived today. The monitors, operating tables and gas supplies are up and running in the theatres. At least that part of the renovations stayed on track.'

There was a nudge at his elbow. Paige had sat down next to him, a large steaming mug of hot chocolate in her hands. 'Did you tell them the rest?'

All eyes turned towards him.

Stefan sighed. 'Paige heard from Franco. Everyone is fine back at the café, but the weather forecast for the next few days is bad. It's unlikely helicopters will be able to get anyone out.'

'Or insulin in,' said Lynn sharply.

Paige looked at her, remembering Bob, their diabetic

man who'd smashed his insulin pen. 'Do we have any at all?'

She nodded. 'Only short-acting. It's different to the one Bob usually uses, but will still work. But he takes a long-acting insulin every evening to give him a steady background of insulin throughout the day. We don't have any of that.'

Stefan nodded slowly. 'Does he have a glucose monitor? I know we have some in the treatment room.'

'He has a sensor which will last another five days.'

They all looked at each other.

'It will be Christmas before then.' Paige said the words that the rest of them had been skirting around.

Christmas Eve was in three days' time. The weather report made it sound as if it could be a strange kind of Christmas.

Paige swallowed and tilted her chin upwards with a look of determination on her face. 'Hopefully by then the road will be clear. If not, there's some Christmas decorations in the chalet we can bring up. We'll need to find some kind of presents for Claudia.'

The seven-year-old. What kind of a Christmas might that be for her? 'At least her mum is with her,' said Paige quickly. 'And there might be jigsaws or games at the chalet we can use.'

The rest looked sombre but nodded. Stefan stood up. 'You guys get some sleep. I'm going to check everyone over and make sure the buzzer system works so they can let us know if they need anything during the night.'

'I'll help.' Paige stood quickly.

Cathy rubbed her eyes. 'Thanks, guys. I can't wait to get to sleep.'

Paige walked alongside him as they checked everyone over. She borrowed a stethoscope and listened to Rafe's chest again. Broken ribs were always tricky. There wasn't a way to magically heal them or make them completely pain-free. The act of breathing alone meant that Rafe's ribs were moving. Trouble was, they really needed him to breathe deeply to avoid pneumonia.

Paige's expression was grave as she pulled back.

'Can I get you some more pain relief?'

Rafe gave a nod and she scribbled something on the makeshift chart beside his bed, and came back a few moments later with some tablets and a glass of water.

Stefan ensured he was as comfortable as possible and had his buzzer before they started the long walk down the corridor.

Paige stopped at the main entrance, running her fingers over the stained glass. 'Do you know anything about this?' she asked.

He stopped beside her. The sharpness and sparkiness he'd seen last night and this morning had drained out of her. For the last few hours, he'd caught himself looking at her and wondering why, at times, her dark eyes looked haunted.

He spoke quietly. 'I do. It wasn't here originally. It was made by one of the first prisoners of war that stayed here for a while. He made a recovery and learned how to make stained glass. He made the two panels, one with the Turaco, the national bird of Switzerland, and one with the Swiss flag, as part of a thank you.'

She traced her fingers over the glass. 'I've never heard of a Turaco before—or seen one. The colours are beautiful.'

The colours were startling—green, purple, blue and a tiny bit of red.

He nodded. 'They are really only found in Switzerland or South Africa. Aren't they amazing?'

'It looks like it should live somewhere tropical. How did it find its way to the Alps?'

Stefan shook his head. He could sense her starting to relax a little, her shoulders dropping slightly, the clench around her jaw easing. She really was incredibly attractive and he was trying not to be distracted. 'I have no idea. I've never asked. To be honest, I'd forgotten these were here.'

She turned around and stared at him. 'How many times have you walked past these in the last few months?'

It was a fair question. He opened his mouth to try and give some kind of excuse, but they all just seemed so lame that he couldn't actually find the words.

She spoke for him. 'Too busy? Not enough time to stop and take a look?'

His mouth felt dry. All of a sudden, the events of the day seemed to flood his body. He was tired—beyond tired. His brain was still churning. It couldn't switch off, planning surgeries for tomorrow, thinking of potential complications for any of his current patients. And he was wondering how long it would take to clear the road. It wouldn't be safe to bring diggers up in bad weather to try and move the debris. Their best chance was a helicopter. But the weather forecast was bad.

'Stefan?' Paige had stepped forward and had her hand on his arm. The heat from her fingertips sent a world of sensations across his skin. 'I'm sorry. I didn't mean to offend you.'

He put his hand on hers. It was instinctive. 'You didn't,' he said gently. 'But you might have hit a nerve,' he admitted.

Neither of them had moved their hands. Something stirred deep inside him. A connection. What was it about this woman?

He looked at the stained glass. 'You're right. It is beautiful. And my great-grandmother told my gran about them. She'd left by the time they were put in place, but she'd looked after the man who made them.'

'Wow. That's a real piece of history.'

He turned to her. 'Want to see more history?'

He was feeling guilty—guilty about all the times he hadn't slowed down to take a breath. To appreciate things like this.

Paige looked curious. 'Yes, of course.'

He had a strange urge to grab her hand, but knew that wouldn't be entirely appropriate. 'Come with me,' he said instead, and led her down the corridor, grabbing keys from the main office, along with a couple of jackets.

She stared at the dirty but bright yellow and orange jacket he handed her.

'It'll be cold. These must belong to the workmen. Better to put something over your T-shirt.' He grabbed two torches and took her down a dimly lit corridor on the opposite side of the building.

The drop in temperature was instantly noticeable and

Paige shivered and wrapped her arms around herself. 'I've never been so glad for heating.'

He nodded. 'The pipes have been put in, but there's still too much to do over here—the electrics, the walls, all the renovations—and it means there's no heating here yet. He came to a set of double doors with panes of glass in the top half. He turned a key and pushed one open with a loud creak.

'This is really the best-kept secret. It should have been torn out a few weeks ago. But with the delays, the workmen just hadn't reached it yet.'

He lifted his hand and let his torchlight sweep over the room. Paige gave a loud gasp.

It was an old traditional ward, with a wooden floor and high hospital beds lined up on either side of the room, next to the dark windows. It was like a hundred black and white photographs that she had seen in textbooks. Or a scene from a historical movie.

He wondered if she would be scared. But, before he could say anything, Paige had switched on her own torch and moved over to the nearest bed, touching the bottom of it. 'Just think of the people,' she whispered. 'Think of the stories. Think of the lives…and deaths.' She moved to the next bed then spun around, letting her light strobe up and down the other side of the room. 'What about all the men who were sent here? I wonder if they were all relieved, or whether some of them were angry about not being able to fight any more.'

This had been a purely instinctive thing—to show her this part of the hospital. And it could have gone horribly wrong. It might have scared her. Or just not interested her at all.

But Paige's face was full of wonder. He could virtually see her brain contemplating the possibilities. Thinking about all the history from years gone by.

All the things he hadn't really had time to consider.

His skin prickled again, but not in the way it had earlier. This time he was uncomfortable.

'I've never really thought about it,' he admitted.

'Your great-grandmother must have had a million stories about this place. The people. The patients. The medicine.' She smiled as she looked at him and he gave a sad shrug.

'I never got to have those conversations. And my gran could remember a few things, but not any of the details. She knew her parents had met here but, like many others of their time, it seemed like my great-grandparents didn't want to talk about the war much. They'd lived it. They didn't want to remember it.'

Paige visibly shivered again. 'Thank you,' she said sincerely. 'Thank you for showing me this place. If we get a chance tomorrow, I'd like to come back and see it in the daylight.'

He nodded and moved back to the double doors. 'The keys will be in the office. They're yours to take any time you want to.'

Her smile was soft. 'Thanks.' She looked down at her dirty workman's jacket and laughed. 'Free use of the jacket too?'

'Absolutely,' he said with a laugh as he locked the doors behind them.

As they walked back down the corridor the heat enveloped them again. All of a sudden the corridor seemed very long. They had the last room, at the very far end. Stefan was conscious they hadn't really had a chance to talk about sharing a suite.

'Do you want me to sleep someplace else?' he asked.

Paige stopped walking and looked at him. 'No, of course not. Why would you ask that?'

He waved his hand towards their suite. 'We were last here. All the other suites had already been taken. I wonder if Cathy, Joe and Lynn wondered if perhaps we were here together, and that's why they left that last place for us.'

'What?' Paige's mouth fell open and her brow furrowed, then she started to nod and her hand came up to her mouth. 'Oh, my. They met us together. It hadn't even occurred to me they might think that.' She started to laugh.

'Am I that bad?' Stefan joked.

'Well, I don't know that yet, do I?' she quipped. 'But seriously, we have separate rooms in there. And I'm sorry for hogging the bathroom earlier. I didn't realise I had a separate shower in the en suite.'

'Don't be silly. It's fine, and those rooms are much smaller, so are the bathrooms.'

Paige nodded. 'I seriously need to find some toiletries.'

'Me too. There are probably boxes somewhere with all those tiny bottles of things that people usually get in hotels. We've just not had cause to put them out yet.'

They looked at each other. 'Tomorrow?'

Then laughed at their simultaneous question.

'I need to sleep,' sighed Paige.

'Me too,' said Stefan.

'We'll definitely hear if one of the buzzers goes off?'

He nodded. 'But we'll need to keep our doors open. So you may well also hear me snore.'

She waved her hand. 'I can probably snore louder. So don't worry.'

She turned back to head to her room, and then stopped and looked over her shoulder. 'Thank you.' Her voice was quiet.

Stefan was confused. 'What for?'

'Being here,' she said, her voice a little shaky, before she disappeared into her room.

CHAPTER FIVE

WHILST THE BED was comfortable, it wasn't the best night's sleep. The wind howled and the trees nearby creaked, making her wonder if they might come down on the hospital. The buzzers went a few times, mainly just for minor things, but the disturbed sleep didn't help.

By the time she'd showered in the morning and dressed in a pair of scrubs, Paige felt as if she'd done ten rounds in a boxing ring. New bruises had appeared on her body—clearly from where she'd fallen with Stefan in the café to shelter.

Strange things were happening with her. Yesterday on a few occasions she'd felt an unusual connection with Stefan. Paige had only had a few relationships—things she'd kind of fallen into. But she'd never really met someone and felt an instant attraction—a buzz—and she part wondered if she was just stressed and this was her brain trying to distract her.

But her brain couldn't make up the little flutter in her chest when her eyes sometimes connected with Stefan's, or the tingle in her fingers when her skin had come into contact with his.

Her life felt like a rollercoaster. One day she'd been at work, then she'd been sent on a recuperation holiday of a lifetime, then she'd been involved in a natural disaster, which now meant she was trapped. If she told someone this story it was likely they wouldn't believe her.

She'd never felt so unsettled. So uncertain or so unsure. This whole situation was madness. But, hopefully, manageable madness. In her head she had already formed a list. X-rays. Assessment. Surgeries. Theatre was not normal for an A&E doctor, but sometimes she'd been called to assist, or ended up in situations in the resus room that weren't too far from theatre procedures. She might need some guidance but she was confident enough that she could assist Stefan.

But all that still couldn't explain that tiny feeling in the pit of her stomach. It had been there for a long time, but coming here had finally forced her to acknowledge it. She might be in the middle of a disaster, but things were stripped back here. She didn't have her own job to think about. She wasn't surrounded by familiar things and friends. Taking those parts of her life away and realising the gnawing feeling was still there made it all the more real.

She walked down the corridor to the kitchen. The sun wasn't up entirely, but all her colleagues were. Tea was made, and a large box of cornflakes and a stack of bowls sat on the counter.

'Don't want to torture people with the smell of toast if we have to fast them for surgery,' said Lynn. 'That would just be mean.'

She pushed the milk towards Paige, who filled her bowl. 'Do we know how we're starting?'

Stefan pushed a list towards her. 'This is the order I think we should do the X-rays. Do you agree?'

She glanced at it and nodded. 'Once we've reviewed, we'll decide the order for surgery or casts?'

The mood was sombre this morning, probably because they were all aware of the storm raging all night. Lynn handed over some charts. 'I decided to formalise our paperwork. Observations, medicines and notes. Found a computer and printer in the office—' she smiled at Stefan '—that thankfully had the generic log-in on a sticky note next to it.'

He rolled his eyes. 'My colleague was site manager here. He's notorious at work for it. Fortunately for him, his wife is expecting twins and he had to fly back to Hollywood at short notice.' He looked up at the ceiling and shook his head. 'You have no idea how glad I am that he wasn't here when this happened.'

They all nodded. Stefan sighed. 'I've checked everyone this morning. Given some more pain meds so we can move to X-ray. There were a few tears. I think shock is finally hitting our patients. Yesterday, they were just grateful to have survived, and to have somewhere warm to sleep. Today, they are stiff and sore from yesterday, and most of them have clocked the weather and know it's likely we'll be here for a few days. Christmas is a big issue.'

'If it comes to it, we can make Christmas work,' said Paige decisively.

'Has anyone spoken to Franco yet this morning?'

They all shook their heads. 'Let's do some X-rays,' said Joe. 'Hopefully by the time we're finished, Franco might have some news for us.'

Ninety minutes later, Stefan and Paige had all the information they needed. Little Claudia definitely needed surgery to pin her tibia and fibula. One of the women with a fractured ankle needed some manipulation and a cast. The other needed surgery, as did the woman with the fractured ulna and radius. Rafe had six rib fractures. He was probably the sickest here, but there was no surgery that could help him. Bruno's head injury was stable, but he still needed observation. Eva, the pregnant lady, was fine, just anxious, and Bob was keeping his blood sugar under control with only the short-acting insulin. The one who was giving unexpected concern was their elderly man with angina. After a comfortable night, settled with some nitrate medicine, Eduardo had started to experience chest pain again. His ECG was mildly concerning.

'In an ideal world we would do emergency bloods,' said Paige. 'But there's no chance of that here.'

Stefan looked around. It was clear he was measuring the range of experience in the room. 'I know the weather isn't good,' he said carefully. 'But, if there's a break in the weather, we might have a chance to Medevac some people out. Eduardo would be my number one patient to get out of here. He needs bloods, and probably somewhere they have a cath lab in case he's heading for a myocardial infarction. Does everyone agree?'

Paige nodded. 'Who would you consider next?'

'That's difficult,' he mused. 'It could depend on how

our surgeries go today. If we could get extra insulin for Bob, he will be fine. If Bruno took a turn for the worse, I'd struggle with the appropriate surgical equipment, or the expertise. He'd be next for me.'

Paige nodded again. 'It's like playing a lottery with people's lives, and I hate that. But we have to try and prioritise.' They'd already decided that both doctors and Joe would be in Theatre today. Lynn would do any casts post-surgery, and Cathy would be keeping an eye on everyone else.

Cathy gave a solemn nod. 'So, if Franco gets in touch, I know the first two patients to get ready for transfer.'

'Don't be afraid to come and get us. Getting someone inside a rescue stretcher is difficult. They might only send the stretcher down in a winch if they think it's too dangerous to send the member of staff. It will likely be based on timing. So come and tell us if you need to.'

Paige's thoughts were circulating back to experiences she'd rather forget. 'I can help,' she said quietly. 'I'm familiar with the stretcher and winch technology. We've transferred a number of patients via the roof of the hospital before.'

Stefan gave a grateful nod. 'Fantastic. Been a while since I've been near one.'

'You've used them too?'

He nodded. 'When I first went to California I was based near Long Beach. Had a short-term role with air and sea rescue.'

Paige was intrigued. Stefan had made a comment last night about being busy. Did the guy ever stop working?

'That's great.' She stood up and stretched her back. 'Are we ready to get started?'

Everyone nodded.

Paige was nervous. Operating theatres were a little outside her comfort zone, but she could see that Stefan was right at home. He moved about with ease. Checking all the surgical tools that were ready. Moving the mobile X-ray machine and checking the drugs on a nearby tray. When he was finally happy he turned to them both. 'Lynn has Claudia and her mum outside. I'll give Claudia some light sedation before I bring her through. Joe, are you happy to monitor her, while I scrub?'

Joe nodded. He had years of experience in Theatre and had a specialist position as an advanced nurse who could also assist in anaesthetics. In the worst possible set of circumstances, it seemed that luck had smiled on them.

Things went smoothly. Claudia had an open reduction and internal fixation of her bones, and a cast applied. After everyone was content, they continued with their other surgeries. Frances had an open reduction and internal fixation of her ulna and radius. Anna required a pin in her ankle, and Greta was luckiest, with her bones still in position, and just required a plaster cast on her lower leg.

Stefan had been cool. He'd admitted reading up on all the surgeries last night—to refresh his brain. Paige was glad to hear him say that. She'd assisted as best she could, conscious of the fact that she would never have managed any of this on her own. He'd been thoughtful and respectful of them all—not like some of the arrogant surgeons she'd met in the past, and she was grateful, because her nerves could have got the better of her. But working alongside someone who was clearly careful and supportive had made her feel much more at ease.

She'd just pulled the pale pink cap from her head when Cathy rushed in. 'You were right. Franco just radioed. There might only be time to get one person out. They have a temporary break in the weather.'

Within five minutes Paige was outside, jacket over her theatre scrubs at a wide space in the middle of the car park. Poor Eduardo was behind a set of doors, ready to be bundled out and into the rescue stretcher.

The *thud-thud* of the helicopter sounded in the distance. The clouds above were thick and heavy and, from ground level, visibility was poor. Stefan had the satellite phone in his hand, listening to instructions. He gave a hand signal to Paige. Three minutes. She nodded. Bruno was also in the background, waiting to see if there would be a chance to evacuate two patients instead of one.

Paige was trying to pretend her heart wasn't thudding in her chest. She breathed in the freezing air and blew it out slowly, trying to count in her head. Anything to calm her nerves down. As the whirring increased above them, the dark body of the helicopter appeared. The side door opened and a man's legs swung over the edge, clearly operating the bright orange stretcher that descended towards them. There was also a small bag attached. Paige untied it with shaking fingers, as Stefan detached the stretcher. Paige could see Cathy talking directly into Eduardo's ear, trying to keep him calm. She wheeled him out and, between the three of them, they manoeuvred him into the stretcher, unable to talk properly because of the noise overhead. Eduardo had his hands across his chest, his GTN spray held tightly in one fist. Paige didn't even want to consider how scary this might be for a man with chest pain. Stefan had given him something to relax him in preparation. But would it work?

As they snapped the last clip into place, Paige gave the signal to ascend. The wind seemed to be picking up, or was it just the backdraught from the rotors above? The stretcher swung perilously as it started to move upwards to the helicopter. But that was normal. Paige knew from experience that the ascent was never in a straight line. How could it be?

Within moments, the operator above had grabbed the stretcher and loaded it on board. There were a few seconds' pause. It was clear the pilot and operator were discussing whether they had time to retrieve another patient. The operator gave a signal. Four minutes. They only had four minutes left.

A second stretcher descended and Stefan sprinted across the car park to the doors for Bruno. Every moment counted. He ran across with Bruno in the wheelchair. Bruno was well wrapped up, and easier to get into the stretcher than Eduardo had been. Within a few minutes the stretcher lifted into the sky, was bundled into the helicopter, the sliding door slammed shut and the helicopter disappeared into the dark clouds above.

It was bitterly cold. But Paige was momentarily frozen to the spot. Stefan bent down at her feet and grabbed the bag, which was still there. He caught her hand and pulled her back towards the hospital, slamming the doors behind them.

Cathy was already inside, tugging off her woolly hat. 'I think we made that by the skin of our teeth,' she said. Then she looked at them both, and obviously caught the expression on Paige's face. 'Kitchen,' she said bluntly. 'I'll make the tea.'

She turned and walked away while Stefan looked at Paige. 'You okay?'

She nodded and swallowed. 'Just absolutely freezing.' She hugged herself in her ski jacket. 'Didn't have time to dress properly underneath. And the noise from the helicopter made it difficult to concentrate. I didn't have a clue what I was doing out there.'

Stefan looked at her steadily. 'You manoeuvred two patients into a complicated stretcher system and ensured they were safe in a limited time frame. You did fine.' He held up the bag. 'Now, let's hope we've got some insulin in here.'

The bag was small, but thick and heavy. They opened it in the kitchen and found well-packaged insulin—both brands that Bob usually used, along with a new fourteen-day sensor. There were also some other drugs, another satellite phone, and some additional items.

Stefan stared at the phone for a few moments. 'Guess they think we might not be getting out of here soon.' He undid the wrapper on something else and frowned. 'What's this?'

Paige inspected the box. It was clearly something electronic. 'I think it might be a booster,' she said as she stared at one of the wires coming off it. 'Maybe to give us some kind of internet provision?'

'We've had barely anything since the avalanche,' said Cathy. 'It might help a lot. If some of our patients could contact their families they might be a bit more settled.'

Joe and Lynn came in. 'All patients that are left are fine.' He glanced at the items on the worktop. 'Oh, insulin, great. I'll take that along to Bob and put the rest in the medicine fridge.'

Lynn stayed near the doorway. She seemed to be reluctant to talk.

'What's wrong?' asked Paige.

Lynn sighed. 'Claudia's mum was quite tearful. Wondered why some people had been evacuated and not her and her child.'

Stefan straightened in his chair. 'We know why. The decision had to be made on a medical basis.'

Lynn shrugged. 'We know that. But they don't understand. Greta's upset too. They're stranded up a mountain after an avalanche, a few days before Christmas. People expect to be with their families at this time of year. It's hard. Particularly when we don't know what comes next.' She gave a soft smile. 'I'm lucky. I'm here with Joe. But if I was up here by myself I'd feel differently.'

Stefan ran his fingers through his hair. Paige could tell he was exasperated. 'I'll talk to them,' he said. 'I get that they're upset. But there has to be some perspective. We're all alive. We're all safe. We're somewhere warm, with electricity and food. We can survive. And people know that we're here. They will try and get us out.' He took a deep breath. 'I get that people are sentimental about Christmas. It's a time of year I love. If I don't get out of here, my dad will spend Christmas alone. But it's one day of the year. And he'll understand. He's a resilient old guy.' There was a real tinge of sadness to his words that struck somewhere deep down inside of Paige. She wanted to ask more. But now clearly wasn't the time.

She held up her hands. 'We can't control the weather. And we all have to take responsibility for the fact we knew there was a weather warning—albeit for the next day—and we still chose to go skiing. I had planned to head down to the town, get some more supplies, and spend the next few days holed up in the chalet. I would likely still have been stranded. But I would have been safe. I would have been warm and comfortable. Just like I am here.'

'You could go back to the chalet if you wanted,' said Stefan, his blue eyes connecting with hers. 'The rest of us don't have someplace else to go. But, if you wanted to, you could go back. There's no obligation to stay.'

Her skin prickled at the back of her neck. Was he testing her? Did he want her to leave? She hated the way she instantly felt inside. As if she could grab the keys to the car, disappear down the mountain and hide in the luxury cabin.

Anyone would be a fool not to consider it.

And she hated herself. Because it did flash through her brain. The thought of not having to be a doctor. The thought of actually having the holiday she was supposed to have. Switching off from it all. Hiding in the chalet with the warm fire, the exquisite library and hugely comfortable bed.

She was a horrible, terrible person. She shouldn't have let even that fleeting thought enter her brain.

'There's no way I'm leaving. I'll only go back to the chalet when the road is clear again and we can all get out of here.'

Cathy gave a nod and poured the tea, but Stefan was looking at her carefully. 'You don't have to.' He cleared his throat and shifted uncomfortably in his chair. 'We've done all the surgeries that we need to. Everyone is stable.'

'If it wasn't so tricky, we could probably have taken everyone back to the café, so we were all together.' Joe and Lynn came back through the door at this point and sat down, picking up mugs of tea as they were poured.

Stefan shook his head. 'Not much point in that. At least we have beds here. And all the food from the chalet. I know the cafés have food, but I'm not sure how much. I'm sure it's much more comfortable in the hospital. We are as well waiting things out here.'

Joe nodded. 'My back is too old to sleep on a floor these days.'

It made perfect sense. And even though Paige had been prepared to spend Christmas alone, she didn't mind being surrounded by other people.

She looked around at her colleagues and stood up. 'Why don't you let me cook this evening? We're all tired. I can make dinner and we can all try and get to bed early tonight.'

Joe, Lynn and Cathy all nodded in assent. Stefan looked at her. 'I'll help.'

She wasn't quite sure what to say. She'd wanted some

space to think, but she could hardly turn down the offer of help.

'Of course,' she agreed in a tight voice.

The rest disappeared down the corridor, likely to one of the other rooms to sit and relax.

Paige made her way over to where they'd placed all the provisions and pulled the cupboard doors open.

Stefan appeared at her elbow. 'Okay, so what dream dinner are you going to make?'

Paige looked around. 'I think it will be simple. Pasta, with a tomato sauce bulked by some of the vegetables while they are still fresh. We can toast some of the bread with garlic butter. Simple, but fine.'

He gave a nod and moved across the kitchen, lifting out a giant pot and filling it with water, and setting it on the hob. Paige grabbed some armfuls of packets and tins. She poured the pasta into the pot and handed him the tins. 'You open these tinned tomatoes and find another large pot. I'll chop all the vegetables.'

It wasn't quite as awkward as she had first thought. Stefan could find his way around the kitchen. He wasn't trying to interfere, just be helpful. After a few minutes, she could feel his eyes on her as she chopped the vegetables.

'Not doing it efficiently enough for you?' she joked. 'I would have given you this job, but didn't want to risk a surgeon's fingers.'

He gave a small smile but shot her a thoughtful glance. 'You did well today. I'm sorry if I didn't say it sooner.'

She looked at him in surprise. 'It was you that did

well. You were doing orthopaedics. I know that's not normal for you.'

He shrugged. 'It's not. I usually deal with facial bones. But I have experience in other surgery, and have pinned and plated before, so it was just a case of remembering all I could.'

She kept chopping. 'You seemed confident.'

'I was pretending.'

She stopped and stared at him, kind of in shock. She gave him a sideways glance and started chopping again. 'Well, I guess I'll need to remember that about you. You're good at pretending.'

'You make me sound like some kind of spy.'

She raised her eyebrows. 'You could be. But, to be honest, if you were some kind of spy, I would have expected you to get us out of here today.'

'You mean, phone my headquarters and ask for the snow-burrowing machine to get through the road block?'

She wrinkled her nose. 'I was thinking more high-tech.' She waved her knife as she spoke. 'You know, the machine that burrows to the centre of the earth, and then spins around and comes out just at the entrance-way to the hospital.'

'Oh, you wanted the big guns,' he joked.

She shrugged and put the onions and courgettes she'd chopped into the pan with the tomatoes, 'I did,' she admitted. 'But maybe you're not that level of spy.'

'You're dissing my spy status?'

'Of course.' She started combining ingredients to make the sauce.

He folded his arms. 'You seem pretty set on getting out of here.'

'Isn't everybody?'

She looked at him, because he hadn't replied. As she stirred the sauce she dug deeper. 'Are you telling me that you'd be happy to stay?'

Now he looked awkward. It was as if the handsome, broad-shouldered man had turned into a four-year-old boy who was shuffling his feet. 'Not…happy. Just not sad exactly either.'

She put down her wooden spoon. 'Okay, you've got me. I'm not touching this dinner until you tell me more.'

'You might get a bad review for your restaurant,' he quipped, clearly trying to change the subject again.

'Well, it's your restaurant, so see if I care.' She winked at him, and he burst out laughing.

He pointed his finger at her. 'So, there you are.'

He said it with satisfaction and she didn't quite get it. 'What do you mean?' She started stirring the sauce again.

'The girl I met in the café before the avalanche. The one that—how do you say it—wouldn't give me an inch?'

Now it was Paige's turn to shift uncomfortably. 'But I've been here all along.'

He leaned forward, putting both elbows on the counter and staring at her. 'But you weren't. You lost your spark.'

Paige was immediately on the defensive. 'Well, let me see, there was an avalanche, there were patients to treat. There were thoughts of being trapped and wondering what on earth happens next.'

Now, she was a bit annoyed. 'Anyhow, don't stand around doing nothing. Find the butter and the garlic, mix it up and put it on the bread. The oven is behind you.'

He raised his eyebrows. 'Bossy.'

Paige shook her head. 'Not at all. The word you're looking for is direct, or I might even let you off with a Scottish word. Crabbit. That's what happens when you have to share a suite with a record-breaking snorer.'

Stefan's mouth fell open and he moved around the counter, coming up next to her. 'You can't get away with that one.' He picked up one of the wooden spoons and wagged it at her. 'You're the one that snores all night.'

'I do not,' she said, aghast. Or at least pretending to be. Her insides were cringing.

'You do so.'

'I'm going to tape you tonight. You literally start snoring the second you close your eyes. And even though there's a wall between us, I can still hear you.'

'Anyone would think you were criticising the renovations that have gone on here.'

'I wouldn't dare,' she sparked back. 'You might start charging me rent.'

Stefan started mixing the butter and pressed garlic together. He looked thoughtful. 'Now, that could actually be a good idea.'

Her phone buzzed and then started playing a tune. After a few seconds Stefan looked at her with his eyes wide. 'Really?'

She pulled her phone from the back pocket of her

jeans, letting the chorus of the eighties pop song 'Last Christmas' fill the air.

'Classic,' she said decidedly, prodding the pasta and deciding it was ready. 'Hurry up with that garlic bread.'

After all her earlier anxieties in the day she couldn't help but notice how relaxed she felt in Stefan's company. Somehow, just being around him, his easy chat and teasing manner seemed to lift her spirits and, as she watched, she wondered if she was having the same effect on him. The restlessness that seemed to plague him appeared to have been pushed away. It was nice just to concentrate on the moment.

He grabbed a knife and spread the garlic butter over the bread, lifting the tray and sliding it into the oven. 'No. You don't get to drop that Christmas tune without an explanation.' Then he looked at her curiously. 'Did you just get a signal on your phone?'

She sighed and pushed it towards him. 'I should be so lucky. No, it's a pre-set alarm.'

'What for?' It was a natural follow-up question, so Paige tried not to let it bother her.

'I take some supplements. It's just a reminder.'

He paused for a second then gave a brief nod. 'And you need your favourite pop band of the eighties to remind you?'

Paige glanced in the pot. The sauce was definitely ready. 'Actually,' she said, as she drained the pasta, 'it's my favourite ever Christmas song. Has been for years. And I won't be moved on that.'

'"Last Christmas" is your favourite ever Christmas song?'

She nodded. 'Absolutely. Just be glad the weather is bad out there. I'd be out in that snow in a flash, trying to recreate the video.'

He rolled his eyes and shook his head. 'Who trapped me with an eighties fanatic?' he joked.

She stirred the sauce into the pasta. 'Actually, I have a whole host of Christmas songs on my phone. I might treat you to all my favourites if you're lucky.'

He started putting out plates for everyone. 'You just make this "snowed-in" event better by the moment.'

She sighed and looked around. 'I actually love Christmas. To be honest, the chalet was my dream come true. Christmas paraphernalia everywhere. A gorgeous setting. Lots of food. And the library. My plan was to spend all day playing "Last Christmas" and just mooching around.'

'Mooching?' He frowned.

She held up her hands. 'You know, flopping from one seat to another, going from room to room, being completely relaxed. I even brought my own advent calendar with me. A proper one. Not one filled with chocolate. You know, the kind you had as a kid, where you open a window each day and see a Christmas picture—a robin, a reindeer, a Christmas wreath, a present.' She stared spooning the dinner onto plates. 'You know, they're very hard to find these days.'

Stefan turned, grabbed some oven gloves and pulled the tray of garlic bread from the oven. 'What can I say?' He shrugged. 'I'm from Switzerland, the land of chocolate. I'm with the kids that like the chocolate advent calendar.'

'Primitive,' she joked as the warm aroma of the garlic bread surrounded them. 'Okay—' she put her hands on her hips '—I think we're ready.'

Stefan grabbed a tray and put some of the bowls of pasta on it. 'Patients first, then us. Let's make sure everyone is good.'

It only took a few minutes to serve the dinner and for Joe, Cathy and Lynn to be attracted by the smell and come to collect their food.

'Where do you want to eat?' asked Stefan.

All of a sudden she realised they were alone. It would be so easy to suggest they eat with some of the patients, or with their colleagues. But, for some entirely selfish reason, Paige didn't want to.

'Any place you haven't shown me yet?' There was a hint of something in her voice, and it surprised even her.

There was a flicker of recognition on Stefan's face. He smiled. 'Sure. Follow me.'

They walked down the corridor with their food, past all the rooms and around another corridor and down a few steps.

'What's this?' asked Paige, as he pushed open a door to a dark space.

He gestured for her to follow. 'Are you scared of the dark?'

'No. But why are you asking that?'

'Because if you don't mind waiting a few minutes in the dark, I might surprise you.' He leaned over and set his food down somewhere. 'Back in a sec.'

Paige had no idea how he knew where he was going. Some hidden part of her brain decided to instantly remind her of every horror movie she'd ever watched. What was that noise? Was that a shadow?

A few seconds later there was a flicker.

And then she gasped.

Dim lights came on. In front of her were a few rows of wide red velvet seats, and in front of them, on the furthest wall, was a large screen.

'A cinema!'

The screen flickered and Stefan's voice came through much louder than before. She jumped. 'Just switching things on.'

The screen came to life, and the soundtrack of a popular dinosaur movie came through the apparently hidden speakers.

Stefan appeared again through a door up a couple of steps at the back of the room.

He lifted his plate. 'Let's grab a seat. Movie's about to start.'

She shook her head. 'You have a cinema in a hospital?'

He shrugged. 'All I can say is that it's one of the most popular parts of the hospital complex in Hollywood. More popular than the gym, or the library.'

Paige still couldn't believe it. She moved along a few seats and sat down. The red velvet chair was sumptuous, deep and well-supported. Stefan sat in the one next to her, his shoulder brushing against hers.

'I can't believe this,' she said as the lights started to dim around them, conscious that they were still touching.

'A cinema?' he asked. 'I don't think it's that unusual.'

She shot him a look as she ate a spoonful of her pasta. 'No. Not the cinema. I can't believe that a few days before Christmas you get a chance to pick a movie—I've told you about my Christmas obsession, and you still go with *Jurassic Park*.'

He grinned in the dark. 'What can I say? Who doesn't love a dinosaur?'

'If it isn't Christmas, I'm a sci-fi girl,' she grumbled good-naturedly. '*Star Trek, Star Wars*...'

He leaned over and whispered in her ear while laughing, his warm breath on her cheek. 'Dinosaurs are sci-fi. Get with the programme.'

There was a definite shiver down her spine. And it was nothing to do with the dark, or the dinosaurs. It was the closeness between them. The hint in the air that had been there from the moment they'd stepped down the corridor towards the cinema. Their teasing and flirtation seemed to have reached a whole different level.

Paige settled back in her chair, trying to pretend this wasn't a completely surreal experience. A private cinema. A handsome man whose warm breath had just been on her neck. And an avalanche. She couldn't make this up.

But if she could, the next part might need a rating that wasn't for dinosaur movies.

CHAPTER SIX

STEFAN LOOKED OUT of the window at the looming dark clouds. It was apparently seven a.m. He'd never seen it so dark at this time of year. It seemed that all the weather reports he'd seen were entirely accurate.

Franco had told him that the people down at the café were getting annoyed and restless. Some supplies were dwindling, and there were no proper wash facilities. Although the chalet was available, the logistics of moving people across the snow in the first instance, then up the winding road, was just too risky. Whilst it was only a five-minute drive from the edge of the resort to the chalet in Stefan's car, it would take a whole lot longer on foot.

Stefan's offer to drive down and ferry people back and forth was declined.

'Too risky,' said Franco. 'Right now, we only have people in two places. If we have another avalanche, it could hit the part near the road again. You, and your patients, are probably safer higher up and near the chalet. I wouldn't take the risk of trying to move these people, when we still can't be sure this snow won't move again.

At least in here they're sheltered. Out there...' He let his voice tail off.

'Have there been any reports of anyone missing or unaccounted for?'

Franco sighed. 'Thankfully not. There were a few accounts of possible missing people, but it turned out they'd already made their way down to the village, or were up here.'

Stefan heaved a huge sigh of relief. 'Good.' He finished the call and went back to the kitchen. He'd been up for the last few hours, reluctant to start working in the main room of the suite in case he somehow disturbed Paige.

The more he got to know her, the more intrigued he was by Dr McLeod. He loved that accent. The way it got thicker as she became more passionate about a subject, or even when she became more relaxed around him.

It was hard being in close quarters with someone with that pull about them. The pull that made him want to look at her every moment and keep looking for her when she moved out of his line of sight.

Stefan was used to being around all kinds of beautiful women. Paige was naturally pretty—pale skin, good cheekbones, wide eyes and long lashes. He liked her. He liked the way her sass could bubble up and overflow. He liked the fact that she'd pulled herself together and started digging with them all after the avalanche. She was out of her comfort zone, but clearly still prepared to try her best.

But there was something about her that didn't quite sit properly. She'd talked a little about her work. She'd admitted she was here for a rest. But he couldn't help but be curious about what her story was. The bruises he'd thought he'd noticed that first day were more visible when she wore scrubs. She hadn't offered any explanation for them. And he hadn't asked. They were fading. They were recent.

Understanding Paige McLeod was like trying to put together pieces of a puzzle. But something else was bothering him.

Himself.

Stefan Bachmann didn't give himself time to think like this. Being stranded up a mountain with limited access to resources was odd. He was writing a million lists. Sending a million emails that he wasn't sure were getting through. The internet had been installed the morning of the avalanche, but it was patchy. The booster that had been dropped to them didn't seem to make much difference.

If he'd been back home, or even up here, with no avalanche, he would be *doing* things. Seeing more patients. Doing online consultations. Painting the walls if he had to.

He couldn't remember the last time he'd taken the time to sit and watch a movie. But last night, with Paige, it had just seemed to fit. It had just seemed right.

And even that made him a little uncomfortable.

Stefan had been born with a nervous energy. His mother had said she could never contain him. The school library had never had enough books. There had never been enough teams to join—football, hockey, rugby. But that energy had changed and been channelled after his mother had died. Once he'd qualified as a doctor, and finished specialising, he'd done voluntary mission after voluntary mission. And he could put his hand on his heart and say that he'd genuinely loved them. But stopping, even for a day, made his brain crowd with thoughts about treatments he should be doing, and people he should be helping. People like his mother. The one person he had failed. Working helped keep him ticking over. To push those guilty feelings from his mind and just focus on the next thing to do.

But now? Being stuck here? He was restless. He was antsy. He could have done with another ten patients or so in the hospital. Not that he wished for a second that anyone else was hurt or stranded here. But just to keep him busy.

The tracker he was using on his computer blinked. It was showing potential breaks in the weather. Trouble was, they were only lasting ten minutes at most. Not enough time to get a helicopter safely in the air and back to the hospital. He knew the journey meant the pilot and his team would be in the air for between thirty and forty minutes minimum—and there didn't look like any predicted breaks in the weather to allow that to happen.

He sighed. They were stuck up here for at least another twenty-four hours. Maybe more. Paige had told him that she loved Christmas. She'd also mentioned how great the chalet was.

Claudia, the seven-year-old, was getting bored. Maybe he could bring some of the Christmas items from the chalet here to try and brighten the place up, make it a little more festive.

Paige had also mentioned some kind of presents. None of the adults would be worried about presents, but a seven-year-old who still believed in Santa definitely would. And it didn't matter that it might not be what she'd hoped for. There still had to be something for a little girl to open on Christmas morning.

It was time for a meeting.

He called all his new colleagues together, made coffee and sat them down in the kitchen.

'Franco called. It looks like the weather will be even worse today and an evacuation won't be possible.' Before they all had a chance to feel low, he carried on. 'I was wondering how you would all feel about trying to make this place look a bit more like Christmas.'

Frowns creased a number of foreheads and he kept speaking. 'We should be safe enough to take a few trips down to the chalet. What about the Christmas tree? And some of the other decorations? I was also thinking about Claudia.'

'Presents.' Lynn, Cathy and Paige said the word together.

They all exchanged glances. 'Is there anything there at all we can use?'

Paige wrinkled her nose. 'There should be. There are board games we can bring up. I'm sure I saw a basket with some kind of crafts. There are books. There might even be more stuff that I just didn't get a chance to find.' She held up her hands. 'I'd only arrived the night before and had a quick look around. Because of the weather, I wanted to ski the next morning, and planned to spend the next day in the chalet.' She gave a smile. 'There could be more that I didn't have time to discover.'

Stefan held up the car keys. 'When we get a break in the weather, will we take a quick trip down?'

Paige nodded and turned to the others. 'Are we worried about anyone today?'

Lynn shook her head. 'All casts are good…fingers and toes are all pink and moving. Eva has had no further concerns with her pregnancy, Bob's diabetes is fine, he's just bored. Rafe needs to be tied to the bed. I've caught him trying to get up a few times by himself and he's not quite there yet. He still needs some supervision.'

Stefan nodded, along with Paige. 'Let us know if you're worried at all again. I'll check Rafe later. Let's introduce Bob to the cinema. It might keep him entertained for a bit.'

'What cinema?' said Joe, Lynn and Cathy in unison.

Paige laughed. 'The hidden one at the end of the corridor. Stefan will show you how to use the computer and set up the films. It's a whole otherworld experience.'

Three sets of eyes widened and Cathy groaned. 'How the other half live.' It was said in jest and the rest all nodded.

When a short break in the weather was predicted, Lynn, Paige and Stefan drove down to the chalet. 'We've got to get the tree,' said Stefan as soon as they walked inside.

'Will we get that in the car?' asked Lynn.

'As long as we leave the boot open,' said Paige. She was looking around. 'Okay, Lynn, the library is along there. I didn't really get a proper chance to look, so you might find some suitable things in there.'

'Can I take anything?' she asked curiously.

Paige was hesitating and Stefan broke in. 'We can send an email and let the owner know what we've done. Here's hoping he might understand, rather than think we've just stripped his chalet clean.'

'We kind of have.' Paige pulled a face. 'I doubt there's anything left in the food cupboards. It was the best-stocked place I've seen.'

Stefan leaned back, looking around more critically. 'You know, there might never have been an avalanche here before, but maybe the owner always had that in mind. They might have had concerns about the road. Even heavy snowfall or black ice could make it unusable.'

'Is this really the best place for a hospital?'

Stefan sighed. 'It's why there's also a helipad in the plans.' He waved a hand. 'From what I remember, it's only a few times a year that the road might be dangerous.'

She leaned on the counter and put her head on her hand. 'And aren't you in charge of that now?'

He sighed. 'I'm beginning to realise exactly what that means.' He glanced over his shoulder. Lynn had gone off to the library. 'Are you unhappy that you're stuck up a mountain with me?'

'Only because you snore,' she said without a moment's hesitation.

'I do not!'

'How many times are we going to have this fight?'

she asked, walking over to the large Christmas tree, trying to decide how best to move it.

There were Christmas garlands along the fireplace, and more on the stairs. 'I think we should take these too.'

Stefan looked out of the window. 'If we try and take all the decorations off the tree, it will take too long. We only have a thirty-minute window. Any ideas?'

Paige nodded and walked into the kitchen, pulling open a drawer.

Stefan smiled and, between them, they wound the clingwrap around the tree to try to keep some of the decorations in place, before tipping it on its side and wrestling it out to the car. Lynn had already loaded up some other supplies, but she had another few boxes that there just wasn't room for.

She looked at them. 'How about I take these up, and come back for the rest?'

Paige checked her watch. 'Is there enough time?'

They all looked at the sky. It was grey, but not as stormy as it had been.

For a moment, no one spoke. 'There's still a few rooms to check over,' said Paige. Her stomach was twisting a little but she nodded. 'You feel okay to drive up and back?'

Lynn nodded. 'It will take longer for the other two to help me unload at the hospital than it will to do the drive.'

Stefan pressed his lips together and put his hand on her arm. 'It looks fine now, but the weather is so changeable. All our patients are fine. If you have any concerns, or the weather gets worse, just stay.' He looked around. 'The chalet is secure and warm. We could manage.'

Lynn gave a nod. 'Don't worry, I'll be back in the blink of an eye.'

She climbed into the car and drove off. Stefan closed the door and turned back to Paige. 'Anywhere else to check?'

She nodded. 'You have no idea how big this place is. In fact, it's a bit like your hospital. A Tardis. Bigger on the inside than it looks from the outside.'

He tilted his head at her. 'A *Doctor Who* fan?'

'Wasn't every child?' Then she laughed. 'And they've started making Christmas specials. It was like someone sent them a note.'

'You didn't?' He actually looked as if he believed she might have.

She tapped the side of her nose. 'You don't get to know all my secrets because you're trapped in a chalet with me.'

Paige led him through to two more rooms near the back of the chalet. One was another sitting room with multiple cupboards, a comfortable sofa and a table and chairs. The other was smaller, with another fireplace and red squishy seats.

'This place never ends,' he said, as he headed into the room with the cupboards. A few moments later he gave a shout. 'What about this…stuff?'

She could hear the question in his voice and wandered through to see him holding a large wicker basket. It was full of wool, knitting needles and lots of little bags filled with pom-poms, sequins, beads and felt.

'Oh, wow.' Paige couldn't wipe the smile from her face. 'This could keep Claudia happy for hours. Perfect. Good find.'

There was a loud roar of wind and they both froze.

'Oh, no...' Paige's heart started to pound. Not because she was worried for herself. 'Will Lynn have made it?'

Stefan put his hand to his pocket and let out a curse. 'The satellite phone is with Joe. Is there a phone in here that might work?'

Paige walked back out to the hallway and picked up the main phone, shaking her head when she heard no tone. 'Let me see if there's Wi-Fi. We might be able to send a message that way.'

There was an older computer in one of the rooms. She fired it up, used the password in the drawer and, after an inevitable delay, it finally connected. The internet seemed spotty. But Paige logged into her account and sent a message to Joe. Within a few minutes she got a response.

She's here. But stay where you are. Too dangerous.

Paige let out a huge sigh of relief. 'Lynn's okay. But Joe must have spoken to Franco. He says to stay.'

Stefan's expression was unreadable. He paced over to the nearest window, pressing his face so close that the glass steamed up with his breath.

'Think I'm making it up?' she quipped.

He shook his head. 'Of course not. But...' he looked around '...what will we do?'

Paige looked at him. 'Are you serious?'

'Yes.' He nodded, and it was then she realised that he was entirely serious.

'Nothing, Stefan. We'll do nothing. We'll wait. Read a book. Sit down. Watch the TV. Rummage around and hope we can find some leftover food.' She moved away from him and walked out into the corridor and along to the kitchen, running the tap. 'Look, the pipes haven't frozen or burst, so I can make you tea, coffee or hot chocolate. We can survive on that if we have to.'

He kept moving. She watched in amazement as he paced from room to room, eventually climbing the stairs. Now, she was curious. She found him in the main bedroom, looking at the mountain through the large window. He'd raised the blind she'd pulled the last time she'd been here, thinking it could protect the room a bit if the avalanche had come this way. He was looking up at the swirling grey and black clouds. It actually made her shudder.

'What are you doing? Are you hoping that a tornado will put down and sweep you off to the Emerald City?' It was easy to joke about the well-known film.

'Will there be something to do there?' he muttered.

The words stung. Was he really so worried about being alone with her? She turned and walked downstairs, taking some deep breaths. It would be so easy to be offended and take his remark personally, but Paige was wiser than that.

She knew exactly how many thoughts were swirling around her own head. Thoughts that she hadn't said out loud to anyone. Maybe Stefan was exactly the same as her.

He'd already mentioned that his dad could be alone for Christmas now. Might he be worried—or feeling guilty? She'd sent a message to her family to let them know she was safe. She'd never planned on spending Christmas with them as she'd expected to be working. She'd told them about the assault at work and that she was taking a holiday for a few weeks.

She put water in a jug and filled the coffee machine, selecting a pod with a coffee with a hint of nutmeg. She was determined to try and be a little festive. The main room was bare without the huge Christmas tree, but there were still other Christmas decorations around, and she lit the fire as the coffee gurgled through in the kitchen.

They were alone. Stranded alone in this chalet. The man whose breath on her skin the night before had sent a dozen sensations down her spine. She recognised he was feeling edgy. But she was feeling edgy too. A night alone together in this chalet might be more than she could handle. The flirtation was already there. Paige took a deep breath, trying to focus herself back on the immediate issues.

Since they were stuck here, she pulled off her boots and jacket, contemplating going upstairs for one of the luxury bathrobes. But the coffee was ready. She grabbed the mug, strolled through to the library and pulled a thriller from the shelves. A few minutes later she was curled up on the red sofa with a blanket on her knees. She could quite easily be stranded here, even if Stefan Bachmann couldn't. As for the tension between them? She would just need to see how things played out.

* * *

The swirling black clouds seemed to echo his thoughts. He'd been rude, he knew that. And he'd have to apologise.

But Stefan made his way back to the computer and sent a message to his father, hoping it would reach him. His father was quite tech savvy. He would be worried, of course he would. Even though they were sometimes thousands of miles apart, his father always knew where Stefan was.

He'd planned to spend Christmas Day and Boxing Day with his father. During the evacuation of patients to the hospital, he'd considered asking Franco for the use of the satellite telephone to get in touch. But it would have been wrong—very wrong.

He'd just made sure his name was on the list of people stuck on the mountain and trusted the people coordinating the rescue to let his father know he was safe. That would be enough for his dad. He would trust Stefan to fill in the details later, knowing that he would be staying to help as much as he could.

His head filled with pictures of his parents' house. A small settee, and two chairs around the fire—one that had been empty for twelve years.

It didn't matter where Stefan had been in the world, at Christmas time he'd always asked his father to join him. Sometimes he'd said yes, sometimes no, dependent on the potential length of the journey. But, if they couldn't be together, Stefan would video call his father at breakfast time, and at dinner time, so they could drink coffee or eat food together, sharing news and stories.

It was hard being an only child. For a time, he'd tried to persuade his father to move to Los Angeles with him, luring him with warm weather and a large, spacious home. But his father had refused. The visits were enough. The heat made his brain foggy, he complained, he preferred the fresh mountain air. Los Angeles was too spread out, he didn't want to spend his life in a car, and a variety of other excuses.

Stefan knew it was much more fundamental than that. His father would never leave the home he'd shared with his wife.

Guilt swamped him again and he drew in a deep breath. Paige didn't get it. She didn't understand that he couldn't bear to be still. He couldn't bear not to be busy. Being snowed in at a luxury chalet might be her idea of paradise, but it was his kind of trap. A trap to keep him still. A trap to make him stop and face his demons.

He swallowed and looked out at the dark clouds. The weather would be like this for the next few hours. He'd have to contain himself. Sitting for just over two hours last night had been quiet enough. Dinosaurs and the floral scent of someone sitting next to him had at least been a part distraction.

He was aware of the sexual tension between them. He was definitely interested in Paige, and was sure she felt the same. But being stranded in a hospital with a whole host of other people was entirely different to being stranded here alone with a very sexy woman. A woman he still had to apologise to.

Stefan made his way back down the stairs. The aroma of coffee drifted towards him. He walked through to the kitchen and found the pods, hoping he was putting it in the correct way before sticking a cup underneath. Most of the cupboards had been stripped, but he found a long thin wall cabinet that contained a stash of undiscovered biscuits.

After a few seconds' contemplation, he found a plate and laid the biscuits out the way he'd seen his mother do in years gone by.

Steeling himself, he made his way through to the room he knew Paige would be sitting in. She didn't even glance up and he knew he had to settle the tension between them.

He contemplated the single armchairs, before biting the bullet and sitting down right next to her, setting the plate of biscuits between them.

'I come in peace,' he said.

'Shoot to kill,' she replied, her face deadpan.

He choked on the coffee he'd just swallowed, coughing and spluttering.

She raised her eyebrows. 'What—you don't like the worst pop song ever about my favourite sci-fi series?'

He started to laugh, in amongst the coughing and choking. 'I can't believe I actually know what you mean. And you're right, it is the worst pop song ever.'

She gave a shrug. 'But it's moved with the times. Memes are everywhere with those words.'

He shook his head and pushed the biscuits towards her. She lifted one and frowned at him. 'Where did you find these?'

'One of the wall cupboards in the kitchen. We must have missed it before.'

'I can live on biscuits for a night,' she said, biting one in half.

He waited a second, trying not to focus on her lips, then dunked his biscuit in his coffee, letting it semi-melt before eating it quickly. He looked up to see her horror-struck expression.

'You didn't just dunk.'

'Of course I did. And don't give me that. I've worked in Scotland. Everyone in Scotland dunks.'

'Everyone in Scotland does *not* dunk. *I* do not dunk,' Paige said indignantly. He liked her when she had that glint in her eye.

'You don't know what you're missing,' he whispered as he stuck his biscuit back into his coffee.

'It's tea you dunk with, not coffee. No one dunks in coffee,' she protested.

Stefan raised his eyebrows and lifted his biscuit back out of his coffee. Then, as if in slow motion, the weight of the coffee-laden biscuit made it waver, then split in the middle, break and land in the coffee with a *thunk*.

Paige was done for. She dissolved into fits of laughter. She had to put her own cup onto the table at the side of the sofa before she rolled onto the floor.

Stefan was sitting frozen, paralysed at the catastrophe that had been his coffee and biscuit. He peered into the cup and shook his head as he glanced at Paige. 'There's no hope, is there?'

She was on her back on the floor at this point. 'Nope—' she laughed '—none at all.'

Stefan reached down and pulled her up by the hand,

landing her halfway onto his lap. 'I'm glad I've managed to amuse you,' he said wryly, liking their close proximity.

But she knew he was joking. He wondered if she might pull away. But she didn't.

Instead, she sort of snuggled into him, leaving them both on the sofa together. She didn't say much—as if she didn't want to draw much attention to their now ultra-close positioning. Instead she grabbed the TV remote. 'Today, I get to choose.'

She flicked through the channels, her warm body heating him. Stefan had no wish to move at all.

'Well, looks like you get your wish, just about everything is Christmas,' he murmured in her ear. He could feel the heat of her body close to his.

She settled on an old Christmas movie. 'Perfect.'

'Perfect,' he echoed. He'd probably seen it a dozen times in his life, but it was one of those Christmas films that no one minded—harmless and entertaining—plus his mind was currently on other things. He definitely needed the distraction.

All of a sudden he wasn't thinking about all the work things he could be doing. He wasn't thinking about referrals, surgeries, or even how many renovations the hospital still needed and estimating the exact opening date.

No. Stefan Bachmann was thinking about something else. Someone else.

Paige leaned back a little, her hair brushing against his nose. She really was comfortable. He moved his arm slightly, settling his hand on her hip. He couldn't pretend he wasn't interested in this Scottish doctor. The girl who loved Christmas but had come up here to escape. Who'd somehow found herself in a baron's hideaway luxury chalet, that was available for people like her.

As the light seemed to fade from outside, warm, dim lights automatically switched on inside the room. The peach glow bathed the side of Paige's face, and he noticed an old wound. It was mainly healed, but it was still red and angry, as if the crust had just fallen off.

He stiffened, automatically worrying about her, all his senses moving into protective mode. Should he really ask questions if he wasn't prepared for the answers?

But Stefan was a doctor. Of course he would. In a soft voice he spoke next to her ear. 'What happened to your head? Were you skiing before? Did you fall?'

He felt her stiffen against him too, but only for a few seconds before she slumped back against him. 'No. That was work. A&E. A drunken patient slammed me into a wall.'

He felt instant rage. The fury at someone attacking a fellow worker. He sat up a little. 'What happened? Wasn't there anyone there to help?'

She sighed and shook her head. 'If you've worked in A&E you know how these things happen in the blink of an eye. You don't have time to think about anything. It's just a minor head wound. The bruises on my back are worse.'

'But it shouldn't happen,' he said angrily.

She turned her head sideways to glance at him. 'We don't all work in the Hollywood Hills, Stefan. I work in the roughest part of Glasgow and see all sorts. Some of the people are the salt of the earth, and would give you the shoes off their feet, others are victims of alcohol, drugs or domestic abuse. It takes all sorts.' He thought she was going to stop, and for some reason he could tell that she normally would have, but instead she took a big breath. 'I've been kind of unlucky. It's the third time I've been assaulted in six months. The second time was actually the worst—I had to go for a head CT. That's why I'm here: After it happened again my boss sent me away for a few weeks. He knew about this place and arranged it for me. They're making changes at A&E, bringing in more staff, and some security. It should all be in place when I get back. I think he feels guilty.'

'He should. You never should have been assaulted once, never mind three times. That's ridiculous, for any hospital, I don't care where it is.'

For a second, he thought he saw her blink back tears, and he was ready for her to come out fighting. But instead she leaned back against him again. 'I'm just tired,' she said quietly. 'Tired of it all.'

Something struck a nerve in him and he tried to understand why he suddenly felt so protective of her.

He placed his hand over hers, squeezing it gently, then stroking the back of her hand. 'I know this hasn't exactly been the time away you wanted, but, if there are changes, things might be better when you go back.'

Actually, he didn't want to say that at all. He wanted to tell her to leave her job and come to Los Angeles. He could talk to friends. Find her a job somewhere half decent. Somewhere you didn't need a bodyguard to keep you safe at work.

There was a long silence. Her voice was shaky. 'What if I don't want to go back?'

Now, he sat up fully and pushed her up too, just so he could adjust his position and they were facing each other. 'Paige, what are you saying?'

A tear slid down her face. 'Do you ever feel like not being a doctor any more? Do you ever think you should find something else to do?'

It was like a punch to the guts. He planned to spend his whole life helping people. He owed that to his mum and dad. He would never, ever consider walking away. How could anyone do that, when they had the passion for the job that he had?

He could see how upset she was, so he answered carefully. 'No, I've never felt like that. And I can't imagine ever feeling like that. Being a doctor was all I ever wanted to do. My mum and dad made a lot of sacrifices to let me go to medical school. I don't have enough hours in the day. I'm always planning my next consultation, or surgery, or trip for Médecins Sans Frontières.' He put his hand to his chest. He wanted to say these words with fervour and passion, because that was how he honestly felt. But he knew he had to tread gently. He wasn't a clown.

'Don't you still feel the passion inside? The buzz when you wake up in the morning? The feeling that, no matter what, you will be doing some good?'

More tears spilled down her cheeks. She shook her head. 'Honestly? No, I don't. I haven't for the last few months.' She put both hands up to her face and covered her eyes. 'I'm the worst doctor in the world. My heart isn't in it any more. When the avalanche hit, I panicked. When you pulled me to the floor, all I could remember was the assaults. I had to come and help, of course

I would do that. But up at the hospital, when you asked me if I wanted to leave?' She swallowed and pulled her hands away from her face. 'For the smallest possible second, I actually thought about it. Who does that, Stefan? Who actually does that?'

His blood felt chilled. This was the total opposite to how he felt about things. How he wanted his life to be. But he could see the pain written all over her face. He lifted his hand to her cheek. 'Maybe your boss was right. Maybe you just need some time away and some space to get your head clear. You did help, Paige. You helped in an emergency situation. And you helped in surgery—something you never usually do. You stepped up. You did that. And you did a good job.'

She nodded slowly, her dark eyes fixed on his. 'But what about later?' Her voice was shaking.

He pulled her into a hug. 'Don't think about later. Not right now. You've just been involved in an avalanche. You're essentially cut off from the world. This isn't the time or place to make life-changing decisions. Don't think about any of this.'

A tune started playing on the TV on the wall behind them, reminding him of the Christmas movie. He wrapped one arm around her shoulder. 'Here, think about Christmas. Think about celebrating. Because if we're still stuck here, that's what we'll do.'

He could sense the tiny tremor in her. He guessed she'd never had this conversation with someone before. And he wasn't sure he was the best person to assist, when he felt so strongly and passionately about his job.

It didn't help that he was currently fighting such feelings of attraction towards her. Paige was beautiful. He'd seen her working…he'd seen her spark. He honestly believed that back home she would be a wonderful doctor. She'd studied hard for years. It had just been an unlucky few months. He should distract her. Let her think about something else for a while.

He wanted to keep talking. But, deep down, something stopped him. He might hear something he didn't like. She might question his passion and his motives. She might uncover his guilt. Things that he didn't need right now.

He looked around. The chalet was warm, beautiful and comfortable. They were safe here. And for some reason that was the thing that struck hardest. Because, above all else, he wanted to make Paige McLeod feel safe.

The Christmas movie danced across the screen. It really was one of her favourites. The flickering fire, the reds and greens of the decorations that were left, and the cosy feel of Stefan's arm around her shoulder, and his warm body next to hers was something she would never even have imagined a few days ago.

But here she was, having just poured her heart out to another doctor, and admitted she might not still want to be one.

She could tell he was surprised, and shocked. Just like everyone else might be if she told them too. But telling someone she'd only spent a few days with seemed like a good testing ground.

He'd been nice, and she got the feeling he might have

been holding back. When he'd fixed those blue eyes on hers it had seemed all right to tell the truth, to try and loosen the heavy weight on her shoulders. Maybe he'd brushed off what she'd said a little, but at least he'd allowed her to talk, to have that conversation, and he hadn't shouted or been angry with her. He hadn't told her she was stupid. He'd told her to take some time, think about something else for a while.

And she was. Stefan Bachmann.

The heat of his body was doing strange things to her. She'd thought he was attractive the first moment she'd met him on the road and he'd raged at her driver. When he'd approached her in the ski café for 'stealing' his chair, she'd enjoyed the gentle flirtation and teasing. It had been fun. And it was a long time since Paige had experienced fun.

As for all the rest? The way her eyes had boggled out of her head when he'd stepped out of the shower, his dedication to his job, and the few surprises she'd found here and there. It all added up to someone she wanted to know more about, and a guy she was immensely attracted to.

Being snowed in, in a chalet in the mountains, had its plus points.

'What would be your ideal dream date?' she asked, her head lying against his shoulder and her eyes now closed.

'Where did that come from?' She could hear the amused tone in his voice.

'Let's call it a cosy enquiry?'

'You're feeling cosy?'

'Who wouldn't?'

He was quiet for a few moments and she nearly opened her eyes, but then he started speaking. 'Dream date is a strange question. I haven't done much dating in a while.'

'Don't tell me.' She was smiling, 'No time.'

'How did you know that?'

Now she did open her eyes and look at him. 'Let's just say, in the few days I've known you, I've kind of got that impression.' She patted her hand on his chest since it was so close. 'So, no secret wife or fiancée in five countries, or a million dating apps and a hundred conversations going on at once.'

He laughed. He actually laughed. 'I can't keep up with one dating app, and one conversation, let alone multiples.' He shook his head. 'Plus, it's hard. I'm going between Los Angeles and Switzerland. I'm doing the jobs for Médecins Sans Frontières and they can take me anywhere. And...' he shrugged '...I do occasionally like to ski.'

She sat up and smiled. 'So you *do* actually take holidays?'

'Occasionally. In fact, that would be my dream date. A day on an off-piste ski run.'

'Seriously?'

'What?'

She let her head flop back. 'I give up. I ask about the dream date, and I get a ski run. Thick, fumbly clothes, skis and poles, danger, speed, and what part of skiing involves touching?' she asked indignantly.

'Ah... So that's what you were looking for.' He was teasing now. 'You wanted dinner in an exclusive restaurant, or on a beach somewhere, with sexy clothes or swimsuits. A private castle. A Learjet.'

Their eyes locked. 'Can't a girl have the simple things in life?'

He moved closer, his nose just a few inches from hers. She could feel his warm breath on her skin and see the shadow around his chin line.

'So, whereabouts did the touching come into this dream date?'

She raised her eyebrows. 'Now, that's a loaded question.'

'Or a lucky one. Do you think being snowed in, in a luxury chalet, will count?' He glanced down. 'We forgot the black suit, bow tie and evening dress.'

She nodded in agreement. 'Formal dress clothes, I've always found them quite restrictive.'

'Me too.' He moved his hand. It was almost back to its former position at her waist, but this time her shirt and jeans had separated a little and his fingers brushed her skin. Paige didn't object. Not for a second.

She put her hand on his shoulder. 'I guess I can make an exception for one day.'

'If we can get to the touching?'

She ran her finger along his jaw line. 'If we can get to the touching,' she repeated.

He moved then, leaning forward and connecting his lips with hers. There was a hint of coffee, but all she could really focus on was the sensations sweeping over every part of her. The kiss deepened, their bodies moving even closer, moulding into each other.

She ran her hands through his dark hair, then bringing them back around to his face, letting his stubble rub against her palms. Heat was rising inside her. Clothes which had felt cosy were now uncomfortably warm.

He shifted his weight and she moved automatically, leaning back into the sofa. His blue eyes fixed on hers. 'Is this okay?' There it was. His accent. Thicker than ever. Sexier than ever. She might have to change her idea of a dream date.

'Yes,' she said with certainty, and his lips started to move over her face and down her neck. In turn her hands slid down his sides, feeling his defined muscles and muscle tone.

Nothing had felt this good. Nothing had lit the fire inside her quite like this. So, for now, Paige McLeod didn't waste a second thinking about anything else.

CHAPTER SEVEN

IT WAS A strange sensation—waking up wrapped in the arms of someone who, a few days ago, had been a perfect stranger.

But Paige wasn't worried. This was an extraordinary situation. Maybe some time when she was an old woman she'd tell her grandchildren about the avalanche and being snowed in on a mountain in the Swiss Alps.

Would she tell them everything? Who could tell?

It was morning. She knew that automatically, but someone had forgotten to tell the weather. It was still pitch-black outside. At this time a few days ago the sun had been clearly visible and people were already heading to the ski runs to hit the first snow.

Today, skiing was out of the question. From the look of it, evacuation might be out of the question too.

She gave Stefan a nudge. 'Christmas Eve, and it looks like we're going to have to play Santa.'

He wrinkled his nose, clearly not quite awake yet. 'What?'

His eyes flickered open and he looked at the window nearest them, which was showing no signs of daylight. Recognition flared in his eyes and he sat up. 'Oh, yeah. Darn it.'

He looked back at her, as if wondering how to be after a night entwined together. 'Okay?'

She smiled. 'Okay, but you're making breakfast—partly because you managed to find some spare food last night.'

He stretched and nodded. 'I'll take the challenge. Why don't you see if there's anything on the news?'

She waited until he left, then climbed up to the bathroom she'd been using. She'd left a few things behind, so jumped in the shower, changed into the last remaining clothes she had, and washed and dried her hair and brushed her teeth. Paige always carried two toothbrushes—a habit she'd got into as a junior doctor, and she'd never grown out of.

By the time she got back down the stairs an aroma was wafting towards her. As she walked into the kitchen it was clear Stefan had mastered the coffee machine. He gestured her to take a seat at the kitchen island. 'What's in there?' She pointed to the oven.

'I found some croissants in the freezer. Unfortunately, we've taken all the butter up to the hospital, so it's marmalade or raspberry jam.'

'Jam,' she said decisively. 'Remind me to let you make breakfast again. I hadn't even found the freezer.'

The oven timer pinged and Stefan slid the croissants out onto a plate, which he put between them. 'Delicious,' breathed Paige. They were hot and crisp on the outside, but fluffy on the inside and perfect with the jam, and the coffee.

'Did you hear anything on the news?'

She shook her head. 'I went up into the shower. I turned it on but didn't really get a chance to listen. It's still so dark. Do you really think there'll be a break in the weather?'

He heaved a big sigh. 'We've got to hope there's at least one where we can get back up to the hospital. I know the likelihood is that everyone is fine, but I'd still feel better if we could check.'

We. He'd used the 'we' word. She wasn't sure if he'd used it before. But this time she'd noticed. It seemed kind of nice.

'We have Christmas presents to take for a little girl,' she reminded him.

'Little girls aren't my speciality, but since we have a whole host of adult females at the hospital I'm hoping for great things.'

The name of the ski resort drifted through from the television in the next room and they both turned their heads in unison and hurried through.

The sight that met them was not pleasant. The TV crew were clearly at the other side of the blocked road. There were yellow and orange road vehicles and equipment all behind the immense pile of snow, trees and debris. If they'd made any kind of indent in it, it wasn't noticeable. The TV presenter was talking rapidly in German, and Paige could catch the odd word. But the message was clear. It would take days to safely clear the road.

The presenter started gesturing with his arms skyward and holding up his hands. It looked as if helicopter rescue might be off the cards too. 'Do you think the rest of the people will have enough food?' Paige asked.

Stefan nodded. 'They've dropped essentials to them too. Food, some clothing, and medicines. Everyone at the café is fine and apparently in good spirits—just all anxious to get home.'

Paige let out a slow breath. At least there was nothing too much to worry about. 'We'll be fine,' she said with a smile.

He leaned his head on one hand. 'The only thing I actually miss is the Christmas cookies.'

She frowned. 'What do you mean?'

'Christmas cookies. They're normally everywhere. Usually start pre-Advent. There's so many different kinds I couldn't even tell you.'

She sat down next to him and mimicked his pose. 'But this is Christmas trivia, and I love it. Tell me your two favourite kinds of Christmas cookie.'

'Oh, that's easy.' His face broke into a huge smile. *Spitzbuben* are jam-filled sandwich cookies and usually have a hint of vanilla, and *Basler brunsli* are chocolate and hazelnut, sometimes with a hint of cinnamon. And *Zimtsterne* are cinnamon stars. My mother made the best in the world of all three.'

His face fell. As if the memory had just slayed him.

The words registered with her instantly. Past tense. She gave his hand a squeeze. 'We might have the ingredients to make some. We took some up to the hospital, and I'm sure there are some other things still in the store here.' Something else struck her. 'What do you have for Christmas dinner in Switzerland? Will we be able to match it?'

The spark had gone from his eyes. He spoke quietly. '*Filet em tieg* and *shinkli em tieg*, usually with potato salad, and sometimes a meat fondue.'

Paige tilted her head to one side. She loved hearing about Christmas traditions. 'What are the first two things?'

He gave a wry smile. 'We like pastry in Switzerland. The first is pork fillet with sausage meat wrapped in pastry, the second is hot ham wrapped in pastry. I'm not sure if we'll have anything like that up at the hospital.'

'There were definitely cans of new potatoes. We could make potato salad out of them. And what about the freezer I never found? Was there anything else in there? Pork fillets or ham or...' she took a breath and licked her lips '...turkey?'

A smile flickered across his lips. 'You want the whole shebang, don't you? The huge turkey with stuffing and gravy—a traditional British Christmas?'

'Truthfully, I'll take whatever we've got, or anything we can magic into something kind of special. Everyone up there will want to be at home. We need to try and make things special, even if it's only for a few hours.'

He nodded and stood up, wrapping his arm around her shoulders and kissing her on the side of the head. 'Let's do a final raid of this place. As soon as there's a break in the weather, one of the others will likely drive down for us and we can make it back up there.'

* * *

It should have been a tense few hours, watching out of the window while checking for messages and drinking even more coffee. But Paige was relaxed around Stefan. Well, as relaxed as a girl could be when it felt as if the human being next to her oozed sex appeal from every pore.

There had been more kissing, more private moments. The news had continued its reporting on the avalanche. There had been no deaths, but a few people had been seriously injured further down the valley and a number of properties and roads had been destroyed.

'Are you going to get an enormous bill for all this?'

Stefan shuddered. 'I'm trying not to think about it. When we signed the contract for the hospital, we agreed to take over upkeep and maintenance of the road. I'm sure there were some clauses, but since I'm not a lawyer I don't pay attention to those kinds of details.'

'Oops…' She smiled. 'That could be expensive.'

He nodded. 'I'm sure that if there is some kind of natural disaster—' he waved his hand '—like an avalanche, then the government take some of the responsibility for emergency aid. I'm hoping it might cover clearing the road. After that? I'm assuming my company will have to pay for some repairs. The road was in reasonable condition, but wasn't great. It might be easier to try and resurface it once the weather is better, rather than wait too much longer.'

'Was the road always like this? You said your great-grandparents met up at the hospital. Did you ever visit with your mum and dad?'

For a moment she wondered if it was the wrong question. There was a hint of something on his face. Then he gave her a resigned look. 'I only came up here once or twice, and because I was so young I never really thought about the road. It's always been like this though—narrow and windy.'

Paige licked her lips. She knew from his previous words that his mother must be dead. She didn't really want to push, but it felt reasonable to ask him a little more. 'Tell me about your parents. Did they always live here? What did they do?'

His blue eyes met hers. His look was cautious, and sincere. 'They went to school together. Grew up in the same village. My father still lives there. I don't think he'll ever move, even though I've invited him out to Los Angeles. He was a printer in a local company. When printing wasn't digital, and much more manual. He dealt with the mechanics of the machinery.' There was a long pause. 'My mum only started working when I went to school. She worked full-time after I told them I wanted to go to medical school.' He gave a sad kind of smile. 'It was expensive for two working class parents. But they were delighted I wanted to go to medical school, and probably relieved I was clever enough.'

'They must have been very proud when you qualified as a doctor,' Paige said.

A wave of sadness crossed over him. It was so clear. 'She never really got to see that part. I was just about to finish medical school when she died.' He shook his head. 'My father phoned to say she was sick, and by the time I got there...' His voice tailed off and she noticed his fists were clenched.

'You couldn't have known.' She touched the side of his arm.

His voice was sharp. 'But maybe I could have, if I'd asked the right questions. Apparently she'd been sick for a while. She'd had symptoms but hadn't had time to see a doctor. I'd only been earning a salary for a few months at this point, and my parents were still helping clear some debts from all the training and living away from home. She was working harder than she should have been. She should have been spending the money on herself, and her care, rather than still supporting her adult son.'

Paige rubbed her hand up his arm. 'But that's the way it is in lots of countries, for lots of trainees. Most people I know come out of medical school loaded with debt.'

There was a flash of anger in his eyes, and she was wise enough to know it wasn't aimed at her. It was aimed at himself. She'd been feeling guilty about considering not being a doctor any more. But Stefan's guilt was even more ingrained—and much more damaging than contemplating a career change.

It was as if a veil came over him, some kind of spell that changed the expression on his face, and his mindset. 'Tell me about your parents,' he said.

He wanted to change the subject. Maybe he felt he'd revealed too much. Paige wouldn't press any further. 'They're both still in Scotland. They split up a few years ago, and I'm an only child, so it makes things a little awkward. My mum met someone else and remarried.

My dad also met someone else, but she died a few years after they met, so he's on his own right now.'

'Do you see them?'

She nodded. 'I do.' She wiggled her hand. 'There's still a bit of animosity, but mostly they are over things. My dad moved to the east coast, so he lives in Portobello near Edinburgh. It's a beautiful town, right on the Firth of Forth. My mum lives in Helensburgh. It's on the water too.'

Stefan wrinkled his nose at her expression and she laughed.

'"On the water" means by the coast or by a river or loch.'

'Ah, I get it. You're lucky. Lots of Scotland is on the water.'

A little alarm sounded on her phone and she pulled it from her pocket, holding it up as soon as she saw the message. 'Look! This might be it.'

She ran over to the window and stared outwards, and upwards. 'What do you think?'

He moved next to her. 'I never even got to see what that was. I'm assuming it's a potential break in the weather?'

She nodded. 'It does look a little better. Still windy. But not quite as grey. Do you think they will come for us?'

Stefan spent a few moments staring outside then smiled in agreement. 'The rest of today will be horrendous. If there's a chance to get out it's now. Let's be ready.'

The two of them spent the next five minutes rushing around, pulling on their jackets, washing cups and ensuring the chalet was tidy, pulling blinds again and checking door locks. By the time they were ready, Paige had managed to bring along another few carrier bags.

As if by magic, Joe pulled up in the car, looking relieved they were ready to go. He gestured with his hand for them to hurry. They climbed in with their packages.

'Everyone okay?' was Stefan's first question.

Joe nodded. 'We will be, once we get you two back to the hospital.'

Snow had fallen again last night but the large tyres and thick tread managed well. Paige was glad that Joe drove slowly, conscious there could be debris blown onto the road by the raging winds of the last day and night. But, apart from a few branches, it wasn't too bad.

Rain and snow started to fall again, and by the time the hospital came into sight it was pure relief. The lights were on, and the stained-glass windows were almost like warm Christmas tree lights, welcoming them home. Joe jumped out as soon as they pulled up at the doors.

Paige reached over and squeezed Stefan's hand. 'Thank you,' she breathed.

'What for?'

'For being you.' She gave him a grateful smile. 'Last night and today weren't half as scary as they could have been. Maybe no one has told you for a while, but you're good company.'

She bent over and kissed his cheek. 'Now, let's get back in and see how our kids are,' she joked.

Stefan was carrying the bags inside as Joe shook his head. 'No helicopter for us today. Winds are just too high. They did mention there might be some possibility tomorrow.'

'On Christmas Day?'

Joe nodded, watching as Lynn and Paige seemed to be whispering together, looking inside some of the new bags. 'Conspiring already. What on earth have you brought back?'

Stefan sighed. 'It looks like we might all become Father Christmas tonight. Paige and I found lots of craft things. We might be able to pull together some small things for Claudia.' He looked at Joe. 'Anything I need to worry about?'

'Absolutely not. Most patients are just a bit fed up. But we're safe, warm and comfortable.'

Stefan nodded. 'Well, I found a freezer in the chalet, and we should be able to bring together something decent for Christmas dinner.'

As they walked down the corridor, he stopped dead. The room to his left was a communal sitting room, and Joe and the others had set up the Christmas tree from the chalet, along with the lights. It looked spectacular. Claudia and her mother were sitting on a sofa watching TV. Eva, Frances and Bob were playing cards at a table. Greta had her foot up on a small stool and was reading a book.

He couldn't help but smile. 'How is everyone?' he asked, walking into the room.

Several of the guests let out a cheer. 'You're back. Are you both okay?'

He nodded and made his way around the room, asking everyone in turn if they had any problems, or needed anything. Bob had a twinkle in his eye. 'What have you done with Paige? Where is our good lady doc?'

'She came back with some more food. I think she's gone along to the kitchen.'

But Bob wasn't finished. 'Must have been a long, long night in that old chalet. Did you have to cuddle up to keep warm?'

Claudia's mother, Marie, looked up and laughed. 'Stop it, Bob. You'll embarrass him.'

Bob held out his hands. 'What, a handsome doc holed up with a gorgeous Scottish girl—everyone likes a good romance,' he said, nodding his head at Greta's book.

Everyone was listening now. All eyes were on Stefan. He didn't mind some good humour, but definitely didn't want to start any rumours. 'Paige and I got on fine. The chalet is like here, warm, comfortable, and I found an undiscovered cupboard full of biscuits. It was a win-win situation.'

He could tell from Bob's suspicious but gleeful glance that he'd been hoping for a whole lot more information, but that was all Stefan was prepared to say.

'Dr Stefan?' The small voice came from Claudia, who had her leg propped up on the sofa.

He moved over and bent down next to her. 'What is it, Claudia?'

'Can you take me home now? I wrote my letter to Santa and he won't know where to find me if I don't get home today.' Her voice was a bit wobbly and her mum shot Stefan a helpless look.

He put his hand out to Claudia. 'Don't worry, Claudia. If you can't get home, Santa always knows where every boy and girl is. I'm sure he'll leave you some presents here, and some others at home. He'll find you.'

'I won't get to see Daddy?'

There was a definite lump in Stefan's throat. He might not have children, but that didn't mean he couldn't empathise or understand how this little girl might be feeling, and how strong her mum was having to be.

'You will get to see Daddy. I promise. But we have to be sure that the road is cleared and is safe to go down, or the winds have stopped and the helicopter can fly safely. We might be here another few days, but you will definitely get to see your daddy again, and you will definitely get to open the presents that Santa leaves at home for you, as well as the ones you get here.'

Claudia's face was still sad, but she looked marginally placated. Stefan gave her another smile. 'It will all be fine. Just wait and see.'

He walked back along the corridor and found Cathy, Lynn and Paige in the kitchen. It was clear they were still plotting. Ingredients were everywhere, along with all the craft materials. 'How is your sewing?' asked Paige.

He tipped his head to the side. 'Really?'

Lynn started laughing. 'Hey, you might be able to stitch skin, but can you sew felt and sequins? We need a stocking to fill with Santa's presents.'

Stefan walked over to the selection of items on the counter. 'I think I can rise to the challenge.'

Cathy turned to the others. 'So, I'll take some of these things along to Claudia and Marie and ask if they want to make some decorations for the tree.'

'Fabulous idea,' agreed Paige. 'That should keep her occupied for a while.'

Joe walked in with a piece of paper in his hand. 'Which Christmas movie are we watching tonight? I found *White Christmas*, *The Santa Clause*, *Santa Claus: The Movie* and *The Christmas Chronicles*.'

'All of them,' said Paige immediately.

'There's no way I can stay awake that long,' joked Cathy.

'Can we take a vote?' said Lynn. 'Watching a Christmas movie in that cinema will be perfect for Christmas Eve. I wonder if we can make popcorn and hot chocolate?'

Stefan shifted on his feet slightly awkwardly. 'What if I said I hadn't actually seen any of them?'

Four faces turned around in horror.

'What?'

'No way.'

'You're joking?'

But Paige just raised her eyebrows. 'Well, that's perfect. That just means you have to sit up with me and watch them all.'

Stefan was conscious of all eyes on him. He gave a good-natured shrug. 'If that's my punishment I can take it. Just remember though, I'm in charge of dinner tomorrow. It could be late.'

'Oh, no,' said Joe with a broad grin on his face. 'Because, before we start the movie marathon, I'll help you prepare everything you need for tomorrow. All you have to do is slide things in the oven, or put them on the stove.'

Paige's eyes were shining. And Stefan was struck by

how good-spirited everyone was being. Like him, they all had other places to be, and would miss Christmas with their family or friends, but none of these guys had complained. Hardly any of the patients had complained either, just looked a little wistful. Yet here they all were, offering to help, pull things together and make the best of their situation. He really couldn't ask for any more.

Paige pulled her hair up into a ponytail and unpacked one of the aprons she'd brought from the chalet, moving over to scrub her hands at the sink. She was always thinking of others, always pulling her weight. He could tell from the expression on her face, and in her eyes, that she was happy right now—comfortable. And that made him think that maybe he could ask for more.

The thought stilled him. His previous relationships had always been fleeting. He'd been too busy with work to pay proper attention to any of the women he'd dated. Things had always ended on good terms, with him generally being told he didn't have time for a woman in his life. But none of his previous dates had the same effect on his heart that Paige was currently having. None of them had made him want to sit down and think about someone else properly.

Maybe this was a false situation. They were snowed in, with limited contact with the outside world. It was the first time in for ever he'd actually been forced to slow down and think.

But thinking brought regrets. The same ones that were on constant repeat. If he'd asked his mother questions. If he'd come home a few days earlier. If he'd taken the time to ask how she was doing, how her health was, how she was feeling. But what young adult actually did that? His head had been in so many other places.

Stefan's mother had died because he was selfish. Too absorbed in the world of learning and medicine to actually use his skills where they would have been most useful.

'Hey.' He jolted at the tug on his sweater. Paige was looking at him with those big dark eyes of hers. 'You okay? You looked like you were in another place.' Her voice was quiet and discreet.

He blinked. 'Yes, I'm fine. Just a bit distracted.'

He could see Joe was staring at the food that had been stashed in the hospital freezer. 'I'd better go and sort things out with Joe, I'll see you in the cinema later?'

She gave him a smile. 'It's a date.'

Paige wasn't quite sure what she was doing with her life. All she knew was that, even though she was in a strange place, and had participated in emergency medical care, she felt better than she had in a long time. And part of the reason for that was Stefan Bachmann.

She couldn't explain it. Couldn't give a real rationale for why she was feeling like this. Were there fireworks? Yes. Was there sizzle? Absolutely. But there was something else.

He was like a warm comfort blanket around her. Someone she could talk to. Someone she could tell the things she hadn't been saying out loud. Then there had been their connection last night...

Cathy and Lynn were sorting out ingredients over on the counter top. She went over and joined them. 'I was thinking, since we are in Switzerland, we could try and make some of their Christmas cookies.'

Both women looked at her in surprise and nodded. 'What a good idea. Do you know what we need?'

She frowned and thought hard. 'Stefan told me the name of the ones his mother used to make. We could look them up and see if we have the ingredients?'

Five minutes later, after a quick search on the computer in the office, Cathy, Lynn and Paige had three separate recipes. All three donned aprons and laid out their ingredients, switching the oven on.

Lynn smiled. 'I should probably warn you that Joe is much better at cooking and baking than me. But, since he's helping with the dinner for tomorrow, we should just leave him to it.' She waggled her hand. 'My attempts can be a bit hit or miss.'

Cathy laughed. 'Well, we're all making something for the first time. If it's a disaster, I can make cupcakes.'

'Deal,' agreed Paige. She pulled out a large pan and set it on the stove. 'And let's not forget the popcorn either. I feel like I'm in my favourite TV baking show. And there is absolutely no way I'd ever win that.'

'Same,' agreed Cathy. 'Didn't a doctor win it once?'

'Well, it certainly wasn't me, but I'll have a bash,' said Paige.

She'd never been in a situation like this before. The most she'd made with friends had been stir fry or beans on toast. Any baking had been very much a solo effort, so it was nice to be amongst colleagues.

As she started measuring out ingredients, she could feel eyes on her. She looked up. Stefan was moving some things from the freezer and into the fridge. Others, he covered over and set out on one of the worktops, obviously to defrost for tomorrow. They might be in an unexpected predicament, but the truth was they were extremely lucky.

A little frisson darted down her spine. This guy was beyond handsome. The crinkles around his blue eyes, his dark hair and tall, lean frame made her mind go to a million places it probably shouldn't. The edges of his lips turned upwards, and for a moment she suspected his mind was in exactly the same place as hers.

At that moment Paige heard the satellite phone sound and she turned to pick it up, hearing Franco's familiar voice. It brought her back to earth with a bump. 'Ah, you got back safely. Are you both okay?'

'Of course. How is everyone with you?'

'Tired. Bored. One man is fractious. Causing trouble and threatening to make his own way down the mountain.'

Paige was shocked at someone being, quite frankly, so stupid. 'What will you do?'

'Well, I can't lock him up, even if I want to. It's dangerous out there. I've been warned there could be another avalanche.'

'Really? No! What should we do?'

'Stay put. The snowfall has been heavy these past few days. They don't think it would be anything like as bad as the first. But temperatures have been fluctuating, so they've given us a warning. Above all, stay put. You will be fine where you are.'

'But will you all? Will you be in the path of another avalanche?'

Around her, four heads shot around at her words.

'No,' said Franco. 'At least we shouldn't be. But they do think the road could be affected. As soon as the weather calms, it looks like they will get us all out by helicopter.'

Paige swallowed and breathed slowly. She'd never been in a helicopter before, and wasn't really looking forward to it. But if that was the only way down the mountain in the near future, so be it.

She ended the call and shared the news.

All faces went serious. There was nothing any of them could do. 'Do we tell the others?' she asked.

'Later,' said Stefan. 'We have no right to keep it from them. But let them all enjoy the movies first.' He moved over, closer to the ladies. 'What are you all up to?'

Cathy answered first. 'Never you mind. Just go and take care of dinner for tomorrow. We'll give you a shout shortly. And remember, you've got sewing to do later.'

He gave a nonchalant wave. 'Don't worry. It will be the best Christmas stocking you've ever seen.'

'Promises, promises,' teased Paige with a twinkle in her eye.

Forty minutes later, the smell of baked cookies, popcorn and hot chocolate filled the room. They piled everything onto trays and made their way down to the cinema, where the doors were jammed open and *Santa Claus: The Movie* was poised to start. All the others—except Rafe, who'd declined to come along—were poised in their seats.

'What's that?' asked Claudia as she saw the trays.

'We have cookies,' Paige said with a smile as she slid the tray onto a table that Bob had set up. Stefan moved next to her and stopped dead. Lynn and Cathy were busy handing out the hot chocolate, so hadn't noticed his reaction.

Paige slid her arm around his waist. 'I paid attention,' she said quietly. 'You told me these were your favourites, and we've attempted to make them, to bring a little bit of Switzerland to the Christmas we have up here.' He was standing very still, staring at the plates of cookies. 'I'm sure they won't taste anywhere near as good as your mum's. But I thought it might be a nice way to remember her.'

He looked at her, his blue eyes moist. 'How did you even remember?'

She smiled at him. 'I know you distracted me with other things, but it seemed important. I told Lynn and Cathy you'd mentioned cookies being a tradition, and which ones you liked. They were delighted to give it a go.' She moved her arm and nudged him. 'Here,' she handed him a small plate. 'Take some and give them a try.'

She noticed the slight tremble to his hand as he picked up one of each of the three kinds of cookie. *Zimtsterne*, *Spitzbuben* and *Basler brunsli* had been recreated to the best of their abilities. Paige picked up a hot chocolate for him and added marshmallows and cream, beckoning him to join her in one of the large comfortable cinema seats. He sank down next to her and stared at his plate.

'Go on then,' she encouraged. It only took him a few

minutes to finish them all. The cookies were small, only a few bites each. 'What's your favourite?' she asked.

'Which ones did you make?' he asked carefully.

She waved her finger at him. 'Oh, no. You don't get to trick me into revealing which are mine.' She straightened in her chair. 'Come on, give us the old *Bake-Off* twinkly eyes criticism,' she said, referring to the chef linked with the TV programme.

'I'm not quite that old,' he said indignantly.

'But you do have twinkly eyes.' She smiled back as he contemplated her question.

He sighed. 'Okay, favourite is always any cookie with jam, so *Spitzbuben* will always win. But...' he paused and gave an appreciative nod '...the *Basler brunsli* were very close to my mum's.'

Paige settled back into her seat as the film started to play. 'Perfect,' she said, reaching over in the dimming light to take his hand.

Stefan was touched. Really touched. He still couldn't understand why he'd spoken about his mum earlier, and he'd been glad when Paige hadn't pushed any further.

But this? This was touching. He wished his dad had been here to see what these people he'd known less than a week had done for him. He would have loved this. And he would have loved the chance to sample the cookies.

The warmth from Paige's hand seemed to pulse through his body. All this couldn't be a coincidence. A meeting on a dark road, then in a café, the avalanche, a woman who could match his abilities with her own expertise, and someone with her own demons. There was a connection between them. Maybe it was timing. Maybe it was where they both were in their lives. Maybe it was just physical attraction. But it felt deeper. Paige got him. They were both dancing around each other. She'd revealed some of her demons, and he some of his. Somehow he knew that, like himself, Paige hadn't really done this before. Hadn't told another human being how she was really feeling.

It should be cathartic for them both. But Stefan was uncertain. Paige had said what he might have expected. It wasn't his fault. It helped to hear someone else say that. But he didn't really believe it. Not deep down inside. In a way he almost wished that the road had opened up again, that things could get back to normal and he could fill his life with work.

But Paige had been here when he'd had to stop and think. Admit how guilty he was feeling. And face the demons that had plagued him for the last few years.

Was he using his feelings for Paige to push his guilt into the background? It didn't seem like that. Both things seemed to have hit head-on. But how could he possibly consider any kind of relationship with his work schedule?

It's time to stop, the voice inside his head said. He'd known it was there all along. If Stefan kept going the way he was, the answer was obvious burn-out. He didn't want that.

But part of what Paige had hinted at really bothered him. She was clearly a great doctor, but a few bad experiences had made her question her career choice. Assault of any healthcare staff was more than criminal, but the fact it had this impact on her made his blood boil.

Paige was arousing every emotion. Desire, protectiveness, lust, curiosity, and maybe a whole lot more.

He just wasn't quite sure what to do next. Despite his workload, his guilt issues, he wanted to let his heart rule his head, ask Paige if she would consider Los Angeles. It would be bold, reckless. It might even be stupid. But as this woman held his hand in the new hospital's cinema, with cookies she'd baked for him, he was sure he was in entirely the right place right now.

This was the place he was supposed to be, and this was the person he was supposed to be with.

He hoped no one would ask him questions about this movie later because, while he was sure it was cute, he couldn't take in a single part of it.

'Hey,' whispered Paige, 'remember your hot chocolate. You need to keep your strength up, you've got sewing to do tonight.'

'We have hours,' he said easily. 'Why do I think you doubt my sewing skills?' His voice was low.

Paige leaned forward. 'Did you hear something?'

He shook his head. 'Hear what?' He took a sip of his hot chocolate and set it on the floor in front of him, listening carefully.

There it was. A muffled shout.

'Guys,' he said in a sharp voice. 'Let's go.'

It was automatic, Cathy, Lynn, Joe and Paige all stood, moving swiftly to the exit. Stefan's mind was on overdrive. The only person missing was Rafe, the Frenchman who'd broken his ribs in the avalanche.

Stefan ran down the corridor to Rafe's room, finding him on the floor next to the bed. He bent down next to him, quickly noticing the wheeze and poor colour.

He opened his mouth to speak, but Paige got in there first. 'He's got a pneumothorax. One of his broken ribs has pierced his lung.' She grabbed a stethoscope from the nearby table and lay on the floor next to Rafe, moving the stethoscope to listen to his chest before giving a nod. 'Right side.'

She turned and rattled off the range of equipment she needed to reinflate his lung. Joe moved instantly to collect the supplies. Cathy wheeled in an ultrasound machine.

Paige and Stefan helped Rafe back up onto the bed, his colour pale, his lips tinged with blue. Stefan slipped some oxygen on him. 'Why did you move? Didn't you press your buzzer?'

Rafe frowned. 'I wa…wanted to get up myself.' He wheezed with every word.

Paige started talking. She was as calm as could be.

'Rafe, one of your broken ribs has punctured your lung. It's collapsed and we need to fix it. This is a relatively simple procedure that I'll be able to do for you. I need you to hold still while I use the ultrasound transducer to find the best place to insert the tube we need to reinflate your lung.'

She moved easily and Stefan could tell that this was a procedure she'd done before. She was confident. She smoothed some gel on the transducer and moved it along the bottom of Rafe's ribs, looking at the screen for the right spot. Stefan recognised it at the same time she did.

As she was doing this, she kept her voice steady and calm, talking to Rafe and being completely reassuring.

She marked the spot on his chest wall, then turned to the sterile pack that Joe had found, along with the local anaesthetic. She moved to the sink, washed her hands, and came back to draw up some local anaesthetic into the needle and syringe. 'I'm just going to numb a little area down here,' she said. 'We'll give it a few minutes and then test it again to make sure you can't feel anything.'

Paige expertly cleaned the area, injected the anaesthetic, then went back and washed her hands again, opening the sterile pack and putting some gloves on.

She waited until Rafe's skin area was numb, then took a small scalpel blade. 'You won't feel anything,' she assured him as she made the precise cut. 'You might feel a bit of pressure, or some tugging.'

Stefan watched as Paige slid the tube easily into position, then connected it to the bottle containing water that relieved the pressure on his lung. A few bubbles emerged. Paige moved, and put a few stitches in position to hold the tube. She leaned back and looked at Rafe, smiling. 'Feeling easier?'

Stefan lifted the stethoscope and listened to both lungs again, to check for inflation. Both lungs sounded good.

'Great job.' He smiled as he looked at her, admiring how smoothly she'd dealt with the whole process, from the second she'd entered the room to when she'd placed the final stitches.

She was a great emergency doctor. It would be a tremendous waste if she didn't return to her job. Didn't keep up her skills that could save lives.

Paige continued to take care of Rafe. She used ultrasound to look again and determine that the lung was completely inflated, then adjusted the oxygen supply. She leant next to the bed. 'Now, for the tenth time, I'm going to ask you to stay in bed and not get up unassisted. We will be able to help you move and bring the tube and bottle with you. Please don't get up yourself again.'

Rafe grunted in response. His colour was much better and his oxygen sats were up.

'I'll stay,' offered Cathy. 'I'll give a shout if I need a hand.'

Stefan nodded and gestured to Paige. She looked initially reluctant, but her shoulders relaxed and she gave a smile, packing up the contents of the trolley and clearing it away.

'I have a surprise,' Stefan said in a low voice.

'Oh?' Paige followed him along the corridor. 'Where are we going?'

'Surprise,' he said as he took her into the kitchen and opened the door to a stockroom. He pulled out a bottle of wine.

She let out a little squeal and clapped her hands together a few times. 'Where did you get that?'

'You didn't remember all the alcohol that was in the chalet?'

She groaned. 'Of course, I hadn't really thought about it.' She licked her lips and stared at the bottle. 'This is the part where I hope that this is cheap stuff and nothing vintage, because the truth is, I would never know the difference.'

'You think Baron Boastful would leave good wine at his chalet?'

'I have no idea.' She sighed. 'What if he visits occasionally himself? Maybe he does keep some good stuff there.'

'In that case, I'm sure it would be locked up.' Stefan found a corkscrew and opened the bottle of wine, pouring it into two glasses. 'Here—' he held up his glass '—let's drink to Christmas Eve.'

Paige grinned and held up her own glass. 'What happened to a quiet night and watching a movie?'

She clinked her glass against his. He chose his words carefully. 'You did brilliantly tonight. I was impressed. You didn't even stop to think. You assessed in the blink of an eye, made a decision and started the procedure. Lots of others might have paused, and second-guessed themselves.'

She shook her head. 'Lots of other doctors would be going in blind. I knew his history, had seen his previous X-rays and knew he has broken ribs. It was clear what the fall had done. Anyone could have done it.'

'But *you* did.'

She stared at him for a long moment. The wine glass stilled on her lips. She rested it on the counter again. 'What do you mean?'

He shrugged. 'I'm just stating a fact.'

She shook her head. 'You would have done the same.'

'I'm not sure I would have done it so well, or so quickly.'

Paige waved her hand. 'You're a surgeon. You could manage a chest tube.'

He gave a reluctant nod. 'I could have. But my skills are in other areas. This particular skill was yours.' He paused and then added, 'And you excelled at it.'

Paige's head sagged and she leaned her elbows on the counter. 'We don't need to do this.'

'We do,' he said determinedly. 'I just watched a brilliant doctor diagnose and treat a patient. Credit where credit is due.'

He could see the struggle written all over her face. Why was he doing this? He knew she was having doubts. But Stefan was struggling too—struggling with the thought that a great doctor was considering throwing her career away and it might just be a blip. One of those moments where a doctor doubted themselves, exhausted by the hours and tasks they'd been doing. He hadn't met a single doctor who hadn't experienced this more than once. He should praise her, he should tell her how good she was. It might be exactly what Paige needed to hear right now and it was all true.

But the slump of her body and head told him this was the last thing she wanted to hear and it actually made his insides ache.

All that training. As soon as that thought appeared in his head he stalled. Maybe this wasn't about Paige. Maybe this was about him? But his life wasn't hers.

His mum and dad had worked like crazy to put him through medical school, with an outcome that no one could have wanted or predicted. He could only imagine the look on their faces if he'd said it had all been for nothing and he was turning his back on his career.

But this wasn't his life, it was Paige's. He'd no idea

what her emotional and financial history was. Scottish students got their university education paid for by the state. They still had to take loans to cover accommodation and food, but they certainly had a better deal than some countries.

Paige lifted her head from her hands. The conflict was clear. 'Thank you,' she said softly. 'I've always known I can do the job. What I don't know is if I *want* to do the job.'

She stood up and he knew the night was about to end in a way he didn't want it to. Not like this. Paige was special, through and through.

He stood up next to her and bent over and kissed her forehead. For a moment they stood there, and she wrapped her arms around his waist and buried her head in his shoulder. He could feel her unsteady breathing against his chest. It made him want to hold her all the tighter.

But Paige pulled back. 'I think I need some sleep. Some time to sort things out in my head.' She pressed her lips together for a few seconds, clearly wondering whether to go on. 'Stefan, we could be out of here tomorrow. You live in Los Angeles. I'm in the UK. We've only known each other a few days...' She paused and Stefan broke in.

'None of that matters. I've met you now, Paige McLeod. We're connected. Somehow or other, we're going to be in each other's lives, no matter what else happens. This won't be goodbye. You have some things to work out, and so do I. But the one thing I have worked out is how I feel about you.'

She looked up at him, her dark eyes drinking in every part of him. 'And how's that?'

'You've captured my heart,' he said simply.

It was everything. He was putting himself on the line for someone in the middle of a career crisis, and in the midst of an emergency situation. If he'd been counselling a friend about this situation, he'd likely have warned them against making any big declarations until they were back home and ready to breathe again.

But this just felt right. He had to say it. He had to be honest. The thought of not seeing, speaking or touching Paige again was already alien to him. And maybe he was calling this all wrong. Now was the time to find out.

She blinked, her eyes shining with unshed tears. The edges of her lips turned upwards and she gave him a soft smile. 'I feel the same,' she admitted. 'This was the last thing I was expecting, but it feels like...' her brow wrinkled as she thought, but she gave a shake of her head and met his gaze again '...it was meant to be. I've never been so connected with someone before. I don't know what will happen next. I guess we just need to find out.'

He kissed her head again, as his heart swelled in his chest. It was everything he wanted to hear, and in another time and place they would have headed straight for the nearest room.

And they would. But Stefan knew tonight that Paige needed some space. And he would absolutely give her whatever she needed.

'I'll be next door,' he said gently. 'If you want a hug, just come on in.'

She reached up and traced a finger down the side of his face. 'Thank you,' she whispered.

'Always,' he replied, and put his arm around her shoulder as they walked along the corridor, and back to the suite.

CHAPTER EIGHT

CHRISTMAS MORNING WAS still dark. But Lynn had managed to get up early, string up some more Christmas lights and link up her phone to play some background music. Paige awoke to the smell of coffee and bacon drifting down the corridor towards her, as she was swamped by the snuggly duvet.

Her first thoughts were for Stefan. He wasn't next to her, and she hadn't climbed into his bed last night. Maybe she should have. But the space had let her make the decision that had been playing in her mind for a while. She hadn't told a soul. But it was as if a huge weight had been lifted off her shoulders.

She was going to take some more time off. She would reassess her specialty, explore her options and decide if she wanted to stay in any part of medicine. She wasn't sure right now what the outcome would be. But she was comfortable with her decision.

The tiny knot that had been in her stomach for as long as she could remember was gone. She would let Leo know as soon as possible, though she suspected he might have already known this was on the cards.

Maybe she would visit Los Angeles? Maybe she would consider a career in another country. All she knew was that she was free to explore that option.

She glanced at the time. It was six a.m. Stefan was obviously up before her as the other room was empty. She wondered if he'd helped with the extra decorations. As she approached the kitchen she realised she was the last one up. The others were sitting having breakfast and whispering to each other.

Cathy gave her a broad smile and put a finger to her lips. 'We don't want to wake Claudia too early.'

'Is everything ready for her?'

The rest all nodded. 'It might not be what she put on her original Santa list, but at least she'll get some presents.'

Joe slid some bacon onto a plate alongside some toast and pushed the plate towards her. 'Wait until you see her stocking. It's a masterpiece.'

She turned to face Stefan. She'd totally forgotten that he'd still had the stocking to stitch last night. Had there been any chance for him to sleep at all?

'What did you do?' she asked with a smile on her face.

He tapped the side of his nose. 'Just wait and see. I bet Claudia will be up soon.'

Now she was intrigued. Paige ate the bacon sandwich she put together and sipped the coffee. Apart from the timing, this was pretty much how she would have spent Christmas morning if she'd been on her own. She might not have got dressed, but her comfortable jeans and T-shirt weren't too big an ask.

'What about the rest of today? Do you need me to do anything?'

Stefan shook his head and looked at Joe. 'We've got it all under control, haven't we?'

Joe nodded in agreement. 'You guys can go and spend time with our patients and leave us to it. Christmas dinner should be ready around three.'

Lynn pulled over a round biscuit tin. 'I put all the extra cookies from last night in here. So there's plenty of nibbles for people.'

'Has anyone checked on Rafe yet?'

Cathy smiled. 'He was fine overnight. I'll leave the check this morning to you. We've got a wheelchair, so he'll be able to come through and eat Christmas dinner with everyone else.'

Stefan asked the one question everyone had avoided so far. 'What about the weather?'

Joe held up the satellite phone. 'They might have a small window around four p.m., and later around six p.m. Franco asked if we had any objection if some of the people from the café were picked up first.'

Stefan frowned. 'Rafe should really be the priority. Are there issues down at the café we should know about?'

Joe held up his hands. 'There are fourteen children down at the café. I think Franco is anxious to try and get them back to their families. Only two of them have parents with them. The rest are with school teachers and were on a school outing.'

Paige nodded. 'That's hard. I can't imagine how upset some of them must have been—their parents too. Is it wrong to let them go first?' She cleared her throat. 'Let me assess Rafe this morning. If I have any concerns I'll let you know. If I think he's stable, I think we should consider Franco's request. Sorry, folks.'

They all nodded. There was a shout from along the corridor. 'Santa's been!' The delight in Claudia's voice was clear.

They all made their way down to Claudia and Marie's room, Stefan putting his arm around Paige's waist as they went. 'Good morning,' he whispered, planting a kiss on her cheek.

'Good morning,' she replied, wishing they were alone.

As they rounded the corner into Claudia's room, Paige's eyes went wide.

The red and green Christmas stocking was bigger than normal—clearly designed to hold all the presents they'd managed to pull together. There was a jigsaw, some chocolate, colouring books and pens, even a small teddy bear. Paige was going to have to email the Baron about all the missing items from the chalet. But the look on Claudia's face right now was worth it.

'Mummy,' she said in amazement, 'this stocking has my name on it. Can I keep it?'

Marie nodded, her eyes filled with tears. *Thank you*, she mouthed to them all.

Paige moved a little closer, looking at the detail on the stocking. It was stitched together from felt, then had smaller pieces of felt cut into a variety of designs and stitched at various points on the stocking. There was a Santa, a Christmas tree, presents and something special. Claudia had just spotted it too.

'Look, Mummy, it's a little bird, like the one in the window at the front doors.'

Sure enough, in multiple colours, Stefan had stitched a little Turaco bird into the design of the stocking.

Paige moved back over to Stefan. 'That's beautiful. I can't believe you had time to do all this. It must have taken hours.'

He shrugged. 'Look at her. It's worth it. This hasn't been the Christmas any of us expected. Here's hoping we can all get out of here later.'

Paige swallowed, realising that she didn't actually have anywhere to go. She could go home, of course, back to the UK. She was supposed to be staying here, still in the chalet. But if the road was going to take days, or even weeks, to clear she would have to be evacuated with everyone else.

'What about your father?' she asked Stefan.

A line creased his brow. 'I haven't been able to contact him yet. It's still early.'

'He'll be disappointed that you won't get home today,' she said sympathetically.

'Maybe. But he'll understand. It will be more important to him that I'm somewhere I can be helping people.'

It was the right thing to say. Paige knew that. But it just didn't feel right.

'Really?' she asked. 'Your father would rather you were working than spend time with you at Christmas?'

When his gaze met hers his expression was guarded, something else lurking just behind the surface. She knew she should delve more deeply.

But this was Christmas Day. It wasn't the right time.

A little voice sounded in her head. Would they have more Christmases together after this one? She certainly hoped so.

It was odd. She just felt so much lighter. Her decision was made and she would live with the repercussions. She would tell Stefan later, when they had some time to themselves.

He blinked again, still looking at her. 'My dad always wants what's best for me, and for others. My parents always put themselves last.'

Paige wondered if it was supposed to sound self-sacrificing, and maybe it was, but it just sounded ultimately sad to her and, from the expression on Stefan's face, to him too.

He lifted his head. 'I have dinner to prepare.' It was as if someone had flicked a switch because all of a sudden he had a broad smile on his face and he was reaching for Joe to encourage him to start helping.

Paige wanted to offer to help too. To encourage Stefan to talk. To ask if he'd ever sat down with his dad and told him how guilty he felt about his mum. But she knew that had never happened. She also knew that Stefan was working himself to death to avoid that conversation. Something really had to give.

She walked down the corridor to check on Rafe. He was looking better and eating a large bowl of porridge that Lynn had made for him. She checked the level in the bottle and listened to his chest again.

She sat on the edge of the bed—against all the rules—and spoke to him. 'There is a small chance that, later on today, we might get a chance to evacuate by helicopter.'

Rafe immediately stopped eating. He glanced at the tube coming out of his chest. 'But how can I be moved with this? Does it mean I can't go?'

She shook her head. 'No, it doesn't mean that. You're stable. We would consider you fit to transfer. It does mean we have to be extra careful. The bottle must be kept upright, and it has to be below the level of your chest. We would strap you into a special stretcher and have the bottle and tube protected and strapped against you for the transfer.'

For a moment he breathed a sigh of relief, and then looked worried again. 'When could this be?'

'Around six p.m. tonight. Long after Christmas dinner—Stefan and Joe are not getting out of that one.' She gave a laugh, and then paused. 'They might be able to get some people out earlier. But there are fourteen children down at the café—some of them with no parents. Franco asked if they could be evacuated first.'

'Absolutely,' said Rafe without a moment's hesitation and a half-shrug. 'After all, where am I going to go? Just to another hospital that's down the valley. My family is back in France. I expect it will be a few weeks before I take a flight back home. Let the kids go first and hopefully some will get to see their families today.'

Paige gave a smile and patted his arm. 'I was hoping you would say that.' She gave him an amused look. 'From the man who didn't want to stay in his bed at all, you've changed your tune.'

He tapped his ribs. 'I've learned to pace myself. I want to get back out and ski. I need to let these ribs heal, and I know I put myself back by having the fall. What can I say? Lesson learned.'

She sighed. 'If only all patients were so obliging.'

He gave her a look of admiration. 'People should be grateful that you're their doctor and listen to you. I'm grateful. You knew exactly what you were doing and didn't hesitate. Thank you.'

She felt a pang in her chest. Moments like this were few and far between. It felt as if people had stopped saying thank you in the health service. Life seemed full of complaints and investigations.

'Thank you,' she said as she stood up. 'It's appreciated.'

He gave a nod and she walked back down the corridor, taking a few moments to go back to the suite she shared with Stefan.

The day was still dark. They might get evacuated—they might not. She certainly wouldn't be able to take the suitcase of belongings she'd brought to Switzerland with her. She would have to get it sent on at a later date.

Paige didn't want to be short of time, so she folded up some clothes, alongside her passport and personal belongings, and put them in a small holdall. She would be ready to go at short notice if needed.

She changed her T-shirt and freshened up her hair and make-up before going back along to the main room. There was a competitive game of Monopoly about to start and she joined in, familiarising herself with the Switzerland equivalent of Mayfair.

The atmosphere was cheerful. People knew there was at least half a chance of getting home later. That, and because the day they had all dreaded being here had actually arrived, made things feel much better. Again, she was grateful to be somewhere safe. Somewhere warm, and with people she now considered friends.

She brought along a pot of coffee and put the extra cookies on plates, and they were soon gone. It didn't take long for wonderful smells to drift down the corridor towards them. She could hear raucous laughter coming from the kitchen, mainly from Joe and his stories. Lynn rolled her eyes. 'He's got new blood for telling all his operating theatre tales. He'll be in his element today.' She leaned forward. 'Let's just hope he doesn't put Stefan off the food.'

The afternoon continued to be dark and gloomy, but the mood in the hospital was jubilant and light. Every now and then Paige would notice someone get a little quieter, or spend a few moments on their own, and that was fine. Christmas was a time for families, and these were exceptional circumstances, all were entitled to their own thoughts.

Joe came along with a whoop of celebration. 'Food is ready, people. Take your places.'

Paige positioned Rafe at the table, the bottle at the side of his wheelchair, and the others took their chairs at the long table.

Cathy, Lynn and Paige went down to the kitchen to help carry the food along, and found themselves bringing trays of potato salad and vegetables. Joe and Stefan followed with silver platters of *filet em tieg* and *shinkli em tieg*. The pastry-wrapped delights smelled delicious.

'I can't wait to try these,' Paige said with a smile as she took one of each and passed the platter down the table.

The dinner was a success, the food delicious. The only thing they didn't do was drink any wine—not if there was a chance of transport later in the evening. Paige offered to wash the dishes, conscious that if they were evacuated she didn't want to leave any mess in the hospital.

Stefan joined her as she loaded the dishwasher and filled the sink for some of the larger pots. He seemed distracted but slipped his arms around her as he finished drying one of the pots.

'When the helicopter comes,' he said slowly, 'will you come with me?'

She held her breath, turning around to look at him. 'Why?'

He was clearly confused by the question. 'Because I thought you wouldn't have somewhere to go. I want to spend more time with you. I'd like you to meet my father.'

She reached and touched his cheek. 'I would love to meet your father, and I would love to spend more time with you. But you have to be ready for that.'

He blinked and pulled back. 'What do you mean?'

She brought down her hand and started knotting the dish towel she'd just used to dry dishes between her two hands. 'I mean, I made a decision this morning. I'm not going to be a doctor any more. Not in A&E at least. Maybe not at all. I still need to figure out that part. I can't keep doing a job that's making me miserable.' She lifted her hand to her heart. 'But until I'd sorted this part of me, and this part of me—' she pointed to her head '—I wasn't going to have room to commit to something new, something different.'

She could see him trying to connect the dots in his jumbled brain. 'You're telling me you couldn't consider starting a relationship until you'd decided to give up your job? That's madness. It doesn't even make sense.'

Paige took a deep breath. 'But it does, for me. And there's something you need to do too.'

He shook his head. 'You've lost me now.'

'Why are you so busy all the time? Why do you plan your life without a moment to spare? Because I know it's deliberate. But do you know it is?'

He stood frozen to the spot for a few minutes. 'I'm busy because, unlike you, I love my work. I want to be busy. I thrive on being busy. I want to do as much as I can to help as many people as possible.'

Paige stepped forward and put one finger on his chest. She wasn't annoyed by the earlier jibe. It had hardly even registered. 'But when do you stop to help yourself?'

She was barely inches from his face. Confusion crossed his face. But only for a moment. Because Stefan did know what she was talking about. He did understand. But was he ready to confront his demons?

'This is ridiculous.' His jaw was tight. 'All I want to do is ask you to come back with me. Ask you to come and meet my father.'

Her hand reached out and touched his. 'And I would love to do that. But I don't want to get in the way of the conversation you need to have with your father.'

'What?'

He was still in denial and, before she had a chance to say anything more, he swung the conversation around. 'And what about you? Aren't you being hasty? After all those years of training, you're prepared to walk away? I mean, I get what happened to you in A&E is totally unacceptable. But you said your boss was making changes and bringing in security—won't that make things better?'

Paige took a deep breath. 'Maybe for others, but not for me.'

'If you don't want to go back there, you could be a doctor anywhere. What about Los Angeles? Why don't you come back with me—take some time to get to know the place, then decide where you'd like to work? There will be plenty of job opportunities for someone with your experience. You could pick and choose.'

'But what if I'm choosing not to be a doctor? Would I still be welcome to join you in Los Angeles?' Her words were sharp, she knew that. But she was getting exasperated. She was getting jittery. In a short period of time, she might find herself hoisted up into a helicopter. It wasn't exactly filling her thoughts with confidence.

And Stefan just didn't seem to be listening. He wasn't acknowledging the fact that Paige could see right through him. That whilst she might have met a wonderful man who made her heart sing, she had to be sure about what she did next.

And that included being sure about him.

She took a deep breath. 'When are you going to realise you can't keep going on like this? Have you ever sat down with your dad and spoken about your mum?

Have you told him how guilty you feel? Have you told him you didn't realise how sick she was and that you wish you could have done something to intervene?'

Stefan pulled right back from her, as if she'd wounded him with her words. But these words weren't harsh. They were just the truth.

'This isn't any of your business.'

She froze. 'You're absolutely right, they're not. But I'd like it to be my business. You just asked me to go to Los Angeles with you. You're inviting me to fly halfway around the world with you. But you're also telling me I can't tell you what I'm seeing, and what I think you need to do. What happens if I come to Los Angeles? Will I ever see you? Or will you continue to work—what is it?—fourteen hours a day, seven days a week? I want to take a chance. But I want to take a chance on *us*, Stefan. If you keep going like you are now, there will never be a chance for an *us*. Can't you see that?'

He walked away, shaking his head, and Paige crossed her hands in front of her heart. She said the words that he really needed to understand—because if he didn't there could never be any chance for them.

'There isn't room for me to love you, Stefan, until you learn to love yourself first.'

And, even though there were tears in her eyes, she turned and walked out.

CHAPTER NINE

THE PAIN STARTED in his chest with every breath. His hands were shaking, and he couldn't get them to stop.

He knew exactly what Paige was saying to him. He just didn't ever want to stop and have that conversation with his father.

He hated that so much of what she'd said was right. He'd been tired lately—exhausted, even—sometimes functioning on four hours' sleep a night. His diary was a whirlwind of dates, surgeries and venues. He consciously said yes to just about everything, juggling dates so he could fit all requests in.

He pulled out his phone and stared at it. He was going to check something but, deep down, knew the answer wasn't something he really wanted to find.

He scrolled. In the last five years he'd had thirty-five days off. One week a year. He'd generally gone skiing somewhere for a few days or seen his father, but that had been it. No down time. Even when he was travelling between countries he was still working. No wonder she was calling him out.

He could picture his father's face right now. His chest

tightened at the thought of bringing up the subject of his mother. What on earth would he do if he found out that his father also blamed him for his mother's death? That was secretly what he feared. His father had been totally devoted to her. He knew that he missed her terribly—just like Stefan did.

There were voices down the corridor, movement, excitement.

Joe was talking loudly on the satellite phone, taking instructions from Paige.

He looked outside. Paige's hair was swept up in a ponytail, she had her outdoor clothes on, and a holdall on her back. She was on her knees, securing Rafe's chest drain bottle.

'Is the helicopter on its way?' he asked, striding down the corridor.

Cathy appeared behind him, pushing another wheelchair with Claudia, and her mother walking alongside.

'There's still a limited timeframe. We're going to try and get Rafe and Claudia airlifted at the same time.'

Stefan could see it was still windy outside. The helicopter would have to drop the stretcher then hoist it back up. It would be dangerous for all involved.

'What's the estimated arrival time?'

'Five minutes.' Paige's voice was calm and professional. She didn't even look in his direction. All her attention was focused on her current patient. She spoke again. 'Stefan, go and assess everyone else for the order in which they'll be evacuated. The helicopter will try and make return trips, but it might not be possible.'

He wanted to talk to her again. But this wasn't the time.

He moved to check over Bob, Frances, Eva, Anna and Greta, helping them into outdoor jackets and giving them a rundown of what could happen next.

The thudding of the helicopter rotors cut through the wind noise. A few moments later, there was an icy blast down the corridor as the front doors were opened.

Stefan pulled the two chairs with the ladies with broken ankles as Bob and Eva walked behind.

The helicopter was hovering over the car park area of the hospital. With trees surrounding the car park, it wasn't a safe place to land but, as Stefan watched, the side door slid open and the stretcher was winched down. Joe and Paige were with Rafe; Joe had the satellite phone between his ear and shoulder.

They wrestled Rafe into the stretcher, positioning his bottle and giving the signal for him to go up. As he lifted up to the helicopter, Joe handed the phone to Paige. The noise from the rotor blades was enormous, Stefan had no idea how on earth Paige could hear anything. But a few minutes later a harness descended, she clipped herself in, put her holdall on her back and, before he knew it, was lifted into the sky.

A sense of dread swept over him. They hadn't had a chance to talk yet. He hadn't told her how sorry he was, and how he'd been too wrapped up in himself to truly understand and appreciate how she was feeling.

The stretcher for Claudia came back down as Stefan ran over to help Joe. The little girl was much easier to manoeuvre and get clipped in. 'What's going on?' Stefan asked Joe as the winch lifted Claudia into the air.

'The doctor on board isn't feeling well. Asked if

someone could help with the transfer.' The wind and backdraught were playing havoc with having any kind of discussion. The harness descended again and they clipped Marie, Claudia's mother, in. She lifted into the sky easily and, as she was assisted in, the door slid closed.

Before Stefan had a chance to think, or say anything at all, the dark helicopter moved off, disappearing into the distance.

Joe put his hand on his shoulder, oblivious to what had just happened between Stefan and Paige. 'They hope to get back in thirty minutes. They can get the rest of our people out then, and will come back for us if there's time.'

His stomach flipped over. He couldn't help but think he'd made a huge mistake in not taking the time to sit down with Paige and talk again.

Stefan swallowed. He had no idea where the helicopter was going. Likely it would be one of the bigger hospitals in the nearby city. Would Paige wait there? Or would she leave?

Deep down, he knew the answer to that.

And, what was more, he deserved it.

CHAPTER TEN

LEO GAVE HER a huge hug as he presented her with a bunch of flowers and gift cards from her colleagues in the department. 'I'll miss you,' he said. 'But I know you're doing what's right for you. Any letter of recommendation you want, just let me know.'

Paige was holding back the tears. Some of her colleagues had been shocked, others not so much. When she'd handed in her resignation Leo had hung his head for a few seconds, then took a deep breath and talked everything through with her. She'd worked her notice, finishing early as she still had holidays owed, and had put some of her things in storage as she planned to go travelling.

Her mum and dad had been stunned, and maybe a little disappointed. But when she'd told them how she'd been feeling about work they'd accepted her decision. She knew that they both hoped that all she needed was a break. Paige was lucky. She had some savings and knew that she would be fine for a few months.

Her stomach gave a little twist and she did the thing she'd been doing for the last few weeks—tried not to think about Stefan. She knew she'd made the right decision about her work life, but had she made the right decision about her personal life? She hated how things had been left, and that even the thought of travelling brought up instant memories of that gorgeous Swiss chalet and the one night she'd spent there in his arms.

Paige sighed as she emptied her locker, put away her scrubs and changed into her jeans and T-shirt. There was a small pang as she closed her locker for the last time and walked out through the front doors of A&E.

Her steps were lighter, and automatically took her over to her favourite café. She smiled as she sat in the bench seat and ordered the specials of the day. Hot chocolate with marshmallows, flake and cream, and some apple tart. She could smell it already and she couldn't help but smile.

There was a creak, and someone slid into the seat opposite. She blinked. No. It couldn't be.

'Hey,' Stefan said softly. 'Long time no see.'

'Sixteen days,' she said without a blink of her eyes.

He licked his lips. 'I'm sorry.'

She pressed her lips together and tried to ignore the rapid beating of her heart. 'I don't need you to be sorry. I need you to tell me what you've done.'

He took a deep breath. 'I spoke to my father.'

'You did?' Her stomach clenched tightly.

He nodded.

'How did it go?' Part of her was dreading the answer.

He bit his bottom lip. 'It probably went as expected. He said my mother was stubborn and he'd told her to see a doctor and she'd refused. The money was a huge aspect for them, and they were both anxious to support me as best they could.' He sighed. 'He doesn't think my mother would have listened to me either.'

She gave a small nod. 'Did you tell him how you felt?'

That had clearly been tougher for him. He closed his eyes for a second. 'I told him I felt responsible. I told him I felt guilty I hadn't been around more to help and give her advice on her health.'

'And what did he say?'

Stefan lifted his head and looked her in the eye. 'He told me he felt guilty too. He should have noticed. He should have stopped her. He said he had no excuse, since he saw her every day.'

'Wow...' Paige leaned back in her seat. 'That's huge.'

Stefan nodded. 'We both felt guilty, and never told each other. He asked me about work, and I told him about you instead.'

'You did?' The tiny hairs on her arms stood on end.

'I did. He was amused, you know.'

Her brow furrowed. 'Why?'

'Because apparently I've never spoken about anyone the way I spoke about you. It reminded him of the way he used to speak about Mum.'

She wasn't quite sure what to say.

'Apparently all I've ever done is talk about my next piece of work. He asked me if I planned to slow down.'

Her skin prickled again. The words caught in her throat. 'What are your plans?'

He smiled. 'It might surprise you to hear I've taken some time off. All surgeries have been rescheduled. The road has been cleared in Switzerland and is getting repaired. We have another project manager, who is taking over the last of the renovations.'

Paige gave a nod towards her flowers. 'And I take it you know that I've just worked my last day?'

The waitress appeared and put two large hot chocolates and two pieces of pie on the table. 'Thought I might as well bring two,' she said brightly.

Stefan gave a nervous smile.

'You've actually taken time off?'

He nodded.

'And what are your plans?'

His hands closed around the hot chocolate glass. 'I have one tiny thing I want to do, but then I was hoping we could make plans together.'

Her breathing caught somewhere in the back of her throat. The second he'd sat down she'd just wanted to hug him, to kiss him. Each of the sixteen days they'd been apart she'd been haunted by doubts—wondering if she'd done the right thing by calling him out and walking away. The temptation to wait for him when she'd stepped off the helicopter and seen her patients to safety had been overwhelming. But the place had been chaos, and it had been easy to slip through the waiting people with her small holdall and find a hotel for the night.

He'd phoned her, texted, but she'd known that they both had things to take care of.

'I'm not sure I want to be a doctor at all,' she said, her voice wavering. 'I need time to find out what is right. And I need the person I'm with to support me, to have my back.'

He reached his hands across the table and took hers.

'I promise I will support whatever you want to do. I'm sorry I tried to push you into staying. I was projecting my feelings and emotions into your situation and I should never have done that. Whatever you want to do, wherever you want to do it—I've got your back.'

She raised her eyes to meet his. 'And if I want to do it in Los Angeles?'

His face broke into a wide smile. 'Then I'd be honoured if you stay with me while you work things out.'

.'No pressure?' she reiterated.

'No pressure,' he said in a reassuring voice. 'Just someone who loves you and wants you to be happy.'

Paige breathed. It was like being back in the Alps and breathing in clean mountain air. Then she twigged what he'd mentioned earlier. 'You said something else—you said you had something to do first. What's that?'

For the first time since she'd known him Stefan looked a little sheepish. 'Yeah, about that. You know how I told you I'd spoken to my father?'

She nodded.

'Well, he was quite insistent about one thing.'

'What was that?'

'That he got to meet the woman who'd captured my heart.'

He nodded behind her, and Paige turned around. There was an older man sitting a few booths behind her, drinking coffee and eating apple pie. He lifted his filled fork towards her with a wide grin, and gave a nod.

Paige's mouth fell open. 'You didn't?'

Stefan smiled. 'He was pretty insistent and, to be

honest, having the two people I love most in the world meet each other seemed like a good idea.'

Paige let out a squeal of delight and jumped up, leaning over the table and grabbing Stefan in a huge hug. 'I'd be delighted to meet your dad!'

Stefan started laughing and stood up, then slipped his hand into hers. 'He's going to love you,' he whispered in her ear. 'Just as much as I do.'

Paige smiled and leaned into his kiss, for now and always.

EPILOGUE

THE ROAD WAS in perfect order as they drove up towards the hospital. 'I can't believe it's a year since it opened,' said Paige, staring out of the window at the snow-capped mountains.

Stefan reached a warm hand over and squeezed her knee. 'I never thought I'd be grateful to an avalanche.'

Paige met his gaze for a second and slipped her hand over his. 'It's so weird being back. I'm not sure whether I prefer the sun in Los Angeles or the air in the Alps.'

'Don't let my dad hear you saying that,' Stefan joked.

They turned the final corner, pulling into the large, landscaped car park that now had a helipad at one end.

The hospital looked even better than the last time they'd been here. New windows had been put into the older building, and Paige could see the state-of-the-art gym. The whole building was finished in a pale cream colour, but the main door remained the same with its stained-glass panels on either side.

'How many patients do you have?' asked Paige.

'Seven,' Stefan replied with a smile. 'Two toddlers for cleft repairs, and five adults, some reconstruction surgery after treatment, a skin graft, and some nose and cheek surgeries.'

The car came to a halt in one of the spaces and they stepped out into the crisp fresh air. 'Any time to ski?' asked Paige, teasing.

'Maybe a little,' he said, slipping an arm around her waist as they walked to the main doors. 'But we have to fit that in between meeting my father for dinner one evening, and Franco the next.'

'I'm sure we'll manage,' she said, putting her head on his shoulder. As they walked up the steps, she looked at him curiously. 'What is it you wanted to show me?'

He tapped the side of his nose. 'Let's say our hellos first.'

They greeted the nursing and theatre staff, general manager, chef and domestic staff. Discretion was key at the alpine hospital. All the staff were professional but the atmosphere was relaxed and easy.

Stefan slipped his hand into Paige's and led her down the corridor to the room that doubled as his office. As they walked in, he gestured for her to sit down.

There was a long white box on the table and Paige smiled, wondering what on earth was going on.

Instead of walking around to the other side of the desk, he pulled over another chair from the wall and sat down next to her. 'I got you a gift.' He smiled, nodding at the box. 'Open it.'

She gave him a curious smile. 'Okay.' She shifted position and lifted the lid of the white box. Inside was a carved wooden plaque. At one end was a brightly coloured Turaco bird, but it was the name and title that caught her attention. She ran her finger along the letters: *Paige McLeod, Counsellor.*

'It's beautiful,' she breathed, one hand going up to her chest.

'I know it's early. But once you qualify, your office will be next to mine. Here, and in Los Angeles.' He waved his hand to the room next door, which was identical to his, only a little smaller.

She couldn't hide the tears in her eyes. He'd supported her every step of the way, just like he'd promised. 'I love the bird. Signifying where we met.' She met his blue eyes. 'Where we fell in love.'

He cleared his throat. 'There's another door plaque underneath.'

She tilted her head to the side, wondering what on earth he meant. 'Why would I need another?'

She lifted the first and looked underneath. There was an identical plaque, with the Turaco bird and a name—only this time it read *Paige Bachmann, Counsellor.*

Her hand went to her mouth and her head turned quickly. Stefan was kneeling on the floor, an open ring box in his hand. 'What do you think?' He smiled. 'And you can have whatever name you like—the question is still the same—will you marry me?'

'Yes!' There wasn't a single moment's hesitation in her answer as she wrapped her arms around his neck, laughing and kissing him.

'Aren't I supposed to put the ring on your finger?' He laughed as she almost knocked him over.

She held out her trembling hand so he could slide

the single pink diamond onto her finger. 'One thing,' she whispered.

'Anything,' he said immediately.

She raised her eyebrows. 'I get the bigger office.'

'Mrs Bachmann,' he agreed, 'can have whatever she wants.' And he picked her up and swung her around as they both laughed.

* * * * *

SAVING CHRISTMAS
FOR THE ER DOC

KATE HARDY

MILLS & BOON

To Chris and Chloe,
who brought back the wonder of Christmas for me.

CHAPTER ONE

NEW JOB, NEW HOSPITAL, and Rachel Halliday was really looking forward to her new start. She'd switched back to her maiden name, and nobody in her new department needed to know how miserable the last couple of years had been. They'd just see Rachel for herself: a good doctor, a supportive colleague, and hopefully a new friend.

Rachel's best friend, Jenny, was a cardiac surgeon at Muswell Hill Memorial Hospital's sister hospital; she'd seen the job on the trust's bulletin board and urged Rachel to apply for it. Rachel had refused; her eldest daughter Meg was in her Finals year at university in Manchester and Saskia, her youngest, was just starting university in Sheffield, so how could she add yet more disruption to the girls' lives? Even though the job was a sideways move and would fit perfectly—a consultant in the Emergency Department, with some responsibility for teaching—she'd resigned herself to sticking it out at Hampstead for another year. By then, she hoped that the pity among her colleagues would surely have died down and something else would've taken her place as the topic to be gossiped about. And if it hadn't—well, then she'd go for the new start.

But Jenny had enlisted Meg and Saskia's support, and Rachel's daughters had set up a family video call to nag her into applying for the job.

'Mum, you've had a horrible two years, with Gran having dementia and you supporting her before she died, and Dad doing what he did, and then the divorce. It's time you did something for *you*,' Saskia said.

'And I've checked out the commute. It's half an hour on the Tube and then a walk through the park, so you don't even have to move house—though, if you decide that's what you want to do, we'll back you,' Meg added. 'We'll even come home and scrub grouting and tidy everything out of sight, ready for the estate agency to take photos.'

'Thank you, both of you, but I'm not planning to move house right now,' Rachel said. Moving house was meant to be one of the three most stressful life events, along with bereavement and divorce; after going through two of them in the last year, she needed a break before she could even consider the third.

'But you can still apply for the job,' Saskia encouraged her.

'They'll be lucky to have you, Mum,' Meg agreed. 'I know it's a sideways move, but it'll be a fresh start—and a new place means new opportunities. Go for it.'

So Rachel had given in to her daughters' urging and applied. She'd been invited for an interview; a few days later, to her delight, she'd been offered the job. And now today, on a foggy and freezing morning in mid-October, she was walking through the park from the Tube station to the hospital, enjoying the way the trees loomed like shadowy blobs and became more like intricate sculptures as she drew closer to them. She loved this time of year, even though today the ground was slippery underfoot and no doubt the waiting room this morning would be full of patients with Colles' fractures who'd put their arms out to stop themselves hitting the ground face-first and broken their wrists. She'd nearly fallen over, herself, just outside the Tube station.

Today was her induction day, but hopefully they could rattle through all the admin stuff fairly quickly and she could get straight into doing what she loved most: treating patients and teaching her juniors. She was looking forward to getting to know her new colleagues. She'd liked what she'd seen of Tim Hughes, the head of the department, at her interview; he'd seemed both friendly and super-calm—just what was needed in the rush of the Emergency Department.

But the second she went to the reception desk to introduce herself and explain that she was due to start in the department today but hadn't been given her key card yet, the receptionist put a hand on her arm and shook her head. 'I'm sorry, Miss Halliday. Mr Hughes sends his apologies, but your induction's going to have to be moved. He's asked if I can direct you straight to Resus, instead. There's been a bit of a bad pile-up on the M1 and they're expecting several patients.'

Given the weather conditions, Rachel wasn't surprised to hear there had been at least one car accident. With a busy motorway and several vehicles involved, it sounded as if the department was going to be stretched. 'Not a problem. Can you tell me where to go, please?'

'I've got the key to your locker.' The receptionist handed over a key with the locker number on the fob. 'The changing room's first on the left through the corridor—there are scrubs on the shelf—and the staff room's next door. Resus is at the end of the corridor, and one of the team there will tell you which room they need you in. It'll be on the whiteboard, too.'

'Great. Thank you very much.'

It didn't take Rachel long to change into green scrubs and her work shoes and dump everything else in her locker, and then she hurried down the corridor to Resus, where she recognised the man standing in front of the whiteboard—Tim Hughes, the head of the department, who'd interviewed her for the job. He was tall, with short dark hair greying at the temples, and the most amazing cornflower-blue eyes that had made her pulse leap inappropriately at the interview.

And now was an even more inappropriate time to remember that flare of attraction. The department was about to become super-busy and there was no room for daydreaming.

'Hi, I'm Rachel Halliday. I believe you're expecting me?' she asked.

Tim nodded. 'Yes—welcome to the team. Sorry your induction day's been hijacked.'

'It's fine, Mr Hughes.'

'Tim,' he corrected. 'We don't stand on ceremony here.'

'Rachel,' she said. 'Reception told me there's been a situation on the M1.'

'Yes. We think one of the drivers had a heart attack, veered across the road and hit the central reservation. The car behind him braked to try and avoid him, but several other cars didn't manage to stop in time.'

Hence the pile-up, Rachel thought. 'What do we know about our patients?'

'There's the one with a suspected heart attack; Sam Price, one of the other consultants, is treating him. I'm dealing with the critical patient with head injuries; there are a few with suspected fractures, and others with soft tissue injuries and shock. We're expecting the ambulances in any minute now, and I'm putting you in Resus Three with Ediye Mosaku to treat a driver who hit the steering wheel. The ambulance crew think he might have a flail chest,' Tim said, gesturing to the white-board on the wall. 'The other patients will be triaged as they get here.'

'Got it,' she said.

'This is Ediye,' he said as a young doctor in scrubs walked into the corridor. 'Ediye, this is Rachel.'

'Our new consultant. Lovely to meet you,' Ediye said with a broad smile.

'Perhaps we can catch up later today, Rachel, when things have quietened down,' Tim said.

'Sure,' she said cheerfully. Though, in her experience, things never really quietened down in the Emergency Department.

He smiled back. 'Good. The coffees will be on me.' There was a yell of, 'Tim!' from Resus One. 'Sounds as if my patient's arrived. See you later.'

Funny how that smile made her heart feel as if it had done a backflip.

Rachel made herself damp down the renewed flare of attraction. She needed to get a grip. Tim Hughes looked as if he was only a couple of years older than she was, and the odds were that he was already in a long-established relationship. If he was single, then he'd probably have as much emotional baggage as she had. Besides, even if he was single and the attraction turned out to be mutual, she wasn't looking for a relationship—not after the events of the past year. Right at the moment, Rachel's focus was on finding out who she was, now she was fifty-two and divorced, and working out what she wanted from life. Starting all over again, trying to find a new partner, just felt like a step too far. She wasn't ready to trust her heart to anyone.

Hoping none of that had shown on her face—she'd be mortified if her new colleagues had spotted that little leap of attraction, or the way she'd talked herself out of it—she turned to Ediye. 'Because it's my first day, obviously I don't know who everyone is yet or what their roles are. But I don't want to patronise anyone by behaving as if they don't know a thing when they're really experienced or push them too far out of their comfort zone by expecting them to know more than they actually do.' She smiled. 'So can I start with you, please?'

Ediye laughed. 'Sure. I've just finished my F2 year, and I'm in my first year of the Acute Care Common Stem training programme. Emergency was my favourite rotation, so I jumped at the chance to join the team. Tim's a really good head of department—he drills it into everyone that you ask if you're not sure about something, and he tries to give the junior doctors as much experience as possible.'

'Brilliant,' Rachel said. It was the impression she'd had at her interview, too, and the way she liked working. 'Have you dealt with a flail chest before?'

'I've seen a couple, and I know the theory,' Ediye said.

'In that case, I'm happy to let you lead, and I'll only step in if I think you need a hand. Ask me whatever you need to know as we're treating our patient; if you need me to take over, that's absolutely fine, and then afterwards we'll have a debrief so we can go over any decisions I made and I'll explain why I chose that particular option.' She smiled. 'Or, rather, you can tell me why I made those decisions, and I'll steer you in the right direction if I need to.'

'That'd be really good,' Ediye said.

A few seconds later, the first three batches of paramedics rushed in. Rachel and Ediye had the last patient, Ben Anstey; once the handover had been done, Rachel introduced them.

'Hello, Ben—I'm Rachel and this is Ediye. We're Emergency Department doctors in Muswell Hill Memorial Hospital, and we'll be looking after you today. The paramedics tell us you hit the steering wheel, and we think you might have broken some ribs.'

'I think so, too, because they hurt like hell,' Ben said, his face pinched.

'We'll give you some pain relief, but first can you take a deep breath for me?'

He did so and winced.

Rachel nodded at Ediye, encouraging the younger doctor to take over.

'It hurts when you take a deep breath?' Ediye asked.

'And when I move,' Ben confirmed. 'It's hard to breathe.' He coughed, and winced. 'Ow. That hurts my shoulder as well.'

'OK. I'm going to put you on an oxygen mask now,' Ediye said. 'That'll help you breathe more easily. I want to examine you, take your temperature and listen to your chest, if that's all right?'

'Whatever you need to do to stop it hurting,' Ben said.

Ediye put him on oxygen and gave him pain relief, then checked his stats and turned to Rachel. 'His temperature's up, his heart rate's too high, his blood pressure's falling and he's got falling oxygen sats,' she said a low voice. 'I notice that part of his chest goes in when he breathes in and out when he breathes out, so I think the paramedics were right about it being flail chest.' Flail chest was a condition where at least three ribs in a row had two or more breaks, so part of the chest wall separated from the rest and moved independently. 'There are decreased breath sounds, so I want to send him for a CT scan to check out trauma to the lungs.'

'Good call,' Rachel said. 'And a possible pneumothorax, because he's got that dry cough and the pain when he breathes radiates to his shoulder.' A pneumothorax was where air leaked into the space between the lung and the chest wall; the pressure of the trapped air then caused the lung to collapse.

Ediye explained to Ben what would happen next and checked if he wanted them to call anyone.

Once the results were back, Rachel reviewed them with the younger doctor. 'Flail chest, a pneumothorax, and the beginnings of contusions to the lungs—all quite common in cases of blunt trauma where you're slammed against the steering wheel,' Rachel said. 'What's your treatment plan?'

'We'll call the thoracic SPR to review the scan and see if they want to take him to Theatre to stabilise his ribs,' Ediye said. 'Meanwhile we need to get the air out from the pleural space, so his lung can reinflate and to reduce his pain.'

'Perfect; but, given that he has flail chest as well, I'd go straight to a chest drain in this case,' Rachel said. 'Have you done one before?'

'I've seen a couple and done one,' Ediye said.

It seemed that Tim Hughes definitely acted on what he'd said at the interview, Rachel thought, pleased. 'Good. You can do this one and talk me through it as if you're teaching me. We need to make sure Ben has enough pain relief so he can take deep breaths, cough and move around—that'll help him to avoid a chest infection. I'll call his wife while you call Thoracics.'

When Ben came back from his CT scan, Rachel said, 'Your wife's on her way in. Reception will send her straight in to us when she gets here.'

'Thank you,' Ben said.

Ediye explained the results of his scan and what they were going to do next. Once Ediye had done the chest drain under Rachel's supervision, Rachel took Ben through some breathing exercises for him to do on the ward to help keep his chest clear.

Ben's wife arrived; Ediye introduced them, explained what they'd done and what was happening next, and finished with, 'If you'd like to sit with him, the thoracic specialist will be with you soon. If you're worried about anything in the meantime, talk to one of the nurses and they can call us in if necessary.'

When they'd left Ben but before seeing their next patient, Rachel smiled at Ediye. 'You did really well with that drain.'

Ediye looked pleased. 'Thanks. Telling you what I was going to do really helped me focus.'

'Good. Let's go and find our next patient.'

It was an incredibly busy morning; as well as the patients from the motorway crash, the waiting room was full of people who'd slipped on the ice and sprained an ankle or fractured a wrist or hurt a knee. Monday morning was always the busiest time in the Emergency Department, and it was way past lunchtime before Rachel had the chance to make herself a coffee in the staff kitchen. She added some cold water so she could drink it down straight away.

'You must be Rachel,' one of the nurses said when she walked in. 'I was just coming to find you. Tim's in his office and asked if you'd come and see him when you've got a moment.'

So much for her break, Rachel thought, and drained her coffee. 'OK. Can I ask where his office is?'

'In the corridor opposite here, at the end on the right,' the nurse said with a smile.

'Thank you.' Rachel washed up her mug and left it on the draining board, then headed for Tim's office.

At the rap on his door, Tim called, 'Come in!'

As he'd hoped, rather than it being one of the suits with yet more paperwork to dump on his desk, their new consultant walked in. 'I believe you wanted to see me?' Rachel asked.

'Yes.' His eyes narrowed. 'It's been crazy this morning. Have you had a break, yet?'

'I was planning to have one now. I just grabbed a coffee in the staff room,' she said, 'and I was about to get the emergency chocolate bar from my bag.'

It was par for the course when they were as busy as they'd been that morning, but Tim didn't like the extra pressure on his staff. 'We can do better than that,' he said. 'I'll take you to the canteen and buy you a sandwich.' He could see the beginning of protest on her face and added, 'No strings. It's your first day and, with that crash, you were pretty much chucked in at the deep end. Plus, we can multi-task. Debrief and lunch at the same time.'

'All right. Thank you. To be honest, I'm glad the induction's been shoved out of the way,' she admitted as she followed him out of his office, and they walked down the corridor together. 'I'd rather be helping patients than spending hours going through admin stuff that I could sort out at home.'

A woman after his own heart. He liked that. 'How's your man with flail chest?' he asked.

'We've admitted him, and the thoracic team are going

to let me know what they're doing. Ediye did the chest
drain for the pneumothorax. She said she'd done one,
so I went by the "see one, do one, teach one" principle
and got her to talk me through it as she did it. And she
was great.'

Tim approved of Rachel's no-nonsense attitude; he'd
liked her at the interview and thought she'd fit in well
to the team. It was good to know his instincts had been
spot on. They'd never let him down in his job. It was a
pity they'd let him down in his personal life. If he'd paid
more attention at home, if he'd let someone else take
over here and gone out to dinner that night with Mandy
and their friends instead of working late because he'd
wanted to make sure his patient made it, maybe she
wouldn't have—

He shoved the thought aside. *Not now.*

At the canteen, he bought them both coffee, sandwiches and cake.

'How was your guy with the head injury?' she asked.

'We got him as far as Intensive Care,' he said, 'and
now it's a waiting game. The guy with the heart attack
didn't quite make it here, and Sam had been called to
treat someone else, so I had to talk to the poor guy's husband and tell him what had happened—which is why
I'm eating my cake before my sandwich.' He grimaced.
'I hate breaking the news that makes someone's world
crumble.' He'd been on the receiving end of news like
that, two years ago, and it had taken him quite a while
to get back to coping. His girls still called him every
day to check on him; and every day he put his work face

on and told them he was doing fine. Which he was—at work. It was home that was tough, especially walking in through the front door to be greeted with silence instead of hearing Mandy bustling about or humming along with the radio as she marked an essay. He didn't even have a dog to welcome him home; much as he would've liked the company, it simply wouldn't be fair on the poor animal, not with the hours he worked.

Maybe he needed a fish.

But a fish couldn't cuddle into you…

Stop. Stop it now. Remember what the counsellor said: focus on the positives. Think of everything you have to be thankful about, everything from the big things to the little ones. The girls, your job, your grandchild-to-be. Your health. Good coffee and loud music.

'Anyway, welcome to Muswell Hill Memorial Hospital.' He lifted his forkful of cake in a toast.

'Thank you.' His eyes caught hers and he realised just how pretty Rachel Halliday was, with those huge grey eyes. Her salt-and-pepper brown hair was cut into a neat bob that framed her heart-shaped face perfectly, and her mouth was a perfect cupid's bow.

Oh, for pity's sake. He knew from her application form that his new consultant was a couple of years younger than he was, and he'd guess her life stage was very similar to his own; she probably had grown-up children who were finding their own way in the world, and maybe the first grandchild was about to make an appearance. Thinking about how pretty she was really wasn't appropriate.

She's here to talk about work, he reminded himself.

'It's not usually *quite* this mad here on a Monday morning.'

'With all that ice, I was expecting a slew of Colles' fractures,' she said. 'I nearly fell flat on my face when I came out of the Tube station.' She smiled. 'Just as well I managed to stay upright, because it would've been a bit embarrassing if I'd turned up in the waiting room on my first day, needing a back slab on my wrist instead of prescribing one for someone else.'

'Just a tad,' he said, smiling back. 'I'm guessing you already know where the lockers and changing rooms are, and the staff kitchen.'

'And now you've shown me where the café is, so I'm pretty much sorted. I just need my key card so I don't have to keep asking Reception to let me in, and my login details so I can access patient records and my email—we did all the notes under Ediye's log-in today.' She looked hopeful. 'Can we skip the rest of it?'

'What, you mean the health and safety bits, the fire procedures, the online policy, the…' He chuckled at the rising dismay in her expression. 'I'll have a word with HR and see if they can give us a workaround. Or maybe one of them will agree to do it as a one-to-one or something and cut it down to half an hour. I'm pretty sure there isn't that much difference between how we do things here and how they did things at your last hospital.'

'Thank you,' she said. 'I don't mind reading stuff or doing an online induction course in my own time, if that helps.'

'Won't your family mind?' The question came out

before he could stop it. 'Sorry. Forget I asked that. It was intrusive.'

'No, it's fine. My daughters are both at uni, so they're only home during the holidays.'

So his guess had been right. She was at a similar life stage to him, with grown-up children, though hers were clearly a few years younger than his. But he noticed that she hadn't mentioned a husband or partner. Mandy had always been a bit fed up with how much time his job took up, and they'd argued about it a lot. Was it the same for other senior doctors? Did her partner get fed up with her always being late home?

Tim couldn't help glancing at Rachel's left hand and noticed that it was bare. There was a bare-below-the-elbow hygiene policy for clinical staff, but plain rings were allowed. Maybe her wedding ring wasn't plain, then. Or maybe she and her partner hadn't bothered getting married. Not that it was any of his business.

But then she said, 'Actually, the girls pushed me into applying for the job here. I'm glad they did.'

'Pushed you?' He was surprised.

She nodded. 'I was going to stick it out in Hampstead for another year, because it's Meg's final year at uni and Saskia's first year, and I think they've had enough disruption over the last few months without me changing everything on top of that.'

Disruption? It sounded as if life had been tricky for her, and he needed to back off rather than risk making things awkward for her. 'Kids are often more resilient than we give them credit for,' he said. His girls had coped with losing their mother a lot better than he had.

Possibly because they'd been able to cry, and he'd stuffed his feelings down. The only times he'd cried in public was when his daughters had been born, and he'd brushed away a tear at their weddings. At Mandy's funeral he'd kept himself under rigid control, knowing that if he let himself crack he'd never piece himself back together.

And he knew, too, that he'd kept his girls at more of an emotional distance than he really wanted to, because he didn't want to lean on them and be a burden. Sometimes he wondered if he'd taken it too far; was he disconnected from them instead of protecting them? And, if so, how was he going to reconnect with them? Mandy would've known how to handle things—but Mandy wasn't here any more.

'My eldest is going on maternity leave in about three weeks,' he said.

'Will it be your first grandchild?' Rachel asked. At his nod, she said, 'You and your partner must really be looking forward to it.'

'Just me, actually,' he said quietly. 'My wife died two years ago.' He blew out a breath. 'Actually, you might as well hear it from me, because someone in the department's bound to tell you, but the rule is no pity, OK?'

'OK.'

Her grey eyes were sympathetic rather than pitying, and that gave him the courage to tell her. 'Mandy had a severe sesame allergy,' he said. 'She was out having dinner with friends—I was supposed to be joining them, but I was held up here.' Even though he knew that her death wasn't his fault, that he couldn't have saved her, that nothing would've changed even if he'd been there, he still felt guilty. If he'd been at dinner with her like he'd promised, at least he could've held her hand in the ambulance and told her he loved her.

But he hadn't been there. He'd been at work.

'Obviously they'd double-checked it with the staff, but there was a mix-up in the kitchen. Nobody realised at the time, but the food had been accidentally cooked in sesame oil. She collapsed, and then she hit her head in the wrong place.' And then there was the bit that had hacked the bottom out of his world. 'She died in the ambulance on the way to hospital.'

'I'm sorry. That's tough, losing your wife so young— and not getting the chance to say goodbye,' Rachel said, reaching across the table to squeeze his hand briefly.

He appreciated the small gesture of kindness. 'Yeah. It's the things you didn't get time to share that you miss the most,' he said. Their first grandchild, due in a few weeks. Their youngest daughter's wedding, last year. Growing old together. All their plans. All the things they hadn't shared because he'd been busy at work; and how ironic it was that now he worked even harder, to fill the gaps and make himself too tired to think when he got home.

'It's not quite the same thing,' she said, 'but I get where you're coming from because I lost my mum earlier this year.' She looked sad. 'In a way, I lost her before she died, because she had dementia. I took a sabbatical to care for her as long as I could.'

'Dementia's a cruel disease,' he said. 'The way it takes someone bit by bit.'

She nodded. 'It was hard on the girls. Towards the

end, their gran kept mistaking them for me when I was their age. But Saskia would sit and read to Mum every evening before dinner, and when Meg was home from uni she'd play the guitar and get Mum to sing old Beatles songs with her.' She smiled. 'She used to do a video call from uni every Wednesday night and get her grandmother singing along with us all.'

'Apparently, music's one of the last memories to go,' Tim said. 'So your mum lived with you?'

'For six months or so. She wasn't safe to live on her own, even with carers popping in,' Rachel said. 'That's why I took time off work and she moved in with us—until she got to the stage where she needed more care than I could give her on my own. Then, much as I hated the idea, I had to find a nursing home.'

He remembered now that the gap in Rachel's CV had come up in her interview, and she'd quietly said she'd taken a break from work to help a family member. Now he understood.

'But I'm glad I spent that time with her. And I guess it did me a favour because it gave my husband the final excuse to leave me for girlfriend number...' She shrugged. 'Well, whatever number she was.'

Her husband had dumped her during her mother's final illness? He winced. 'That's tough.' Not just the affair, but the timing. Even though Mandy's mum was really difficult, Tim wouldn't have complained if she'd had a terminal illness and Mandy had wanted to move her into their home to look after her in her final months. When you were partners, you took the rough with the smooth and you supported each other; you didn't just go off and find someone else with fewer complications when things got difficult. Rachel's ex clearly hadn't shared Tim's views.

'It's been a bit of a tricky couple of years,' Rachel said.

And that was a huge understatement, Tim thought.

'But the girls and I got through it.' She smiled. 'And now I get to do something for me: a new start in a new job. No pity or set-up dates required.'

'Oh, the set-up dates.' He groaned. 'Tell me about it. I know people mean well. But when friends invite you to dinner, and you think you're simply going to spend a nice evening with friends you've known and loved for years, eating and talking too much; and then you turn up and they introduce you to someone suitable, and there's all the expectation...' He shook his head. 'Not my idea of fun.'

'At our age, if that "someone suitable" has always been single, I've found they tend to be very set in their ways,' she said. 'And I've had enough of having to bend over backwards to please someone else.'

It sounded as if her ex had been a bit demanding, Tim thought. 'Absolutely. And, if they're divorced or widowed, there's a broken heart to deal with on top of your own. Dating isn't for me. I'm perfectly happy to be on my own.' It wasn't quite true—he was horribly lonely, and the house echoed—but at the same time he wasn't quite ready to join the dating mill. Especially at this time of year. He was dreading the run-up to Christmas. All the songs of loneliness that seemed to be on every radio station, whatever one he flicked to; all the reminders of happy families, when his own was fractured.

'I'm happy on my own, too,' she said, raising her own coffee.

'And that's why I've learned to eat cake before sandwiches,' he said. 'Do the happy stuff first.'

'That's a great idea. Except,' she said, gesturing to her own plate, 'when the sandwich happens to be a hot brie and cranberry panini. Then I'm afraid there's no contest. Cheese first, all the way.'

'You're a cheese fiend?' he asked.

'Totally,' she admitted.

'Then there's a shop I need to introduce you to,' he said. 'Which I guarantee will make me your new best friend.'

She laughed. 'I like the sound of that, though you'll have to make do with being second-best friend, or else Jenny—my bestie—will scalp you. Let's just say she's a cardiac surgeon who does kickboxing in her spare time.'

'Super-scary, so don't mess with her. Got it. Second-best friend will do fine,' he said, and lifted his mug. 'Here's to new friends.'

'New friends,' she echoed.

How weird that her smile made him feel more settled than he'd been in months. Not that he was going to examine that too closely. 'Right. What else do you need to know about the department? We have team nights out, every so often—anything from cocktails to curry to clubbing.' He smiled at her. 'And other things that begin with a different letter of the alphabet.'

'Pints, pizza and…let me see…paddle-boarding at Paddington Basin?' she suggested.

He couldn't help laughing. 'Nice one.' Instinctively, he liked this woman. Rachel was definitely on his wavelength and she seemed to share his sense of humour, too. 'I admit, I tend to skip the clubbing nights. Not because I'm too old, but because the music's not quite my scene.' He grinned. 'I still tease my girls, though. I threaten to take them clubbing, wear a really loud and embarrassing shirt, get the DJ to play something especially for me, and have a good old dad dance right in the middle of the dance floor—making sure everyone knows I'm with them.'

She looked sad for a moment. 'Steve wouldn't even consider saying that as a joke, let alone really go somewhere with them. He doesn't bother doing anything with the girls.' She shook herself. 'Sorry. Ignore me. Not your problem.'

Or his business, he thought. 'Would you go clubbing with your girls?'

'Probably not—like you, the music isn't my scene— but I still go to the odd gig with them. They love Bryan Adams as much as I do, so I take them with me to see him whenever he plays in London,' she said. 'There's really nothing better than singing your head off to songs you love with thousands of other people.'

'Loud enough so the band has to turn the sound up. I agree. That's the best sort of stadium gig,' he said. 'Though I have to admit I love the tiny venues as well, when there's maybe fifty of you and a seriously good guitarist.'

'I'm hoping to find something they'll both like when

they're home for the Christmas holidays.' She smiled. 'I love Christmas.'

Whereas Tim found it incredibly hard to bear, nowadays. But he was the head of the department, and his staff had to come before his feelings. 'Now you've mentioned Christmas, make sure you catch up with Ediye before you go today. She's in charge of organising the department Christmas meal and Secret Santa this year, so she'll get your name on the list. It's the last week of November.'

'I'll do that,' she said. 'And I'd better get back to work. We still have a waiting room full of patients.'

'Not to mention the joys of paperwork. And I have a meeting with the suits this afternoon, so I need to play nice.' He rolled his eyes.

'Thank you for lunch,' she said, 'and for making me feel welcome.'

'Pleasure.'

And how strange it was, Tim thought as they chatted on the way back to the department, that he felt lighter of heart than he had for a long, long time. Something about Rachel Halliday made him feel as if the world was in kilter again. Or maybe it was just the relief of knowing that they'd made the right choice in appointing her: a warm, lovely woman who would be great with the patients and staff alike. Of course it was that. Work. It had to be.

CHAPTER TWO

'I'M SORRY I couldn't make dinner last night,' Jenny said.

'You're a surgeon, Jen. You can hardly stop in the middle of an operation and tell the rest of your team that you have dinner plans and they'll just have to carry on without you,' Rachel said. 'It was fine. I got your message, and I had stuff in the fridge so I could make myself dinner.'

'Which had better not mean just a cheese sandwich,' Jenny said.

'A toasted cheese sandwich—with good bread, chutney and a salad—is one of life's joys,' Rachel said. 'No, actually. For your information, it was salmon baked with lemon and thyme, roasted veggies and wilted greens.'

'Mediterranean food. Just what a cardiac surgeon likes to hear,' Jenny said. 'So how was your first day in your new job?'

'Great. The team's lovely, and Tim, the head of the department, is one of the good guys—he managed to talk HR into letting me do most of the induction stuff online. *And* he bought me a brie and cranberry panini to welcome me to the team.' She grinned. 'So I got my cheese fix yesterday anyway.'

'Sounds good. And how are the girls?'

'Saskia's settled in really well, Meg's busy planning her dissertation, and they're doing tag team texts to nag me to eat properly. Which,' Rachel said, 'is probably in collusion with their godmother.'

Jenny batted her eyelashes. 'I couldn't possibly comment.'

Rachel laughed and raised her glass of red wine in a toast. 'Thank you. It's good to know you all have my back.'

'Of course we do.' Jenny smiled. 'We love you.'

'I love you, too. And I'm so glad you're not doing the set-up dates any more. Tim said it's the same for him.'

'He's divorced?'

'Widowed. Don't get ideas,' Rachel said, seeing the interest on her best friend's face and guessing what Jenny was thinking. 'We're going to be friends.'

'It's always good to make new friends,' Jenny said. 'But I still worry about you being lonely.'

'I have my girls, I have you, I have other friends and I love my job. All the loose ends are tied up with Steve. Apart from wishing I'd had the sense to ask him to leave, years ago, I'm doing fine,' Rachel said with a smile. Tim Hughes really was going to be just friends with her. He understood that she wasn't ready to start all over again, because he was in exactly the same place that she was. Friends was good. Friends would be enough.

And she wasn't going to think about the way his cornflower-blue eyes crinkled at the corners and made her heart do a little skip.

* * *

'Hello, love.' Tim handed his daughter a bouquet of bright orange gerberas. Flowers weren't really enough to bridge the gap he suspected he'd put between them, but it was a start. And you didn't always have to say things out loud, did you?

'Oh, Dad. They're gorgeous. Thank you.' Hannah gave him a hug. 'Oof. Either you've got fatter since last week or I have,' she teased, 'because I can't get my arms all the way round you.'

Tim chuckled and rested his hand on the bump. 'Good evening, little one.' His smile broadened when the baby kicked in response. 'Knows their granddad's voice, I see.'

'Good, because we're so lining you up for babysitting duties. Come and sit down while I put these in water.'

'You're the one who should be sitting down, not me.' He took the flowers back. 'Sit. Just remind me where you keep your vases and tell me which one you want.'

'Were you this bossy when Mum was pregnant with me?' Hannah asked.

'Absolutely. So there's no standing at the top of a stepladder to paint the nursery ceiling. If you want it done, ask Jamal or me. Got it?' His heart ached. This was when Hannah needed her mum to tell her all the little stories about what it had been like to be pregnant with her, to share the experiences and reassure her and make her laugh instead of worrying. But Mandy wasn't here—and Tim could only tell Hannah stuff from the outside, not how it actually felt to carry a baby. 'Your mum rested when I told her to, though she refused to put up with my cooking. You're lucky that Jamal can cook, because if you'd had to rely on me you would've been stuck with scorched baked beans on burnt toast every day of the week for months.'

She looked at him. 'Dad, you are—?'

'Yes, of course I'm eating properly,' he cut in, reassuring her. 'I'm not that bad. Half of what I tell you about my cooking is for dramatic purposes.'

'Not convincing, Dad—I used to live with you, remember.' But she let him usher her into the kitchen, directed him to the cupboard where she kept her vases, and sat down at the table while he put the flowers in water and started making them both a mug of tea.

'So how's your week been?' she asked.

'Good. My new consultant started on Monday. Just as I'd hoped, she fits in very well with the team.'

'Consultant?' Hannah looked interested. 'So she must be in at least her late thirties, then.'

'She's nearer my age, actually,' he said.

'Oh.' Hannah raised an eyebrow. 'Would she be single?'

He rolled his eyes. 'Don't *you* start. Actually, she is, but don't get any ideas. I think we'll become friends, but no more than that.' Even if Rachel Halliday was really pretty and had a warmth that drew him, he wasn't looking for love. He was just getting through the days. 'Nobody will ever match up to your mum, Han.'

'Soph and I don't want you to be lonely, Dad,' Hannah said. 'Mum wouldn't have wanted that, either. And it's been two and a half years. That's a long time to be on your own.'

'I know, love.' He brought their mugs of tea over. 'And I'm fine as I am. Really.' It wasn't strictly true, but Tim didn't want his daughter worrying about him. He'd find his way through this, in his own time. 'Now, tell me about your week.'

On Thursday morning, the paramedics rushed in with a middle-aged man who'd been cutting wood with an electric saw. They'd called the department beforehand, so Rachel had already got the surgeon and anaesthetist on standby, and when the patient arrived she asked Lorraine, the triage nurse, to bleep the surgeon.

'I'm Rachel, one of the doctors, and I'll be looking after you today,' she said.

'Dave Fleetwood,' he said, 'but everyone calls me Woody because of my name and because of what I do.'

'OK, Woody. Can you tell me what happened?' Rachel asked.

'I was cutting some wood. It slipped, and my left hand ended up under the blade,' he said. 'I'm not sure how bad it is because I blacked out and Baz—my best mate, and thank God he was working with me—put my fingers in a plastic bag with ice.'

'That's quick thinking.' The situation was time-critical, Rachel knew. The longer that the blood supply had been cut to a body part, the lower the chances were that the surgeons could reattach it. From the amount of blood on the dressing covering his hand, it looked as if this case could be tricky.

'I'll give you some pain relief,' she said, 'and the surgeon's on his way down. I'm going to send you—and the fingers your friend saved—for an X-ray, so we can get a better idea of whether we're looking at crush injuries as well as laceration and what the surgeon's going to need to do. Can you remember when you last had a tetanus vaccination booster?'

He shook his head. 'No idea.'

'We'll add that in,' she said. 'Did you hit your head at all when you blacked out?'

'No,' he said. 'Baz caught me and sat me on a chair.'

'That's good. Can I ask, how old was the blade?'

'Pretty new,' he said, 'so hopefully it doesn't mean there was any gunk on the blade and it's not going to get infected.'

She unwrapped the dressing; there were three fingers missing, and his little finger looked damaged as well. 'OK. I'll clean this up, give you some pain relief and a tetanus jab, and then we'll get you to X-Ray. Can we call anyone for you?'

'Baz called my missus when the ambulance came,' he said. 'She's on her way in now. I feel so bad about this. We were supposed to be going away, this weekend. It's our wedding anniversary. But I'm not going to be able to drive us there, and she can't drive.' He bit his lip. 'We'll book a taxi. I'll be out of hospital by then, won't I?'

'That's one to ask the surgeon,' she said with a sympathetic smile.

The surgeon had come down to the department by the time the X-ray files were through to her computer.

'This isn't looking great,' Mr Gupta said as they reviewed the X-rays together. 'You can see there's a lot of damage to his little finger as well as the three he's severed. I'll try to save as many of his fingers as I can, but with that level of damage I think he's going to need to prepare for the worst.'

'Poor guy,' Rachel said.

Lorraine came into the office. 'Rachel, I've got Mrs Fleetwood in the relatives' room. The whiteboard says her husband's with you.'

'Yes. He's on his way back from X-Ray,' Rachel said. 'We'll come with you to collect her.'

In the relatives' room, Lorraine introduced the anxious-looking woman as Suze Fleetwood.

'Is Woody going to be all right? I mean, Baz said on the phone he'd cut half his fingers off. He lives for his job. If he can't do stuff with wood any more, I just don't know what he'll...' Looking distressed, Suze shook her head.

'Mrs Fleetwood, let me introduce you to Mr Gupta, the hand surgeon,' Rachel said gently. 'He'll be helping your husband in Theatre.'

'I'm going to do my very best for your husband, Mrs Fleetwood, and I'm good at my job, but I'm afraid I need you to prepare yourself for the fact I might not be able to save all his fingers,' Mr Gupta said. 'It's going to be a very long operation. I'd say it's likely to take more than twelve hours, so I'd advise you to either get some rest at home or call some family or friends to come and be with you, because waiting here on your own will give you too much time to worry.'

'Twelve *hours*?' Suze looked shocked. 'And you

might not...' She dragged in a breath. 'Working with wood—that's what he loves, more than anything. Making furniture. He's a proper craftsman. If he can't do that any more, then it'll be the end of the world for him.' She looked distraught.

'We'll do our best for him,' Mr Gupta said gently. 'And we can do a lot with prosthetics, nowadays. Rehab will take time, but with support I promise we'll be able to help him. He doesn't have to lose everything.'

'Can I see him before he has the operation?'

'Of course you can,' Rachel said. 'He's on his way back from X-Ray now.'

'You can come to the doors of the operating theatre with him,' Mr Gupta added, 'but then, as I said earlier, I'd advise getting someone to come and sit with you in the cafeteria or the relatives' room. We'll let you know as soon as there's any news.'

'Let's go and wait for him at the cubicle,' Rachel said.

Woody was wheeled into the cubicle just as Rachel pulled back the curtain, his face pale with pain. 'Oh, Suze, I'm so sorry. I've ruined our anniversary. I can't drive us to the hotel now. I'm not even sure I'll be able to go away.'

'Idiot,' she said, and kissed him. 'None of that matters. As long as I've still got you—I don't care about posh hotels and cocktails. It's *you* that's important. And thank God you're still here. When Baz phoned, it terrified the life out of me.'

Rachel had to swallow the lump in her throat. She'd found out the hard way that the posh hotels and cocktails had been more important to Steve than she was. Much as she would've liked to be loved the way that Suze Fleet-wood clearly loved her husband, the idea of signing up for dating apps and putting herself out there felt way too daunting. How did you find love again when you were middle-aged? How did you deal with all the emotional baggage of a potential partner as well as your own?

Though, right now, she needed to concentrate on her patient's needs rather than her own insecurities. She introduced Dave to Mr Gupta, who talked him through the operation and answered as many questions as he could.

'I'm going to have a word with the anaesthetist and scrub in,' Mr Gupta said. 'Can you take Mr Fleetwood to Theatre Six, please?' he added to the porter.

'We can still have cocktails and bubbly at home, when you get out of hospital,' Suze said. 'And I'll cook you a steak, just the way you like it. Even if I have to cut it up for you and feed you like a baby.'

Woody gave her a watery smile. 'I love you, Suze.'

She kissed him. 'Love you, too. Always have, always will.' She turned to Rachel. 'Thanks for doing what you've done, Doctor.'

'You're welcome,' Rachel said. 'All the best—and happy anniversary to you both.'

'Cheers, love,' Woody said. He was smiling again now, even though he was clearly worried sick; he'd definitely perked up as soon as his wife had arrived.

Suze held his good hand and walked alongside the trolley as the porter wheeled him out towards Theatre. And Rachel squashed the little sad bit of longing for a love like that in her own life, wrote up her notes, and went to find her next patient.

* * *

On Friday, when Rachel had finished writing up her notes before lunch, she headed for Tim's office. 'Busy?' she asked.

'Depends,' he said.

'Coffee and a sandwich? My shout, as you paid last time.'

'All right. And it'd be good to catch up and see how your first week's gone,' he said.

Once they were settled with lunch, he said, 'Right. Hit me with it. The good, the OK, and the things that need changing?'

'I love my colleagues, I love the team spirit here, and Mr Gupta managed to save three out of my patient's four fingers from the other day—that's the excellent stuff. The paperwork's bearable and thank you for persuading HR to let me do the online stuff at home instead of dragging it out. And the things that need changing—well, the head of department would be all right if he kept his promise to introduce me to the best cheese shop in the world,' she said with a grin.

'That,' he said, 'can be arranged.'

'What are you doing on Saturday?' she asked.

'Laundry,' he said with a groan.

'Me, too. But can I tempt you out for an hour?'

He was silent for a moment, and she suddenly wondered if he thought she was hitting on him. 'As friends,' she added swiftly.

Was that relief she saw in his eyes? Either way, it was a reminder to her not to get too close to him.

'All right. I'll meet you at the Tube station at ten,' he said.

'Perfect,' she said, and switched the topic back to the safe topic of work. 'How's your head injury patient doing in ICU?'

'Holding his own,' he said. 'And your flail chest?'

'Discharged today. His wife popped in earlier with a tin of biscuits, a jar of coffee and a box of teabags for the staff room.'

'Ah, that's kind,' he said. 'But the bit I like best is hearing that someone who was rushed into us on a trolley is well enough to be discharged and go home.'

'Absolutely,' she agreed.

On Saturday, Tim waited outside the Tube station. Just friends, he reminded himself, feeling the little bubbles of excitement fizzing through his veins. Platonic friends, that was what they'd said they'd be. This wasn't the start of a relationship. He wasn't even looking for a relationship. But the bubbles of excitement increased as he saw her walking towards him. He lifted a hand in acknowledgement; as soon as she saw him, she smiled, and his heart felt as if it had done an anatomically impossible pirouette.

'Good morning, Mr Hughes.' Though she wasn't being formal in the slightest. She was being cheeky, and he liked her sense of fun.

He grinned. 'Good morning, Ms Halliday. Ready for some intensely serious discussion about cheese?'

'Certainly am.'

He resisted the impulse to take her hand. Not appropriate, he reminded himself. But he chatted lightly to her on the way into the high street and realised how much he'd missed making inconsequential chatter with someone he felt instantly comfortable with. It was weird how it felt as if he'd known Rachel for years instead of for barely a week. They'd just clicked.

He led her through a couple of the back streets and stopped outside a shop. 'Ta-da.'

'Muzzy's Barn,' she said, reading the sign. 'OK.'

But as soon as they stepped inside, he heard her soft 'oh' of delight.

The cheese counter was dedicated to small artisanal cheeses; there were locally made chutneys, pickles, jams and jars of sauces; there was a deli section with a barrel of gleaming olives; there were artisanal bread and pastries, displayed beautifully; there were locally produced fruit, vegetables and eggs; and there was a section for locally roasted coffee and blended teas.

'It's like an indoor farmers' market,' she said. 'And, look—they even have a specialist vegan section.' She smiled. 'My youngest is vegan. I'm definitely coming back here and stocking up, before she's next due home. There's some non-dairy cheese there I've not seen before and it might have the right texture.'

'I take it vegan cheese isn't a hit with you?' he asked.

'Cashew-based soft cheeses are lovely, and I've found something that's not far off Camembert,' she said, 'but I've yet to find something with the right texture to replace a decent Cheddar.' She smiled. 'Though, actually, I've liked nearly all the things Saskia and I have made together. I think our favourite's been the caponata sauce. And these,' she added, taking a jar of capers off the shelf and adding it to her basket, 'are so going in the next batch I make.'

'So you like cooking?'

She nodded. 'And experimenting. Now the girls are both at uni, my best friend's my usual guinea pig.' She gestured to the counter. 'My new second-best friend, if he chooses, could be my guinea pig to say thank you for introducing me to such a wonderful shop.'

She was inviting him to dinner as a friend and co-conspirator, not as a date. Which was a relief and a disappointment at the same time. 'I'd like that,' he said. 'But I'm afraid you get a choice of burned beans on charred toast or a takeaway in return. Hannah—my eldest—says I can't cook because I forget to keep an eye on things and can't follow a recipe. Which is a bit ridiculous, given that I can follow procedures to save a life. Her words, not mine.'

'I'd guess that work matters to you but cooking doesn't,' she said.

'Mandy did the cooking and I did the washing up,' he said. 'I'm guessing you had a similar arrangement?'

'We had a dishwasher,' she said, and looked away.

Her marriage had clearly been very different from his own close partnership. 'Sorry. I didn't mean to stomp over a sore spot.'

'It's fine,' she said. 'Let's go and look at the cheese.'

She seemed out of sorts, but he didn't know her well enough to know how to fix it. Being bright and breezy would be tantamount to sticking his fingers in his ears, closing his eyes and singing *La-la-la, I can't hear you.*

Feeling awkward and cross with himself, he followed her to the cheese counter.

To his relief, she started talking with the young woman behind the counter about the different cheese, trying several; and then she turned to him to encourage him to do the same. By the time she'd added half a dozen different sorts to her basket, she was smiling again.

'Shall we stop and have a cup of coffee?' he suggested. 'The café here is very good.'

He wasn't surprised that she opted for the Parmesan shortbread to go with her coffee.

'This is seriously good,' she said after her first bite. 'I think it's as good as the cheese biscuits Mum taught me to make. I used to bake them for school fundraisers and family parties, and if people knew I was making them I'd get a bunch of texts begging for a doggie bag, so I always had to make an extra batch.'

'Sometimes the Emergency Department staff bring in things they've baked and leave them in the kitchen for everyone to share,' he said.

'Would that be a hint, Mr Hughes?'

'Just a teensy, tiny one,' he said.

She laughed. How pretty she looked when her eyes crinkled at the corners, he thought. Those were real laughter lines. Rachel Halliday might have had a rough couple of years, but she was definitely the sort of person who looked for the good in life.

'OK. Next time I do some baking, I'll bring them in,' she promised.

'I used to cheat,' he said, 'because Mandy used to make brownies for me to bring in. Nowadays I cheat and just buy a ton of brownies from the bakery down the road.'

'You don't fancy trying to make them yourself—burned baked beans aside? I have an easy one-step recipe—you just dump everything in a bowl and then mix it together.'

He shook his head. 'It'd just be a waste of ingredients. Baking isn't my thing.'

'I miss baking for school coffee mornings,' she said. 'And, as I'm an only child, I miss cooking big family meals. The Sunday roast, or the curry night. The nearest I get to it is batch-cooking a lasagne and putting individual portions in the freezer.' She smiled. 'Though Steve's family have told me I'm not getting away from them that easily and, in their view, I still count as part of them.'

'That's nice.' Thought he wasn't surprised that her ex's family wanted to keep her close. Rachel Halliday was lovely, the sort of woman whose smile made the day feel that little bit brighter. 'So what does my new second-best friend do on her days off?'

'Read, go for walks, maybe go to the cinema or the theatre—I don't mind going to see things on my own if nobody else fancies going with me,' she said. 'Sometimes I dance around the house, singing my head off to the old stuff. Oh, and I'm a bit of a crossword addict. What does my new second-best friend do?'

He'd been a hermit for the last couple of years, except for when his best friend or the girls had dragged him out. And he knew he spent too much time at work. It was easier to fill his head with paperwork that needed doing rather than face the emptiness of his house. He just hoped it would get better when Hannah was on maternity leave and he could do a bit of babysitting. 'I go to the odd gig,' he said. 'And I try to avoid dinner parties when I suspect I'm going to be set up with someone.' He paused. 'Maybe we could go for a walk together, some time.'

'I'd like that,' she said. She glanced at her watch. 'And I need to stop taking up all your time.'

'The laundry's winning, now you've got your cheese?' he teased.

'Afraid so.' She smiled. 'I learned the hard way that it's easier to do things in smaller chunks; if you let them build up, they're a lot more daunting and take a lot more mental effort.'

'Good point. I, too, ought to do some laundry.' He couldn't quite bring himself to admit that he paid a cleaner to do his ironing as well as keep the house clean. It sounded too entitled.

'Thank you for bringing me here,' she said.

'My pleasure. I'd better let you go, as I need to pick up a couple more things while I'm in town,' he said. It wasn't actually true, but he didn't want her feeling obliged to offer to wander round the centre of Muswell Hill with him. Particularly as he was aware that he did actually want to spend more time with her, and that was a dangerous thing. He wasn't quite ready to move on from the past, and he had a feeling that it was pretty much the same for her. For both their sakes, it would be much more sensible to leave things be.

'I'll see you on Monday. Thanks for the coffee,' she said.

'My pleasure,' he said.

And oh, that smile. It warmed him all the way through and made him want to ask her to stay a bit longer. But that really wouldn't be a good idea. He had nothing to offer her; and he didn't want to make life complicated for either of them. So he smiled back and left the café.

CHAPTER THREE

RACHEL WAS ON a late shift on Monday; just after she'd started, an elderly man was brought in with a suspected AAA—an abdominal aortic aneurysm, which was a bulge in the main blood vessel running from the heart to the abdomen. As the swelling grew larger, the walls of the blood vessel grew thinner, and if the aneurysm ruptured the patient could bleed to death.

'This is a tricky one,' Samir, the paramedic who was doing the handover, said. 'John Reynolds, aged eighty-six. He had a fall this morning and he'd got pain in his lower back—the paramedics who saw him thought it was probably a fractured hip and took him in to his local hospital. No fracture, but they think it's an AAA. Apparently, he had a small one twenty-five years ago, but he took the advice to stop smoking, change his diet and start exercising, and according to him he's been fine ever since. He hasn't been on any medication at all, for the last seven years.'

Rachel raised her eyebrows. 'That's quite unusual, at his age.'

'I gather he's quite independent,' Samir said, 'and

he doesn't think very much of his GP, which is why he refuses to go to appointments—he says he'll go to the walk-in centre if he has a problem. Anyway, he says he's been really well in himself, until he fell today.'

'Any history of falls?'

'According to him, no. Today was different because he tripped over the cat. Right now he's worried about his cat, he's got a pain in the middle of his tummy, and both legs hurt.'

'Got it. Any next of kin?'

'His daughter, Marnie. She's on her way here,' Samir said. 'And she says the neighbour's looking after the cat, so we can tell her dad not to worry. I've already told him, but I think he could do with the reassurance if you don't mind repeating it.'

'Of course,' Rachel said. 'Thanks, Samir.'

When Samir brought the patient in, Rachel introduced herself swiftly. 'Samir tells me you've had a fall and thought you'd broken your hip, Mr Reynolds, but the local hospital couldn't see anything on the X-ray and thought you might have an aneurysm.'

'I told them, that was twenty-five years ago now,' Mr Reynolds said. 'I'm fine.'

'What hurts?' she asked gently.

'My tummy, and both legs,' he said.

'Did you hit your head at all when you fell? Can you remember blacking out, even for a few seconds?'

'I might've hit my head, but I don't remember blacking out,' he said.

'Would you mind if I examined you and did a couple of tests?' she asked. When he gave his consent, she added, 'Marnie's on her way in, by the way, and she says to let you know that your neighbour's looking after your cat, so don't worry.'

'Smudge. He's a dear little thing. But he got under my feet, this morning—he was fretting, because I was late giving him his breakfast—and that's why I fell,' Mr Reynolds said. 'I felt such a fool. I couldn't get myself up again and I had to press my bracelet to get someone to come and help me.' He rolled his eyes. 'Marnie will say she told me so.'

'To be fair,' Rachel said, 'I used to worry about my mum having a fall. I made her wear a bracelet, too—that meant she could keep her independence and I wasn't worried sick about her all the time.'

'You girls worry too much.' He patted her hand. 'Tough as old boots, me.'

'Let's have a look,' she said.

But she really wasn't happy with the feel of his stomach; his blood pressure was lower than she would've liked, and his heart rate was too fast. There were definitely signs of a bleed, somewhere. 'I'm going to send you for a CT scan,' she said, 'just to give me a better idea of what's happening. And I'm going to take some bloods to check a couple of other things.'

When the blood tests results came back, she really wasn't happy. His blood wasn't clotting properly and the balance of acids and alkalis wasn't right. The CT scan showed a mass in the psoas muscle—the one in the back of the abdominal wall that went down the leg. The mass could be a cyst but, together with the other symptoms, she thought it was likely to be a haematoma.

It wouldn't be an easy fix, because the muscle was hard to get to; plus there was a bleed on the brain that she wasn't happy about, either.

She headed for Tim's office. 'Got a couple of minutes?' she asked. 'I could do with a second pair of eyes on something.'

'Sure.'

She gave him a swift patient history and brought up the scan results on his screen. 'I'm thinking a psoas bleed, plus he hit his head when he fell and he's got a bleed there as well. And his bloods are all over the place.'

'I agree—that scan looks like a psoas bleed, and it's one for the surgical team,' he said. 'I think the best we can do is to sort his bloods here, if we can, and admit him to ICU for monitoring until the surgeons can get him on the table.'

By the time John Reynolds came back from his scan, he couldn't wiggle his toes and had no feeling in his feet or his right leg. Rachel's instincts were all on red alert: the symptoms meant that his peripheries were shutting down, and the bleed was getting more serious. She spoke to the surgical team and got him admitted to ICU. When his daughter arrived, Rachel took the time to explain what was happening and took her up to see her father. 'They'll have the most up-to-date information about how he's doing,' she said, 'and the surgeons will see you before they take your dad to Theatre.'

'He's done so well,' Marnie said. 'Most of his friends are gone, now, or are in nursing homes. That's why I suggested he adopted a cat, to give him a bit of company.'

She bit her lip. 'I feel so guilty now. I can't believe he tripped over Smudge.'

'You couldn't have predicted the fall,' Rachel reassured her. 'And you'd persuaded him to wear an alarm on his wrist, so he could call for help, so you did the right thing there as well.'

Marnie nodded. 'I was panicking in case he'd fractured his hip and would have to go into a nursing home for months—he'd hate it, even though my neighbour works in one that's good and they'd look after him there as well as I would. But he's in better shape than some of *my* friends, and he can give most of them a good thirty years.'

'It's hard to lose your independence,' Rachel agreed. 'I felt really guilty about my mum going into a nursing home, but she needed more care than I could give her, and it was the best way to keep her safe. If your dad needs extra rehab after here, it won't be for a hugely long time. He'll cope—and, as you say, he'll have the cat for company when he gets back to his own place.' She just hoped that the surgeons could fix that bleed.

But, at the end of her shift, Theatre called down with the bad news: John hadn't made it off the operating table. Rachel could feel the tears pricking her eyelids. She forced herself to blink them away so she could deal with her last patient professionally, but by the time she'd changed out of her scrubs she was swallowing hard.

'Are you OK?'

She glanced up at Tim. 'Fine,' she fibbed.

He clearly wasn't buying it. 'What happened?'

'The patient I saw you about—he didn't make it.'

'I'm sorry.' He patted her shoulder awkwardly. 'You did your best for him. You did all the right things. A psoas bleed is hard to fix, and a bleed on the brain as well was a complication too many.'

She was incredibly aware of him. Where his hand had touched her shoulder, even though her scrubs had been a barrier between their skin, she tingled: which was crazy, not to mention inappropriate. Tim was her boss, and he was treating her in exactly the same way that he treated everyone else in the department. Ediye had told her that when they lost someone, Tim always squeezed their hands and reminded them that they'd done their best and they couldn't save everyone.

'Yeah, I guess,' she said.

'It's always hard when you lose a patient,' he said. 'But you've got nothing to reproach yourself about. We can't save everyone—we try to, but it's not humanly possible.'

'I know.' But it didn't stop her wishing she'd been able to fix things. Or that sudden longing to lean on him. For goodness' sake. She was an experienced doctor. She knew that some conditions just weren't fixable, and she didn't need to lean on anyone.

His blue eyes were filled with kindness—and was there something else, too, or was she deluding herself? 'See you tomorrow,' she said.

Though she was still out of sorts when she got home, both from losing her patient and from struggling with her inappropriate feelings towards Tim.

'He's your head of department,' she told herself out loud. Ha. As if that mattered. Plenty of people dated colleagues. 'And he's not looking for anything from you other than friendship. That's what you agreed. So stop thinking about him in any other sense.'

Despite her pep-talk, she couldn't get Tim Hughes out of her head. She liked him. More than liked him. But she didn't want to make a fool out of herself by making an unwanted move. Could she even trust her instincts any more? If she made a mistake, and what felt like mutual attraction really was nothing more than a platonic friendship, working together would be incredibly awkward.

Baking, when she got home, made her feel a bit better. The next morning, she left a box of the cheese biscuits in the staff kitchen, with a note.

Help yourself, from Rachel.

And she left a smaller box of them on Tim's desk with another short note.

Thanks for being kind yesterday. Enjoy, with best wishes from your second-best friend.

Tim was on a late and caught up with her just before her break. 'Those biscuits you left me: are they the ones you were telling me about? They're amazing.'

'I put some in the staff room as well,' she said, 'but I know how quickly they vanish at family get-togethers, so I gave you a separate box because I wanted to make sure my fellow cheese fiend did actually get some.'

'You,' he said, 'are a superstar. Thank you.'

Funny how his praise made her feel so warm inside.

On Friday afternoon, Tim sought her out in the office where she was filling out paperwork. 'Are you busy tonight?'

'I have a hot date,' she said, 'with the ironing.'

'I saw what you did there. Very good.' He laughed. 'Seriously, though, are you busy? I was going to a gig with my best friend tonight, but he's been called in to do some very tricky spinal surgery and he can't make it. It'd be a pity to waste the ticket.' He named a band she'd loved in her early twenties. 'They're playing a tiny gig in Camden, as a warm-up for their new tour. Would you like to come with me?'

'I'd love to,' she said. 'How much do I owe you for the ticket?'

'Nothing, because it would've just gone to waste.'

'Then maybe I can buy you a pizza and a beer first,' she suggested.

'All right, it's a deal.'

A deal, not a date, she reminded herself: even though she had that funny, fluttery feeling in her stomach when he smiled at her. 'Let me know what time it starts and where,' she said, 'and I'll find us a table somewhere nearby.'

She booked a pizza place near to the venue for an hour before doors opened and texted him with the details. When she got home after her shift, she reminded herself there was nothing romantic about this and she was simply going to a show with a friend; she dressed casually in jeans, low-heeled ankle boots and a plain black T-shirt that wouldn't make her feel sweaty in the heat of the club. Tim was already at the pizza place when she arrived, and raised his hand to greet her from their table; again, she had to ignore that funny fluttery feeling in her stomach.

She enjoyed chatting with him about music and was delighted to discover that they had quite a crossover in their tastes. They spent a while swapping tales about gigs they'd enjoyed and their favourite albums, and Rachel couldn't remember the last time she'd enjoyed herself so much.

In the venue, they managed to find their way to the front. The support band was good, and the main band was three songs into their set when some lads behind them decided they wanted to make a mosh pit, pushing into the crowd before them and swaying back again.

'We can move to the side away from them, if you want to,' Tim said. 'Or I can stand here as a buffer.' He frowned. 'I don't see why we should have to miss out just because they're being selfish.'

'I'm happy to do whatever you want,' she said.

Tim shifted so he was standing behind her, with one arm either side of her braced against the barrier to protect her from the worst of the shoving. It made her feel warm all the way through; Steve wouldn't have taken her to see the band in the first place, let alone acted so protectively, and she really appreciated how safe Tim made her feel.

Plus, if she was honest with herself, she really liked having Tim's arms round her. It would be oh, so easy to let herself act on the attraction she felt towards him and let their relationship move past a simple friendship.

But was that what Tim wanted, too, or was he just being gentlemanly?

Asking was out of the question. She didn't want to risk making things awkward between them, either at

work or as part of their new friendship. But she was
aware of every movement he made, every brush of his
body against hers.

After the gig, Tim saw Rachel home to Hampstead. She
lived in a gorgeous period terraced house; he guessed
that, like himself and Mandy, Rachel and her ex had
bought the house years ago, before property prices had
gone completely insane. He walked down the tiled path
to the front door with her and waited while she extracted
her key from her jeans pocket—all the while trying
not to think about how well the soft denim hugged her
curves.

'Thanks for—well, protecting me at the gig,' she said.

'You're very welcome. I'm only sorry that those lads
had to be selfish and spoil it for everyone else.'

'It's not your fault, and I still enjoyed myself. The
music was great.' She gave him a slightly shy smile.
'Would you like to come in for coffee?'

If he had any sense, Tim thought, he'd say no and
make the excuse that they had work tomorrow. He'd already got too close to Rachel tonight, standing at the gig
with his arms round her. He'd done it primarily to protect
her from the pushing of the lads behind them; but he'd
enjoyed being close enough to her to feel the warmth of
her body and breathe in the sweet vanilla scent she wore.

He opened his mouth to make the excuse, and a completely different set of words tumbled out, because his
common sense clearly wasn't working in sync with his
mouth. 'That'd be lovely.'

She opened the front door and ushered him in to a hallway with black and white chequered tiles.

'This house is too big for just me. I'm kind of rattling around in it,' she said. 'But I'm not planning to downsize until both the girls have finished uni and are settled. I want to make sure they always have a home.'

He nodded. 'I know what you mean. Mandy and I kept dithering about downsizing, once the girls had graduated, and then we decided we needed room for any future grandchildren to come and stay. I'm kind of glad we did, especially now Hannah's going to have her first baby, but being the only person in a family home feels a bit...' He wrinkled his nose. 'As you say, rattling around.' And he wasn't ready to lose all the memories, starting over in a new home.

'The room on the left was Mum's room,' she said, gesturing to a door in the hallway. 'It's the guest room, now. The girls and I painted it over the summer. There's a bathroom en-suite, so if you need the loo that's probably the quickest, or there's a bathroom up the stairs and straight in front of you.'

She led him past the door on the right, which he assumed led to the living room, and through to the kitchen. There was a beech dining table with six chairs on one side of the room, in front of large French doors; the kitchen cabinets were all cream, and there was a pine dresser with blue glassware and pretty china cups and saucers on display. The room was tidy and the work surfaces uncluttered; there was a vase of flowers on the windowsill, next to a narrow tray which held three terracotta pots full of fresh herbs.

'Would you prefer coffee or tea?' she asked.

'Coffee, please—decaf, if you have it, and just a splash of milk.'

'I stick to decaf at this time of night, too,' she said, taking a jar from the fridge then shaking grounds into a cafetière.

'What, no posh coffee machine?' he teased.

'No—not when all the pods end up in landfill,' she said. 'This is a bit old-fashioned, but it works just fine, and I can save the grounds for mulch in the garden.'

'My girls have nudged me into a few eco changes, over the years,' he said. 'I can't quite bear to give up my coffee machine, but Sophie found these metal pods that you fill yourself, wash up and reuse rather than dump in the trash.'

'That's a good idea,' she said. 'I might look into doing that.'

He noticed the photographs held to the outside of the fridge with magnets. 'Can I be nosey?'

'Sure.'

There were photographs of Rachel with two girls who were clearly her daughters, and others with an older woman who looked so like her that it was obviously her mum. There was another snap with the four of them in front of a Christmas tree; Rachel and her mother were wearing Santa hats, the girls were sporting hairbands with reindeer antlers, and they were all laughing and holding up a glass of something bubbly.

'We took that one the Christmas before last,' she said, 'when Mum could still join in.'

Two Christmases ago. It had been his first Christmas

without Mandy, and he'd made sure that he was working a split shift so he was too busy to even think about what he was missing. Then he'd gone home and curled up in a bed that was way too wide and, knowing nobody would see, sobbed his eyes out for an hour.

Last Christmas had been rough, too. He'd worked a double shift to block it out.

This Christmas… He was dreading it. The misery and the memories and the loss, bound together with the guilt that he wasn't there enough for his girls. But working was the only way he knew how to keep everything from battering his heart. He could block out his feelings with work. He'd rather patch up the drunks who'd lost their temper and ended up in a family fight than ruin Christmas for either of his daughters by sitting brooding in a corner. Yet, at the same time, he felt guilty for not being there enough for them.

It looked as if Rachel loved Christmas as much as Mandy had. He'd bet she would make a traditional wreath for the door with her daughters, just as Mandy had, and put up a real tree, scenting the air with pine. The fir tree that Mandy had nurtured and brought in every year had remained outside for the last couple of years, completely neglected. Tim hadn't even been able to face putting up a small artificial tree, let alone decorating it, and he'd left all the Christmas cards in a heap on the sideboard rather than pegging them up on a string over the door.

He didn't know what to say. Part of him wanted to run and avoid any discussion about Christmas; yet part of him wanted to stay. Could Rachel help him see things differently and find a way back to all the warmth and the wonder?

As if she'd guessed what was going on in his head, she handed him a mug of coffee. 'Let's go and sit down.'

'Thank you.'

Not Christmas, he decided as he sat at the table opposite her. Think about anything except Christmas and all the happiness he'd taken for granted would carry on and on and on—but had abruptly stopped.

He stared out of the patio doors. Of course. He couldn't see it in the dark, but there was obviously a garden out there. And she'd said earlier about keeping her coffee grounds as mulch. This would be a safe topic of conversation. 'Are you much of a gardener?'

'Not really,' she admitted. 'The garden's mostly shrubs because one of my ex's friends started a landscape gardening business years ago and we asked him to design us something low-maintenance and child-friendly.' She smiled. 'And thankfully he comes back every autumn to prune everything for us and sort anything out that isn't quite working. But I've got also little clumps of spring bulbs from pots that the girls bought me over the years, and I planted out when they'd stopped flowering. The troughs on the patio are a bit bare at the moment, but in the summer they're full of wildflowers; it helps to bring the butterflies and bees into the garden.' She looked at him. 'Are you a gardener, then?'

'I'm not much of anything, really,' he said. Apart from being a workaholic. 'We have a few roses and things in the garden.' Things he'd neglected horribly, along with the fir tree, because nothing had felt right without Mandy.

'It's hard to find the time to do everything,' she said. 'I've learned not to beat myself up about it. With a job as demanding as ours, something has to give.' She chuckled. 'With me, it's the oven. I pay someone to clean it for me. And my living room only really gets a dusting and a proper hoovering when I know someone's coming over, because the kitchen is my favourite room in the house and it's where I spend most of my time.'

'It's a nice room,' he said. Warm. Comfortable. Inviting.

'The French doors and the windows make it really light in the daytime,' she said. 'And I'm not a big one for telly. I'd rather sit here with a mug of tea and read or listen to music.'

'That sounds good to me.' Tim was relieved that she'd managed to get his head to change gear; but she'd also given him something to think about.

I've learned not to beat myself up about it... Something has to give.

She was right. He was struggling—and he'd been struggling for a long time. Maybe it was time he admitted it, instead of beating himself up about it or trying to block it out with work. But the words stuck in his throat.

He finished his coffee and lifted his mug. 'I'll wash this up before I go.'

'No need,' she said, taking it from him.

'And I'd better let you get some sleep. Thank you for coming with me tonight.'

'Thank you for asking me. I really enjoyed it.'

He honestly meant to just kiss Rachel's cheek, as he would with any of his and Mandy's joint friends. But somehow his lips ended up touching the corner of her mouth. She froze. He was about to pull away and apologise, when she moved closer, and her lips brushed against his.

His mouth tingled where her lips touched his. The next thing he knew, they were really kissing; his arms were wrapped round her waist and hers were wrapped round his neck. And there was a warmth spreading through him, as if a long, icy, lonely winter had finally ended and spring was starting to break through.

He broke the kiss and rested his forehead briefly against hers. 'I'm sorry. That really wasn't meant to happen.'

'It hadn't been my intention, either,' she said. 'I know neither of us is looking for a relationship.'

'This thing between us was meant to be strictly friendship,' he said.

'It's what we agreed. I kept telling myself the same.' She rested her palm against his cheek, and her grey eyes were huge and serious. 'Except, if I'm honest, I *like* you, Tim. And I liked it when you put your arms round me at the gig tonight to protect me.'

If she could be honest about it, so could he. 'Me, too. I mean, about liking you. And about liking holding you tonight at the gig. It just felt right, being close to you.' He bit his lip, aware that neither of them had moved; his arms were still wrapped round her waist and hers were round his neck. 'So what do we do now? Pretend this didn't happen?'

'Right now,' she said drily, 'you couldn't get a blade of grass between us, so we can't exactly deny it's happening.'

'There is that,' he admitted. But where did they go from here? What did she want? What did *he* want? He wasn't sure. This whole thing scared and thrilled him at the same time. 'What do we do?' he asked.

'I don't know,' she said. 'Maybe I'm a bit set in my ways, but the whole idea of starting all over again, at the age of fifty-two, terrifies me. I don't even know where to begin dating again. How do you even meet someone?' She shook her head. 'I know there are internet dating sites, but how do you know people are telling the truth on their profiles? And going to a speed-dating evening or what have you just isn't my thing.'

'I've never done it. But I imagine it's like being on parade, pretending to be someone you're not, and being judged by people who don't know you.' He grimaced. 'Which sounds even worse than the set-up dates.'

'At least your friends *know* the people they're trying to set you up with and can reassure you that you've really got something in common, and that they're nice,' she agreed. She looked at him. 'So what happens now?'

He wanted to date her. At the same time, the idea made him antsy. What if it went wrong? Working together would be awkward. And what if it went right? Would that mean wiping Mandy completely out of his life?

As if she guessed what he was thinking—or, more likely, she had similar doubts—she said, 'Just so we're clear, if things do happen between us, I'm not trying to replace Mandy.'

'Thank you,' he said. 'And I'm not trying to replace your ex.' He paused. 'I really like you, Rachel, and I don't want to wreck what could be a really good friendship. But, at the same time, I think there's something else between us. Can we keep things low profile for now, until we've worked out where this thing between us is going and what we both want from it?'

'That's a really good idea.'

He kissed her. Just because he could. He'd almost forgotten what it felt like to kiss someone, and he really liked the feel of Rachel's mouth against his. 'Is it weird that I feel like a teenager again?'

'No,' she said, 'because so do I. Though I haven't dated anyone else since I met Steve, nearly a quarter of a century ago, and I don't have a clue what dating etiquette is, nowadays.'

Neither did he.

'What about the set-up dates?' he asked.

'They don't count,' she said, 'because if I accept an invitation to go and see my friends it isn't the same thing as accepting a date to have dinner with someone I've only just met.'

'I haven't dated anyone else since I met Mandy, which is even longer ago,' he said. 'So don't expect me to be smooth and suave and sophisticated.'

She laughed. 'I promise, as long as you don't expect me to be a siren.'

He gave her an assessing look. 'You have siren potential.'

'Honestly? I'd rather be in jeans and boots and a big

sweater, out for a long walk, than wearing high heels and a slinky dress at a cocktail party.'

'Me, too. Walks rather than cocktail parties, that is.' He rubbed the tip of his nose against hers. 'Are you off on Sunday?'

'Yes.'

'So am I. I'm going to my daughter Hannah's for dinner in the evening but, if it's not raining, how do you fancy a walk in Richmond Park on Sunday morning to see the deer? Maybe grab some lunch while we're out?'

'Going with the flow? That,' she said, 'sounds wonderful. Even if it rains, we can still go and see the deer; we'll just need to remember an umbrella and waterproof coats.'

'Great.' He kissed her again. 'I'll see you on Sunday. Shall I meet you here?'

'You live in Muswell Hill, right?'

He nodded.

'Then let's meet at Hampstead Heath station, because there's a direct overground train from there to Richmond.'

'All right. I'll see you on Sunday at Hampstead Heath station,' he confirmed. 'What time?'

'Quarter past nine?' she suggested.

'Perfect. See you then.' He stole a last kiss. 'Sweet dreams.'

CHAPTER FOUR

SUNDAY MORNING WAS Rachel's first 'first date' in nearly a quarter of a century, and she wasn't sure whether she was more excited or apprehensive about it. Part of her was dying to tell her best friend about it; but on the other hand she and Tim had agreed to keep this just between them, for now. Which made sense. If things went wrong, then Jenny would see the fact that Rachel had actually dated someone as the green light to set her up with someone else—whereas if things went wrong, she'd want a lot more time to regroup.

Despite what she'd told Tim about being more comfortable in jeans than in a cocktail dress, she made an effort with her hair and actually wore lipstick. She glanced out of the window, noting that it was frosty outside, and opted to wear her walking boots, slipping an umbrella into the pocket of her waterproof jacket.

Tim was waiting for her outside the train station. 'Hi.' He greeted her with a smile, then bent to kiss her cheek.

'Hi.' And it suddenly didn't matter that it was cold and damp and grey. It felt as if the sun had come out. Just being with him made the day feel brighter.

He held her hand all the way on the train to Richmond, and on the bus to Richmond Park itself. It was
sweet and cherishing and endearing, all at the same time.

'It's the perfect autumn day,' he said. 'I love this time
of year, when it's frosty and a bit misty, and you can
crunch through the leaves.'

'"Seasons of mist and mellow fruitfulness",' she
quoted. 'I used to love taking the girls to the park, all
wrapped up in scarves and gloves and coats, and we'd
look for conkers.'

'So did we. It feels like five minutes ago and twenty
years, all at the same time,' he said. 'Let's head this way
and see if we can find the deer.'

He held her hand as they walked through the park,
too. If anyone had told Rachel when she was fifteen that
it was just as thrilling to hold hands with someone in
your fifties as it was when you were in your teens, she
would never have believed them; yet it really was just
as heady and exciting. She could feel the blood thrum-
ming through her veins and butterflies in her stomach.
It was crazy. She hadn't been looking for a relationship.
And she definitely didn't want to repeat the heartache
she'd felt after Steve's final betrayal. Yet at the same
time, she was enjoying the anticipation and excitement
of a first date: those fizzy, sparkly feelings about all the
possibilities opening up before her.

The sun finally broke through the clouds, dispel-
ling the mist and turning the frosted grass and bracken
into glittering silver where its rays shone through the
branches of the almost bare trees. Here and there, the
last few leaves hung from the branches in shades of yel-

low and copper and ruby, the colours bright against the darkness of wet bark; fallen leaves had drifted like copper snow beneath the trees. It was the most gorgeous late autumn morning; then they rounded a corner and saw a red stag standing in the bracken, his head lifted and his antlers looking as if they were crowning him.

'Oh, look at him! He's beautiful. So majestic.' Rachel took her phone from her pocket and took a few snaps of the deer at a safe distance.

A second deer came to join the first, and then a third and fourth, the colour of their coats almost blending with the bracken; the females grazed with the stag looking over them, and Rachel stood watching them, with Tim's arms wrapped round her and his cheek pressed against hers.

'Aren't they stunning? This is the perfect Sunday morning,' he whispered against her ear. Then he kissed the spot just behind her ear and sent desire licking up her spine. She couldn't remember the last time she'd felt that heady, powerful need to kiss someone. Part of her worried that she was rushing into things, but the impulse to kiss him was too strong; she turned round in his arms so she could kiss him thoroughly.

When she broke the kiss, they were both shaking.

'I think a whole herd could've stomped past us, just now, and we wouldn't have noticed,' he said huskily.

She stroked his face. 'You're telling me.'

Was this weird, long-forgotten feeling blooming through him happiness? Tim wondered. He'd spent the last two and a half years burying himself in work, keeping himself too busy to think and to feel. But with Rachel, he was content. Something as simple as walking through the park, enjoying the autumn landscape and each other's closeness, had made him feel so much brighter.

His first proper date since he'd lost Mandy.

And there was something about Rachel Halliday that drew him, that made him want to step out of the shadows with her and seize the brightness. Maybe this could be his second chance. And this time he'd try harder to get it right, to balance his work and his life a bit better and reconnect properly with his daughters.

But in the meantime, he was going to live in the moment. Enjoy the gorgeous surroundings of the park with someone who noticed things, but who didn't feel the need to fill every moment with chatter. The more time he spent with Rachel, the more he liked her.

By lunchtime, they'd walked up an appetite; they found the café and loaded their trays with hot soup, fresh bread and a shared bowl of rosemary salted chips.

Rachel smiled as they sat down at one of the tables. 'Jenny would be nagging us about our salt intake if she saw this. But I think that hot, crispy chips *need* salt.'

'Agreed—plus we have wholemeal bread and vegetable soup, which is good for our gut biome,' Tim said. 'I reckon that cancels out the chips.'

'Good point,' she said.

There was a dimple in her cheek when she smiled; it was so, so cute. He smiled at her. 'I was wondering what made you decide to become a doctor?'

'I wanted to be a nurse or a doctor right from when I was tiny,' she said. 'I was always bandaging my teddy bears when I was a toddler, and my favourite Christmas present ever was a doctor's kit from my godmother. I used to take everyone's pulse and pretend to listen to their heart through my stethoscope.'

He could just imagine that.

'I was lucky,' she said. 'Mum always championed me, even though it was a bit of a struggle for money for me to go to university.'

'What about your dad?'

She shook her head. 'He hasn't been in my life for a very long time.'

Tim winced. 'I'm sorry. I didn't mean to bring up difficult memories.'

'Not a problem,' she said. 'I was lucky in having the best mum in the world. I have no regrets. So how about you? What made you want to be a doctor?'

'I was fascinated by science when I was at school,' he said. 'You know, all the kitchen science experiments—the vinegar and baking soda volcano, making a battery for a clock with a potato and zinc and copper wire, that sort of thing. My gran had been a chemist, so she encouraged me to do the experiments. But then she died from a heart attack when I was about ten. I missed her hugely, and it made me want to be a doctor, so I could save other people from having to lose their grans.'

'But you chose emergency medicine rather than cardiology?'

'The emergency department was my favourite rotation, in my houseman years,' he said. 'I like the mad pace, and the fact that we can actually see the difference we make to people's lives. What made you pick emergency medicine?'

'It was pretty tough to choose between emergency medicine and obstetrics,' she said. 'I really loved bringing a new life into the world, those first moments when you look into a baby's eyes and see all the wonder. But even more than that I love being able to save someone's life, being able to give people hope when they'd been expecting the worst.'

'There's nothing like it,' he agreed.

'Was anyone in your family a medic?' she asked.

He shook his head. 'As I said, Gran was a chemist, but it was industrial rather than pharmaceutical. I come from a long line of lawyers. That's what I was supposed to be, too—especially as I was my dad's only son. Even though my older sister has made a much better lawyer than I would ever have been, he wasn't very happy when I sat him down and explained that I wanted to be a doctor and I wasn't going to follow in his footsteps. I don't think he ever forgave me.' He smiled wryly. 'I always felt I was a disappointment to him, and I guess that's one of the reasons I worked so hard early on—I wanted to make him proud of me.' He shrugged. 'I guess it became a bit of an ingrained habit, and I carried on. Though I swore I'd never be like him with my girls—whatever they wanted to do, I'd support them and make sure they knew they'd always have my backing.'

'What do they do?'

'Hannah, my eldest, is an English teacher; she followed in her mum's footsteps. She's about to start maternity leave.'

'When's the baby due?' she asked.

'The middle of December,' he said.

'A Christmas baby. How lovely.' She smiled. 'Christmas will be really special for you, this year,' she said.

Tim had been blocking that out, because he had no idea how he was going to cope with it. He found Christmas hard enough as it was. Adding his first grandchild as well, a reminder of all the things he couldn't share with Mandy any more...

But Rachel had asked him about his daughters, and he didn't want her to notice that he was brooding. 'Sophie, my youngest, has set up her own digital marketing consultancy for small businesses. Don't ask me what she actually does, because she talks about stuff I really don't understand,' he said. Hoping to head the conversation far away from Christmas, he asked, 'What about your girls?'

'Meg's reading music in Manchester. She's already sorted out a place for her PGCE next September because she wants to teach music—the subject, that is, not an instrument.'

'What does she play?' he asked.

'Piano and guitar, though actually she can play any instrument she picks up. I think she's good enough to make a living professionally, but she says hardly anyone makes a decent living as a musician, and she doesn't want to be a session musician. She'd rather have a settled job in teaching and play in a band on the side for fun.'

'It sounds as if she's very sensible and practical,' Tim said. A lot like Rachel herself.

'She is,' Rachel said.

'What about your younger daughter?'

'Saskia's at Sheffield, reading biochemistry. She wants to work in a research lab and save the world—I think she'll do it, too, because she has a huge heart.'

Also like Rachel herself, Tim thought. The more he was getting to know her, the more he liked her.

They went for another wander through the park, and then Tim saw Rachel back to her house and kissed her goodbye on the doorstep.

'You're very welcome to come in,' she said.

'It's kind of you to ask,' he said, 'but Hannah's expecting me.' Part of him was tempted to ask Rachel to come with him; he knew his daughter wouldn't mind. On the other hand, he didn't want to rush this—and a selfish part of him wanted to keep Rachel to himself for a little longer. 'I'll see you tomorrow at work,' he said, 'and maybe we can go to the cinema in the week? I don't mind what we see, though I'm not a huge fan of gory stuff.'

'Me neither,' she said. 'I was planning to go and see that new comedy drama—the one that's been tipped for several awards.'

'I'd quite like to see that, too,' he said.

She smiled. 'All right. I'll check the listings and book something. Which evening's good for you?'

'I'm on early shifts Tuesday, Wednesday and Thursday,' he said, 'so any of those work for me.'

'OK. I'll sort it out and let you know,' she said.

Another date. Part of Rachel worried that this wasn't a good idea. She wasn't looking for a permanent relationship, and her experiences with Steve had made her wary of trusting her heart to anyone else. On the other hand, she liked what she'd seen of Tim, and she wanted to get to know him better. And it would be nice to see a film with someone else, so they could chat about it afterwards.

In the end, she booked tickets for the Thursday evening.

'Do you want to grab something to eat, first?' Tim asked.

'I thought we could eat at the cinema,' she said.

'There's a café?'

'Not exactly. Instead of normal cinema seats, they have sofas with tables, so you place your order on their app, and the staff bring the food and drink to your table,' she explained.

'What a great idea,' Tim said. 'As you bought the tickets, I'll buy the food and drink.'

They shared several dishes between them and a bottle of Pinot Grigio, and Rachel thoroughly enjoyed the film. And most of all she enjoyed holding hands with Tim all the way through the second half: being with someone who was actually present, instead of checking his phone every five minutes.

As the screening finished reasonably early, Tim suggested having coffee at his place.

'I'd love to,' she said.

They chatted about the film all the way on the Tube and then as they walked to Tim's house. He led them down a tiled pathway to a large Edwardian terraced house with a large bay window.

'It needed a bit of work when we bought it, but it had so many original features and we fell in love with those,' he said. 'Those six-over-two panes in the windows, the spandrels in the porch, and the leaded lights in the door.'

'It looks lovely,' she said.

'Let me give you the guided tour,' he said, opening the front door. 'Hallway, obviously.' The hallway had its original geometric tiled flooring, with the wooden panelling beneath the dado rail painted a soft dove grey, and the wall above painted cream. He gestured to a door on the left. 'Obviously the downstairs toilet isn't original, though we went for Edwardian-style fittings when we could afford it.' He led her through the first door. 'Living room.' The walls were painted Wedgwood blue, with cream paintwork; there was a huge mirror over the original cast-iron fireplace, and overstuffed bookshelves either side of the chimney breast. There was a large geometric-patterned rug on the polished floorboards, and the navy sofas with their cushions embroidered in jewel-like colours looked incredibly comfortable. It would be the perfect reading nook, she thought.

There was a collection of photo frames along the mantelpiece. 'Can I be nosey?' she asked.

'Sure.'

The photos were a similar mix to the ones in her own house: Tim's wedding to Mandy, graduation photos of themselves with their own parents and then with their daughters, and a couple of what were clearly much-loved candid family snaps taken in the garden or on holiday. She could see that Tim's daughters had inherited his dark hair and cornflower-blue eyes rather than Mandy's blonde hair and lighter blue eyes. And they seemed a warm, close, loving family—much like she'd tried so hard to make her own to be.

'Mandy looks a really lovely person,' she said. There was a sunniness about her in the photographs that made Rachel think they would've been friends, if they'd ever met.

'She was,' Tim said. 'But I'm not comparing you to her. You're very different. Both lovely, in your own ways.'

Rachel smiled. 'I wasn't fishing for a compliment.'

'I know. But it's kind of awkward…' He tailed off.

She knew what he meant: his very new girlfriend seeing photographs of his late wife. Yet this was still very early days between them; and she'd never been the jealous type. Right now, there was nothing to be jealous about. And, even if it did work out between them, she believed that hearts expanded and there would be room in his life for both herself and his memories of Mandy. 'It's fine. I've always thought that feelings aren't like a piece of cake where you have to grab the plate back and chop off a corner to give to someone else.'

'Because then all you'd be able to offer someone is a pile of crumbs,' he said.

'I'd be more concerned if you'd put all the photos away in a box and were pretending that Mandy never existed. I still have a couple of framed photos in the house with Steve, the girls and me, because there were some good times as well as the rough bits. At the end of the day, he's still their dad and I don't want to cut him out of their lives.' Her ex was doing a good enough job of that by himself, she thought.

'Fair point. This is obviously the dining room,' he said as he took her through to the next room. The walls were painted sage-green; again there was cream paint-work and polished floorboards, an original cast-iron and tiled fireplace, and there was a large table in the cen-tre with eight chairs. The curtains were a green Morris print; there was a reproduction of Monet's *Water Lily Pond* on one wall, and another of two little girls in a garden of lilies.

'John Singer Sargent,' he said, noticing her gaze. 'Mandy loved that painting since the moment she first saw it in the Tate. I bought her a proper art print, and had it framed for her birthday a few years back.'

'It goes really well with this room,' she said.

'Yeah.' He took her through to the kitchen. 'Mandy was the cook. I'm afraid I just shove stuff in the micro-wave or the toaster,' he said with a wry smile, 'and even then, you can't assume that I checked the toaster settings before I shoved the bread in.'

It was the kind of kitchen that cried out to be the hub of a family home, with its grey-painted cabinets and beech worktops and a matching table and chairs at one end. Though it looked more like a showroom kitchen than one that was used, Rachel thought; there were no herbs or plants growing on the windowsill, and there wasn't so much as a newspaper on the table. There was a calendar on the wall, but there were no dates filled in, and she noticed that the page on display was still that of the previous month. Rachel could've wept for him; it was obvious that he was lost without the centre of his family.

He took her through to the final room, which led off the kitchen. 'This is the garden room. We had it built when the girls were teenagers, though we did re-use the original back door.' The wall that wasn't glass had been painted cream, with a large clock set on it, and the whole thing was light and airy. There was a large potted palm in one corner, and an oversized clock on the wall; fairy lights were draped artfully round the window frames and the top of the painted wall, and the sofa and chairs looked incredibly comfortable, piled with cushions. She could imagine his girls here with their friends, just as her daughters would've been: mugs of coffee on the table and music playing as a background to chatter and laughter.

'Righty. I promised you coffee.' He led her back to the kitchen. 'Take a seat.' He measured coffee into a metal gadget she assumed was the reusable pod he'd told her about and set the machine running while he took two mugs from the cupboard.

'Tell me about Mandy,' she said.

'We met at uni. Mandy was doing her teacher training year, and I was in my last year—I was a year older than her,' he said. 'We were both out with a group of friends. Someone jostled her at the bar, and she ended up spilling the best part of a glass of red wine over me.'

'A bit of a different way to meet,' she said with a smile; though she was pretty sure that Tim would have laughed it off rather than having had a hissy fit about wine spilling over his clothes.

'She asked if she could take me for a pizza, the next night, to apologise for covering me in wine. I said she didn't need to apologise, but I liked the way she smiled so I said yes to the pizza, and we'd go halves on the bill.' He looked wistful. 'We just clicked, and we talked for hours, that night. We just didn't notice the time, and the staff ended up having to ask us to leave because they wanted to close the restaurant.' He smiled. 'We got married just after we graduated. The first year was a bit tough—you know what junior doctor hours are like, and it was her first year as a secondary school teacher—but we got through it. We were a team. The plan was that she'd make assistant head of department and I'd be a registrar before we started trying for children—but Hannah had other ideas and made her appearance a year or so earlier than we'd expected.' His face softened. 'Becoming a dad—I thought I knew it all, being a medic. I mean, I'd even delivered a baby. But nothing prepared me for how it felt when I looked into our little girl's eyes for the first time. That rush of love just blew me away. And it was the same when Soph arrived. I'm not one to cry in public, but I bawled my eyes out when I first held them,' he confessed. 'And both our girls have been brilliant, this last couple of years.'

'The perfect family?' she asked lightly.

'No, a *normal* family,' he corrected. 'We don't always agree on things. Mandy and I used to row over me working too hard, and I admit I missed most of the girls' sports days.' He wrinkled his nose. 'I was late for parent-teacher evening a few times, but I never missed one of their performances—whether it was one of the girls singing "Twinkle, Twinkle, Little Star" at an end-of-term nursery school concert, right through to Hannah playing Lady Macbeth in sixth form and doing the whole "out, damn'd spot" bit. I was always there, as near to the front as I could get, and made sure they could see me clapping and cheering them on. We used to take them out for dinner after the performance to make a fuss of them and tell them how proud we were of them.'

Meg and Saskia couldn't say the same about their own dad, Rachel thought with a pang. Two times out of three, Steve had found an excuse why he couldn't make it to a school performance, and he'd almost never made parent-teacher evenings, saying that Rachel was much better at dealing with them than he was. Only now, with the benefit of hindsight, had Rachel realised it hadn't been work keeping him away: it had been a stolen date with his latest mistress.

Tim put a mug of coffee in front of her.

She took a sip. 'This is perfect,' she said. 'Thank you.'

'My pleasure.' He opened a tin marked *Biscuits* and wrinkled his nose. 'Stale digestives. Not the sort of thing you should offer a guest.' Then he rummaged in a cupboard and emerged waving a packet of biscuit curls, which he decanted onto a plate. 'I hoped I still had these. I'll replace them before Hannah drops round next—it's her latest pregnancy craving,' he said.

Tim Hughes was definitely the sort of man who'd notice something like that and act on it, she thought, touched. The little things added up and made a lot.

'Tell me about Steve,' he said.

'We met at a party when I was doing my last year as

a house officer,' she said. 'He was a friend of a friend. He worked in advertising, so he had the gift of the gab and a boatload of charm—and the most soulful brown eyes. You know how it's impossible to resist a spaniel?' At Tim's nod, she continued, 'It was like that with him. One look and I'd just melt. And he made me laugh. I thought I'd found my perfect partner. We'd been together for almost a year when he took me to this little café opposite the Eiffel Tower for breakfast. I'd ordered an almond croissant, and it came out on a plate with *Veux-tu m'épouser?* written in chocolate beside it, and on top of the croissant there was a tiny paper case with a solitaire diamond nestled in it.'

It was nothing like Tim's own proposal to Mandy on a beach in Northumbria, when they'd gone for a walk, got totally drenched in an unexpected rainstorm, and he'd apologised but she'd just laughed off the fact that they were both soaked and freezing. That moment, he'd realised she was the one he wanted to spend the rest of his life with, and he'd asked her to marry him. No ring, no witnesses, nobody to document the moment. Just the two of them, a kiss and a promise they'd both kept until she'd died.

Then he realised Rachel was waiting for him to respond. 'Very romantic,' he said, trying to be diplomatic. Though if she wanted grand, flashy gestures from him, she'd end up very disappointed. That wasn't who he was.

'It did kind of sweep me off my feet. I said yes. And I thought we were happy,' she said. 'Steve was working his way up the ladder at work, so he had to put the hours in; and, as you said, there's never any time when you're a junior doctor because you're always on call. But then I fell pregnant with Meg, and I had really hideous morning sickness. Not quite hyperemesis but getting on that way.' She paused. 'That was when he had his first affair.'

Tim stared at her, shocked. His *first* affair? That meant her husband must've had more than one fling. And the timing, when Rachel had been so vulnerable, pregnant and suffering with morning sickness... Even though he knew it was none of his business, he couldn't help asking, 'Why did you stay with him?'

'I was going to leave him,' Rachel said. 'I talked it over with Mum, hoping that she'd let me come back to stay with her until I could find a flat for me and the baby. But she'd been there, too. When she found out my father was actually working his way through her friends, she left him. But her parents were from the generation who didn't believe in divorce—they said she'd made her bed, so she had to lie on it.'

'Harsh,' Tim said.

She nodded. 'My dad was about as reliable at seeing me and making maintenance payments as he was at being faithful, so we struggled a lot when I was little. Mum didn't want my life to be as tough as hers had been, and she talked me round. The way she saw it, being a single mum is really difficult. Not just financially, but the fact that you're the one who has to make all the decisions, and you haven't got anyone to share the worries with, or anyone who can take over and let you sleep when you're bone-deep tired and terrified of letting yourself drift off in case you're sleeping so heavily you don't wake when the baby cries. And she persuaded me that maybe Steve had made a mistake because I'd had a tough pregnancy and he simply wasn't coping with seeing me so poorly and knowing he couldn't really do anything to help me.'

Tim didn't think that was anywhere near a good enough excuse, but it wasn't his place to say so.

'Except,' she said quietly, 'Steve did exactly the same thing when I was pregnant with Saskia. For him it was more of a three-year itch than a seven-year itch. He was good with the girls when they were little, and I wanted them to grow up in a stable home rather than waiting for a dad who never turned up, the way I had, so I put up with it.' She grimaced. 'I always knew when he'd started an affair, because he'd be late home all the time and suddenly start having to work weekends at the office; and I always knew when it ended because he'd be back to being home at a normal time and he'd bring me flowers every Friday night.'

Tim had always brought Mandy flowers on a Friday night: not because he'd had a guilty conscience, but because he knew how much she loved fresh flowers and he'd liked to see the pleasure in her eyes when he gave them to her. It had been one of the little rituals that helped cement a marriage.

'Looking back now, I guess I'd always known that Steve was selfish, but in the early years I managed to justify it to myself,' Rachel said. 'He had a high-pressure job.'

And a doctor in the emergency department had a

low-pressure job? Tim didn't ask the question, but he felt cross on her behalf.

'He was busy at work.'

That went for doctors, too. Tim's crossness intensified. 'So I guess you wish you hadn't listened to your mum?' he asked.

'Sort of,' she said, 'though Mum did give me one really solid bit of advice: to keep my money separate from Steve's and have a joint account just for bills. She'd had money when she got married to my dad, but everything had been in their joint account, and he cleaned her out when she left him.' She gave him a wry smile. 'Steve was almost as bad with money as my dad was. He liked designer clothes and very posh restaurants. When he bought me flowers, the bouquets were always really fancy ones from an expensive florist. I always felt so bad about him spending so much money on something so frivolous; I would much rather have had a cheap bunch of daffodils or what have you and given the rest of the money to charity.'

Oh. So she *didn't* like flashy gestures. Tim was relieved. 'So what made you finally leave him?'

'I didn't. He left me,' Rachel said. She shrugged. 'Ironically, I had been planning to leave him once the girls were both settled at uni. But then Mum was ill with dementia.' She grimaced. 'I'm not proud of myself for manipulating Steve, but he'd just come out of an affair, and he was always a bit more likely to agree to things when he was feeling guilty. I told him I wanted to take a sabbatical and move Mum in with us for a few months, to look after her for as long as I could. The girls wanted her to be with us, too. But then Mum started calling him by my dad's name, and Steve got really upset about it. He couldn't see that she was confused and didn't mean to call him by the wrong name.'

'It sounds as if you married a man like your dad, and maybe when your mum was ill, she could see that,' Tim said carefully.

'And maybe he realised it, too. He definitely resented the time I spent with Mum, thinking I should've been focusing on him. Eventually he gave me an ultimatum: either I had to put Mum in a home, or he'd leave, because what we had wasn't a marriage any more.'

Tim winced. 'I know I shouldn't judge, but that's *incredibly* mean-spirited. Your mum was ill and you wanted to support her and spend time with her.'

She nodded. 'I called his bluff. And he left.' She looked away. 'It turned out he was seeing someone else. I'd just been so busy with Mum that this time I'd missed the signs. It was before the no-fault divorce rules came in, or I would have agreed to that. But Steve decided to sue me for divorce on the grounds of unreasonable behaviour.'

The more Tim heard, the more he disliked Rachel's ex. How could anyone be that self-centred?

'Unfortunately for him, my solicitor was very good, and Steve discovered that the courts didn't see things in quite the same way that he did. Adultery, on the other hand, did count as unreasonable behaviour—on his part. It got a bit acrimonious, though we're just about civil now, for the girls' sake. And because, once probate from Mum's flat had been agreed, I bought him out of our house.' She looked bleak. 'Actually, I did move my mum into a nursing home, towards the end, and I felt so guilty about it. But Mum needed more care than I could give her, and I wanted her to be comfortable. I visited her every single day. The staff were brilliant—when I came into the reception area, they used to tell me what kind of night she'd had and what sort of mood she was in, and whether she'd taken part in activities. They were so upset when she died. A dozen of them came to her funeral.'

Tim reached across the table to squeeze her hand. 'I'm sorry about your mum. And I'm sorry your ex didn't support you through her last illness. No wonder you're wary of starting another relationship. It must be so hard to trust again when someone's treated you like that.'

'Yes—and that's trusting my own judgement as well as trusting someone else,' she said. 'But it's been hard for you, too. You were happy with Mandy until she died, and you never expected your life to change so suddenly.' She looked at him, her grey eyes wide with sincerity. 'I hope you know I'm not trying to step into her place in your life.'

'I do,' he said. 'It's different—and it's kind of weird, dating again after all these years with one person. I've no idea what the dating rules are nowadays.'

'Neither have I,' she said. 'So let's make a pact. We'll just be ourselves and not what we think each other wants us to be.'

'That works for me,' he said, and chinked his empty coffee mug against hers. 'Here's to getting to know each other and being honest with each other.'

'Getting to know each other and being honest with

each other,' she echoed. 'And ourselves.' She glanced at her watch. 'I really ought to be going.'

'I'll see you home,' he said immediately.

She shook her head. 'You don't have to do that. I'll be fine.'

'At least let me walk you to the station,' he said. 'I know you're perfectly capable of looking after yourself; but, apart from the fact that it's the way my parents brought me up, there's a very selfish bit of me that means I don't quite want to let you go.'

To his relief, she agreed; and he walked hand in hand with her to the station.

'Thank you for this evening. I really enjoyed it,' he said.

'Me, too. And thank you for the coffee.'

He kissed her lightly. 'My pleasure. See you tomorrow.'

And he was smiling all the way home. It was still early days between them but letting her a tiny bit more into his life felt good. Maybe, just maybe, she was the one who'd help him move on from the yawning ache of loss—just as he might be the one who could help her move on after an unhappy marriage to a truly selfish man.

CHAPTER FIVE

'PETER BELLINGHAM, AGED FIFTY-SIX,' Lorraine the triage nurse said. 'He had chest pains, and I've run an ECG but it's clear. He's got a headache and a temperature, he's been feeling unwell for about four days, and he looks as if he's got mumps. He didn't want to come in and he's convinced it's all a fuss about nothing, but his wife insisted on bringing him in.'

'Thanks, Lorraine,' Rachel said, and introduced herself to the patient and his wife when they came through.

'I don't know why we're here. It's just a bug,' Peter Bellingham protested. 'The nurse said my ECG was fine and it's not my heart.'

'But you've got a headache and a temperature, you've had chest pains, and there's the swelling in your neck,' Rachel said. Bilateral, she noticed, around his jaw and lower neck. 'What do you do, Mr Bellingham?'

'I'm a plumber,' he said.

'So if someone's got a dripping tap, or their sink is a bit slow in emptying, would you advise them to sort it out quickly or just leave it until, say, they have their yearly boiler service?'

'Get someone out,' he said, 'because if you leave that sink it'll end up being blocked and it'll be a lot more hassle and cost more to sort out.'

'That's precisely why you're here,' Rachel said with a smile. 'Because if you leave it, you could end up with complications. Would you mind if we examined you?'

'It's just a bug,' he insisted. But then he sighed. 'All right. Go ahead, because it'll stop Sheena worrying when she really doesn't need to.'

She checked his lymph glands and looked in his mouth. His tongue was swollen, as were the tissues under his tongue. She noticed that his submandibular area was tense; it could be a dental abscess, which in turn was causing something more serious. 'Mr Bellingham, have you had any pain in your teeth?' she asked.

'No. Just my neck.'

'I think you might have something called Ludwig's angina,' she said, 'but I want to put a camera down your nose to look at the top part of your airway.'

He frowned. 'Angina? Isn't that to do with my heart? I think one of my uncles had angina—isn't that right, Sheena?'

'I think so,' his wife said.

'Ludwig's angina isn't to do with your heart. It's a type of cellulitis—a bacterial infection involving the inner layers of your skin,' Rachel explains. 'It causes swelling in your neck, which you've already noticed, and swelling in the floor of your mouth.' And it was time-critical, because when the tongue started swelling it could become difficult to stop the airway being compromised. 'I'm going to put a spray up your nose, so it won't be so uncomfortable when I put the tube with the camera in. Are you OK with that?'

He looked fed-up but agreed.

Rachel went to fetch the camera, and bumped into Tim.

'Camera?' he asked, glancing at the instrument in her hand.

'I've got a patient that I think has Ludwig's angina,' she said.

'That's rare. Dental abscess?'

'I think so,' she said. 'But obviously I need to check. If he'd left it much longer, I might've had to give him a tracheotomy to preserve his airway. I still might.'

'Along with the possibility of sepsis and complications,' he said. 'Give me a yell if you need an extra pair of eyes, but your treatment plan sounds the same as mine would be.'

'Cheers,' she said, buoyed by his support.

The camera gave her a good view of her patient's vocal cords, and the swelling was obvious. 'Mr Bellingham, I'm going to send you for a CT scan to see if any pus needs draining—but I think you have an abscess under your tooth, and it's given you a bacterial infection which is causing the pain, the lump in your neck, and the fact you're finding it harder to swallow. The maxillofacial surgeons will have to remove that abscess for you, under a general anaesthetic, and we'll give you antibiotics to sort out the infection. You'll need help breathing until it's all settled down, so we'll need to admit you. And you're lucky you didn't delay it much longer, because it can lead to sepsis—which can be fatal.'

'I could've died?' He looked shocked. 'I thought my wife was just making a fuss.'

'No. You made a good call,' Rachel told his relieved-looking wife.

He shook his head. 'And I don't understand how it can be a tooth abscess when my mouth doesn't hurt.'

'Not all abscesses hurt,' Rachel explained. 'But I'm glad you got it checked out. If you'd left it longer and your throat had started swelling, we might've had to give you a tracheotomy.'

'What, where you have to put a hole in my throat?' He looked shocked.

'In other words, stop being a stubborn middle-aged man,' Sheena Bellingham said, her teasing belied by the worried look in her eyes.

'You did the right thing, making him come in,' Rachel reassured her.

Once Mr Bellingham had the CT scan and Rachel had called down the maxillofacial surgeons, he was taken off to Theatre.

She saw Tim briefly in the staff kitchen during her break and filled him in on her patient's progress.

'That's good to hear. Now, I'll keep this really quick, because it isn't work,' Tim said, clearly mindful that someone else from the team could come into the kitchen at any minute. 'When are you off duty next?'

'Wednesday,' she said.

'Perfect. If the weather's reasonable, do you fancy a day at the beach?'

'That'd be great,' she said. 'Actually, I prefer the beach in autumn and winter.'

'Me, too. I'll call you tonight after work,' he said, 'and we can decide where to go.' He gave her one of those gorgeous smiles that reached his eyes and made her stomach flip, then headed out of the staff room to his office.

True to his word, he video called her later that evening. 'I've been looking at our options. If we go by train, we can reach Brighton in an hour. So we can have an ice cream on the pier; perhaps a look round the Pavilion, if we can get tickets; and a wander through The Lanes, mooching about in the art galleries and antique shops,' he said. 'Or we can get to Rye in about the same amount of time, catch a bus and find ourselves a nice sandy beach to walk along, then go back and explore the town.'

'That's pretty hard to choose,' she said. 'How about we do one this month and one next month?'

'Great idea,' he said, and took a coin from his pocket. 'You call.'

'Heads Rye, tails Brighton,' she said.

He tossed the coin and checked it. 'Heads,' he said, showing her the coin lying on the back of his hand. 'Rye it is.'

'I can't remember the last time I went to Rye. I was probably quite young,' she said.

'It'll be fun,' he promised.

They caught the train from St Pancras on Wednesday morning, then the bus from Rye station to the beach. The weather was perfect; the sun turned the sandy beach to gold, and the sea was a beautiful bright blue. Rachel enjoyed walking hand in hand along the beach with Tim, hearing the swish of the sea as the waves rolled lazily onto the shore and hissed back again. The wind whipped by them, making the top layer of sand spin across the beach; she kissed him, tasting the salty air on his lips. 'This was a great idea of yours,' she said. 'Just us and the sand and the waves.'

When they'd finished their walk and Rachel had taken a couple of snaps of them together, they caught the bus back into town and wandered through the charming cobbled streets, enjoying the view of the higgledy-piggledy half-timbered houses with their mullioned windows. They stopped in a charming ancient pub with heavily beamed ceilings and found a table by the inglenook fireplace with its roaring fire.

'According to the website,' Tim said, 'this place used to be home to smugglers.'

'So those cutlasses on the walls might've once belonged to a pirate,' she said.

'And it's haunted,' Tim said. 'There's a priest's hole in the chimney breast, and that door behind me led to what were once secret tunnels.' He smiled. '"Watch the wall, my darling."'

'You've lost me,' Rachel said.

'It's a poem about smugglers. I can't remember who wrote it, but Hannah did it with her Year Sevens and I remember her doing the lesson prep for it round our kitchen table with Mandy.' He laughed. 'They did the entire thing in pirate speak. And I think Hannah borrowed a pirate hat and eyepatch to teach it.'

'Arr, that be a great idea,' Rachel said, in her best pirate voice, and he groaned.

After lunch, they explored the narrow streets a bit more before taking the train back to London.

'We ought to make a list of places we want to see,' Tim said. 'And things we'd like to do.'

'Hampstead Pergola,' she said. 'And that's open all year round. So we could go later in the winter if it's snowing, or wait for the wisteria in the spring, or just go and see the autumn leaves everywhere right now.'

'All three work for me.' He took his phone out. 'And I've always wanted to do one of those tours when you get to see the Tube stations that aren't open to the public any more. Like going back in time.'

'I'd like that, too. And Hampton Court. For the maze,' she said.

'We could go by river. It'd be fun.'

Between them, and with the help of a couple of websites, they came up with a list of museums, parks, stately homes and unusual buildings they wanted to visit by the time the train pulled into London.

'Thank you,' Tim said when he saw her home. 'I've really enjoyed today. And making our list. It's been a while since I let the world in. You've given me a new perspective.'

'You've done the same for me,' she said. 'Right now is the most fun I've had in a long time.'

He kissed her lingeringly. 'Me, too. I'll see you tomorrow at work.'

On Friday the following week, they spent the morning wandering round the museum at the Royal College of Physicians, fascinated by the seventeenth-century surgical instruments and the collection of everything from bezoar stones to leech jars, and then Tim glanced at his watch. 'Righty. Time for lunch.'

'Are we going to the museum café?' Rachel asked.

'No. I have a table booked somewhere I think you'll really like. And it's a nice day, so it's a pretty walk.'

They headed towards King's Cross and the Regent's Canal; the trees with their remaining few leaves were reflected perfectly in the water, looking incredibly pretty.

'So where are we heading? Islington?' she asked.

'Not quite,' he said.

A few minutes later, he stopped beside a narrowboat with 'The Cheese Barge' painted along its side. 'We're having afternoon tea for lunch,' he said. 'Except there's no cake.'

'Afternoon cheese,' she said with a smile. 'Sounds perfect.'

And it was: finger sandwiches, a mini cheese toastie and a mini English muffin topped with Welsh Rarebit, two warm cheese scones, and then a range of cheeses paired with very posh crackers, celery and grapes.

'And there's a pink sugar mouse,' she said, delighted. 'Tim, this is genius.'

'Isn't it just?'

After lunch, they walked along the canal to the Angel and caught the Tube back to Hampstead. They were curled up together on her sofa, kissing, when the front door banged.

'Mum, we're home! Surprise!' Meg and Saskia came into the living room, still wearing their coats because they were clearly too eager to see her to take them off and hang them up first; and then, seeing her move away from Tim on the sofa, they stopped dead. 'Oh.'

Busted, Rachel thought. Very busted. She hadn't been ready to tell her daughters about Tim, yet, but it looked as if she was going to have to explain. 'Let me introduce you,' she said. 'Meg, Saskia, this is Tim. My boss.'

He coughed. 'That's merely in admin terms. We work as a team in my department.'

'*Your* department,' Rachel teased.

Meg and Saskia looked at Tim, at how close he was sitting to their mother, and then at each other. Rachel could feel colour rising in her face. No doubt her mouth was slightly reddened and swollen, too. Ridiculously, it felt as if she and Tim were the teenagers and her mum had come in unexpectedly to find them kissing on the sofa, rather than her being the mum and her adult children being the ones walking in.

'It's nice to meet you, Tim,' Meg said politely, and held her hand out to shake his.

'Very nice,' Saskia added, shaking his hand in turn. 'It's about time Mum had something lovely going on in her life.' She gave Rachel a pointed look. 'Don't try to tell us you're just good friends, either.'

Yeah. She'd known that one wouldn't work.

'Do you mind?' Tim asked.

'No. Provided you don't behave like our dad did,' Saskia said bluntly.

'No. That's not who I am. And, if things work out between your mum and me, I wouldn't try to take his place,' he reassured them. 'Since you've both had a long train journey—Manchester and Sheffield, if I remember rightly—you must be in severe need of a mug of tea. Sit down with your mum and I'll go and put the kettle on. Milk? Sugar? And would you prefer tea or coffee?'

They smiled approvingly at him. 'Thank you. That's so kind. Coffee for me, please—just milk,' Meg said.

'Me, too, please,' Saskia said. 'Except—'

'You're vegan, so you need non-dairy milk,' he said. 'That's in the cupboard underneath the kettle, right?' he asked Rachel.

'Yes, it is,' she said, grateful for both his tact at giving her some time alone with her daughters, and the kindness of making them a hot drink after their journeys.

Meg and Saskia took off their coats and placed them on the back of an armchair; the second Tim had left the room, they pounced. 'You kept him quiet, Mum,' Meg said.

Rachel winced. 'It's early days. *Very* early days.'

'Do you like him?' Saskia asked.

'Yes,' Rachel confirmed.

'Then that's all right,' Meg said. 'Because he seems to like you, too.'

'I can't believe he knew about me having non-dairy milk,' Saskia said. 'Dad never remembers, and I've been vegan for two and a half years.'

'Tim's one of the good guys,' Rachel said softly. 'He notices the little things.' Though she couldn't say it was because of his job, because Steve would've needed to pay just as much attention to detail in his own job. The difference was, Tim didn't put himself first, second and third. Not that she wanted to point out Steve's faults in front of his daughters; she wanted to try and keep that

relationship as uncomplicated and smooth as possible.
'So you're both home for the weekend?'

'Yes. I know we should've checked you were off duty,
first, but we just wanted to see you,' Meg said.

She hugged them both in turn. 'You never, *ever* have
to ask to come home. You live here. And I've really
missed you both.'

They hugged her back even harder. 'Love you, Mum,'
Saskia said.

Tim came back in with tray of coffee and biscuits for
all of them, then sat chatting to Meg and Saskia about
their courses, and Meg's plans for teaching. Somehow,
it felt natural for him to stay for dinner; Tim confessed
he was hopeless in the kitchen but insisted on doing the
washing up. And when Meg got out her guitar after dinner, they all ended up singing along, something Rachel
knew Meg had always wished her dad would do with
them, but Steve had never quite had the patience.

When Tim had left, Meg said, 'I really like him,
Mum. I think he'll be good for you.'

'We might be good for each other,' Rachel said, 'but,
as I said earlier, we haven't been together long and we're
keeping it low profile. I don't want to rush into things.
As far as everyone at work is concerned, we're just good
friends.'

'Does Jenny know you're seeing him?' Saskia asked.

Rachel laughed. 'Yes. According to her I was glowing
after our dance aerobics class last week, and it wasn't
just because I'd put in extra effort that evening. She
made me tell her everything. We met her for a drink,
and she likes him.'

'Obviously he works with you, so that's how you met him. Is he divorced, too?' Meg asked.

'Widowed,' Rachel explained. 'There was a tragic accident, a couple of years ago. His wife was allergic to sesame. She went out to dinner with friends, and her food was accidentally cooked in sesame oil; she collapsed and hit her head in the wrong place.'

Saskia winced. 'How awful. Poor woman. And poor Tim.' She paused. 'Does he have kids?'

'Two girls, a bit older than you,' Rachel said. 'Hannah, the elder one, is an English teacher and is expecting her first baby in a few weeks, and Sophie has a marketing consultancy.'

'What are they like?' Meg asked.

'I haven't met them yet,' Rachel said.

'You're so lovely that they're bound to like you straight away,' Saskia said.

'Or see me as someone trying to step into their mum's shoes,' Rachel said quietly.

Meg shook her head. 'Even if they worry about you doing that, they'll know as soon as they meet you. That isn't who you are—unlike *some* people we could mention.'

Rachel sighed, knowing they meant the way their dad had foisted various girlfriends on them; he'd split up from the woman he'd left her for and moved on several more times since. 'I don't want you to fall out with your dad. He does love you, you know.'

'Mum, let's be honest about it. The person Dad loves most is himself,' Saskia said. 'He's never been in the running for Dad of the Year. We've learned not to expect anything from him, and that means we never feel let down. On the rare occasions he does actually do something thoughtful, then it's a bonus.'

'I'm sorry,' Rachel said. It was easy to see things in hindsight, but maybe she'd been wrong to stay with him and put up with his behaviour for all those years. Maybe she should have asked him to leave when the girls were small. Being a single parent had been a struggle for her own mother, but perhaps it would have been better for her daughters if Rachel had been a single parent. She'd never discussed it with them, not wanting to make their relationship with their father even rockier; but she had a nasty feeling that, despite the way she'd tried to protect them from knowing about their dad's affairs, they'd picked up on it anyway.

'It's not your fault, Mum,' Meg said.

'Anyway. Let's talk about something else. Are you off at any point, this weekend, and can we do something?' Saskia asked.

'I'm off tomorrow,' Rachel said, 'and I'm working a late on Sunday. So I'm all yours tomorrow and Sunday morning.'

Meg flicked into the internet. 'It's another fortnight until the rink's open at Somerset House, or I'd suggest ice skating and hot chocolate.'

'I know we've got our own personal emergency doctor, but do you really want to risk falling over and hurting your wrist or your hands so you can't practise a piece, when you've got Finals this year?' Saskia asked.

'Good point,' Meg said. 'We'll have to think of something else.'

'How about the Natural History Museum, followed by cake somewhere nice, then back home to watch *Mamma Mia*?' Saskia suggested. 'We haven't done any of that for ages.'

'Fine by me. Mum?' Meg asked.

Rachel nodded. 'We can order a takeaway tomorrow night. There's a new Thai place that's just opened round the corner, and apparently, they have really good vegan and veggie options. I was waiting until you were home to try it out.'

'That,' Saskia said, giving her a hug, 'sounds perfect.'

Rachel thoroughly enjoyed having the girls home; they reminisced their way through the Natural History Museum, found a gorgeous indie patisserie for cake, sang their way through *Mamma Mia* and discovered that the new takeaway lived up to its reputation. They went for a walk on Hampstead Heath on Sunday morning and had a leisurely brunch at a café before the girls waved her off to work and promised to text her to let her know they were back safely at their respective flats.

She didn't see Tim until after their shift on Monday, when they'd arranged to go for a drink.

'I liked your daughters very much,' he said. 'They're very like you.'

She smiled. 'Thank you.'

'And, considering I've met your girls... I was wondering if you'd like to meet mine. I've told them about you, and they've suggested having dinner at my place.'

'You're cooking?' she asked warily, remembering that he'd said how awful his cooking was.

'Um, no,' he said, 'nothing so dangerous. Hannah's

going to make a lasagne, I'm buying the salad and garlic bread, and Sophie's going to make tiramisu. Is there anything there you can't eat?'

'No—it all sounds lovely,' she said.

Though she felt a bit daunted on the Wednesday night as she walked to Tim's house from the Tube station, carrying wine and chocolates. Were his daughters going to feel that she was trying to take over from their mum? And was this too soon in any case? Was she rushing into something that would end up making her feel even lonelier than she'd been before she'd started her new job?

But Hannah and Sophie were warm and welcoming, as were their partners, and made sure she was part of the conversation. Rachel thoroughly enjoyed dinner and insisted on helping to clear the table afterwards. 'As a guest, I really hate being waited on hand and foot. I'd much rather muck in and help, so everything's done more quickly and nobody's left stuck on kitchen duty.'

Tim shooed her back out of the kitchen. 'I'm stacking the dishwasher while the coffee's brewing. Honestly, there's almost nothing to do.'

'Thank you for inviting me tonight,' she said to Hannah and Sophie when she went back to the table with them.

'My pleasure,' Hannah said. 'This is my first official week on maternity leave, and making lasagne gave me something to do, seeing as *someone* banned me from decorating the nursery.' She gave her husband a mock glare.

Rachel smiled. 'I remember being yelled at for using

a chair as a stepladder so I could put curtains up in the nursery.'

'Don't give her ideas,' Jamal groaned.

'I'll try not to,' Rachel promised. 'I just wanted you both to know that this thing between your dad and me is very new, and I'm absolutely not trying to step into your mum's shoes, even if things develop between us. I lost my mum earlier this year and I miss her very much, so I have an idea how you must feel.'

'Thank you,' Hannah said.

'Can we be honest with you?' Sophie asked. At Rachel's nod, she continued, 'We worry about Dad being lonely. He has a habit of cocooning himself in work when he doesn't want to talk about things. Since Mum died, he's even kept us at a bit of a distance. But he's loosened up over the last few weeks, so I'm guessing that's your influence.'

'Maybe,' Rachel said. 'My daughters worry about me being lonely, too. And they liked your dad very much when they met him.'

'Dad's pretty awesome,' Hannah said.

Rachel smiled. 'Yes, he is. He's a great doctor—and he's a really nice man.'

'How do you feel about board games?' Sophie asked, eyeing the bare table speculatively.

'Love them,' Rachel said.

They ended up playing Trivial Pursuit. 'Women versus men, I think,' Hannah said.

'I'm hopeless at the sport questions,' Rachel said, 'so I hope you're good.'

'Better than Dad is,' Sophie said, laughing. 'Give

him a football question, and nine times out of ten he'll get it wrong.'

'Bring it on, because we're so going to win—right, Jamal and Calum?' Tim asked, blowing on his finger-tips and polishing his nails on his sweater.

'If you lose,' Sophie said, 'you're buying us choco-late, Dad. A bar each. A *big* bar.'

'You're the one who's going to be buying chocolate, sweetheart,' he teased back.

It turned out to be a noisy game, with many accusa-tions of the other team having super-easy questions and a lot of laughter. Rachel enjoyed it thoroughly and was shocked to realise how late it was when they'd finished their second game.

'I'd better head for home,' she said, 'because I'm on an early shift tomorrow and my boss is a bit grumpy.'

'Very grumpy, because he's buying all the chocolate,' Sophie crowed. She and Hannah high-fived Rachel then gave her a hug.

'It was really nice to meet you,' Rachel said.

'It was really lovely to meet you, too,' Sophie said. 'We'll have to do this again.'

'Maybe we could have dinner at my place, next time,' Rachel offered. 'I enjoy cooking. Just let me know of any dietary requirements.'

Before they left that evening, Hannah said, 'Rachel's lovely, Dad. I think Mum would've approved of her. She was very careful to let us know she isn't trying to insert herself in Mum's place.'

'Nobody will ever take your mum's place,' Tim said. 'This is something new.'

'And we're glad,' Sophie said. 'We think she'll be good for you.'

Tim thought that Rachel would be good for him, too. Particularly as his daughters liked her.

But.

There was a niggle that wouldn't go away, no matter how hard he tried to ignore it or squash it.

Being a workaholic meant he hadn't been there for his wife when she'd needed him. Would it be the same with Rachel—even though they did the same job, and he was pretty sure she'd understand where he was coming from? Would this all just crash and burn?

Given how unhappy her marriage had obviously been, he didn't want to hurt her. So he was going to have to be really careful. No matter how attractive he found her, they needed to take it slowly. Sensibly.

CHAPTER SIX

'HANNAH AND SOPHIE really liked you,' Tim said when he managed to snatch a coffee break at the same time as Rachel, the next day.

'It's mutual,' she said. 'They're lovely. And that tells me what a gorgeous woman Mandy was, too.'

Then Ediye came into the rest room. 'I know you're both on a break,' she said, 'but I'm in over my head. I have a patient with suspected sepsis.'

Tim and Rachel exchanged a glance. Sepsis was potentially serious, but both of them thought that Ediye was experienced enough to handle the situation.

'And she has motor neurone disease,' she said.

Motor neurone disease was a disorder that affected the nerves controlling the muscles, and eventually made the muscles weaken and waste; it could affect movement, speech and breathing. Although there was no cure, the symptoms could be treated. But MND meant they'd need to take a lot more into account where sepsis was concerned.

'I'll come now,' Rachel said. 'Catch you later, Tim.'

Ediye introduced her to Ginny Morton, their patient, and her partner Bella.

'Ginny was a pharmacology lecturer,' Bella said. 'MND hasn't taken away her intellect, but she can't speak any more. She communicates with her eyes— one blink for yes, two for no.' She wrinkled her nose. 'We do use an alphabet chart, but it's slow and frustrating when you blink to spell a word.'

'I can imagine,' Rachel said. 'Ginny, I'm sorry that I need to ask Bella to answer for you, but Ediye tells me you might have sepsis so, with your background, you'll know why I want to assess you as fast as possible. Can I check you're OK with that?'

Ginny gave a single blink, and Rachel squeezed her hand. 'Thank you. And you're happy for me to examine you?'

Another single blink.

'Thank you. Are you in any pain?'

Two slow blinks. 'That's good,' Rachel said.

The breathing difficulty was apparent; when Rachel listened to Ginny's chest there was little air going in. Given the motor neurone disease, Ginny's ventilation muscles were probably impaired. Her heart rate was faster than Rachel was happy with, and her blood pressure was on the low side; the signs were all pointing towards a severe infection.

'So when did the breathing difficulty start?' she asked.

'Today,' Bella said. 'She was tired, yesterday; this morning, her breathing was bad, and her temperature was up. That's why I called the ambulance.'

'You did the right thing. Ginny, I'm going to send you for a chest X-ray,' Rachel said, 'because I'm not happy about what I'm hearing through the stethoscope. I think it's likely to be an infection, and I'm going to give you some broad-spectrum antibiotics, as well as some fluids and medication to get your blood pressure up. And I want to admit you for monitoring.' She looked at Bella. 'The antibiotics should kick in fairly quickly, but I'm worried about Ginny's breathing. I'd like her in so we can react quickly if her breathing gets worse. But I'm pretty sure we can get her through this and back home.'

'Good. Because I'm not ready to...' Bella's voice wobbled.

Guessing what the other woman wasn't saying—that she wasn't ready to say goodbye to the woman she loved—Rachel gave her a swift hug. 'Hang on in there,' she said. And she was really glad that she, rather than Tim, had helped Ediye with this case. She had a feeling it would've brought back too many memories for Tim, opening up his scars from losing Mandy.

At the end of November, it was the department's Christmas meal. A couple of evenings beforehand, Tim was curled up with Rachel on her sofa. 'Is it bad to admit that I'm dreading the Christmas meal?' he asked.

Rachel frowned. 'Why are you dreading it? From what I've heard, it's the highlight of the department at Christmas, and everyone loves you doling out the Secret Santa presents.'

'But it's the start of Christmas.' Tim wrinkled his nose. 'And you know what Christmas is like in the department. All the winter ailments, the fractures from icy days, and then Christmas itself when people start drinking and falling out, and we have to spend half our time patching them up.'

'Yes, but that's only some of the population,' she reminded him. 'Most people enjoy the chance to spend time with the people they love, eating too much and playing board games and...' She looked at him. 'What's this really about, Tim?'

He shook his head, not wanting to put it into words. 'Nothing.'

She folded her arms and stared at him, waiting.

He sighed and gave in. 'OK. Mandy really, really loved Christmas. She always made a big thing of it—the decorations, the music, the food, the Christmas get-togethers. I've had two Christmases where I just haven't been able to face her not being there on Christmas Day, and I've worked late so I don't have time to think. I've been a coward and made my girls go to their in-laws for Christmas Day, because I know I can't make them the sort of Christmas their mum did.' He grimaced. 'And it worries me that they might think I'm pushing them away.'

'I'm sure they understand,' Rachel said.

Something in her expression made him wonder if they'd confided in her. He sighed. 'I know I could order Christmas and get it delivered in a box, but that'd feel wrong, too, because it isn't what the day's meant to be about. And it feels wrong to celebrate Christmas in our house, when Mandy was the centre of it.'

'I think,' she said, 'you're panicking. And it sounds to me as if you're trying too hard.'

'How?'

'This is going to sound harsh, but you need to accept that you just can't have Christmas like you did with Mandy, not any more. It's always going to be different now,' she said.

And that was what he couldn't handle.

'But different doesn't mean that you're pushing her out of your life or pretending that she never existed,' she said, reaching out to hold both his hands. 'If you start accepting that things will change from year to year, it means you can cherish your memories of the good times instead of focusing on what you've lost. The last Christmas you had with Mandy was very different from your first Christmas together, yes?'

'Yes,' he agreed. 'That last Christmas, it was dinner for sixteen because everyone came to us. A roast turkey, veggie options, all the trimmings, three puddings, crackers and charades and board games. But our first Christmas—we spent it in a pokey little flat, where we barely had the space to put up a tiny artificial Christmas tree. I was working an early shift, and Mandy was determined to cook Christmas dinner for us and our parents because it was our first Christmas together. We didn't have space for a dining table, so everyone was going to eat off trays. She'd got everything planned and this mammoth timetable. Except the oven went wrong, so she couldn't even cook the pigs in blankets, let alone the turkey.' He smiled, remembering. 'She probably should've admitted defeat and begged one of the parents to let us cook at their place instead. But Mandy refused to give in and did the lot on the hob. She diced the turkey and made it into a kind of Christmas stew, including the pigs in blankets and stuffing balls. There was a mountain of mashed potato, and the most vile boiled sprouts.' He smiled. 'And it didn't matter.'

'Because you were together. Which is entirely what Christmas is about,' she said gently.

'On the first of December,' he said, 'she always made Christmas Stew. So we could remember and laugh about it.' He blinked hard. 'The sprouts got better, though.'

She squeezed his hand. 'Mandy sounds like an amazing woman.'

'She was. And I know she'd be furious with me for moping and acting like a wet weekend at her favourite time of year. I know I need to move on. And I want to move on. I really do.'

'You know that with your head,' she said, 'but not with your heart.'

'I don't know how to change that,' he said. He'd been trying. But Christmas felt like an enormous iceberg sliding into his path.

'How about this: even if Mandy had still been here with you, Christmas would've been different this year because you might have a new grandchild to celebrate with,' she said. 'Next year, it will change again, because the baby's going to be old enough to start realising what's going on, and the year after that new traditions might start—Christmas carols and mince pies at nursery, going as a family to take the baby to see Father Christmas, or maybe everyone spending Christmas at Hannah and Jamal's rather than everyone congregating at yours.'

Tim knew Rachel had a valid point, but he still couldn't make himself feel it.

'You're a Christmas-aholic, aren't you?' he asked.

'I'm afraid so,' she said. 'Last Christmas was awful. Mum was battling pneumonia and she didn't know any of us. Steve had just slapped me with the divorce papers. We were supposed to be going to his family's for Christmas Day because Steve wouldn't be there, but at the last minute he decided to go and take his new girlfriend. Thank God, my sister-in-law warned me he'd changed his plans; I ducked out of going, because I wasn't sure whether he was going to be sniping at me or ostentatiously snogging his girlfriend every two minutes to show me what I was missing.'

Tim felt another surge of dislike towards Rachel's ex. Christmas was a time to try and heal the rifts, not widen them. And didn't the man care about the hurt he was causing his daughters?

'The girls didn't want me to be on my own on Christmas Day, so we stayed at home and had a very nontraditional Christmas dinner. Which was fine. We still managed to find the love. We caught up with Steve's family later, when Steve had gone off skiing. And this year,' she said, 'we're making up for it. We'll be doing all our old traditions, with extra chocolate and gin.'

Making up for what they'd missed. He understood that, but he couldn't find the heart to do it himself. It was just too, too big.

Rachel was clearly trying to help him, so he'd try and meet her halfway. 'What are your family traditions?'

'The girls and I always have a Christmas movie night—when Mum was alive, she joined us, too. We all put on a Christmas jumper, we make big mugs of hot chocolate laced with cream liqueur—a vegan version for Saskia—we start working our way through the Christmas shortbread, and we cuddle up on the sofa under a fleecy throw and watch movies. Usually there's at least *Love Actually* and *Elf.*'

It was just the sort of thing that Mandy had done with their girls.

'We used to go skating at the Natural History Museum or Somerset House, though with Meg being in her Finals year we're giving it a miss this year—the last thing she needs is a sprain or fracture that means she can't practise a piece for her exams. And I always make them stockings.' She grinned. 'I don't care that they're eighteen and twenty-one, and neither do they. They still hang a stocking on their door, and I fill it after they've gone to bed. Lots of little things that I pick up during the year, plus the last-minute stuff that I don't want to be out of date. I normally include a chocolate reindeer and a sugar mouse, a decoration for the Christmas tree, a miniature bottle of flavoured gin, make-up, nail varnish and something ridiculous to make them laugh, like a wind-up toy. I've got personalised plectrums for Meg, this year, and packets of herb seeds for Saskia.' She looked wistful. 'I used to make a stocking for Steve, even before we had the girls; I always bought a crazy gadget from the shop at the Science Museum for his desk, a miniature bottle of brandy, and Christmas-themed chocolate.'

Tim noticed what was missing. What went in Rachel's stocking? 'What about you? Didn't you get a stocking?'

'Once the girls were old enough to stop believing in Santa, they collaborated with Mum,' Rachel said. 'Even last year, when Mum could barely string a sentence together, they made time to sit with her and chat about Christmases past. I have no idea how they managed to help her write a Christmas card to me—it must've been before the pneumonia really knocked her for six—but that's the most precious gift I could've had. The last Christmas card, in her own handwriting.' Tears shimmered in her eyes for a second.

Tim put his arms round her and held her close. 'And this is your first Christmas without her.'

'Yes. She died in January,' she said.

'The first Christmas without them is the roughest one,' he said. 'But your mum will be here with you in spirit. She'll be there in your memories. That'll never go away.'

A single tear spilled over her lashes, and he kissed it away.

'That goes for you, too, you know,' she said shakily.

'Yeah. Mandy always did stockings for our girls, too. I do them, now, because I don't want them to miss out.' It was about the only thing he managed to do for Christmas.

'I bet they really appreciate it,' she said.

He nodded. 'But I don't have Mandy's touch. It feels like going through the motions. They're always nice about it, but I'm sure I've fallen short, and I don't understand where I'm going wrong.'

'Maybe,' she said, 'we can do a joint shopping trip. One just for stocking fillers.'

It filled him with dread and anticipation in equal measures. He had a feeling that Rachel loved Christmas even more than Mandy had; he wasn't sure he could live up to her ideals, and he didn't want to let her down. But, given that this was going to be her first Christmas without her mum, he didn't want to back away from her either.

'I assume you put up a real tree, rather than an artificial one?' he asked.

'Yes, because I love the scent. I always buy it on the first of December. And I've still got the tree decorations that the girls made me at nursery—the yogurt pots painted like a bell with a pipe-cleaner clapper, the salt dough Christmas tree with the splodges of paint for baubles. It doesn't matter that they're getting a bit tatty now, because they were made with love. And I make my own front door wreath.'

Of course she did. Tim felt even more inadequate. He'd avoided any kind of Christmas decorating for the last two years, because it had just been too hard to make the effort. With every stretch, the paper-thin walls around his grief had shredded even further.

'Even last year, I made a wreath for the door,' she said. 'I took all the bits to Mum's room. I chatted to her about the times we'd made wreaths together, I made a playlist of Christmas songs she loved, and I sat there holding her hand and singing until she fell asleep. Then I worked on the wreath until she woke up.' Her smile was bright, though tinged with sadness. 'I'll make a Christmas wreath for her grave, too, this year. An eco one, full of berries to feed the birds. She loved watching the birds in the garden.'

So had Mandy. And there was a huge lump in his throat. Rachel was so brave about this. Why couldn't he be brave, too?

'What are you doing for Christmas, this year?' she asked.

'Working,' he said. 'The girls will go to their in-laws, just like they have for the last two years. It's fine.'

'Do your girls love Christmas?' she asked gently.

He nodded.

'Do you want to be with them?'

'Yes,' he said, 'and no. Yes, because I'm their dad and of course I want to spend family time with them. I love them.'

She waited.

The old doctor's trick, of waiting until your patient told you what was really wrong, worked just as well on someone who wasn't a patient, because he found himself admitting, 'And no, because I feel so inadequate and I can't do things the way their mum did, and I find Christmas just too much.'

'Have you talked to them about it?'

'No. I'm not great at talking about feelings. I never have been.' He glanced at her and could see on her face that she was thinking, *But that's what he's doing right now.* 'It's different with you,' he said. 'I can talk to you.'

'Why?'

'I don't know.' He shook his head. 'I just can.'

'I'm taking that as a compliment,' she said. 'Did you have any traditions that you did with them particularly?'

'Obviously Mandy and I took them to see Santa when they were tiny, but they're too old for that now.'

'What about going to a carol service, or to one of the Christmas markets, or just out for a walk to see the Christmas lights?' She smiled. 'I would suggest ice skating, but with Hannah being so close to her due date it wouldn't be fair for her to have to sit on the sidelines and watch.'

'I used to take the girls to see the Christmas lights when they were small,' he said, 'and I kind of feel I ought to let the people in the department with small kids have the time to spend with them, because mine are old enough to wait.' He shrugged. 'I know Hannah has a baking session with Sophie for the school Christmas fair. They make gingerbread reindeer and mince pies. But you know how hopeless I am in the kitchen. I'd just get in the way if I tried to help.'

'Maybe you could be their official barista and washer-upper, if you want to join in,' she suggested gently. 'Or maybe you need to make a new tradition, something they didn't do with Mandy. Something to make new memories that will help you smile when you remember the old memories, like your Christmas Stew, instead of wanting to howl inside because you can't do the old stuff any more.'

'I…' He looked helplessly at her. 'I don't know where to start.'

'You could do some things with me, maybe,' she said, 'and if you think it's something the girls might like to do with you then you can suggest doing it with them, too.' She paused. 'I happen to be working on Christmas Day as well. Meg and Saskia are volunteering to serve dinner at a shelter, and we're going to make a proper Christmas dinner for the three of us on Boxing Day. The whole thing—a vegan filo pastry thing for Sophie and turkey for Meg and me, all the trimmings, a fresh pineapple and really good ice cream for pudding. We're going to raise a glass of Prosecco and gin to Mum and eat way too much chocolate.' She looked at him. 'Why don't you all come to us on Boxing Day: you, your girls and their partners? That way, it'll be something new; and because it'll be here, rather than at your place, it means you won't have constant reminders of Mandy not being there.'

He just stared at her, not knowing what to say.

'It's not a way of pushing Mandy away or pretending she didn't exist,' she reminded him. 'It's helping you come to terms with things so you can remember the good times and smile. So you can enjoy Christmas again with your girls—all the important family stuff.'

'That's incredibly generous of you,' he said, 'and bits of me really want to say yes. But it's taking up time you'll want to spend with your girls. It's not fair to just expect them to host people they don't know.'

'I'm pretty sure they'll say yes,' she said.

So was he, because he'd met them and he'd had the distinct impression that they'd both inherited their mum's huge heart. But he wasn't taking any of it for granted. 'Ask them first,' he said.

'All right,' she said, 'and then you ask your girls.'

* * *

As Rachel had expected, Meg and Saskia agreed immediately. And Hannah and Sophie were delighted to accept the invitation.

Hannah—after Tim had checked that Rachel wouldn't mind if he gave her number to his daughters—called her. 'It's really kind of you to ask us, Rachel.'

'It's not kind of me at all. If anything, it's totally selfish,' Rachel said.

'How do you work that out?'

'I miss having a really big family Christmas, because my family now is just my girls,' Rachel explained. 'Even though my ex's family get on with me and still see us, it's a bit too awkward still for me to accept an invite to a family thing if my ex is going to be there.'

'It's going to be really good spending the time with Dad, but he hates Christmas because...' Hannah stopped. 'Sorry.'

'Because your mum loved Christmas and he can't cope with it without her. I know, love,' Rachel said gently. 'Probably because I never knew your mum, he's able to talk about her to me and be honest about how he feels. I'm hoping I can make him see Christmas a bit differently this year. I'm not pushing your mum out at all—I know I've already told you that, but I really want to make sure you and Sophie don't feel I'm intruding. I'm simply hoping that he can make some new memories that will help him remember how to enjoy the old ones and also keep him close to you.'

'That,' Hannah said, 'would be amazing—and it means this'll be the first good Christmas we've had in three years. But it's also not fair to expect you to do everything. What can we do to help?'

'How about,' Rachel suggested, 'you bring pudding? Maybe Sophie can make her amazing tiramisu or something. But honestly, the best thing you can bring is yourselves and a smile. Oh, and let me know of any—' she balked at the word 'allergy', not wanting to trample on a sore spot '—dietary requirements. There's going to be a vegan option, because of Saskia. It's a filo pastry snake filled with veggies, pearl barley, apricots and spices, and she's making a spicy tomato sauce to go with it.'

'That sounds good.' Hannah chuckled. 'Dad tells me you're as much of a cheese fiend as he is. So we'll bring cheese, too. And a vegan one for Saskia.'

'Perfect,' Rachel said, 'and I'll make cheese biscuits.'

'The ones you took into the department and Dad raved about? That sounds wonderful.'

'We have board games,' Rachel said, 'and including one where you have to play kazoos and guess the song. Meg usually plays the piano so we can sing our heads off. And there will be chocolate.'

'I can't wait,' Hannah said.

It was the first time in three years that Tim had actually enjoyed the team Christmas meal out, and it was all thanks to Rachel. They were still keeping their relationship quiet at work, but he couldn't help glancing at her when he donned a Santa hat to hand out the Secret Santa presents. And, even though she was sitting at the other end of the table from him, she met his gaze every so often and gave him an encouraging smile. He danced with everyone in the team after the meal; his dance with Rachel wasn't the slow one he longed for, though he consoled himself that at least it helped him keep up the pretence at work that they were just good friends because it meant he wouldn't slip up and accidentally kiss her in front of the department.

Because they lived in different parts of the city, they left the party separately; but Tim had arranged beforehand to catch a taxi from his place to Rachel's. When she opened the front door to him, he smiled. 'You look absolutely gorgeous in that dress, Ms Halliday.'

'You scrub up rather nicely yourself, Mr Hughes,' she teased back. 'Can I tempt you to a glass of wine?'

'Yes, please.' He handed her a bottle of chilled pink Prosecco.

'Thank you. Nice choice,' she said. 'Come into the kitchen.' She deftly opened the bottle without spilling a drop, poured them both a glass, and handed one to him. 'So did you enjoy tonight?'

'Yes,' he said, 'thanks to you. But I wish I'd had a chance to dance with you a bit more.'

'That can be arranged,' she said, putting her glass on the worktop and picking up her phone. 'Christmas mix?'

'Something slow and bluesy is more what I've got in mind,' he said.

She found a playlist on her streaming app and connected her phone to the speaker. 'Like this?'

'Perfect,' he said, as Fleetwood Mac's 'Need Your Love So Bad' came on. He put his own glass down, hung his jacket over the back of a chair and drew her into his arms. 'This is what I wanted to do earlier,' he said, 'but not in front of everyone. I don't want to make things awkward for us at work.'

'I know. It's sensible,' she said. 'Though at the same time it makes me feel a bit like a dirty little secret.'

'You're not a dirty little secret. Not at all,' he said. 'It just saves the complications, that's all. The people who are important know. The rest can wait until we're ready.'

'I guess.' She rested her head on his shoulder and swayed with him to the music; he closed his eyes, enjoying the feel of her arms wrapped round him and the warmth of her body against his. He wasn't sure which of them moved first, but then he was kissing her, his eyes closed, everything focused on the way her lips moved against his.

He really, *really* liked this woman.

And he wanted more. Except it wasn't fair to rush her. He was meant to be taking this slowly.

Gently, he broke the kiss and dragged himself out of her arms. 'I'd better go before I outstay my welcome.'

She held his gaze, her grey eyes huge. 'Maybe you're not outstaying it.'

His heart rate speeded up a notch when she added, 'We're both on a late tomorrow, so we don't have to be up early.'

He caught his breath. 'Are you asking…?'

'If you like porridge for breakfast. Oh, and just in case you were wondering, I bought a new bed after I split up with Steve, and I've redecorated the room.'

'There won't be any comparisons,' he said softly. 'For either of us. Though I probably should warn you it's been a while since I've slept with anyone, and decades since I slept with anyone except my wife.'

'Me, too,' she said. 'So maybe we both need to get the awkward stuff over and done with. This isn't going to be perfect. It's going to be different.'

'But it's still you and me,' he said.

'Bring your glass,' she said, scooping up her own glass and the bottle; she took his hand and led him up to her bedroom.

It was a pretty room with a wrought iron bedstead, floral curtains and pale blue walls. She put her glass and the bottle on her bedside table and switched on the lamp; he placed his glass next to hers.

'Are you sure about this?' he asked.

'Bits of me are scared that this is rushing it. But bits of me have wanted this since the first time you kissed me,' she admitted.

He appreciated her honesty. 'I'm not sure if I'm more thrilled or scared.'

'Born again teenagers, the pair of us,' she said.

Slowly, slowly, she removed his tie and undid the buttons of his shirt. Her hands were shaking, he noticed; just as his were when he undid the zip of her dress.

Colour bloomed across her cheeks as she turned to face him. 'I don't have a condom but, just so you know, I haven't slept with anyone in two years and there's absolutely no chance I can get pregnant.'

'I haven't slept with anyone since Mandy died,' he said, wanting to reassure her that she didn't need to worry about STDs; as a doctor, she'd be very aware of their effects. 'And I don't have a condom, either. But if you want to wait, there are other things we can do.'

'So there are,' she said, and her smile made his heart feel as if it had just done a backflip.

She stepped out of her dress and hung it over the top of her cheval mirror; though he noticed how tense her shoulders were.

'The thing about being a born again teenager rather than an original one,' he said, stepping out of his trousers and hanging them on the cheval mirror too, 'is that we do our own laundry and tidy up after ourselves.'

The ridiculous joke made her laugh and took the tension out of her, to his relief. He drew her into his arms and kissed her; when the kiss turned heated, he scooped her up, pushed the duvet aside and laid her against the pillows.

'You're beautiful, Rachel,' he said, 'and you make me feel things I never thought I'd ever feel again.'

'It's the same for me,' she said, stroking his face.

He made love with her, enjoying finding out how and where she liked to be touched, what made her gasp with pleasure; and in turn he enjoyed the way she explored him.

Afterwards, he cradled her in his arms. For the first time in years, the bed didn't feel too wide. It didn't matter that he was lying in a strange bed, because he was getting to know the woman lying in his arms—and it felt as if he was finally coming out of the darkness that had smothered him for the last two years.

The next morning, Rachel woke, warm and comfortable; then she turned over and realised the bed beside her was empty.

A little flutter of panic went through her as she opened her eyes. Clearly, they'd taken it too fast last night and she shouldn't have asked him to stay. It was obvious that he'd woken before her and had left, feeling embarrassed and ashamed about what they'd done, and too awkward to face her.

But when she sat up, planning to change into her workout gear and run her own shame and embarrassment off before she went to work, she glanced over to the mirror and realised that Tim's trousers and shirt were still there. *He hadn't left.*

A few moments later, she heard footsteps on the stairs, and he appeared in the doorway, wearing just his boxer shorts and carrying two mugs of coffee.

'Good morning,' he said.

She could feel her skin heating. For pity's sake; she was fifty-two, not nineteen. 'Morning,' she mumbled.

He put both mugs of coffee on her side of the bed—he'd obviously taken the bottle and glasses downstairs when he went to make coffee—then bent down to kiss the tip of her nose. 'At our age, the walk of shame is supposed to be when we've forgotten that we're driving and had one glass of wine too many. But I'm dropping thirty years and being the med student who goes home the next morning in his party clothes from the night before.' He climbed back into bed beside her. 'Regretting it?'

'No. And yes,' she admitted. 'I don't regret what we did; but I do feel a bit awkward this morning and I don't really know what to say to you.'

'"Thank you for the coffee, Tim" would do,' he teased.

She smiled. 'Yes. Thank you for the coffee. Maybe

I'll have worked out the etiquette for this sort of thing by the time I'm eighty.'

'You'll still be beautiful when you're eighty,' he said. 'That bone structure and those amazing eyes.'

She hadn't expected the compliment and it felt all the sweeter. 'Thank you. You've got gorgeous eyes, too. It was the first thing I noticed about you, when you interviewed me. The colour of cornflowers.' She felt brave enough to trace the line of his jaw and steal a kiss. 'You'll be beautiful at eighty, too.'

'So what happens now?' he asked.

'We could have breakfast together. Here, I mean,' she said. 'And we're on a late. So we don't actually have to have breakfast until late…'

'I like your thinking,' he said, and leaned over to kiss her.

CHAPTER SEVEN

OVER THE NEXT few days, Rachel felt happier than she'd been in years. At work, she and Tim kept things polite and professional with each other, but since that night together things had changed outside work: he was more tactile, easier with her, and she enjoyed the closeness. By unspoken arrangement, he stayed over the nights before they were both on a late shift, and it was so good to wake in his arms and feel that the day would be full of sunshine.

One evening, she took him to the Christmas market on the South Bank as part of the plan to make Christmas less difficult for him. As they walked through the crowds between the wooden chalets, Christmas music was playing, and the air smelled of spice and oranges. There was a nip of frost in the air, and they could see people's breath like mist rising up to the twinkling lights as they chattered and laughed.

She bought them both a hot chocolate, liberally laced with cream liqueur, and they browsed the stalls that sold all kinds of Christmas decorations and gifts, from wooden ornaments and toys to jewellery to candles.

'These stars are gorgeous,' she said. 'I'm definitely buying these for the girls' stockings, this year.'

Tim, too, bought a selection of stocking fillers for his daughters; then they grabbed something to eat from one of the food stalls before walking over Waterloo Bridge and wandering over to watch the skaters at the Somerset House ice rink.

'You know, if we hang around here much longer, we're going to end up working,' Tim said. 'At the very least, there's going to be a Colles' fracture, not to mention sprains, strains and a lot of bruising.'

She tucked her arm through his. 'I know ice skating is maybe not the safest thing, but my girls used to love going here, or to the rink outside the Natural History Museum. It's the combination of the lights, the music, the smell of hot chocolate and the Christmas trees.'

'I have to admit, I'm not really a fan of skating,' he said, 'even if you exclude the Emergency Department aspect of it.'

'I'm not brilliant at actually doing it,' she said, 'but I used to love watching Torvill and Dean. They were so graceful, gliding across the ice and doing those amazing jumps and pirouettes. And I loved her outfits.'

He chuckled. 'You're so showing your age—we must have been students when they won the gold medal.'

'I know.' She laughed back. 'The music I'd choose for ice skating shows my age, too. Robbie Williams...' she sang a snatch of 'She's the One' '...and George Michael.' She grinned. 'And "Last Christmas" is still my favourite contemporary Christmas song ever.'

'Mandy's was Mariah Carey,' he said.

'An excellent choice,' she said. 'I love that one, too. Mandy had good taste.'

'I think,' he said, 'you would've liked each other.'

'I do, too,' she said, and squeezed his hand. 'Have you been to see the Christmas lights at Kew Gardens?'

'No. Mandy went a couple of times with the girls, but I was working.'

'Drop the guilt,' she said, 'and think of the people you helped on those nights. People who were in pain—people who might have died. You made a difference.'

'I guess.' He paused. 'Have you been to Kew?'

'I went with Steve, three or four years back.' She shrugged. 'But it was a work thing, so he spent the whole night networking. I'm planning to go on my own this year and just enjoy the lights and the music and the Christmassy feel.' It was part of her plan to do things for herself again, but maybe it would help Tim, too. 'You're welcome to join me, if you like.'

'Actually, that sounds really nice,' he said. 'And, just to prove I'm serious, I'll book the tickets now.' He grabbed his phone and flicked into the internet. 'Thursday night?'

'Thursday night works for me,' she said.

'This is way better than I remember it,' Rachel said when they were partway through the trail at Kew. 'This is amazing. It must've taken hours to put all those lights over the trees—especially all the way to the top of that beech tree.'

'And those colour-changing butterflies,' he said.

'Though I think my favourites are the ones where the lights look like snowflakes falling.'

There were little wooden huts on the way, selling Christmassy food and hot spiced cider; and there was a mini fairground in the middle, with old-fashioned rides and Christmassy music played on a steam organ.

'I always loved the gallopers when I was a kid,' Tim said, gesturing to the horses on the carousel.

'Me, too,' Rachel said. 'This will be perfect for your grandchild in about two years, with the train and the pedal car and the swing boats.'

'And Father Christmas, with real reindeer,' he said. 'Actually, I think the girls would really like this.'

'Make a date with them,' she said.

'I will,' he agreed. Rachel's delight in Christmas was making it so much more bearable for him, this year. And maybe this would become a new tradition, something to look forward to. With her.

The trail took them over a bridge, where the reflections of the lights in the water were stunning; through a light arch, which felt like being in a cathedral; and then an area where the lights on the Christmas trees changed in time with the music. Finally there were lasers projected onto water which sprayed across the lake.

'Thank you for coming with me,' he said when they finally left the gardens. 'That was spectacular.'

'Wasn't it? I can't work out what I liked most,' she said. 'I think all of it, actually.'

But it wasn't just the prettiness of the lights and the fabulous presentation, Tim thought. What had made it magical for him was Rachel. Walking hand in hand with her, stealing a kiss, sharing a smile. In the few short weeks he'd known her, she'd chased so many of the shadows away. And he was starting to think that maybe, just maybe, he'd found happiness again.

The following evening, they were both on a late shift when the paramedics brought a little girl into Resus. 'This is Willow Patterson—she's a year old in two days' time,' Samir, the paramedic, said. 'Mrs Patterson, her grandmother, has come in with us, and Willow's parents are on their way in. She went limp and then started fitting, and her gran called us straight away.'

'Do you know how long the seizure lasted?' Rachel asked.

'Twenty minutes,' Samir said.

Rachel and Tim exchanged a glance. Febrile convulsions were common in that age group, but the fit lasted typically for about five minutes. In this case, it could be encephalitis or epilepsy causing the seizure. And very young children could become extremely unwell very, very quickly.

'In the van, her eyes kept going to the left for about fifteen minutes,' Samir said. 'We've put her on oxygen. Her temperature's a bit higher than normal, but nothing I'd be worried about.'

'OK. Mrs Patterson, we're going to give her some medication to control her seizure, but the medication depresses breathing so we'll need to help her breathe for a little while,' Tim said. 'It's going to look scarier than it is. You're welcome to stay, or if you want to wait outside for her parents to arrive, that's fine.'

'I'll stay,' Mrs Patterson said. 'Can I hold her hand?'

'Yes,' Tim said. 'Rachel, would you mind bagging while I give her the meds?'

'Of course,' Rachel said, sorting out the oxygen mask and bagging. 'Mrs Patterson, do you know if Willow has ever had a fit before?'

'I'm pretty sure she hasn't,' Mrs Patterson said. 'Ellie—my daughter-in-law—would've said.'

'Has she had a high temperature or any other symptoms of a virus over the last couple of days?' Tim asked.

'She felt a bit hot this evening after Ellie gave her her dinner,' Mrs Patterson said. 'She ate just fine—but Ellie thought she was teething. She and Stu were going to call off going out, but I told them I'd give her some teething crystals and she'd be fine with me.' She looked distraught. 'We were just having a cuddle and a story before I put her to bed, but then she went limp and started having a fit. I panicked and called 999.'

'Which was exactly the right thing to do,' Rachel reassured her. 'Her temperature isn't high enough for it to be a febrile convulsion, but about one in twenty people have a one-off fit in their lifetime. This doesn't mean she definitely has epilepsy, though we'll want to keep an eye on her and check her over.'

'Oh, God. If anything happens to her, Stu and Ellie will never forgive me. They haven't been out for months. I sent them out to see a film and have dinner, so they could have some couple time,' Mrs Patterson said.

'It's not your fault,' Rachel reassured her. 'These things happen. Once the medication's taken effect and she's breathing OK on her own, we'll try and wake her up. You can help us with that, if her mum and dad haven't managed to get here by then.'

'She's such a happy little girl. She's just learned to clap and she's so pleased with herself, doing "If you're happy and you know it",' Mrs Patterson said, looking anxious. 'It's not going to change her, is it?'

'We'll know more when she's awake,' Tim said. 'I remember my girls loved clapping songs.'

'So did mine,' Rachel said with a smile, knowing that he was trying to take Mrs Patterson's mind off the scary unknown.

A few minutes later, when Willow had just been taken off oxygen, her parents arrived, looking shocked. 'I can't believe this. It's the first time we've left her in months,' her mum said.

'We know it's not your fault, Mum,' Willow's dad reassured the older woman. 'It would've happened if we hadn't gone out.'

Tim took them swiftly through what had happened and what they were doing. 'We need to get her to wake up so we can assess if the seizure's had any effect,' he said gently.

'Come on, darling. Wake up,' Willow's mum said, rubbing the little girl's cheek. 'Wake up.'

'Show Daddy how you clap with Grandma,' her dad added.

Willow's grandmother sang the first verse of 'If you're happy and you know it' and clapped.

Still Willow didn't wake, and Rachel exchanged a glance with Tim. The longer the baby was unresponsive, the more likely there were to be problems.

Finally, to their relief, the baby woke and started crying.

'Mum-Mum, Da-Da,' she said, stretching her arms up to her parents.

The fact that she was able to recognise her parents was a really good sign, and relief flooded through Rachel.

Willow's mum scooped her up and held her close; the baby clutched her and whimpered.

'It's going to be all right, now,' Willow's dad said, enfolding them both in his arms.

'Now she's awake, we're going to send you to the paediatric department so they can assess Willow properly,' Rachel said. 'They might want to keep her in overnight, but if they do you can stay with her.'

'I'm never leaving her again,' Willow's mum said, her face pinched. 'Never.'

'Her gran did everything right,' Tim said gently. 'These things happen. But when Willow's been assessed they might have a better idea about whether she has epilepsy, and they can give you advice on how to handle any future fits.' He stroked the little girl's cheek and smiled at her mum. 'It's nice to see those big blue eyes. Take care.'

Once the Pattersons had gone up to Paediatrics with Willow, Tim gave Rachel a hug. 'You were thinking of your girls at that age, weren't you, and how easily something like this could've happened to them?'

She nodded. 'I'm guessing you were, too.'

'Yeah. It's a scary thing, being a parent. Everything you think you know suddenly goes out of your head, and instead there's this great fog of panic.' He gave her

a wry smile. 'I'm going to be terrified every time I baby-
sit my new grandchild.'

She smiled back. 'You might get that initial panic,
but in an emergency you'll switch back to doctor mode.'

'There is that,' he conceded.

In the middle of December, Rachel and Tim were
walking through Hampstead Heath. There was a mini
Christmas fair going on, with a few stalls and a band
on a small stage with a keyboard, a drum kit, a guitar
and an amp, playing Christmassy music. When they
started playing 'Last Christmas', Tim looked at Rachel.
'They're playing your song. It'd be a shame to waste
it.' He gave her a bow and held out his hand. 'Dance
with me?'

She laughed and stepped into his arms.

It was wonderful, Tim thought, dancing under the
trees with Rachel's arms wrapped round him and her
cheek resting against his, with all the fairy lights twinkling round them. All they needed now was the lightest,
lightest sprinkling of snow as the final touch...

And then he heard someone say, 'Look at those two
dancing together. It's lovely to see an older couple still
so in love with each other.'

Love.

Was he in love with Rachel?

Her warmth and sweetness had seeped through the
barriers he'd built round his heart, gently undoing all
the fetters without him even noticing, because he'd been
focused on enjoying the brightness she brought to his
days. He was even starting to think that he could actu-

ally handle Christmas, this year—and it was all thanks to her. The world had started to feel bright and sparkling again, since the first moment he'd kissed her. Waking up in her arms in the morning made him feel that the world was full of sunshine. He was learning to see the joy again.

He almost—almost—told her. But he didn't want to say it for the first time in the middle of a crowd. Instead, he just let himself enjoy the moment, dancing with her under the fairy lights.

When the song came to an end, he smiled at her. 'Shall we take a selfie?'

She smiled back at him. 'Sure.'

He pulled his phone out of his pocket and stared at it in horror as the notifications filled the screen. Missed calls from Hannah and Jamal. Sophie, too.

And the text that stood out made his blood run cold.

Baby not moving. Going to hospital.

Oh, Christ.

No.

Hannah couldn't lose the baby. She couldn't.

And then he thought of Mandy, going to hospital in the ambulance but never making it there.

'Tim? What's wrong?'

'My phone. Must've been on silent.' He couldn't bear to voice his fears out loud. Instead, he showed her the screen.

'Oh, no. Poor Hannah. She must be worried sick. And you must be, too,' she said. 'But, Tim, remember that it doesn't always mean there's a problem. Hannah's in her last month, right? It could be that the baby's head is engaged so she won't feel so much movement, or the baby's simply in a deep sleep. The chances are, by the time she gets to hospital, she'll be feeling movements again.'

'But what if…?' The words stuck in his throat. What if the baby died? What if Hannah died? His clever, capable daughter, so like her mother. Surely Fate wouldn't be so cruel as to repeat itself? He wouldn't lose his daughter and grandchild, the way he'd lost his wife?

He'd been so busy having fun with Rachel that he hadn't taken care of his daughter.

'Tim,' Rachel said, dragging him from his thoughts. 'We're not far from my place and it'll be quicker to walk there than call a taxi. I'll drive you. Which hospital?'

'I…' He couldn't think straight. 'Hackney.'

'OK. Call her,' she said, giving his phone back. 'Tell her you're on the way.'

Hannah's phone went straight to voicemail. So did Jamal's. And Sophie's. And Calum's.

He was shaking so much; he couldn't type a text. He called Hannah again and left a voice message. 'It's Dad. I'm on my way. Hang on. It's all going to be all right.' Even though he was terrified that it wouldn't be. He was the parent. It was his job to reassure her. 'I'll be there as soon as I can. Love you.'

It felt as if it took hours to walk to Rachel's, even though it was only a few minutes, and his brain was too scrambled for him to talk—though at least he'd remembered which hospital. She didn't push him, simply switched the radio to a classical station and drove him to Hackney.

'Do you want me to come in with you?' she asked.

Yes. No. He didn't know. Panic and worry had rendered him completely hopeless. 'I...'

She squeezed his hand. 'Look, I'm not going to intrude. Go and see Hannah. Call me if you need *anything*. That goes for all of you. OK?'

'Thank you,' he whispered, and wrapped his arms round her.

'It's going to be all right,' she said.

Exactly the same reassurance he'd given Hannah. And he knew it was just as hollow. Mere words. Because nobody could know for certain.

'Call me when you can and let me know how she is,' she said. 'Give her my love.' Her eyes held his. 'Remember what I said. Anything you need, I'm here. Just call me. Even if it's stupid o'clock.'

He nodded; his throat too thick with fear to let any words out.

It wasn't a rejection, Rachel reminded herself as she drove home. It was obvious that Tim's worries about Hannah and the baby had brought back memories of Mandy's death. He needed space and time. She'd done what she could to support him.

She just hoped that everything would be all right. There were several reasons why a baby's movements decreased—as well as the ones she'd given Tim, there was the chance that Hannah had overdone things that day. Plus, babies were often wide awake when the mum was trying to sleep and less active during the day.

Please, please, let everything be all right, she prayed

silently. Let it be the Christmas Tim and his family needed, full of love and happiness and the joy of a new baby.

Be strong, Tim told himself as he walked up to the maternity department reception.

'My name's Tim Hughes. My daughter Hannah's been brought in because she couldn't feel the baby moving, and she needs me here,' he said. His glance flicked automatically to the whiteboard; Hannah's name was there, right under the word 'emergency'. 'Would it be possible to see her, please?'

'I'm afraid we can't allow visitors,' the receptionist said, 'but I can get a message to her and you're very welcome to go into the waiting room.'

Tim dragged in a breath. 'Sorry. As a doctor myself, I should know the protocol,' he said.

'But you're also a dad,' the receptionist said, 'and you're worried about your daughter. Actually, I think her sister's in the waiting room.'

Tim forced himself to smile. 'Thank you.'

The receptionist directed him to the waiting room, and Tim strode swiftly there. Sophie stood up as soon as he walked through the door, and he wrapped his arms round her. 'How's Hannah? How are *you*? I'm so sorry.' The words tumbled out.

She held him close. 'Everything's OK, Dad. They gave her a scan and the baby's okay. They gave her a glass of orange juice and the baby's moving again now.'

'It's the sugar in the juice. Energy,' he said. 'Are they

giving the baby a non-stress test? Did they say why the baby wasn't moving?'

'I don't know, Dad. The main thing is, she's getting checked out.'

'I should've been here.' But he'd focused on himself and his own needs instead of on his daughters. He hadn't been there when they'd needed him. 'I'm so sorry. My phone was on silent.' He dragged in a breath. 'I don't know how. I was out with Rachel.'

'Where is Rachel?' Sophie asked.

'I, um—she went home.'

'Right.' Sophie looked surprised. 'How did you get here?'

'Rachel drove me. She said it'd be quicker than waiting for a taxi.' He raked a hand through his hair. 'I said I'd call her and tell her…when I know what's happening. She…um…sends love.'

'She could've stayed,' Sophie said.

'Better not,' Tim said.

Sophie gave him a strange glance. 'Calum and I will give you a lift home when we've seen Han and know she's OK.'

'Thank you.' He hadn't even thought about getting home. 'Where is Calum?'

'Gone to get coffee. You just missed him.'

'Right.' He held her close. 'I'm sorry. I've let everyone down.'

'Han was a bit upset when you didn't call,' Sophie said. 'She even asked me to ring the hospital, because we both thought you were at work.'

It was a fair point. But he'd replaced work with Rachel. Made himself even less available.

And it had to stop.

Now.

He'd tell Rachel tonight, once he knew Hannah and the baby were both all right.

The waiting seemed to last for ever, but finally Hannah and Jamal appeared in the waiting room.

'They've checked us out thoroughly, given me a scan and done a non-stress test, and they're happy for me to go home,' Hannah said. Her voice was wobbly. 'The baby's fine. Just really deeply asleep when I couldn't feel the usual movements, they think.'

'And she'd been overdoing it,' Jamal said. 'Which means we need to tag team her and make her rest.'

'I'm fine,' Hannah said, lifting her chin. 'I just panicked a bit, that's all.'

Tim hugged her. 'I'm so glad it's all right. And I'm so sorry I wasn't there.' He should've been there. He could've reassured her—both as her father and as a medic. 'I'll take the first shift in looking after you.'

'Dad, you've got work,' Hannah said. 'And you'll all drive me potty if you fuss. It's fine. I have all your numbers, and I'll call if I'm worried about anything. I don't need a babysitter.'

'My phone was on silent,' Tim said. 'It won't be, in future. I'll make sure it's diverted to the admin team if I'm at the hospital.'

Hannah's face crumpled, and she burst into noisy sobs.

Guilt flooded through him, and he stroked her hair, holding her close. 'It's OK, Han. It's all going to be OK.'

'I was so scared, Dad.'

'I know, baby. But it's all fine. You have Jamal. You have Soph and Calum. You have me. It's fine. They've told you what to do if you're worried in future?'

'Drink juice or have a snack. Lie on my left side and count the movements. If I'm still worried, come straight in.'

'Then it's fine,' he said. 'It's all going to be just fine.'

He went home with Hannah and Jamal and took the Tube home rather than making Sophie and Calum drive out of their way. And then he called Rachel.

Rachel snatched up her phone as soon as she saw Tim's name on the screen. 'How's Hannah?'

'Fine. They did a non-stress test and a scan, and they think the baby was deeply asleep. They've sent her home.'

'I'm so glad,' she said. 'Is there anything she needs? Anything I can do?'

'No.' He was silent for a moment. 'Rachel—I'm sorry. I can't do this any more. I can't be with you.'

It took her a moment to process what he was saying. He couldn't do this? He didn't want to be with her? 'Why? What have I done wrong?'

'It's not you—it's me,' he said.

Dread trickled down her spine. Everyone knew that phrase; it was the nice guy's get-out.

'I'm sorry. I just think it's better if we stick to being colleagues from now on,' Tim continued.

Rachel didn't understand. She thought things had been going well between them. They were in tune with

each other. They got each other's jokes. They liked each
other's families. They *fitted*. She'd thought they had a
future; but it seemed Tim hadn't felt the same. She was
too shocked to know what to say. So much for finally
moving on from the misery of her marriage and this
last lonely year, because Tim had just pulled the rug out
from under her. She shouldn't have trusted him with her
heart so quickly.

He didn't want to see her any more.

Though she supposed that the bright side was that
at least Tim hadn't cheated on her before dumping her.
He'd merely made love with her and let her fall in love
with him.

'I need to concentrate on my girls,' he said.

It felt like an excuse. A flimsy one, kindly meant
to spare her feelings, but actually it did the reverse. It
felt like a hundred paper cuts ripping across the confidence she'd built back up, each little tear bleeding into
another and making her realise how fragile that confidence had been.

'Of course,' she said. She wasn't going to fall apart
and let Tim realise how deeply she felt about him. She'd
made enough of a fool of herself, already. 'I'll see you at
work. I'm glad everything's all right with Hannah and
the baby.' Then she quietly ended the call and put her
phone back on the coffee table.

It was over.

All the dreams had popped into nothing, like the useless bubbles they'd really been all along—except she
hadn't wanted to see that.

And she definitely wasn't feeling any of the spirit

of Christmas that had bathed her for the last few days when she'd been making memories with Tim. Thankfully it was still the middle of December, so Meg and Saskia wouldn't be home for another few days. It would give her enough time to get herself back under control again and pretend that everything was fine, just as she'd pretended for the last year. But, right at that moment, the house felt unbearably empty, full of echoes, all the promise of Christmas snuffed out.

She drew her knees up and wrapped her arms round them, then rested her face on her knees and cried out all her loneliness and despair. The one good thing was that they'd kept their burgeoning relationship quiet at work, so nobody would know what a stupid mistake she'd made.

If he'd stayed with Rachel, Tim thought, he would've let his girls down again. But breaking up with her had made him feel just as guilty, because he knew he'd hurt her. Let her down, the way he'd let his girls down.

He'd done the right thing. He knew that.

So why did he feel so miserable about it?

The next few days at work were truly awkward. Rachel was fine while she could concentrate on a patient or teaching one of the students or juniors who'd been assigned to her, but when she was in her office writing up notes or doing paperwork for a training schedule, she was acutely aware of where Tim was in the department—and she just missed him.

Stupid, stupid, stupid.

He'd made it clear he didn't want to be with her.

So she'd focus on the bits of her life that did work: being a mum, being a doctor and being a friend. Anything else wasn't going to be on her agenda in future.

On the Friday afternoon, the paramedics brought in a woman in her late sixties. 'This is Mrs Dilreet Kaur,' Samir said. 'She hasn't been feeling well all week but she thought she was just coming down with a bug. Today, she'd been feeling a bit short of breath and nauseous, and then some pain in her jaw and her back—nothing in her chest, so she didn't think it was her heart.'

Women often had different symptoms from men when having a heart attack, Rachel knew, and were more likely to feel the pain in their jaw or back rather than the classic heart attack symptom of crushing pain in the chest.

'She collapsed, and her friend called us,' Samir continued. 'We've given her some aspirin, and we did an ECG in the ambulance on the way here, which shows it's a STEMI.' He handed her the printout from the ECG. 'She's on oxygen, but I'm not happy with her sats.'

'Thanks, Samir. I've already put a call up to the cardiac team,' she said. 'Has anyone called her family?'

'Her friend called her son,' Samir said, 'and he's on the way in.'

'Great. Thanks, Samir.'

Between them, they transferred Mrs Kaur from the trolley to the bed. 'Mrs Kaur, I'm Rachel Halliday, one of the doctors in the Emergency Department,' Rachel said. 'Samir put some wires on you in the ambulance so he could monitor your heart, and I'm just going to attach those wires to my monitor here so I can do the same thing,' she explained as she hooked Mrs Kaur up to the monitor.

'What's happened?' Mrs Kaur croaked.

'You've had a heart attack,' Rachel said gently. 'What's happened is that your arteries around your heart have become narrowed by a gradual build-up of fatty deposits called atheroma, and a piece of atheroma has broken off along with part of your artery wall. A blood clot formed to repair the damage, and it's blocked your artery.' A STEMI—an ST segment elevation myocardial infarction—meant there was a total blockage. 'Your heart muscle hasn't had the blood and oxygen it needs, and we need to treat you to restore the blood flow. I'm going to do some things here in the department to make you feel better, and then we're going to send you up to the cardiac unit for tests to see whether they're going to treat you with medication or surgery.'

'I'm sorry to be such a nuisance,' Mrs Kaur said.

'You're not a nuisance at all. I'm here to help,' Rachel reassured her. 'Please ask me if there's anything you're worried about. Your friend called your son, and he's on the way in.'

'What kind of surgery? Will I have to have a transplant?'

'No. It's something called an angioplasty—using a tube called a catheter with a balloon at the end. The surgeon will put it into one of your arteries and guide it up to the bit where your artery's blocked, then inflate the balloon to open the artery again. If they can't do that, they might have to do a bypass—that's where they take a blood vessel from another part of your body and attach it to the artery above and below the blockage, so the blood's diverted—'

The rest of Rachel's words cut off as Mrs Kaur went pale, slumped and stopped breathing. The monitor showed that her heart had gone into ventricular fibrillation; it was an arrhythmia that often happened just after a heart attack, when the heart muscle hadn't had enough blood flow and became electrically unstable.

'Crash team!' Rachel yellowed. 'Nita, I'm going to need you to put a ventilation bag on her. I'll start the compressions.' She changed the angle of the bed so Mrs Kaur was lying flat, then tilted her head back and lifted her chin to open her airway. Nita, the nurse working with her, put a ventilation bag in place, and Rachel started pushing down hard on Mrs Kaur's chest to the rhythm of the Bee Gees' 'Stayin' Alive', making sure she was going down at least five centimetres. After the first thirty compressions, she paused so Nita could give two rescue breaths with the mask; the monitor showed that the heart rhythm was still VF, so she kept going for another thirty compressions. Two breaths. Still VF. She and Nita carried on, looking up when the doors to Resus burst open—and of course it would have to be Tim.

But their patient was much more important than the tension between them, right now. 'She's in VF. I'm doing chest compressions and Nita's bagging,' Rachel said. 'We're coming up to two minutes.'

'I'll attach the defib,' he said. 'OK. Charging. Let me know when you're at two minutes.'

Push, push, push.

Her wrists were hurting. 'That's two minutes of chest compressions,' Rachel said.

'And clear,' Tim said.

Everyone stood back, and he delivered the first shock. Mrs Kaur remained motionless.

'Rachel, we'll swap for this cycle,' Tim said.

It was hospital protocol to change the person doing the chest compressions every two minutes, to avoid fatigue and make sure that the compressions were deep enough.

Rachel recharged the defib while Tim and Nita continued CPR.

'And clear,' she said, delivering the second shock.

'Still VF,' Tim said, as they swapped over. 'Nita, can you sort out the adrenalin and amiodarone for me?' He got her to repeat the dosages back to him. 'That's great. Cheers.'

After the third shock, Tim administered the two injections. One more shock, and finally Mrs Kaur's heart was beating in sinus rhythm again.

'Well done, everyone,' Tim said.

By the time Mrs Kaur was stabilised, the cardiac specialist had come down and Rachel did the handover. Back in the office, she wrote up the notes, relieved that they'd managed to get their patient back; yet, at the same time, she felt so sad. Tim hadn't even been able to meet her eyes when he'd said well done to the team.

This wasn't going to work.

But she'd only been at Muswell Hill Memorial Hospital for two months. How could she possibly walk out of the job now? She'd be letting her colleagues down.

She'd just have to put up with it. And maybe at the next team meeting she could suggest taking over doing the staff rotas. Then she could make sure that she and Tim were on different shifts, so they'd have to see as little of each other as possible.

Next year, maybe she'd be able to make another fresh start, somewhere else. Another city, perhaps. And she definitely wouldn't make the same mistakes again.

CHAPTER EIGHT

'DAD, WHAT DO you mean, Christmas is off?' Hannah asked.

'We're not going to Rachel's any more.'

'Is she all right?'

Guilt flooded through Tim. Of course his eldest daughter's first thought would be of an accident or something, after what had happened to Mandy. 'It's not that. It's just not appropriate any more.'

'Why not? I thought you were dating her?'

Tim was struggling to find the right words to explain when Hannah sighed. 'Oh, Dad. What went wrong?'

'Me,' he said.

'Nope. Not getting it.'

He sighed. 'You know what I'm like. I'm a workaholic. That's why I wasn't there for your mum. And I wasn't there for you, when you had that scare and you needed me—I was repeating the same old mistakes.'

'You weren't at work,' Hannah pointed out. 'You were with Rachel.'

'And I wasn't concentrating on my family, the way I should be.'

'Dad, that's crazy. And everything was all right. And you came as soon as you got my message.'

'Which was later than I should've been,' he said stubbornly.

'So you're the one who ended it?'

'Yes.'

There was silence the other end, and then another sigh. 'OK, Dad. I'll let Soph know for you.'

He knew that she'd let him off the hook and it was way more than he deserved. 'Thanks, love.'

'I've got to go now,' Hannah said.

'All right. I'll call you later in the week.'

An hour later, Tim was scrubbing the kitchen clean—not that he used it much, apart from reheating things in the microwave, but the physical activity was giving him something to think about other than how miserable he was and how much he missed Rachel—when the doorbell rang.

He opened the door to find both his daughters standing on the doorstep; Sophie was holding a box of muffins.

'This is an intervention,' she said. 'Because Hannah and I can't just stand aside and watch you throw away something so good.'

Tim was too shocked to protest. The next thing he knew, he was seated at the table with a mug of coffee and a blueberry muffin in front of him.

'We knew you've been miserable all week,' Sophie said, 'but we couldn't work out what was wrong—if you were stressed about work or something—because you always close off and bury yourself in work.'

'It drives us potty,' Hannah said, 'but it's who you are, and we've learned to deal with it. Well, up to a point. But I told Soph what you told me about splitting up with Rachel.'

'Honestly, Dad. Right now it feels as if you're the teenager and we're the parents,' Sophie said. 'You're the head of a department at a busy hospital. We know you're clever and we know you save lives every day. So how can you be so utterly *hopeless*?'

He stared at her, taken aback. 'Hopeless?'

'Rachel's lovely. She's perfect for you. Since Mum died, you've been lost and lonely and we've been at our wits' end trying to work out how we can help you,' Hannah said. 'And then Rachel came into your life, and you started to smile again. It meant we had our dad back. We were even going to have our first proper Christmas for three years.' She rubbed her bump. 'What could be my baby's first Christmas. A new start. And now you've wrecked it.'

'And neither of us can understand why. Rachel's not Mum, and she's not trying to be Mum. She's herself,' Sophie said. 'She's lovely. So tell me why you dumped her, because what Han said made no sense at all. I'm convinced it's preggy brain making her muddle her words.'

'I'm convinced it's preggy brain, too,' Hannah said, 'because what Dad said makes no sense.'

'I let your mum down. I wasn't there enough. I've put my work before my family, in the past—and I've just replaced work with Rachel. I'm making the same mistakes.'

'That,' Sophie said, 'is a really feeble excuse, Dad.

Yes, you're a workaholic, but that's only part of who you are. We know it's because Granddad was frankly a rubbish parent; he always put you down when he should've been proud of you.'

Hannah gave a wry laugh. 'When I decided to do my PGCE, Granddad told me that English teachers were ten a penny and I ought to do a conversion course and be a lawyer instead, and I gave him a lecture on psychology and how rubbish he was. He sulked for *months*.'

Tim blinked. 'Oh, my God. He said something that awful to you? I had no idea.'

'It's OK. I said I hope he'd never been that rude to my mum, who was one of the wisest people I know and who did a job that was every bit as important as his, even if she didn't earn as much as he did. That I planned to follow in her footsteps and be a brilliant teacher who'd use poetry and Shakespeare to inspire kids to be the best they could be. And that, actually, money isn't the only measure of a job's value,' Hannah said. 'Then he said the nonsense about only saying it so I'd fight back to prove him wrong and get good grades.'

Tim went very still. 'He did that to me.'

'I know. I told Mum about it, and that's when she told me what he'd said to you, and that he'd always made you feel you were a disappointment to him.'

'Just so we're very clear on this,' Tim said, 'I'm hugely proud of both of you, and so was your mum. We wanted you to do what *you* wanted, not what we thought you ought to do.'

'And we appreciate that,' Sophie said.

'I'm just so sorry he...' Tim blew out a breath. 'If I'd known, I would've read him the Riot Act.'

'Way ahead of you, Dad. When he said it, I told him that putting people down all the time was the quickest way to make them feel crap about themselves rather than this "fighting back to prove him wrong" nonsense, and if he ever did it to Soph then I'd know about it and I'd scalp him. With a blunt instrument and lots of salt,' Hannah said.

Tim marvelled at his daughter's bravery at facing down her grandfather's bullying.

'When Mum told us what he'd done to you, Han went round to see him with his favourite cake to lull him into calmness. Then she told him you were a brilliant doctor who deserved much, much better from him, and she battered him with Shakespeare,' Sophie said, laughing. 'She followed it up with a poem every single day until he admitted he was in the wrong and you'd made the right career choice.' She grinned. 'You know, Han, maybe you need to do that to Dad.'

'There's no need to batter me with Shakespeare. I apologise when I'm in the wrong,' Tim said. 'I still can't get over the fact you tackled your granddad, Han.'

'He needed to be put straight,' Hannah said. 'It's not the way to treat people. Though,' she admitted, 'it's probably easier to stand up for yourself if you don't have to live with that person and feel their disapproval every second of every day.'

'You and Mum always believed in us,' Sophie said. 'You've always made us feel as if we could do anything we wanted—and we're so glad you weren't like

Granddad. I think that would've turned us into worka-
holics, too.'

'Though you still repeat your mistakes, Dad. You're
as stubborn as Granddad, in your way,' Hannah said.
'Yes, you used to fight with Mum about your ridiculous working hours. But she loved you anyway, because
she understood what drove you and how you wanted to
care for people. That you wanted to save people so they
wouldn't miss their grandmothers as much as you did.'

'Mum wouldn't have had you any other way, Dad,'
Sophie said. 'Think about it. She had a vocational job,
too, and she understood how important your job was
to you.'

'And Rachel will understand even more, because she
does the same job as you. Her daughters will know how
much she loves them, just as we know how much you
love us,' Hannah said. 'But they'll also know that emergency doctors are really, really driven and they need to
save people. It just goes with the territory.'

'Don't feel you're being disloyal to Mum by getting
serious with Rachel,' Sophie added. 'Mum wouldn't
have wanted you to be alone for the rest of your life.
She would've wanted you to find someone who loved
you for who you are and wouldn't want to change you.
Someone who'd support you and get on with us and be
part of all our lives, while acknowledging how important
Mum was to us—and that's exactly what Rachel does.'

'I'm glad you were out with her instead of shutting
yourself away on your own. It's about time you light-
ened up and got on with enjoying life. Mum would've

scalped you for the way you've been since she died,' Hannah said.

'But I wasn't there when you called me,' Tim reminded her.

'Your phone was on silent. It happens,' Sophie said. 'You know what I think?'

He knew she was going to tell him anyway and steeled himself. Sophie and Hannah had inherited their mother's straightforwardness.

'It's an excuse because you're scared.' Sophie looked at him. 'Dad, I love you, and this isn't a nice thing to say, and I'm only telling you this so bluntly because being subtle doesn't work with you.' She took a deep breath. 'I think you're scared that if you get close to someone, you might lose her, the way you lost Mum. So you dumped her rather than risk losing her.'

Tim thought about it. Was Sophie right?

'Soph's right. Dad, there's always a risk. It's better to let people in than to keep them at a distance,' Hannah said gently. 'Be honest about your worries. I panic that I won't get the baby to term. Jamal's terrified that I'm going to get a pulmonary embolism after I've had the baby and die. There's always a risk with everything you do, but you have to put it in perspective. Live your best life, the way Mum did.'

It was as if his daughters had thrown a bucket of cold water over him.

And, once the shock had passed, he could see clearly again. He'd refused to let himself see it, but his girls were absolutely right.

'I've screwed up,' Tim said. 'Big time. Rachel's ex was a selfish jerk who let her down—and I'm no better.'

'Of course you're better than that,' Sophie said.

'Just call her and tell her you screwed up,' Hannah said.

'How?' Tim asked.

'If you're honest with her, tell her how you feel and why you said whatever you did, she'll understand. It sounds as if you hurt her, but you can fix that. It might take time and it'll definitely take effort—but she's worth it. *You're* worth it. Now, eat your muffin and think about it,' Sophie said.

Hannah nudged her sister. 'Are you sure you want to stay as a marketing tycoon, Soph? You'd be an awesome teacher. All the Year Ten boys would be so terrified of you that they'd actually do their homework.'

'You seriously think I want to spend my working day in a room that smells of feet, farts and way too much body spray?' Sophie teased back. 'No chance. I want all the glamour of fancy coffee and posh biscuits, courtesy of grateful clients.'

Tim tuned out his daughters for a moment.

Be honest with Rachel. Tell her why he really dumped her. Admit that he was scared of failing her or losing her and hadn't wanted to take the risk.

She'd probably find a solution, with that calm common sense of hers. But he didn't want calm common sense. He wanted her to love him, the way he was pretty sure he loved her. Though how could he ask that of her?

'Dad? Earth to Dad,' Sophie said.

'Sorry. I zoned out for a second,' he said. 'What did you say?'

'I said, I hope you're going to talk to her. Make it right,' she said. 'We're going, now. So call her. And then, when you've sorted it out, tell us.'

After he'd waved them off at the front door, he called Rachel. He was more than prepared for her to let it go through to voicemail and ignore him, but she picked up. 'Tim.'

'Rachel.' And then he went all tongue-tied. For pity's sake. He saved lives every single day. That meant communicating well with your team. Why couldn't he communicate with Rachel now?

'What do you want?' she asked, after an awkward silence.

'To see you. To talk,' he said. *To apologise.* The words stuck in his throat like sand.

'No,' she said. 'I don't think we have anything to say to each other.'

'But—'

'Sorry, Tim. You were right. It's not going to work between us. We're much better off sticking to being just colleagues.' Her voice was totally expressionless. She was freezing him out. 'I'll see you at work.'

She didn't even give him the chance to say goodbye before she ended the call.

Oh, hell.

What was he going to do?

If she wasn't even going to talk to him, how on earth could he tell her that he was sorry, and he'd made a huge, huge mistake?

Wanting to clear his head, he walked to the parade of shops round the corner and bought some flowers, then headed for the cemetery. He knelt in front of Mandy's grave, taking out the faded flowers from the previous week, wiping down all the surfaces and then replenishing the water in the vase and putting the new stems in place.

'Mand, it's all going to hell without you,' he said. 'I thought I'd found someone I could maybe be happy with. Not replace you—I could never replace you—but someone I can share my life with.' He blew out a breath. 'Except I was stupid. I got scared that I'd mess it all up or I'd lose her—not that I even admitted that to myself—and I pushed her away. I was hopeless with you, neglecting you and the girls for work, and I didn't want to make all the same mistakes over again. Especially because her ex was totally selfish. She deserves better than that. *You* deserved better.' He sighed. 'I love you, I always will, and she understood that. And I... I love her, too.'

Maybe it was his imagination, but he had the impression of warmth around him, as if he were being hugged, and he could smell the gardenia perfume he'd always associated with Mandy. And he could almost hear her voice saying, *Your heart expands to make room for love. I want you to be happy. Talk to her. Open up.*

And she was right. He needed to talk to her; his mistake had been trying to phone Rachel. Even a video call wasn't good enough. This was something he needed to do face to face, so she could look into his eyes and see that he was completely sincere about everything.

Though, before he tried to arrange a meeting, Tim knew he needed to work out exactly what he wanted to say.

'Sometimes it's useful when our parents are a bit less clued up on social media,' Sophie said. 'Rachel's friends list is open rather than hidden. All we need to do is find her daughters and get in touch with them.'

'Meg and Saskia, Dad said they were called,' Hannah said.

'Let me search the list. Yep, there's a Meg and a Saskia. They have a different surname—but Rachel's divorced, so that figures,' Sophie said. 'Righty. I'll send a direct message to both of them and see which one comes back first.'

Hello! We haven't met yet but our dad Tim was seeing your very lovely mum. Except he's done something stupid—he broke up with her because he thought it would be best for her.

She added an eye-roll emoji.

Which is EXTREMELY stupid of him because they're good for each other. Dad's eating himself up with guilt, and Rachel won't speak to him so he can't explain why he's made such a mess of things. Can we do a joint intervention to stop them ruining what we think would be a good thing for both of them? Cheers, Sophie and Hannah.

She showed the message to her sister. 'Anything you'd change?'

'Nope. It's perfect,' Meg said. 'Send it.'

Within half an hour, Meg had messaged Sophie back.

Your dad's lovely, too. Agreed we need to act. We'll work on Mum and get her to talk to him. Cheers, Meg and Saskia.

'So now all we have to do is hope he doesn't mess it up,' Sophie said.

Rachel's phone pinged to signal an incoming text. Meg.

Got a moment for a chat?

The years of practice she'd had in pretending that nothing was wrong would come in useful now. Even though she was miserable, she'd make sure she sounded smiley for her daughters. She texted back.

Sure.

The phone rang immediately with a group video call from her daughters.

'Is everything OK?' Rachel asked.

'No,' Saskia said. 'When were you going to tell us that Christmas—or rather Boxing Day—was cancelled?'

'How did you know? Did Tim tell you?' She frowned. But how could he have done? She hadn't given him her daughters' numbers.

'No. His daughters got in touch with us,' Meg said. 'They found us in your social media account friends' list and sent us a message.'

'Uh-huh.'

'What happened, Mum?' Saskia asked.

'He wasn't ready, and he wanted to call it a day. It's fine.' Rachel turned up the wattage on her smile in the hope of convincing her daughters that it really was fine. 'We can be civilised colleagues at work.'

'He made a mistake, breaking up with you, Mum,'

Meg said. 'And he didn't do it for the reason you said, because he wasn't ready. It was because—oh, you need to talk to him about it.' She sighed. 'Mum, don't assume he's going to be like Dad. They're nothing alike. Dad never felt guilty when he'd had yet another affair.'

Rachel flinched. So much for thinking that she'd protected their girls.

'Whereas Tim's eating himself up with guilt,' Meg finished.

'Guilt about what?'

'You need to talk to him, Mum. For both your sakes,' Saskia said.

Almost on cue, her phone pinged.

'Who was that text from?' Meg asked.

'Tim.'

'What does he say?' Saskia asked.

'He wants to talk and wants to know when's a good time for him to call round.' She narrowed her eyes. 'Does this have anything to do with you?'

'Probably Hannah and Sophie,' Meg said. 'We're staging a two-part intervention. Daughters to parents.'

'We're hanging up now, Mum,' Saskia said. 'Call him. Then let us know how things go.'

Before Rachel had a chance to protest, the screen went black. Followed immediately by a text message from Meg.

CALL HIM NOW!!!!!!

Call Tim. Talk to him. But what was there to say? He'd walked away from her—just as her ex had, and just as her father had.

Then again, if she didn't talk to him, she knew Meg and Saskia would nag until she did.

She texted him back.

I'm free now.

He texted back.

Be with you in about half an hour.

Should he take flowers? Chocolates? Wine? Tim thought as he booked a taxi.

No. None of it was enough.

What he needed to give Rachel was something more important. Total honesty.

He rehearsed the words in his head all the way from Muswell Hill to Hampstead; but the second he'd paid the taxi fare and pressed her doorbell, they all vanished. Why the hell hadn't he been sensible and written them down?

Rachel opened the door, unsmiling. 'Tim.'

'Thank you for agreeing to see me, Rachel,' he said quietly.

'Come in.' She stood aside. 'Coffee?'

'Yes, please.' Because at least then he could have something to do with his hands.

This was crazy. In his thirty-plus years as a doctor, he'd kept a cool head; he'd performed CPR countless times, dealt with horrific fractures and trauma injuries, done emergency tracheotomies to secure airways, all the while reassuring his patients and his team. Yet, at the idea of talking about emotional things, opening up to Rachel and telling her what was in his heart, he was terrified and didn't even know where to start.

He took off his shoes, hung his coat on the bentwood stand in the hallway, and followed her to the kitchen. 'Is there anything I can do to help?'

'It's fine.' She gestured to the table. 'Take a seat.'

He sat at her kitchen table, tapping the ends of his fingers against each other, while she made coffee. Maybe he should try small talk. Except he didn't know what to say.

She placed a mug in front of him and sat opposite him.

'Thank you,' he said. 'For the coffee. And for agreeing to see me.' He took a deep breath. 'I'd prepared a speech. But I should've written it down, because all the words have just vanished out of my head.' He spread his hands. 'I'm sorry. I'm truly sorry I hurt you. What I said to you... I was in panic mode. I wish I could take it all back.'

'You said,' she reminded him, 'that you couldn't be with me. "It's not you, it's me."'

He winced as she made the exaggerated quote marks with her fingers, but he knew he deserved it.

'You said you couldn't be with me any more. That you needed to concentrate on your girls.' Her face tightened. 'I've been thinking about this ever since. I think what you really meant was that I wasn't enough for you. Just as I wasn't enough for my dad, and just as I wasn't enough for Steve.'

'What? No! It absolutely wasn't that.' He stared at her, horrified. 'Is that really what you thought?'

'What other reason could there be?' she asked tightly.

'You're enough for me. Of course you're enough for

me. I love you.' And then he stared at her, aghast at what he'd just blurted out.

'You love me,' she said drily. 'And that's why you dumped me.'

He raked his hand through his hair. 'I know it doesn't sound as if it makes any sense.'

'It doesn't just *sound* it. It doesn't make sense at all,' she said.

'It's all a mess,' he said. 'My job came first, most of the time, and I know I wasn't there for Mandy and the girls as much as I should've been. Worst of all, I wasn't there at the end.' He dragged in a breath. 'I know I couldn't have saved my wife. Nobody could've saved her, not with the brain injury caused when she hit her head. But I should have been right there by her side in the ambulance, holding her hand on the way to hospital and telling her I loved her when she died. I'll never be able to forgive myself for that.'

'You were saving someone's life at the time, weren't you?' she reminded him.

'A seventy-year-old woman with a heart attack. Just like my gran. The same age Gran was when she died. She even looked like Gran. I needed to be sure I'd saved her. I thought that dinner could wait, that nobody would mind me being a bit late—that Mandy would be there, the way she'd always been.' He turned the mug round in his hands. 'Work was always a bit of a bone of contention between Mandy and me. I work ridiculous hours. I always have. It started as a way of proving to myself that I was going to be a really good doctor, that I'd be there for my patients and make a proper difference.' He swallowed hard. 'Partly it was because I wanted to save other families from what we went through, losing Gran. And partly...' He shook his head. 'I told you Dad was disappointed I didn't follow him into law. Actually, he was more than disappointed. He said I'd made a huge mistake and one day I would come crawling back to him and admit he was right.'

'That,' Rachel said, 'is utter rubbish. Did he ever admit he was wrong?'

Tim gave a mirthless laugh. 'Not quite. After I made consultant, he said that my being a doctor was his idea all along and what he'd said was his way of pushing me. In his view, if he told me I was useless and I'd never be able to do it, then I'd fight back to prove him wrong and I'd excel.'

Her eyes widened. 'That sounds a bit "sorry, not sorry" to me.'

'That's what I thought, too.' He shrugged. 'I guess I can see where he was coming from—but it just made me angry all the time. I'd wanted him to support me instead of sniping. And I swore I'd never be like that to my kids, trying to push them into what I wanted them to do instead of helping them live their own dreams.' He looked away. 'I had no idea at the time, but he did exactly the same thing to Hannah. He told her teachers were ten a penny and she should do a conversion course and be a lawyer. Except she faced him down where I didn't. She's braver than I am.'

'People react in different ways,' Rachel said. 'It's what makes us human, not robots.'

'But I repeat my mistakes,' he said. 'I nearly wasn't

there for Hannah when she had that scare with the baby, and my phone was on silent. She couldn't get hold of me when she needed me.' He shook his head. 'I panicked. I told myself I was letting my family down again—except this time the reason I wasn't there wasn't work, it was because I was concentrating on myself. Because I was with you. And I know how unfair that is.'

'Yes, it is,' she said. 'You're using me as an excuse.'

'I'm sorry. It's…' He swallowed hard. If he told her his fears, then maybe she'd understand and give him a chance to make things right between them. 'I haven't even been honest with myself,' he said. 'Deep down, I'm scared to take a risk again. What if I fell in love with someone and lost her, the way I lost Mandy?'

'There aren't any guarantees,' she said. 'All you can do is make the most of what you have. Because, if you shut yourself off, all you have is loneliness—and that means you've lost anyway.'

'When I met you, I realised you'd had a rough time, but you were brave about it.'

'Was I? I seem to remember telling you I didn't have a clue about how to pick myself up and start all over again.'

'But you didn't wallow, the way I have. You made things the best you could for your daughters. And you just got on with your life.' He blew out a breath. 'I'm making a mess of this, now. I'm not great with emotional stuff. I…didn't expect to feel the way I do about you, so quickly. I told myself we'd be friends, and that's honestly what I intended to happen.' He met her gaze. 'Except, the more I got to know you, the more I liked you. It felt as if all the clouds were melting away and the sun was coming back out. I was happier than I'd been in years.'

'That's how I felt, too,' she said. 'Then I realised how stupid I'd been. I'd let you close and trusted you—and then you backed off. And it was obvious I wasn't enough for you.'

'You *are* enough for me,' he said. 'You're everything I want, Rachel. You're kind and you're funny and you're clever. You make my heart feel as if it's doing somersaults when you smile. Even if I'm having a bad day at work, stuck with the suits, I think about seeing you and it makes all the clouds go away.'

This was making even less and less sense, Rachel thought. If he felt like that about her, why had he dumped her? 'So why did you back away?' she asked.

'Because I panicked,' he said. 'I know we do the same job, and you get where I'm coming from about wanting to save people, because it's the same for you. But you've already been married to someone who didn't put you first. How can I ask you to be with me, when I know I always put my job first? I can't ask you to make that kind of sacrifice.' He shook his head. 'I never meant to hurt you, Rachel. But there wasn't a choice. If I stayed with you, I'd end up hurting you by not putting you first. If I ended it between us, I'd hurt you—but not as much as if you started to rely on me and then I let you down.'

'That's pretty twisted logic,' she said. 'But the point is that *you're* the one who made the choice, Tim. You didn't discuss it with me or try to find out how I felt about the situation. Right now it feels as if you used me as an excuse for your fears, instead of giving me a say in my own future. Yes, you're right. I spent nearly a quarter of a century with a man who started off as Prince Charming and swept me off my feet, and then became completely self-centred. I would never have married Steve if I'd realised I was marrying a man like my dad, the sort who'd always put himself first and didn't bother with his kids. I wanted someone who'd love me for who I was, who'd make a family with me, who'd love my mum and love our future kids. And, yes, I made the choice to stay with him and put up with the things that made me unhappy. Maybe that was the wrong decision. But now I'm in a place where I'm comfortable making my own choices.' She took a deep breath. 'And I don't want to be with someone who uses me as an excuse not to face up to his own fears.'

'That's fair.' He looked at her. 'And I don't want to use you as an excuse. I want to face up to those fears. And I'll do it, Rachel. I won't be able to make them go away overnight, but I'll make the effort. Because I want you. I want to be with you.'

'But how do I know I'm enough for you, when I wasn't enough for Steve or my dad?' she asked. 'How do I know I can trust you?'

'You don't,' he said. 'That's fear talking. Something you need to face and make go away, just like I need to face my fear that I'll let you down. And I think that's something we can't do on our own. We need someone else's perspective to make us see things how they really are, instead of what we think they are.' He reached across the table and took her hand. 'Shall I tell you how

I know you're enough for me? Because I was lucky enough to have a really good marriage. I loved Mandy, and I know she loved me—even when we drove each other crazy. She taught me that you don't have to be perfect to be worth loving.'

Rachel thought about it. Was Tim right? Could she be enough for him? Could she let herself trust him again?

'I love you,' he said. 'It isn't the same love I felt for Mandy, because you're not her—and I don't want you to be her. I want you to be *you*, just the way you are. But I know my love's true and it's real, and it'll grow deeper with every day.' He blew out a breath. 'You know what we said weeks ago about middle-aged people being set in their ways? I'll try to be less set in my ways, but I don't think I can stop being a workaholic. It's part of who I am.'

'And I understand that,' she said, 'because I have the same job as you. Emergency medicine means you can't walk away. You need to be there and get your patient through the crisis. It's not the sort of job where you can leave a task until tomorrow. You can't even plan your day, because that's the whole point of emergencies: you never know what's going to happen or who's going to need you.'

'Actually,' he said, 'you can kind of plan your day. You don't know who your patients will be and you don't know what conditions they'll present with, but you know who's on your team and you know they're going to try their best to help people, too, and you'll get through it because you'll work together.'

'Which means,' she said, 'you're reliable. You're not

going to let your team or your patients down. Just as you won't let your family down.'

'I can't guarantee I'll be home on time—or, if I'm working, that I'll even manage to get there for a family party or dinner out with friends,' he said.

'Neither can I,' she reminded him. 'If there's an emergency doctor in the family, everyone knows that and works round it. It's all about reaching a workable compromise and having a good support network. I had Mum and you had Mandy.' She paused. 'You're being too hard on yourself. Has it ever occurred to you that only a kind man who really cared would be so worried about missing things and letting people down?'

'No,' he admitted.

'Think about it,' she said. 'You told me you knew I'd be enough for you because you'd had a good marriage and Mandy taught you that nobody has to be perfect to be worth loving. I'm telling you I know you're enough for me and it's OK for you to be a workaholic, because I was married to a man who didn't care enough—and you're the complete opposite of that,' she said.

'So where do we go from here?' he asked.

She knew what she wanted, but she wasn't quite brave enough to say it first. 'What do you want, Tim?'

'The short answer: you,' he said immediately.

She shook her head. 'That's glib. I mean, *really*. What do you want?'

This was important, Tim knew. If he got it wrong now, he'd lose her. And he needed her to know that he was being completely sincere.

'I want to share my life again,' he said. 'But not with just anyone. I want someone who makes my heart beat faster when she smiles at me. Someone I really like as a person as well as loving her. Someone who enjoys the same kind of things that I do and will maybe push my boundaries a bit. Someone who'll be happy to blend her family with mine. Someone who'll encourage me to catch up with my best mate while she catches up with hers—someone who understands that you need to do things separately as well as together and give each other space to be who you are.'

Was that hope he could see in her eyes?

It made hope glow in his own heart, too. More than glow: it burst from a flicker into a steady flame.

'I want a real partnership,' he said. 'With someone who'll let me support her and take up the slack when she's rushed off her feet, and who'll be there for me when I need support. With someone who won't mind that when I'm in charge of sorting dinner it'll be a choice of takeaway or cheese and crackers. With someone who'll know that I'm not perfect, that I have all these doubts and these fears, and I'll try my hardest to overcome them—but who understands that those fears won't go away overnight, and I'm going to need prodding from time to time.'

He squeezed her hand. 'That someone is you, Rachel. But it will only work if that's what you want, too.' It was a terrifying question to ask; but she'd been brave enough to ask him. He'd make himself be brave enough to ask her. 'What do *you* want?'

She said nothing, and his stomach cramped.

What if he wasn't what she wanted?

But then she cleared her throat. 'I want a real partnership,' she said. 'With someone who'll celebrate the good times and support me through the tough times. Someone who'll do their fair share—I don't mean necessarily half of each chore, but someone who'll empty the bins or clean the windows I can't reach or notice when the laundry basket's full and put a load of washing in the machine without making a fuss about it. Someone who'll make a family with me. Someone who'll be honest and stay faithful.'

He could do all that.

'But I don't want just anyone,' she said. 'The one I want makes my heart beat faster when he smiles, just as I do to him. He's the one who makes the morning feel bright and shiny and new when I wake and see him next to me. He's the one who'll know just from looking at me when I walk in what kind of shift I've had—and whether I need a hug, or coffee made with a bit of cold water so I can drink it straight down, or to be danced round the room and reminded that life's good.'

He could do all that, too.

'I'm ready to move on,' he said. 'And I want to move on with you. I'm not offering you perfection, because perfection isn't real. But I'll give you everything I am,' he said. 'I'll respect you, I'll appreciate you, I'll compromise with you—and most of all I'll love you.' He squeezed her hand. 'I'm sorry I hurt you and I'm sorry I made such a mess of things. I love you, Rachel. Will you give me another chance?'

'Take a risk?' She squeezed his hand. 'Together.'

'Together,' he agreed.

At last, she smiled. 'Yes. Because I love you, too.'

He released her hand, pushed his chair back and walked round to her side of the table. When she stood up to meet him, he wrapped his arms round her and kissed her. 'I love you. Here's to the future.'

'The future,' she echoed.

Just then, both their mobile phones beeped with a couple of messages.

'Mine are from my daughters,' Rachel said. 'They say, "Well?"—with four question marks.'

'Snap,' Tim said. He grinned. 'Even though I'd quite like to have you to myself, this evening, I think we might need to make a video call first…'

CHAPTER NINE

'AND CHRISTMAS STARTS NOW—a day late,' Rachel said with a smile. 'The turkey's in, the pigs in blankets are cooking, the veg is all prepped, your filo pastry snake is resting in the fridge, Saskia…and I think we've earned Buck's Fizz.'

'It's so nice to see you happy,' Saskia said. 'I'm glad you and Tim talked properly and sorted it out. He's lovely.'

'He is. I think Mum would've liked him.' Rachel poured orange juice into three wine glasses at the kitchen table and topped them up with Prosecco.

'Happy Christmas, Mum.' Meg raised her glass. 'And this next year's going to be so much better.' She smiled. 'Even with exams.'

'Seconded,' Saskia said.

'Thirded,' Rachel said, not to be outdone. 'Right. Pancakes.' She'd made the batter before she'd started the veg; she cooked a pile of them swiftly on the hob, while Meg made coffee and Saskia brought out everything else.

'Do you remember when you used to use a squeezy

bottle to draw pancakes in the shape of Rudolph, and give him a raspberry for a nose?' Saskia asked.

'And we'd have them with tons of golden syrup and sprinkles,' Meg added.

'And now look at us,' Rachel teased, gesturing to the table. 'Vegan pancakes with blueberry compote and dairy-free Greek yogurt.'

'Things change,' Saskia said. 'And next year will be different again. You might not even be living here, still.'

'Wherever Tim and I decide to settle,' Rachel said, 'it will always have room for both of you. And, just so you know, he said it two seconds before I could.'

'We're just glad to see you happy,' Meg said. 'And we're really looking forward to meeting his family properly today.'

'Me, too,' Saskia said. 'It'll be lovely to have a big family Christmas again.'

Just turning into your road, Dad. x

Tim scanned Hannah's text and texted back.

Locking front door now. x.

Jamal managed to park outside their gate, and Tim opened the boot of the car to stow the champagne and chocolates he'd bought as his contribution to Christmas dinner before squeezing into the back next to Sophie.

'Merry Boxing Day,' he said.

'Merry Christmas,' Hannah said. 'I'm so looking forward to meeting Rachel's daughters.' She turned her head to smile at her father. 'And we never thought we'd see you looking happy at Christmas again.'

'I'm happy,' he said gently.

'And we're glad,' Sophie said.

* * *

An hour later, everyone was sitting round Rachel's dining room table, with a glass of champagne—sparkling elderflower for Hannah, and for Jamal who was driving—and Rachel was carving the turkey. The girls had bonded immediately, and by the time they sat at the table it felt as if they'd all known each other for years instead of for a few minutes. Tim had been tasked with making Hannah sit down and stay put, and everyone else had brought in dishes of veg and trimmings, until the table was practically groaning.

Sophie had made eco crackers from recycled paper, containing a packet of wild flower seeds, a terrible joke contributed by Tim and a challenge card to do over coffee. Everyone tried Saskia's filo pastry 'snake' and pronounced it delicious; and the room was filled with conversation and laughter and the clinking of cutlery against china.

If she could preserve a moment in time, Rachel thought, it would be this one: having a full house again, feeling part of a big family, and with everyone relaxed and talking and laughing.

She met Tim's eye and was pretty sure he was thinking the same.

Even clearing up was easy; Meg sat at the piano, playing Christmas songs and making Hannah sing along while everyone else cleared the table and Rachel stacked the dishwasher.

They were in the middle of having a very rowdy game of Monopoly when Hannah excused herself from the table. 'I swear this baby's dancing on my bladder.'

She'd just walked out of the dining room when they heard a wail of distress.

'Hannah?' Rachel rushed out to the hallway, followed closely by Tim and Jamal.

'I'm so sorry. I didn't make it to the loo in time.' Hannah grimaced. 'If you can let me have a cloth, I'll clear up.'

'Honey, it's fine,' Rachel reassured her. 'It'll take me seconds to do it.'

'Sweetheart, given that you're a week overdue, are you quite sure that was your bladder?' Tim asked.

Hannah looked horrified. 'You mean—that was my waters breaking?'

'It's a possibility,' Rachel said, 'but don't panic yet. Have you had any kind of contractions?'

'I've felt twinges on and off all day, but they're just Braxton-Hicks. Twinge—ow!' Her face turned pale. 'This one isn't weak!'

'Hold on to me,' Rachel said, and Hannah clung to her arm during the contraction.

'We're going to get you to the kitchen, you're going to make yourself comfortable leaning on the back of a chair, I'll get you a glass of water, and we'll plan what we do next,' Rachel said.

'Is your hospital bag in the car?' Tim asked.

'Yes, with my pregnancy notes.' She gave them a watery smile. 'Jamal says I need to take them everywhere.'

'Yes, you do,' Jamal said. 'Oh, my God. Are you really in labour, Han?'

'It's looking that way,' Rachel said. 'It's just a matter of how fast it's progressing.'

In the kitchen doorway, Hannah had another contraction; this time, it was clearly sharp.

Rachel glanced at Tim, guessing that, like her, he'd realised how short the time was between contractions and that his daughter was actually in advanced labour.

The main thing was to make sure that the parents-to-be—and grandfather-to-be—didn't start worrying. Especially given Hannah's recent scare about the baby's movements. Which meant giving them distractions. 'Jamal, can you time the contractions for me? Tim, can you tell the others and grab Hannah's hospital bag? And, Hannah, you're doing brilliantly,' Rachel said. 'Keep breathing for me. Nice and deep.'

The next contraction came in five minutes, by which time Tim had told the others, brought in the hospital bag and followed Rachel's directions to get the thermometer, blood pressure monitor and stethoscope from the kitchen drawer where she kept the house medical supplies, and the magnetic pad and pen from the front of the fridge.

'Do you want me to examine you?' Tim asked.

Hannah shook her head. 'I love you, Dad, but—' she grimaced '—I'd rather you were at the non-business end with Jamal, talking to me.'

'Understood. And it's all going to be fine, sweetheart,' Tim said.

'Rachel, I know it's a lot to ask,' Hannah said, 'but would you? Examine me, I mean?'

'I'd be honoured,' Rachel said. 'Tim, can you take down all the stats for me?'

'For the midwifery team's records?' Tim asked. 'Ready when you are.'

Rachel took Hannah's pulse, temperature and blood pressure, and Tim noted down the readings.

'Just as well I'm in a doctor's house,' Hannah said shakily.

'You're going to be fine,' Rachel reassured her. 'Most people would have a thermometer with their medical kit, and the blood pressure monitor's a middle-aged person thing,' she said, trying to make Hannah smile. 'I'll agree that the stethoscope isn't standard, though.' She checked the baby's heart. 'All sounds good. Do you want to hear, Hannah? Jamal?'

While Tim helped Hannah with the stethoscope, Rachel felt Hannah's abdomen to check the baby's progression. This definitely felt like established labour.

'Tell me when your next contraction ends, and then I'll examine your cervix,' she said.

She was shocked to discover that Hannah was already eight centimetres dilated.

'Your hospital's in Hackney, right?' she checked.

'Yes,' Jamal confirmed. 'We were going in tomorrow for Hannah to be induced.'

'Hackney's a good three-quarters of an hour's drive from here, plus we'll need to get you up to the ward.' Rachel squeezed Hannah's hand. 'Hannah, I don't want to frighten you, but realistically I don't think you're going to make it to hospital. We'll call an ambulance, but I think there's a very good chance your baby's going to arrive before they do, because you're in active labour, and you're already eight centimetres dilated.'

'You mean—I'm going to have the baby here?' Hannah's eyes widened.

'You need to call your midwife,' Rachel said, 'and I'd like to talk to her, too. Not because I think there's anything to worry about at all, but just a quick professional chat, and you'll need to give her your permission to talk to me. Is that OK with you?'

'I…' Hannah looked dazed.

'I've delivered several babies,' Rachel reassured her, 'as well as having my own. Your dad's delivered babies, too. This might not be quite according to your birth plan, but your antenatal team probably told you that babies have a habit of ignoring birth plans.'

'Yeah,' Hannah said shakily.

'Make the call, sweetheart,' Rachel said. 'And, Jamal, can you ring the ambulance?'

Hannah called the hospital and spoke to her midwife, while Rachel swiftly read her birth plan, then handed the phone to Rachel. 'My midwife's called Naseera,' Hannah said.

'Thanks.' Rachel smiled at her. 'Hello, Naseera. My name's Rachel, I'm an emergency medicine consultant, and we're with Hannah's dad, who's head of the Emergency Department where I work,' she said. 'Hannah's doing fine, but I think we're looking at precipitous labour.' The normal length of labour for a first-time mum was around thirty hours; precipitous labour was where the baby was born within three hours of regular contractions commencing, with a sudden onset of intense contractions and little time between them. 'Is there anything Tim and I need to know about?'

'No complications during pregnancy and the baby's the normal size for dates,' Naseera said. 'Obviously you know Hannah was going to be induced tomorrow. She says you don't think there's time to get here.'

'No,' Rachel said. 'We've called the ambulance, but I think this baby's going to get here first. The good news is, Tim and I have both delivered a baby.'

'Am I on speaker phone?' Naseera asked.

'No.'

'Good, because I need to ask—given your specialty, I assume it's quite a while since you or Tim delivered a baby?'

'Yes.'

'OK. Obviously you can't list them for me, because we don't want Hannah to worry, but I'm just checking you know the potential complications of precipitous labour?' Naseera asked.

'We do,' Rachel said. With a fast labour, there was a risk that Hannah's body didn't have enough time to stretch slowly and prepare for the baby's birth and might tear. There were potential complications such as heavy bleeding, a retained placenta and even shock after giving birth, plus a greater risk of infection for the baby.

'All right. You've got the ambulance on its way, and I'm here if you need backup advice over the phone,' Naseera said.

'Thanks. We'll keep you posted,' Rachel promised, ended the call and handed the phone back to Hannah. She could see the worry etched on Tim's face and gave him a reassuring smile.

'OK, Hannah. I've had a look at your birth plan, and I think we can tweak it,' she said. 'Just for now, keep standing, so your contractions work with gravity. I think you might be more comfortable giving birth in the living room, plus we can keep it nice and warm for the baby, so I'll get that prepped.'

'But—I can't,' Hannah said in horror. 'I'll mess up your living room.'

Rachel gave her a quick hug. 'No, you won't. Everything will clean up. The important thing now is you, and how you want to do this, and what position you want to deliver in. We'll try our best to do as many of the things you planned for the birth, but the tough thing is that I don't have anything to give you for pain relief.'

'I've got a TENS machine in my hospital bag,' Hannah said.

'We can help you put it on, but there might not be enough time for the endorphins to work, sweetheart,' Tim warned her gently.

'I can run you a warm bath, for pain relief,' Rachel said. 'Though you won't have the space to move around.

'No, I'll manage.' Hannah bit her lip. 'Though I'm scared. I thought I'd be induced tomorrow, and everything would be in hospital. This feels out of control.'

'I promise you, love, your body knows exactly what to do,' Rachel said. 'Let it guide you. And music can help your body release endorphins. Have you got a birth playlist, or is there any kind of dance music you really like?'

'I've got birth playlists on my phone,' Hannah said. 'It's a bit like my running playlist for the hard bit, and then something gentle for when the baby arrives. They said at antenatal, you match your music to your mood.'

'Perfect. We'll connect your phone to my speaker. I

assume you did breathing exercises at antenatal classes?' Rachel asked.

'Yes,' Jamal confirmed.

'Can you breathe with Hannah while I get the living room ready?' Rachel asked.

Between them, Sophie, Calum, Saskia and Meg followed Rachel's directions. They put a shower curtain on the carpet to protect it and stop Hannah worrying and covered it with clean sheets; there was a stack of clean towels ready to dry the baby; and they put the heating on to make sure the room was warm enough for the newborn.

'If the doorbell goes,' Rachel said, 'that'll be the ambulance.'

'We'll go into the kitchen when Hannah's in the living room, so she's got a bit more privacy and we're not too noisy for her,' Meg said. 'Yell if you need anything. Cup of tea, hot soapy water—whatever it is, we'll be on it.'

'Thank you.' Rachel hugged her.

Between them, Jamal and Tim supported Hannah through to the living room, and Rachel brought her portable speaker through.

'We'll keep you walking about,' Rachel said, 'and we've got plenty of pillows. There's a shower curtain under those sheets, so there's nothing at all to worry about. You'll be meeting your little one very soon, and we're all here to support you. Anything you need, you tell us, and we'll sort it.'

'Can I have just the lights on the tree?' Hannah asked. 'Or will that be too hard for you?'

'I'll use the torch on my phone if I need light,' Rachel said. 'Let's make this how you need it.'

'Twinkling lights,' Hannah said. 'And music.'

Jamal connected Hannah's phone to Rachel's speaker.

'I want the upbeat one until I need to push,' Hannah said, 'and then I want the piano one.'

Jamal pressed 'play', and the beginning of The Beatles' 'Here Comes the Sun' floated into the air.

'Great choice,' Tim said. 'Are we walking or dancing?'

'Dancing,' Hannah said.

'Keep breathing in through your nose and out through your mouth,' Rachel said, 'and pant through your contractions. And we'll dance until you feel you need to do something different.'

Tim sang along, and Rachel joined him.

When a contraction hit, Jamal encouraged Hannah through the panting.

'You're doing brilliantly,' Tim said.

Four songs later, the ambulance still wasn't there—but Hannah was ready to push.

Rachel examined her. 'OK. The baby's crowning. Let's get you on your hands and knees.' And please, please, don't let this be complicated, she begged silently. Please don't let the cord be looped round the baby's neck. Please just let this work. Let this be a Christmas of joy for Tim and his family.

'I'll change the music,' Tim said, and switched the playlist. Jamal knelt beside Hannah, supporting her and telling her he loved her.

'When you feel the contraction,' Rachel said, 'push.'

Fauré's 'Sicilienne' floated into the air as the lights twinkled on the Christmas tree, and Hannah began to push.

Tim put his hand on Rachel's shoulder, letting her know he was there if she needed him. 'Good girl, Han. Keep going,' he said softly.

'That's the head delivered,' Rachel said. 'You're nearly there, Hannah. Next contraction, and your baby will be here.'

Hannah pushed again.

'That's great. The shoulders are through,' Rachel said.

And finally, the baby slid into her hands. She wiped his mouth and nose then checked him over, adding up the Apgar score. One for Appearance: normal colour with hands and feet slightly blue. Two for pulse, with it being over a hundred per minute. One for grimace, which he'd done when she wiped his mouth and nose. Two for activity, when his little legs kicked. And two for respiration, because he gave the cry she'd been waiting for. 'Apgar of eight, Tim,' she said quietly.

She dried the baby; Jamal helped Hannah to move to a sitting position, and Rachel put the baby directly on Hannah's chest so they were skin to skin, covering them both with a clean towel. 'Welcome to the world, baby,' she said softly. 'Well done, Hannah. We still need to deliver your placenta, but it's fine. There's nothing to worry about.'

'What about clamping the cord?' Hannah asked.

'No need to rush it,' Rachel said. 'The baby's getting

lots of lovely stem cells and iron through the cord. We can wait for the paramedics.'

'You did it, Han,' Tim said, his voice cracked with emotion.

Jamal was sitting next to Hannah, his arm round her shoulders and his head leaning against hers, stroking their newborn son's cheek. 'He's amazing, Han. You're amazing.'

'Our baby boy,' Hannah whispered.

'Let's give them a moment,' Rachel mouthed to Tim, and they quietly moved away to the far side of the room.

'That,' Tim said, 'was such a privilege. To be there when you delivered the baby, to see his eyes open and all that wonder...'

'The perfect Christmas present. Even if he was a little late,' Rachel said.

'We were both working yesterday, so today counts as our Christmas,' Tim said. He smiled. 'And this is definitely a different Christmas, a change none of us quite expected.'

'A newborn for a new Christmas,' she said. 'A new start.'

He wrapped his arms round her. 'Our first Christmas all together as a new family—and now with our newest family member. I'll remember this for ever. We'll be talking about this when we're eighty.' He smiled. 'Today, my daughter needed me—and I was there for her. Just as you were.'

'Just as I know you'd be there for my girls, if they needed you,' Rachel said gently.

'Rachel, will you...?'

He didn't get to finish the question, because the doorbell rang to signal the arrival of the paramedics.

Once the paramedic had clamped the cord, Jamal cut it; then she checked Hannah over. 'Everything's fine. There's no need to go into hospital,' she said. 'Just speak to your midwife.'

The rest of the day was spent celebrating the baby's arrival. Hannah and Jamal hadn't brought the car seat with them to take the baby home, so Rachel persuaded them to stay overnight, and she and Tim would collect the car seat in the morning. She persuaded Sophie and Calum to stay, too.

Later that evening, when they'd made a drawer into a temporary crib for the baby, the new parents had gone to bed, and everyone else was chilling out listening to Meg play the piano, Tim took Rachel into the garden to steal a moment.

'Today's changed everything,' he said. 'I'll never dread Christmas again.'

'The day we delivered little Arun. One of the best days of my life,' Rachel agreed.

'Before the paramedics rang the doorbell, I was going to ask you something.' He smiled at her. 'Today's just underlined what I already knew. I love you and I want to spend the rest of my days with you. Will you marry me, Rachel? Make a family with me, be my love and my wife?'

'I love you, too,' she said. 'Yes.'

'That,' he said, 'is the best Christmas present of all.' And then he kissed her.

* * * * *

COMING SOON!

We really hope you enjoyed reading this book.
If you're looking for more romance, be sure to
head to the shops when new books are
available on

Thursday 22nd December

To see which titles are coming soon, please visit
millsandboon.co.uk/nextmonth

MILLS & BOON

MILLS & BOON®

Coming next month

RULES OF THEIR FAKE FLORIDA FLING
Juliette Hyland

"I wrote up that contract." Her cheeks turned bright red, and she looked everywhere but at him. "If you're willing to go along with it, I'll owe you."

He was thrilled! She'd chosen him, and he planned to spend his time with Aurora making her smile and laugh. "Have a seat, please." He knew he'd never demand repayment. "What are the rules, Aurora?"

She moved to his couch, sat down and waited for him to join her, before pulling out a sheet and handing it to him.

He raised a brow as he looked at it. "This is a real contract."

"I doubt that it would hold up in court. But one of my college roommates sent me the template they use for PR relationships."

"What?" He'd been serious about the contract, but he hadn't expected a real one.

"Oh, sometimes celebrities have a relationship just for the press...usually right before a big movie or television launch. They have specific contracts regarding how everything will go." Aurora brightened as she outlined the information.

"Do you secretly love celebrity gossip?" He almost laughed but kept it in as Aurora nodded, not wanting to make her feel bad.

"My guilty pleasure." She shrugged.

"Never understood that phrase." Asher clicked his tongue. "If it's something you enjoy then it's just a pleasure. No need to feel bad about it."

"Sometimes, I can't believe you're a neurosurgeon." Aurora clapped her hand over her mouth. "I didn't mean anything bad by that. It's just that you are so silly, happy, hot and down-to-earth…" Aurora sighed and closed her eyes. "Sorry."

"No need to apologize. All of those were adjectives I love hearing. You find me hot?" Asher reached out and tapped her knee. He pulled back almost instantly, intently aware of the tingling in his hand. The desire to leave his hand on her knee, to offer comfort…but he wouldn't deny the desire hovering in his soul either.

"You have to know you're attractive." Aurora put a hand to her cheek.

He wished there was a way to draw the embarrassment from her, but for the first time in forever no jokes came forth to lighten the moment. So he went with the truth. "You're very attractive too."

He saw her swallow. Then she pointed to the contract, "Are you okay with this?"

Asher blinked and tried to refocus. "Rule one: Remember this is a fake relationship. No falling in love."

Continue reading
RULES OF THEIR FAKE FLORIDA FLING
Juliette Hyland

Available next month
www.millsandboon.co.uk

Copyright © 2022 Juliette Hyland

MILLS & BOON

THE HEART OF ROMANCE

A ROMANCE FOR EVERY READER

MODERN

Prepare to be swept off your feet by sophisticated, sexy and seductive heroes, in some of the world's most glamourous and romantic locations, where power and passion collide.

HISTORICAL

Escape with historical heroes from time gone by. Whether your passion is for wicked Regency Rakes, muscled Vikings or rugged Highlanders, awaken the romance of the past.

MEDICAL

Set your pulse racing with dedicated, delectable doctors in the high-pressure world of medicine, where emotions run high and passion, comfort and love are the best medicine.

True Love

Celebrate true love with tender stories of heartfelt romance, from the rush of falling in love to the joy a new baby can bring, and a focus on the emotional heart of a relationship.

Desire

Indulge in secrets and scandal, intense drama and plenty of sizzling hot action with powerful and passionate heroes who have it all: wealth, status, good looks…everything but the right woman.

HEROES

Experience all the excitement of a gripping thriller, with an intense romance at its heart. Resourceful, true-to-life women and strong, fearless men face danger and desire - a killer combination!

To see which titles are coming soon, please visit

millsandboon.co.uk/nextmonth

MILLS & BOON
A ROMANCE FOR EVERY READER

- **FREE** delivery direct to your door

- **EXCLUSIVE** offers every month

- **SAVE** up to 25% on pre-paid subscriptions

SUBSCRIBE AND SAVE

millsandboon.co.uk/Subscribe